MARCO LOBO

JINCAN

The Shaman's Poison

Two men, worlds apart, team up to pursue a killer
through California's Gold Country.

JINCAN, The Shaman's Poison
A Graystone and Shen Novel
by Marco Lobo

Published by

Christopher Matthews Publishing
PO Box 571
Gleneden Beach, OR 97388
541-961-7641

Interior layout, cover design by Suzanne Parrott
Cover Art, "JINCAN", ©2019 / Suzanne Fyhrie Parrott

Library of Congress Control Number: 2019911358
Genre: *Historical Thriller / Suspense*

ISBN: 978-1-944072-03-2 (pb)
ISBN: 978-1-937333-99-7 (epub)

10 9 8 7 6 5 4 3 2 1

Printed in the United States of America.

A Graystone and Shen Novel

MARCO LOBO

JINCAN

The Shaman's Poison

Two men, worlds apart, team up to pursue a killer
through California's Gold Country.

Christopher
Matthews
Publishing

To the 9 of you
My siblings, my dearest friends

ACKNOWLEDGEMENTS

Research for this book centered around two deaths that occurred in July of 1850 — Macau's 75th governor Pedro da Cunha, and that of President Zachary Taylor — they happened on opposite sides of the earth, both were sudden and said to be caused by cholera.

Da Cunha died little more than a month after arriving in Macau, and there is not much written about the circumstances of his demise. I relied on a healthy dose of imagination as well as several books addressing the politics and history of Macau. Geoffrey Gunn's book *Encountering Macau: A Portuguese City-State on the Periphery of China, 1557-1999*, provided cultural and political perspective as did Jonathan Porter's *Macau: The Imaginary City.*

Delving more deeply into Chinese cultural beliefs, I read Feng Shui practitioner, Joey Yap's *Chinese Traditions and Practices*. I also admit to having watched several online videos showing different forms of Chinese martial arts as well as the correct use of traditional Chinese weapons — thank you YouTube! Likewise, there were numerous online resources that provided rich information on San Francisco's and California's history, the argonauts, and the Chinese diaspora in America. Thanks also to the US Marshal's Service for information provided on their website.

Ralph Andrist's book *The Gold Rush* provided information about gold mining as well as the Chinese battle in the gold fields, and Jesse Holland's book *The Invisibles* opened my eyes to the issue of slavery and slaves in the White House.

The now-defunct *Philadelphia Bulletin* helped immensely with a fly-on-the-wall viewpoint of the turbulent time, while Holman Hamilton's book *Soldier in the White House* provided a political perspective.

Creating two flawed characters like Graystone and Shen required a deeper understanding of the frailties of the human mind. Graystone's black dog, Shen's ghosts, their wounded psyches, and their need of one another as shadow-selves, required the poring through several sources. One of note being Anthony Storr's *Churchill's Black Dog, Kafka's Mice, and Other Phenomena of the Human Mind*.

Finally, it would be remiss not to mention the many helpful suggestions I received from my dear friends at the Tokyo Writers Workshop.

BOOK ONE

THE PATH

1

1850
CHINA, GUANGDONG PROVINCE

SHEN WONDERED IF THE RED CROWN OF A CRANE could be used, and whether such an animal could be found in these southern provinces. 'Triple smile death powder' was said to make a man smile deliriously, even as he passed his last breath. If such a poison truly existed, where would he procure it? Surely such inquiries would draw unwelcome attention to him. What about 'heartbreak grass'? Natural and easy enough to come by, but then he questioned his ability to convert the flower's bright yellow blooms into a lethal dose. Furthermore, he had heard that after ingesting it, the victim might take several hours to die, and if seen to in time by one knowledgeable of such matters, there were antidotes.

No, Shen thought. His mission was to fulfil a final oath to his deceased master. Failing to do so would be an act of betrayal, shaming the memory of the great Li Taotai; causing his spirit to wander restlessly. Shen shuddered at the shameful thought, an accusatory memory that his master's demise was due to his failure to shield him when most needed.

Death had to be immediate. The poison, however, would have to make it appear that the death was natural. If seen as murder, the intended victim being a foreign official, it would certainly invite calamity. China was in no state to endure more imperialist abuse, but more importantly for Shen, the debacle would besmirch the name of his late master — the district administrator for Guangdong Province.

Pushing away frightening thoughts of Li Taotai's restless spirit, Shen decided that he needed a toxin that transcended all worldly impediments — one that harnessed the dark forces of the spirit world. And so he decided to approach the only man he knew capable of such craft, Wu Peng the shaman.

Through incense smoke, flickering candlelight revealed Wu's gaunt features. The glow allowed barely enough light for the old man to write in his notebook. Eight Taoist trigrams were embroidered into his cap; cosmological symbols representing the fundamental principles of reality. Four of the trigrams represented *Yin*: 'sense', 'think', 'feel' and 'will.' The other four represented *Yang*: 'body', 'soul', 'spirit' and 'awareness.' A string of wooden beads dangled from the shaman's neck. At the end of it, a rough lump of turquoise lay over his dark robe.

Shen had been sent before by his master to procure potions from Wu Peng, so knowing what was to come, he readied himself for an uncomfortable interrogation — information claimed to be necessary 'to better understand a victim's nature.' He was aware that secrets Wu extracted from his clients could be every bit as venomous as his potions. This time, Shen resolved to provide the barest amount of information.

Over cups of steaming tea and speaking as if the subject of murder was nothing more than inclement weather, Wu began, "Why have you come to me?"

"I need a poison."

Wu took a noisy slurp of tea and then set the small cup down. He cleared his throat and responded, "There are poisons of all kinds, designed to do different things." His voice was low and rasping. "Some are earthly in nature, others rise from the realm of shadows. They can be used to create sexual urges, or for seduction. I'm well-known for lust potions as you might recall." He grinned, his eyelids narrowed. The creases on Wu's thin face looked to have been carved out by a sharp blade. The Taotai had spent a small fortune on potions that he believed would enhance his manly prowess. Wu bobbed his head conspiratorially at Shen. "Other potions can be made for ensuring great wealth, or the perpetual poverty of an enemy. Say you wanted a victim to go mad, to lose their hearing or use of their limbs. A different formula is required for each. Then, there are, of course, poisons used for killing. But still, you must consider the manner of death — quick and painless, or prolonged and agonizing. Well?"

"I want to kill a devil," Shen said. "It must be quick and certain. I don't care about whether it causes pain, but the death must appear natural. Can you make such a poison?"

Wu left Shen's question hanging while he sipped his tea. "I can," he finally said peering over the rim of his teacup, "but I need to know more." He put the cup down and looked at Shen through half-closed eyelids.

"There's not much more to say."

"There's always more. You mentioned a devil. I presume you meant a foreigner, not a real demon. That would require something very different."

Shen nodded. "A foreign devil."

"Ah, there so are many amongst us now. Perhaps you could tell me which one."

"It's better that I don't. Possessing such information could be dangerous for you." Shen held the old man's eyes for a moment to ensure his warning was understood. "Perilous," he added.

Wu swallowed, his Adam's apple shifted impressively over his skinny throat. A glitter reflected in his eyes gave the impression of an animal waiting for a chance to strike. "You can rely on my discretion. Now, tell me, which devil, does he dwell nearby?"

Shen took a moment to think of a reply, something to obscure the truth. "Not far from here," he managed feebly.

Wu made a clicking sound out the side of his mouth and then said, "If you won't tell me who, or where, then at least I need to know when he arrived. To make a chart, you see." He dipped the tip of his brush into the inkwell and then held it up, ready to make an entry in his book.

"This one arrived recently."

The shaman tilted his head quizzically, brush still poised.

Shen pursed his lips and blew out slowly. The candlelight fluttered. "About a month ago, in May."

"When, in May?"

"End of the month."

"*Ah*, the time of the new moon." The shaman nodded and then lowered his head to write.

"What does he look like?" Wu continued.

Shen recalled the arrival of his intended victim. He had gotten close to the dock, joining a crowd to watch the man come ashore. "He is not a big man, about fifty years of age."

"Where did he come from?"

"From Africa."

Wu's eyebrows rose. "I see. A black devil, then?"

"No, not a black man, but I understand he was a ruler of blacks."

"*Ah*," Wu said with a nod. He dipped his brush in the inkwell and made another entry.

"What about his clothes?"

Shen showed his annoyance with a noisy breath. "Do you really need to know how he was dressed? Your queries lead me to believe that your interests go beyond what is required for making a poison."

The old man forced a snake-like hiss through clenched teeth. His face twisted as if he'd taken a bite of rotten meat. He spoke rapidly. "I've told you before. Every little thing you tell me is of help. Based on the knowledge, I will determine the type of poison best suited to the individual. For example, one clad in leather imitates a particular kind of animal with that kind of skin." The shaman's eyes lit up, voice and gestures growing more animated as he spoke. "One covered in smooth silk might be more like a reptile, or even an insect. The victim's background and mannerisms are vital knowledge if I am to make the perfect poison."

"What you hear must be kept secret." Shen stared into the old shaman's eyes, "or there will be consequences. Do you understand?"

"People come to me because they know I can be trusted with information of the most private nature. Now, if you don't mind, the clothes."

Wu's response didn't appease Shen's concerns. He had to remind himself he had little alternative to being here. He raised his eyes and stared into the ceiling dense with incense smoke, trying to picture the governor's attire. "A plume of feathers stuck out of his hat."

"Feathers . . . trailing down from the back?"

"No, they stuck straight up from the front, like a cockatoo's." Shen held a hand above his forehead with his fingers fanned out to show what he meant.

"I see. A soldier's hat perhaps?"

Shen nodded. "One worn by a foreigner of high-rank," he said before he could stop himself.

Wu lowered his eyes and wrote in his book. "Continue."

Shen cleared his throat. "When I saw him, he had on a short, light-colored jacket."

The shaman wrote and then looked up expectantly, brush hovering.

Shen turned his eyes up. "His legs were covered in dark trousers . . . tight-fitting, tucked into shiny black boots."

"Was he armed?"

"Armed? No. Yes, a sword. I remember now, a sword hung off his belt. I noticed it when he turned to talk to the welcoming party. It was long and thin, in an ornate scabbard. A flimsy thing more for show than to be of practical use as a weapon, I thought."

The shaman wrote a few characters in his notebook. "How did he walk?"

"Walk?"

"Did he strut like a bird? Was he crouched over? Did he march?"

"I understand now."

"Then, proceed."

"He carried himself confidently."

"How so?"

"With the gait of an arrogant master. It showed on his face, the bearing of a man ready to teach us a lesson, if you get my meaning."

"I do." Wu smiled, looking as if he had deciphered a code. "An apt description. Thank you. And was he accompanied by a female?"

"I didn't see a wife."

"Do you know anything about his state of health?"

"A little only. It is not good, I believe. He seems to have been unwell recently."

"Most intriguing. Tell me more about his condition."

"A foreign doctor has been calling at his house. To treat precisely what, I don't know. It could be anything, a stomach upset from a change of diet, or something more serious."

"Anything else you noticed about this. . ." the shaman looked down at his notes, "arrogant master?"

"That is all I know. Now, I want to know about the poison, how to handle it," Shen said.

"I will give it to you in a flask." The shaman held his thumb and forefinger apart to show its size. "You must never get the poison on your skin, and you must not open it until you are ready to use it. When you do, try not to breathe the fumes. Do you understand?"

"I do."

"The victim will have to consume it. Mix it in his food or drink, or even better, try to pour it directly into his mouth. It must get into his blood, so an open wound or a blade coated with it could also do."

Shen nodded. "How long will it take to work?"

Dishes clattered in a nearby room. There was a familiar scraping sound and the hollow knock of a wok in use, the hiss of frying oil. The smell of cooking garlic wafted in, mixing with the aroma of incense.

Wu turned his head towards the door and then back to Shen. "You have to go now," he said.

"You haven't answered me. I asked you how fast death would come."

The shaman spoke quickly. "If he swallows a complete dose, death will be swift — a minute, maybe less."

Dishes clattered again. "You must leave now," Wu said.

"When will . . ."

"Come back in two days. Bring payment." Wu wrote on a new leaf in his book and tore the page out. He waved it in the air a few times to dry the ink and handed it over. He closed his book and then got up.

Shen looked at the amount written on the paper. "It's more than I paid the last time, a lot more."

The last time? That was something I did for your master. Besides, each potion is different."

"I still come on behalf of my master."

"You want it or not?"

"I will return in two days," Shen said.

The shaman smiled. "You know the way out," he said, snuffing out the candle with a pinch. Turning away, he left Shen in the smoky room.

Stunned by the price asked, Shen looked at the paper again but couldn't make out the numbers in the darkness. He folded and pocketed it, shaking his head at the exorbitant sum, aware of having revealed too much.

He groped his way to the door and paced slowly through a dim corridor. In one of the rooms he passed, he saw the shaman seated at a table with his wife. Wu had his head down, picking at his food. His wife was scolding him. The old man heard Shen passing the doorway and raised his head momentarily. The dejected look on his face almost made Shen feel sorry for him.

Shen passed another room with a large workbench at its center. This was where Wu concocted his potions, he guessed. Down the hallway, the shaman's wife could still be heard berating the old man, and Shen took the opportunity to sneak a look in the workroom. He tiptoed in. This space was not as dark as the rest of the house, daylight filtered through a window partly obscured by a wooden screen. An old apothecary cabinet sat at one end of the room. The other walls were lined with shelves holding glass jars of all sizes. At first, he thought they held ingredients for creating medicines: jumbles of leaves, twigs, and whatnot; but movement in one of them caught his eye, and he ventured nearer.

Closer inspection revealed that each jar contained different kinds of animals. In one, a centipede as long as his forearm waved its scythe-like pincers. He looked into another container, in which shiny black scorpions slithered under rotting wood and dried leaves. A hairy spider as large as his open hand reared up when he approached, revealing its fangs. Another of the containers held a few brightly colored frogs; they inflated thin membranes over their throats and began to make high-pitched *peeps*. Shen backed away into a corner, clattering into stacked wire cages. He turned to see snakes flicking their tongues at him.

He ran from the room stumbling his way out of the house into dazzling sunshine. Shen raced across the garden and escaped through the front gate.

2

LUNCH HAD BEEN A GRIM AFFAIR, awful food seasoned by his wife's bitter pestering. Wu placed a palm over his slightly bloated stomach; it felt warm to the touch. Later it would be worse, he knew, when unbearable gas pains would have him spending a great deal of time on the chamber-pot.

"*Gi-ga, ga-ga,* constantly, like an angry duck," he grumbled. He'd long endured the woman's bad humor silently and dutifully. Voicing objection, he'd learned, would send her into rageful counter-attacks. There were times when he had thoughts of 'taking care of her' — a simple enough task for a man of his skills — a slow, excruciating demise caused by a spell would serve her right. After a vicious tongue-lashing, he sometimes had notions of dealing with her with something quicker; a snakebite perhaps. But no, casting a spell in the home they shared would set spirits loose under his own roof. Who knows what could happen? Besides, she hadn't always been such a fiend. They had endured long years together, and she had borne him two strong sons, both now grown and with families of their own — the elder, a successful merchant and the younger and up-and-coming government official, already a source of secret information.

At his workbench, he climbed atop a tall stool that put him within easy reach of the ingredients used for creating potions. He opened his book and studied the notes he'd written at his meeting with Shen.

Wu snickered at Shen's gullibility, of believing the story about needing to know about the victim's clothes or how he walked. Shen's defenses had been sloughed away like the skin of an overripe plum. Certainly, there were things that would make a poison more potent for a particular individual; time and date of birth for instance, but not feathers on a hat. A cockatoo — really! The old man chuckled at the memory of his client's fingers fanned out above his forehead.

He had gained valuable information from Shen, a good description of the man he wanted to kill, one whose identity he believed he had deciphered. It would be confirmed when he heard about the death. It was then that the information would become the most valuable. He didn't care to prevent a murder; whatever the outcome, it was predetermined by universal laws. But to know the murderer's identity opened up many possibilities. Knowledge was currency that could be used to buy favors, traded for other secrets or for money, or to force one into doing anything he wanted doing.

To concoct a poison simply to kill someone was child's play. A death that needed to look as if of natural causes, called for more finesse; for the skills of a master. Wu wiggled his fingers playfully at the thought of creating another potion. The last time he was asked to prepare something of that nature had been several months earlier. Picturing the client in his mind, he recalled the man's slight stature and that the client's mannerisms were a little feminine. The little man paid a rather high price without a flicker of hesitation. "Why weren't they all like that?" he mumbled to himself.

When Wu asked questions about the victim's appearance, the man responded openly. The client even pulled out a folded portrait of a white-haired foreigner in a military uniform. He said the man was a high-ranking government official and that the victim lived far away, over the Pacific Ocean and all the way across the vast continent of the United States. Wu learned that the victim had to die on or around America's Independence Day, July 4th, today's date he realized. Keeping the poison for so long would reduce its potency, but it would still work, *yes, it will,* he reassured himself. He had used the date to search for a symbol that would guide him in creating the poison. Now, vaguely curious as to the victim's identity, he dismissed the thought — the old devil would very likely be dead by now, or would be very soon. Like Shen's order, it was for a poison that mimicked death by natural causes. He believed, however, that since the prey lived so far away, he wouldn't be able to profit from it beyond the hefty fee he had already charged. Besides, he had already sold the portrait of the elderly foreigner along with the scant knowledge he had.

Wu decided to use the same method to create a poison for Shen. He flipped the leaves of his book to the records of the previous order. An oracle script he had drawn identified the page he wanted. The date inscribed at the top showed that he had met the man half a year earlier. Now he remembered cautioning the client that though the poison would still work after several months, it would lose potency and that death would be certain, but slower.

Gu was an ancient form of a Chinese character depicting a kind of poison. The pictograph could also be interpreted as 'bewitch', or 'to drive to insanity', and quite appropriately, he thought while studying it, 'intestinal parasite.'

Under the character, he had drawn a hexagram.

The eighteenth hexagram of the *I Ching* held special meaning for him. Known as *Ku*, it represented a bowl, filled with breeding worms.

The shaman's excitement grew as he thought about what he was about to do again. The notebook trembled in his hands. He tried to calm his mind while pondering the meaning of the symbol. *The wind blows low on the mountain. Thrown back, it spoils vegetation.* The words conjured an image of decay, preventing improvement. *Debasing attitudes and enhancing corrupt human society.* This was about conflicting attitudes, politics he decided. *The superior must remove stagnation by stirring up public opinion, as the wind stirs up everything, and must strengthen and tranquilize the character of the people.* Yes, good leaders should be as mountains, providing tranquility and nourishment to all that grows in their vicinity. But if they don't, then they must be removed . . . one way or another.

Wu considered how the two clients had come to him for the same thing half a year apart. Both wanted poisons to kill high-ranking government officials and for the deaths to appear natural.

There was no such thing as coincidence.

He reflected on the date and the season. With the earth's rotation, America's Independence Day would be a day later here in China, tomorrow. High summer. He imagined the weather over there to be hot, so the interpretation was that decay must come from heat miasma. Mists that seep from the ground — evil heat and noxious *qi* that is harmful to man. The shaman's heart quickened. *Jincan,* Golden Silkworm, he thought gleefully; an ancient method of creating a potent venom. Not a silkworm at all, the name was reputed to have originally come from Kashmir. A funerary decoration made from pure gold.

He slipped off the stool and picked up a large earthenware pot from a corner of the room. Grabbing it by its handles, he struggled back to his workbench and lifted the container onto it. Incantations were painted across the container's rough beige surface. Under a glass lid, the pot's flat base was separated into five compartments like upright walls of a five-pointed star, designed for ease of removal as a single piece.

Wu turned to the jars lining the walls, he ran his gaze over them. Five animals were needed. The task was to combine them, creating a poison that would hold the potency of all five creatures at once. The next step was to select which creatures were to be used to make the *Jincan.*

It was to be a gladiatorial contest, each animal of the quintet fighting for survival by using its particular lethality. For it to be a proper battle, it was essential to select creatures that were well-matched in size and potency. His excitement mounted at the thought of watching such a competition. He went to his jars of animals and peered into each one, moving sideways slowly, occasionally pausing to touch each vessel and consider the suitability of its inhabitants.

His first selection made, he picked up a pair of bamboo tongs and went to a container that had been fashioned into a terrarium. He removed the dewy enclosure's glass cover and used the tongs to brush aside thick leaves inside it. Not seeing the animal, he turned the leaves over one at a time until he spotted a frog hidden at the bottom of the miniature rain forest. The bright blue amphibian with a blackish mottled back was no larger than the upper section of his thumb. It didn't try to escape when he gripped it with the tongs. The little frog's back contained a powerful venom that native tribes of China's mountainous areas used to poison the tips of their arrows. A speck of it was enough to kill a man. He released the frog into a compartment of the pot and covered it.

Wu chose a wolf spider next. It took more effort to catch the fleet-footed arachnid. But with the aid of a set of smaller tongs, he managed to grab hold one of its legs and tugged it from its lair, a small hole in a rock. He examined the feisty warrior before putting it into a compartment next to the frog.

The next two creatures were a centipede with a red back and yellow legs and a black scorpion. As his final competitor, Wu selected a creature that lived in his garden: a wasp. Wu went out to the hive that was in a tree in the far corner of his garden. He lit an oily rag below the hive, gray smoke drove off most of the hive's residents; the few left behind were dazed and docile. He grabbed one carefully by its back and returned to his workroom. At his bench, taking great care not to injure the body of the sluggish insect, he carefully snipped off its wings and placed it in the last compartment.

In nature, these animals, each from quite a different habitat, were unlikely to come across one another. If they did, their instincts would likely be to avoid each other. Except for the wasp that had woken up and was batting the stubs of its clipped wings about angrily, ready to jab its sting into anything and everything, they had no reason to fight. Wu had to give them one. He hopped off his perch and went to his medicine cabinet. This *yaochu* had been passed down through several generations of medicine men. It held 42 drawers each marked with what it contained. He hooked his forefinger through a metal loop and pulled open one of the square drawers. Rifling through a stack of neatly arranged paper packets he found one with the character *chán* 饞, 'gluttony', written on its front.

Wu uncovered the pot and sprinkled a substance resembling white pepper onto each of his combatants. The powder's odor made his stomach gurgle. His mind filled with images of his favorite dishes, those of his childhood prepared by his mother and meals shared with intimate friends.

The animals reacted instantaneously, moving about their little cells in search of food. Wu lifted the glass lid and removed the partition before quickly closing it again.

The frog, normally a creature that waited patiently to flick out its tongue at a passing ant or baby cricket, was first on the attack. Oblivious to its own safety, it went for the noisy wasp, clamping its toothless mouth over the head, intent on gobbling it down whole. The wasp moved its tail around and repeatedly jabbed at the frog. The black scorpion rushed at the fighting duo and grabbed the business end of the wasp with its pincers and began to gnaw at whatever part of the animal it could, striking and injecting venom from its own tail. Locked in combat, the three creatures rolled about. All the while, the frog continued to secrete poison from sacs on its back, smearing the pot's bottom with a venomous paste. They tumbled into the centipede which wrapped itself around the scorpion and attacked indiscriminately with its poisonous bite. The eight-eyed wolf spider leapt onto the centipede, and now the combatants were a writhing ball, gnashing, stinging and biting — entangled in spider silk, thrashing about in poisonous puddles. They fought until one at a time, each of the animals succumbed to its wounds. Even as they died, so strong was the desire to eat that through their dying breaths, they continued trying to gorge themselves on one another.

In the end, the pyrrhic victory went to the wolf spider. Wu sprinkled more of the powder onto it. Though nearly dead, the spider continued eating, well beyond what it was capable of. This was the critical part, for after gorging on its foes, the main ingredient of *Jincan* had to be harvested: the victor's feces.

3

1850

CHINA, MACAU

MACAU'S 75ᵀᴴ GOVERNOR, PEDRO ALEXANDRINO DA CUNHA emitted a long, quiet moan. Slapping the back of his hand against his hot brow, he turned his eyes towards the little brown medicine bottle. The dose he had taken earlier had enfeebled him and caused him to take to bed. He had woken up with a splitting headache, his stomach feeling worse than before.

He had intended to spend a few hours working in his office, but now half a day was lost, and there was plenty still to be done. As it was a Saturday, Cunha decided to stay home for the rest of the day and go over his plans in the small study adjoining his bedroom.

His regent, Queen Maria II of Portugal had been very specific about what she expected of him — to push the Chinese very hard. He had been hand-picked for this job by the queen herself, telling him that he, as the former governor general of Angola, was the perfect man to establish a new colony. In Africa, he'd enacted tax reforms, built roads, even started a newspaper. The first step was to officially establish Macau as a colony. As of now, though occupied by the Portuguese since the fifteenth century, the land he was on still officially belonged to China.

Nearly a year had passed since the murder of Cunha's predecessor, Governor Amaral. *Poor Amaral,* he pondered, *a brave man, but lacking the talent needed of a true statesman.* He dipped his pen into an inkwell and held it over a blank sheet of paper. A tiny globule began forming on the pointed tip of the nib. His mind went blank. "Come on, Pedro," he grumbled.

"What is it? What is it?" he asked himself, mesmerized, by the growing shiny black pearl. It hung there heavily until, at last, it dripped off the nib and splattered onto the paper, breaking the spell. A slow, deep breath made his head spin. He set the pen down before any more mess could be made.

Gripping the edge of his desk for support, Cunha pushed himself up from the chair. He shuffled to the large windows that looked out towards Macau's harbor. It was stifling in the room, but the doctor had insisted he keep all windows tightly shut to keep out dangerous vapors. The governor would have defied the doctor's orders if not for the commonly held knowledge that disease was caused by pestilential vapors that seeped out of the ground. And in this part of the world, as it was in Africa, the vapors could cause cholera. His drenched shirt stuck to him. He put a hand over his churning stomach.

From the window, Cunha could see the frigate, Dona Maria II. The 32-gun warship he'd sailed on from Lisbon was an ominous sight in the little harbor. At anchor next to it was the Don Joao I with its 22 guns. In addition to Macau's garrison of 500 men, he had a small contingent of soldiers recently brought in from Goa. Cunha allowed himself a smile. *In a week, when I'm better, I'll sail up the Pearl River and threat-*

en Canton. The Chinese had witnessed the destructive power of modern weapons of war, and it had scared them enough to hand over Hong Kong. He hoped that no bombardment would actually be necessary, that merely the threat might be enough.

Beyond the warships, lining the other side of the harbor stood a row of waterfront warehouses. From a distance, the large white structures were impressive, hinting of a robust trading port. One of the first things Cunha had done after his arrival was to make an inspection of the trading houses. Close up, the buildings were less impressive. Paint peeled off the three and four-story buildings. Some of the grander ones boasted large verandas that ran along the entire upper floors.

He had gone inside a couple of them for a look. Expecting hives of commercial activity, he entered near-empty rooms. Though the cavernous depots were still in operation, but for a few crates and baskets stacked against the walls, they were mostly bare. Most the large business owners had moved their operations to Hong Kong where they had built grand warehouses along the harbor front of the new city of Victoria. Hong Kong was sovereign British territory. It operated under British law and was not subject to the whims of the Chinese Emperor.

Standing by the window, his head reeled from the exertion of the short walk across the room. Things were going to change, but right now he needed rest, to shut his eyes for a while. He crossed through to his adjoining bedroom, closing the study door behind him. He went to the bedroom's main door and turned the key. Locking the door, he left the key in the keyhole.

—◆—

Enfolded by the roots of an ancient banyan, in the moonless night, Shen was near invisible. 'Perfectly safe to touch', Wu had assured him when he had gone back for the poison. But could he trust the old man? The thing felt hot enough to blister skin. He slipped a hand between the cloth buttons of his tunic and felt the bottle. His fingertips sensed only the natural warmth of an object heated by his body. Shen ran his thumb over the stopper. He pulled his hand away, wondering if the sense of foreboding from just touching it was purely his imagination. Utmost care had to be taken that the poison's sinister nimbus wouldn't prevent him from using it this night. He remembered the shaman's warning that to allow a single drop of the potion to come into contact with his skin would mean excruciating sickness and imminent death. Death would, however, appear natural, mimicking 'blue death', cholera.

He peered through the tree's gnarled tendrils. The mansion showed no obvious signs of life. Upstairs rooms had gone dark hours ago, but armed sentries patrolled the governor's grounds, dictating a high degree of vigilance on his part. It was still the Hour of the Pig, when most animals slept soundly; he decided to wait a little longer. Shen looped both arms over his knees and pulled them in closer. He settled back, waiting patiently, fingering the vial of poison through the fabric of his shirt.

Shen felt a trickle of sweat run down his back, and he sneaked another look at the governor's mansion. He blinked away mosquitoes that had landed on his eyelashes. Clad in black from head to toe, he didn't bother swatting at the insects swarming about his face. Head tightly wrapped, only his eyes were exposed. For the past week, Macau had been shrouded in a clammy fog. The constant drizzle had pooled into perfect hatcheries for mosquito larvae. On this morning the rain had given way to intense sunshine that battered the ground like a blacksmith's hammer, driving moisture into Macau's already stifling humidity.

The hours of rat and ox gave way to the Hour of the Tiger. He got to his feet, grabbed hold of vines and pulled himself into the tree's leafy boughs. Halfway up, he crawled along a thick branch that extended towards a verandah.

It hadn't taken much for him to learn the layout of the governor's mansion. He had watched the house for a few days observing the comings and goings of servants. Shen had followed one of the local girls to the market and befriended her, seducing her with flattery and gifts of sweetmeats. The kitchen-maid had told him all he needed to know. The ailing governor needed little food. Following the devil doctor's instructions, she shopped for a few simple things: guava, green coconut, and onions which the cook made into soups to replenish the liquids Cunha had lost through bouts of vomiting and diarrhea. More importantly, he learned from the girl that a second-floor verandah led directly into the governor's bedroom.

He leapt a two-meter span from the end of the branch to the verandah. His cloth shoes made no sound as he landed, bending his knees to absorb the momentum of the drop. No turning back now. If caught, he would take the poison himself. When the governor was dead, his final mission would be complete. He would leave forever, not just Macau but his beloved China—for somewhere far away, *Gum Saan*, Golden Mountain, where so many of his compatriots had already gone in pursuit of riches. He had given thought to other far-away places, but *Gum Saan* seemed the best, somewhere he would never be found; a place to make a new life, and if fortune smiled on him, then riches as well.

Shen firmly gripped the cool brass doorknob. He waited, listening for any sounds of movement from inside the room. Expecting to have to force the door, the knob turned effortlessly. The verandah door stuck briefly against its frame before creaking open. A breeze blew in and flapped the curtains as he went through. He closed the door behind him and stood still, allowing his vision to adjust to the darkness. The bedroom smelled of sickness, the odor of vomit and excrement. Absent, however, was the sound of rhythmic breathing expected of a man in deep slumber. Shen looked at the white face of a clock on a shelf. It was just after 3.00 a.m.

Governor Cunha lay under a mosquito net suspended from the ceiling. Moving closer, he saw the governor lying on his left side, facing the wall and away from him. Shen pinched the diaphanous curtain and lifted it over the governor, flipping it to one side.

As soon as he opened the vial of poison, it released a putrid stench that cut through the stink of the full chamber pot. His eyes stung and watered. He avoided breathing in the fumes by holding a sleeve against his mouth and nose.

It would have been easier to slit his victim's throat, but with tensions as they were, China could not afford to pay compensation or to fight another war. What better way than to explain away the fatality of a new arrival than by a sickness as common in these parts as cholera? Shen had to admire the shaman's expertise, the ability to combine poisons taken from different beings, that when inflicted would imitate infection from an entirely different source.

Cunha's head was turned away from Shen — he needed a better angle to use the poison. He leaned over intending to dribble the venom slowly through the side of Cunha's slightly parted lips that were coated with flecks of dry vomit. Still, Shen couldn't detect any movement at all coming from the governor, no sound of breathing or movement in his chest. He prodded the governor's back — nothing. The man was stiff and lifeless; dead. Had someone had gotten to Cunha before him, and on this very night?

Shen's immediate thought was that he had failed the Taotai again. The idea of it caused him to lurch backward bumping into a bedside table. It wobbled, and a pitcher and glass tipped over and crashed to the floor.

Shen hastily resealed the empty vial and pocketed it. He heard shuffling from outside the door. There was a knock, a muffled voice, "Your Excellency?" The brass knob turned, but the door didn't open. Shen saw the circular bow of a key protruding from the keyhole.

He hadn't counted on a sentry being right there. *But of course*, Shen chided himself. After the previous governor's murder, this one would be given a higher level of protection.

A voice called from the other side of the bedroom door. Polite knocking became frantic banging. "Your Excellency!" A thud jarred the door. Shen imagined an armed sentry hurling his shoulder against the heavy wooden barrier.

Another crash and the sound of splitting wood made Shen back away from the bed. He turned for the verandah door and hurried through it. Closing the door, he leapt from the verandah railing onto the branch and made his escape down the banyan tree. Above him from inside the bedroom came a crash of wood.

He walked as calmly as he could along the dark harbor front, all the while his thoughts confused as to who could have beat him to the deed of killing Cunha, of cheating him of his final promise to his deceased master, rejecting the notion that the death was indeed a natural one. Reaching the sea wall, he threw the vial as far out into the water as he could. The little bottle arced and plopped into the sea.

Hazy light woke Shen from a deep sleep, muddled thoughts floated to the surface of his mind. As his head started to clear, he tried to block out the memory of his failure of the night before, but the thought became ever stronger — the non-fulfillment of his oath.

He wrestled with the dilemma. Did it matter? After all, Cunha was dead.

But for a blemish at the periphery of his consciousness, the realization should have filled him with a pleasure that given time might have evolved into sheer bliss. Searching for the truth of that obscure thought brought him the understanding that his final task, his life in the service of Li Taotai, had ended for good. Then the shadowy thought surfaced, and his mood darkened, it had ended in failure.

The governor's death was of little consequence to him. His master had often ranted about China's humiliation at the hands of foreigners. As a Chinese, Shen felt bullied by 'western devils', was appalled by them. But they confused him too; he wondered how such uncouth people could subdue China so easily.

A new thought came to him — a frightening one — the devil ships. What of them? The killing of Amaral had triggered a retaliatory attack. Now yet another governor would be sent to press for Portugal's grander designs. Would the ships have to be dealt with too? Perhaps, but that was not his problem. He had never needed to make weighty decisions or consider their consequences, he had just done what the Taotai ordered. With the Taotai he had the guidance and protection of a wealthy patron, now any number of enemies might want revenge against him.

Shen needed to consider what to do with the rest of his life. But first, he had to know what was being said about the governor's death.

No place was better for catching the latest gossip than a busy marketplace, and in Macau, tittle-tattle was fresh and abundant as the produce offered for sale. He headed for the market, bought breakfast at a food stall and then mingled with early-morning shoppers, many of them servants of Macau's households. He listened to their chatter while enjoying a sticky rice-dumpling filled with salted pork fat. Lanes were abuzz with gossip, and he searched for any mention of the governor, catching bits of conversation as he strolled by each stall. Macau's serving class brought news, real or merely hearsay from their employers' homes to the market. It spread through the marketplace and later from house to house, eager lips delivering it into even more impatient ears. Repeated through recurring chains of speaker and listener, stories were embellished until they bore little resemblance to their origins.

Shen picked words out of the air, not always entire words, some were a smattering of floating syllables, but enough for him to grasp on to and seek out more of the same. The sounds took form and soon he had enough to follow. He pursued a stream of words through the market's crowded lanes as if they were a trail left by grains of rice spilled from a leaky shopping basket: 'dead', 'cholera', 'vomit', blue', 'governor.' Eventually, he reached the wellspring; the mouth of a plump gray-haired matron, holding court in front of a fish stall. He pushed into a small group listening to her.

"And why should we believe you, auntie?" a young man asked.

"Why indeed," the orator sneered. "Because, unlike you, who still carries the smell of breast milk yet to dry," she paused, allowing time for her audience to mock the red-faced youth, "everyone here knows that I run the household of Doctor Pedro Cordeiro. That's right, the esteemed white doctor. And when I say I know something, you can be certain of it because I heard it from the doctor's very own mouth."

Though she'd probably delivered the sermon several times already, it pleased Shen that she did so again without any encouragement. She spoke slowly, savoring her place at the center of attention. In the background, the fish monger's chopper punctuated her speech with whacks that severed scale, flesh, and guts. "After breakfast, I heard the good doctor discussing the details with his nurse. He'd been called to the governor's mansion during the night. By the time he arrived, it was already too late."

"What caused his death?" asked a woman.

The doctor's housekeeper responded with an air of authority, as if she were the doctor herself. "It couldn't have been anything other than the 'blue death', cholera, caused by *Zhàngqì,* miasma. With the rain and fog we've had, how could it be anything else?" Her audience mumbled and nodded their agreement.

"How can you be sure it wasn't murder, like the other one?" the youth asked again, having recovered from the tongue lashing.

"Hah! You again. A child with a head as empty as a green pepper. Don't you know that the previous governor was decapitated, his arm hacked off? Not a scratch on this one's body I tell you, just a bed full of shit and vomit. What kind of poison could do that?"

A man squeezed in between two people at the front. "Poison?" he asked. "Who has been poisoned?" The matron began her story again. Shen peeled away into the crowd.

By noon, although the original story of Cunha's death by cholera still made the rounds, Chinese whispers ensured that it was joined by other versions. One was that Governor da Cunha had been poisoned by his household staff and that they were now all under arrest. By far the most outlandish story he'd heard was that the ghost of the governor's dismembered predecessor had appeared in the bedroom carrying his own severed head — and Cunha had shat himself to death. Shen could only shake his head and chuckle when he heard that one. *Death by defecation, truly!*

So, no poison was necessary after all. The governor had apparently died of natural causes, but sooner or later there would be some trouble coming of this. He had purchased the poison. There was a link to him through the shaman. The time had come for him to plan his departure from Macau. He held an image in his mind of a gleaming mountain of gold, *Gum Saan*. He didn't know exactly how to get there, but he knew who to ask. His late master, the Taotai, had dealings with Yan Chow, Macau's most successful merchant.

4

SHEN HAD MISGIVINGS ABOUT SEEKING ADVICE from one who devoted his entire life to the pursuit of profit; unfortunately, there were few he could turn to now. He suspected that Yan bought secrets from the shaman and feared that when news of the governor's death reached the shaman's ears, he would surely reach the conclusion that Shen had been the assassin. If the Shaman were to betray him, he would make good on the warning he had delivered to the old man.

He hadn't seen Yan for over a year, not that he'd been in hiding, but given his close association with the Taotai, had thought it best to keep out of sight. He wove his way through Macau's busy streets towards the teahouse where Yan took his midday meal. From the entrance, Shen spotted Cheng, Yan's bodyguard standing at the back of the noisy restaurant. He declined an offer from serving staff to be shown to a table, preferring to stand by the doorway, waiting for Cheng to notice him.

The bodyguard's watchful eyes scanned the bustling restaurant, stopping when they locked onto Shen's. The men nodded politely in acknowledgment of their mutual standing as members of a clandestine fraternity. Shen wondered if he'd detected something more in Cheng's demeanor, an expression of sympathy perhaps, from a man with a benevolent master looking pitifully at a man who'd lost one.

Yan sat by himself at a table large enough to seat half a dozen patrons. He tilted his head when Cheng leaned over to whisper in his ear. Shen saw Yan frown at what was said. Yan looked up and beamed; Cheng waved Shen over.

The wealthy merchant's smile broadened with each step Shen made towards the table. Yan wore a blue silk robe and sported the compulsory Qing hairstyle; a shaved forehead with the rest of his hair plaited into a long queue that hung down his back.

"Ah, Shen Xiling. How long has it been?" Yan asked, gesturing for Shen to sit across from him.

"Too long, Master Yan. I hope you will excuse my insolence," Shen replied with a bow before taking his seat.

Yan summoned a serving girl. He ordered steamed buns and a fresh pot of tea to be brought and then returned his attention back Shen. "Well, you had things to do I suppose. The Taotai, I am sorry to have missed the funeral. Quite an affair, I understand." Yan lowered his head.

Shen also bowed at the memory of his deceased master. "Li Taotai felt it his duty, you see. . ."

"Entirely. Quite noble of him, really."

"As a Qing official, he administered the 'five punishments' judiciously," Shen said.

"I can attest to that," Yan responded.

"In the end, a lapse in judgment was what led to his sentencing—punishment of the fourth-level—exile to a distance of 2000 *li*."

Yan leaned forward, "But, then why was he executed?"

"I understand your confusion, it wouldn't be a decision taken by a lesser man, but my master pleaded with the magistrate to raise his sentence to the fifth level. He felt he couldn't live with the disgrace, no matter how far away, so he chose death over banishment."

"I see," Yan said, pinching his chin and nodding. "Let's not forget the beating of 100 strokes that would have come with fourth level punishment."

"Which, if he survived, would have meant living in perpetual pain," Shen added. "He wanted something more certain."

"Still, I suppose death can be regarded as a kind of exile, one without having to endure a prolonged embarrassment," Yan said with a wry smile. "Wise to the end, yes, the deed of a wise and judicious man."

Shen nodded solemnly. Both men were quiet for a minute, allowing the loss of the Taotai to wash over them.

A clatter of dishes broke the silence. Yan spoke first. "If I might ask . . . the method of execution?"

"Strangulation. I was allowed the honor." Shen stood briefly and put his hand over a red silk sash tied around his waist.

Yan looked round to his bodyguard standing behind him listening to the conversation. "The duty of a dedicated servant." Cheng gazed at Shen and bowed reverently. "And you, Shen Xiling, how is it that you have escaped scrutiny? My people informed me that you were involved in the affair of the assassination of the former governor, a year ago."

Shen saw no point in denying the allegation. Yan rewarded his spies well for accurate information. "Involved, yes, though not in performing the deed itself."

"The repercussions resulted in a catastrophe for China."

"What was the Taotai to do? The foreign devils tore up the graves of our ancestors," Shen said. "His actions were for the honor of all Chinese."

"He should have recognized it for what it was, a provocation, a trap. What you called a lapse in judgment, caused the destruction of a large Chinese fort, one of the empire's key southern defenses. It exposed the Pearl River all the way through to the heart of Canton." Yan smiled as he spoke. "Anyway, a catastrophe for China but not for me. I should thank you for whatever part you played in it."

"Thank? I don't understand, Master Yan."

"The Portuguese victory over China has given them a stable base here. As a merchant, that is exactly what I need."

The conversation paused while the server brought the order of *bāozi*, steamed buns with meat filling, another girl set a teapot on the table to brew. *"Dà Hóng Páo."* Yan said making a show of waving in fragrant steam rising from the pot and sniffing noisily at the tea's chocolaty aroma. The servers departed and Yan started again. "Do you know anything about what occurred last night at the governor's mansion?"

Shen's heart thumped. If Yan wanted a stable foreign-controlled trading port to work from, then Cunha's death was an impediment. Yan couldn't possibly know of his involvement so soon, could he? He struggled to keep his voice steady. "Only what I heard in the market this morning, that the new governor succumbed to the 'blue death.'"

"Yes, that's what I heard too." Yan spoke with the air of a man who knew more than he let on.

An image flashed through Shen's mind: a red sash pulled taught between his fists, his master's wrinkled face looking up, uttering his final words, instructions, 'kill the next one too.' He gathered himself. "I know nothing of what happened last night. As for your concern over my culpability for what occurred last year, so far I have gone unnoticed. The assassins are being hunted, but as you know, they have so far evaded capture. I can't rely on that being the case forever. If they are caught, under torture, my name will be revealed, which is why I believe the time has come for me to leave China. For that reason, I've come to seek your advice. I'll pay of course — the Taotai was generous with me."

"There's no need for talk of money between old friends," Yan said shaking his head with a laugh. "As I said, you helped me substantially, though inadvertently perhaps, but it turns out that I am in your debt. My opium business has grown magnificently, as has my coolie trade."

"Is there honor in trading the sweat and blood of our compatriots?"

Yan tutted. "Shen Xiling, that word again. You make too much of it. Honor and profit are two separate matters. I wouldn't be able to call myself a true merchant if I decided that certain types of goods were appropriate for trade and others were not. If something is in need, it has value, and a merchant's calling is to use his knowledge of its demand to his advantage. There is a high demand for Chinese workers. Besides, it is their contracts I deal in. Naturally, men go along with the contracts to wherever they are transported."

Yan's mention of transport reminded Shen of he'd what he had come to discuss. "And where do you send these . . . contracts?"

The question hung in the air for a moment, Yan's face turned contemplative, as if cogs in his head were clicking away like the innards of a clock. Yan looked down at the teapot. "It is ready," he said pouring tea into small cups. Both men sipped, bobbing their heads appreciatively at the smoothness of the *oolong*.

Yan put his teacup down. "Yes, the contracts. Many go to Cuba where they work in fields, just as on farms in China, but for better pay. And also to Peru, but there it's quite different, they're employed as diggers, miners."

"For gold? Silver?"

"Afraid not. In Peru, they dig for guano."

"Is that some kind of precious stone?"

Yan laughed. "It is precious, but not in a way you might think. Guano is simply bird manure."

"There's profit in bird shit?"

"Indeed. Even in that. How strange life is, *eh?* Over centuries, sea birds visiting coastal areas to nest have been depositing their waste there, which it turns out, is rather valuable as fertilizer."

"So, just like the night soil collected by farmers."

Yan nodded.

"What about getting to other places?" Shen said.

"Is there somewhere in particular that you're interested in?" Yan asked, refilling the teacups.

"I want to know how one gets to *Gum Saan.*"

"Yes, well . . . many have started traveling there too of course, but generally, those going to Gold Mountain are different; free of labor contracts."

"Tell me, Master Yan. How does one get there?"

"Have you considered it carefully? Do you really want to go? If you stay in China, I might be able to protect you, provide work from time to time as needed."

Shen had anticipated the offer. If he stayed, it would only be a matter of time before Yan betrayed him. "With the Taotai gone, with no family ties, it's best to leave."

"You're not such a young man. Not to say you are old, not at all, but such adventures are for the young, or those running from something."

"Or someone wanting to make a new start. Please, tell me," Shen said.

Yan slurped his tea noisily. "Well, if you are certain."

"Under the circumstances, it's only a matter of how I should go about it."

"Perhaps we can help one another then."

"How can an ignorant man like me help you?"

"I could use a man like you to extend my business affairs."

Shen slanted his head quizzically. "Work for you in *Gum Saan*?"

"Other than merely disappearing, you'd have a proper reason for going. Such an arrangement could work well for both of us, don't you think?"

Shen looked down, fingering the rim of his empty teacup. "I'm not sure."

Yan picked up the teapot and leaned forward to pour. Shen tapped his knuckles gently on the tabletop in a simulated *kowtow* while Yan filled the cup.

"There has been talk," Yan said, "of the governor's death last night." He sipped his tea but kept half-closed eyes on Shen, tipping the teacup back, peering through wisps of steam.

"What kind of talk?" Shen brought the teacup to his lips.

"Just idle chatter, but nonetheless, talk of," Yan paused, leaned forward and lowered his voice, "poison." The word slithered slowly out of Yan's mouth like a viper. It dropped to the table and slid across to Shen and then sank its fangs into his throat.

Shen choked on his tea. Did Yan know, or was the crafty merchant just fishing for information? Only hours had passed since the murder. The latter, Shen decided, but did his reaction give him away?

"Are you alright?" Yan asked.

Shen dabbed his mouth with a napkin. "It's nothing. Marketplace rumors can be so far from reality."

Yan laughed. "Yes they can, we've all heard our share of foolish gossip, but there's a ring of truth to this one. Anyway, what do you think of my suggestion of your doing some work for me?"

Shen could feel Yan trying to own him, tentacles reaching out to envelop him in a cocoon of lifelong obligation — the cocoon of a golden silkworm. Shen heard the shaman's words: *You can rely on my discretion.* If the shaman hadn't yet sold Yan the information, he soon would. He had to be silenced. In the meantime, Shen thought he'd better play along with Yan. "I suppose such an arrangement might work."

"Good, good." Yan poured more tea.

"What would I have to do?"

"I want to extend my business activities."

"Opium?"

"That, and more, reaching out to wherever our countrymen go — I need someone I can trust to help me with it, and since you want to go anyway . . . ."

"I am not a businessman."

"Don't worry about that. You have other talents. Special skills in what you already do. There will be some other work, but don't worry, you'll catch on, a smart fellow like you. I have dealings with a shipping company that works out of the port of Xiamen. They sail to *Gum Saan.* If you wish, I could arrange your passage to America."

"I would be most grateful for such a kind arrangement," Shen said, *and be in your debt,* he thought.

"So be it." Yan beamed. "I'll let you know details about our specific business arrangements later. I'll send word to your house."

"I live at . . ."

Yen held his hand up. "We know where to find you." Yan laughed and glanced up at his bodyguard who returned a sly grin. "Don't look so surprised, Shen. But now there are

46

things we must discuss, this is as good a place as any to have a chat." Yan gestured to their surroundings. Many diners had finished their meals, and the restaurant was beginning to thin out. "Unless you're in a hurry to go elsewhere."

"I have nowhere to go now that the Taotai is gone."

Yan nodded benevolently. "As I said, you have specific talents that will serve me well once you're in *Gum Saan*, but being on your own there, you should know a little about how money is made and used."

Shen couldn't comprehend why a successful merchant would consider him as a business partner. He suspected the man of something more, and that man being Yan, of something sinister. The merchant attempted to instruct him on how to conduct business, the machinations of a world he knew existed but until now had managed to avoid getting involved in. He thought it might do him good to learn something of the world. Under the Taotai, his work had been hard and often dangerous, but trading for profit had never been his responsibility.

The session started simply enough. The idea of selling something for more money than you paid for it seemed logical, but then Yan had said, "Remember, always buy at the right price. Your profit is made when you buy, not when you sell." *How could that be true?* Shen asked himself. And then there were other bewildering things: obtaining goods of the appropriate quality, transporting them, safe storage and the setting of prices. And when all that was done, Yan had spoken of collecting money, and to top it off, doing something that he referred to as 'making money work for you', whatever that meant. He didn't want to ask, just bobbed his head in the hope that it wouldn't be mentioned again.

Yan suggested that Shen bring with him a small amount of opium to America. He qualified it by saying that it needn't be of the best quality. "After all," Yan reasoned, "few of the Chinese who go to *Gum Saan* would have ever smoked the best, and if white-devils take to it as I think they will, they'd never be the wiser." Shen saw the logic of it. Though not a regular opium user himself, the Taotai was, and his household only ever used the very finest quality of specially prepared *yan-gao*, purified opium paste ready for smoking. Opium merchants seasoned the high-quality paste for at least three years in sealed ceramic jars to enhance its flavor and natural potency. Poor households and low-class opium dens sold an inferior product that was often mixed with dross scraped out of spent pipe bowls. "And once they have a taste for it, I'll send you more," Yan said.

The session ended with Yan saying, "I'm sure all this may seem a little confusing at first, but you'll soon understand it. It will become part of your life, like the air you breathe. You are Chinese after all, what could be more natural than making a profit?"

Now, I'm sure there must be things you need to do to prepare for your departure, however, before I bid you farewell, a further word of advice."

"Of course, Master Yan."

"Learn the tongue of the 'Red Hairs' before your departure from our shores."

"I am grateful for your wisdom. Fragrance clings to the hand that offers flowers." Shen bowed deeply. By the time Shen left the teahouse, the sun was low; he followed his long shadow as he moved through the marketplace towards his house.

The idea of a long journey, one Shen would probably never return from, filled him with both excitement and dread. He decided he would use Yan to get away, and then he would disappear into the American wilderness.

That night, Shen's dreams were filled with horrifying visions. A nightmare woke him breathless and bathed in sweat, still seeing images of emaciated men overseen by a richly dressed overlord. They toiled in a rocky, dry landscape strewn with corpses. Vultures stripped flesh off decomposing cadavers and plucked their eyes out. When he fell asleep again, his next dream was nothing less than rapturous. He stood knee-deep in gleaming gold coins; an image he clung to, resisting the fingers of morning sunlight that tickled his closed eyelids.

5

SHEN CHASTISED HIMSELF FOR BEING SO STUPID. Going to a puppet-master like Yan in the first place, tumbling into such a quandary was a stark reminder that without the Taotai's guidance, his actions required a great deal more forethought. He recalled his master's words disciplining his impulsive behavior. "Actions of a typical 'horse'," he'd said, referring to Shen's birth-year animal. "You must learn to heed advice, be less impatient."

Yan was right about him no longer being young. He'd already lived through more than three 12-year cycles. He still felt the vitality of a younger man. His hair was still mostly black, though the sparse whiskers on his chin would reveal patches of gray if allowed to grow.

Daily martial arts exercises kept Shen in superb condition. Rising from the bed, he strode barefooted out to the courtyard. He lived in one of his late master's numerous properties; the smallest and oldest one. He wondered which of the Taotai's family now owned it and if they knew of its existence whether they cared. It suited him well enough —

surrounded by farmland and far from prying eyes, he'd never paid rent. When he left on his journey, the empty courtyard house would likely fall into decay.

He lowered his head while passing the faded depiction of a tiger over the *bagua*, the eight trigrams of Taoist cosmology. The Taotai had been an ardent devotee, and Shen too had come to appreciate its infallibility, of what gave meaning and balance to everything in the universe.

In the open courtyard, he looked down into rainwater collected in a large ceramic urn, grateful that the reflection was not clear enough to show the wrinkles that had started to appear at the corners of his eyes or the whitish scar on his cheek, a small memento of a long-ago job. He cupped his hands in the cool water and splashed it over his face, rubbing the sleepiness away. He pulled off his shirt and prepared for his morning exercise routine.

Standing rigid, he stilled his mind, focusing *qi* on various parts of his body. The inner-strength practice calmed him as he walked around the courtyard in a circle, crouching into a variety of low stances. Facing the center, he changed direction as he went round executing the bare-handed fighting forms of the *baguazhang*; entwining footwork and a snake-like form, twisting, utilizing his whole body with smooth coiling and uncoiling motions. He practiced strikes with fist, palm, fingers, and elbows. He went through a routine of kicks, throws and joint locks used for grappling an opponent.

He moved on to weapons training.

Shen considered archery practice but then glanced over to a weapons rack. He decided to begin his practice with a pair of deer-horn knives. Gripping one of the curved blades in each hand, he executed movements designed to parry and trap longer weapons. The slow, graceful motion made him appear as a man dancing while waving fans.

He replaced the knives with a fighting staff, a *gun*. As a younger man, his workouts with a *gun* had been far more vigorous, employing high leaps and rolls on the ground. Having wielded staffs in numerous fights, by now he understood which moves were the most useful to him. The workout started by kicking one end of the stick up, catching it in both hands and thrusting it outwards held horizontally like a barrier, blocking and forcing back imaginary opponents, going high and then low. He hopped and spun the staff while moving forward, stirring the air in wide circles, creating a vortex of energy that could deflect weapons and drive a foe backward. He changed direction, circling, smashing and thrusting; aiming the end of the *gun*, smashing at head level and then bringing it behind him to jab at a groin. The exercise ended with a leaping spin and a loud slap of the staff to the ground.

To complete his morning ritual, he chose a *dadao*. The broadsword's curved blade was set at the end of a long handle. Shen practiced the 'walking broadsword' style where man and sword continually followed the other's fluid movements. The weapon's balance and weight gave it considerable power for slashing and chopping. Shen cradled it in the crook of his left arm with the blade facing upwards, he raised both hands up, gathering *qi* and then went through a series of motions, alternately crouching and stepping with knees raised high, arms rotating like wings. He turned and slashed with the blade before throwing a hard punch at the throat of an imaginary enemy. The movements had names like 'Five tigers killing a herd of sheep' and 'crouching dragon'; the stances too were named after animals they imitated: monkey, cat, horse.

He had a simple credo regarding the art of assassination. To always seek the advantage, not to show forgiveness, and to keep his actions secret. He assigned expressions to the three principles, reciting them as he practiced with the heavy blade.

"*Jiànfēng zhuǎnduò*," 'see the wind, set the helm', he said slicing the air, completing a turn. Shen crouched low and jabbed the broadsword. He bounded up, leaping across the courtyard, coming down with the point of the blade in the ground. "*Yánchéng bùdài*," 'punish severely, show no mercy', he shouted. He completed a series of fast, explosive moments of sticking, hooking and slicing. "*Yǐnqíng bùbào*," 'secret circumstances, without illumination', Shen hissed, ending the workout.

Shen sat cross-legged in the center of the courtyard and went into a meditation, the name of this style of contemplation, *guan*, literally meant 'observe.' Its symbol was the *Yijing's* 20th hexagram. He allowed his mind to float freely. Eventually, through a swirl of color, a face appeared in his mind's eye. Unclear at first, like an object floating to the surface of a pool, but soon he started to recognize its features — Yan's face. As he observed the merchant's face, it began to change. A moment later, the face transmogrified to that of the shaman. The old shaman's face held firm, and Shen's mind started to make sense of the image, of what the meditation was showing him. If Yan suspected poison, he would get to the shaman sooner or later, if he hadn't already done so. Though he had given a clear warning to the shaman, he was certain now that the old man would sell the information. Should he silence the shaman now?

Delivering death had long been part of Shen's very existence, but he had never killed without being ordered to do so by his master. Killing the shaman would be his decision alone, for nobody's gain but his own. Shen had limited knowledge of the greater world. His experiences were confined to the goings-on of his former master's household in which the Taotai placed great trust in his abilities. Taken in as a child, he was trained as a servant. Hard work and dedication eventually earned him his master's confidence; then began his training as an assassin. He learned to kill much in the same way as he learned to do household chores; instructed by his elders, paying attention to every detail, and by practice.

His first assignment, a simple test, was at the age of thirteen when he was ordered to silence one of his master's rivals. His teacher, also in the Taotai's employ went over the plan with him but stayed back watching as Shen knifed his victim in the back as he staggered home drunk. There was nothing elegant about it, and Shen had spewed copiously after he stopped running.

Shen had learned not to raise questions of right or wrong about the business of killing. Those weightier matters were for people who could afford to sit in tearooms and discuss murder, even order it, but never have to perform it themselves. He knew of many bungled attempts. Some would-be assassins simply didn't have the requisite martial skills. Some that did, over-complicated their tasks by cluttering their heads with thoughts of morality, only to hesitate at vital moments with disastrous results. Others faltered, feeling pity when their victims begged for mercy, resulting in their own deaths, or worse — being caught — the true mark of an amateur.

Shen had been taught how to do things, but he hadn't been taught to think things through, to make decisions or understand their consequences. It was one of the reasons why he sought out Yan Chow, an elder, a man of the Taotai's station, to tell him what to do. He was inclined to follow advice from an elder, to question his own feelings in favor of dubious counsel. He reminded himself that things had to change. *Decide*, he told himself. *Do what you need to.*

He typically did his work at night. Darkness was a trusty companion for any assassin and to have such a co-conspirator was usually an advantage, but not in the case of a shaman. Night was their realm. To kill a shaman, he would need to have the upper hand, get him into bright daylight. He decided to leave immediately for Wu's house; to get to him before Yan did.

The shaman lived a couple of hours walk from Macau's border with China. The house backed against the foot of a hill. A stream burbled near the front gate, perfectly balancing the residence to elements of wind and water. Though a wall shielded the shaman's property from prying eyes, from the hilltop, Shen could see all he needed to. His impulse was to kill Wu immediately, but remembering the Taotai's words, he waited. He camped overnight and through the next day, just observing.

Remembering the interior of the dark house caused a brief shiver. With luck, he wouldn't need to enter. Other than the shaman's wife, a servant also lived there. Shen had seen both women on his previous calls to the house. He watched them tottering about the garden in the early morning. The corpulent, gray-haired wife wobbled away on her bound feet aided by the thin servant.

At mid-morning, the shaman's wife left the compound with her maid. One of the servant's hands steadied her mistress; the other gripped the handle of an empty shopping basket. Shen had only to wait an hour before the wife returned. Her swaying motion, one who in her youth would have been referred to as a 'lotus gait' and regarded as being erotic, was now an ungainly shuffle. With each step, the grimace on her face told of the pain she felt in her twisted feet. The maid followed behind, gripping a squawking and flapping chicken by its legs and with a bundle of vegetables in the shopping basket. Shen didn't think the two women would pose a problem. If they interrupted his work, he would have no qualms over eliminating them both. He hoped there would be no other visitors. If anyone else showed up, the same fate awaited them.

The women entered the house. From the hilltop, Shen heard raised voices. A moment later, the shaman came out in a rush and puttered around the garden, presumably to avoid further contact with his wife. He stayed outside until a shout from the house summoned him for his midday meal.

The shaman's time alone in the garden while his wife prepared lunch, when it happened again the next day would be Shen's opportunity. He couldn't be absolutely sure it would occur again, but if it didn't, he would simply wait for another chance.

Light rain woke Shen just before dawn. Shen pulled on a straw rain-cape from his pack. He briefly entertained the idea of entering the dim house while everyone was still sleeping but steadied himself, again remembering to stay with his plan. "Pulling on seedlings will not help them grow," he mumbled.

He watched the house for the next few hours. Then at about the same time as on the previous morning, his patience was rewarded. The shaman's wife opened the front door and looked up at the sky. She held a hand out, feeling raindrops on her palm and then turned inside. Shen heard her bark out an order. The servant exited the house first and opened an oil-paper umbrella. She held it over her mistress, disregarding her own discomfort as rainwater dripped down her back.

Shen observed the two women depart for their daily shopping. He descended the hill and entered the compound over a wall at the rear of the house. Once in the garden, he concealed himself behind thick bushes. In another hour, bright sunshine replaced the drizzle. The sound of buzzing insects came from near his hiding place. He looked up at the branch of a tree to see wasps emerge from a hive and fly out into the clearing sky.

The wife returned from shopping, trailed by the maid carrying a full basket and the closed umbrella. After she entered the house Shen heard an angry exchange, then the shaman emerged, scuttling out like a hermit crab evicted from its shell by a rival. This time he carried a book in one hand.

Muttering under his breath, Wu ambled from one flowerbed to another all the while referring to his book. He stooped to touch his plants, rubbing them between his fingers and sniffing them, continuing to move closer to Shen. From inside the house came sounds of a chopper striking a wooden block. The shaman looked up briefly, muttered something and then continued: crouching, inspecting his medicinal plants, consulting his book. At one point, the old man stood up and looked around as if he sensed something amiss. He tilted his head up and smelled the air, looking towards Shen's hiding place. Shen flattened himself against the grass, glad for the added concealment of the straw rain cape he still wore.

Wu stepped closer, reading his notes, crouching, touching, sniffing. The chopping stopped. The hiss of frying began. Wu moved to within a few paces of the waiting assassin.

Shen rose from his crouch and stepped aside to a clearing. He wanted his quarry to recognize him, to understand what was to come.

At first, the shaman didn't realize what he was looking at. He wondered why a scarecrow was standing at the end of his garden. Then he understood. He reeled back in shock, tripping over the hem of his gown and almost falling over.

He dropped his book and bean to stoop to retrieve it from the damp ground.

"Don't move," Shen said.

Wu straightened, his eyes going from the book to the stranger and then back to his precious book and up again. "Who . . . So, it's you! Why did you sneak in here like a common thief?"

Shen answered by moving a step closer. In bright daylight, the shaman looked frail; a gray-skinned, shrunken old man.

The shaman took a step back. "You can't need more venom already, it worked well enough, didn't it?" he said with a nervous laugh.

"What do you know of it?"

"What I meant to say . . ."

"You have too much to say. I'm here to make sure you keep silent."

Shen's reply hit the shaman like a sharp slap on the face, but he recovered swiftly. "What is it you think I will do?"

"I know exactly what you intend to do if you haven't already done it."

"Surely, you cannot know my intentions."

"Did you not understand my warning about what would happen?"

The shaman shrugged innocently. "I understood it very well." He spoke like someone trying to soothe a petulant child. "I know the kind of man you are, I would never betray your confidence, or anyone else's for that matter."

"Shit gushes from your deceitful mouth. There is only one way to stop you."

The shaman shook his head in denial, clasped his hands, and bowed his head. He moved two paces closer.

Shen wasn't fooled by the shaman's solemn demeanor — the man could not be trusted.

"Come now. You can't think I would tell anyone," the shaman said in a conciliatory tone, taking another step, "you are mistaken. Who would I tell?" One of his bony hands reached into a sleeve, his foot stepped back, both knees were slightly bent.

Shen recognized the attack stance. Wu's hand came out of his sleeve in a flash, flicking something. Shen pivoted his torso and tilted his head to one side. A dart nicked the edge of his ear as it whizzed past. He touched his ear and felt a trickle of blood. His fingertips tingled where he felt the broken skin. He wiped his fingers on his wet rain-cape.

Wu reached into his other sleeve.

Shen was lucky to have evaded the first dart; he didn't want to give his opponent a second chance. He sprung forward, arm coiled to strike, knuckles of his hand bent so that they formed a blade-like edge. In the half-second that he flew through the air, his vision blurred. His strike had been aimed at Wu's sternum. Expecting to feel the old man's bones splitting under his knuckles, his fist caught only air. When his leading foot hit the ground, his leg buckled. Shen could barely see. The greens and browns of the garden melded into hazy forms. Head reeling, he fought to stay on his feet. He felt the fabric of Wu's robes brush the back of his hand. Shen made a fist and struck out blindly, hoping to connect.

Wu yelped in pain. Shen heard a snap of bone as he caught Wu hard on the shoulder. Shen moved forward, aiming higher this time, throwing a series of lightning-quick punches at his unseen target. This time his knuckles connected with Wu's temple; a glancing blow but hard enough to drop the old man.

Shen saw a blurry shape on the ground moving away from him. He wondered if the poison from the dart to his ear was enough to kill him. Shen had to finish the shaman and get away quickly before he fell. He stepped cautiously towards the blurry shape as it kept backing away. "Have mercy," he heard faintly. The words sounded as though they were spoken through a closed door.

Shen's vision worsened, his head began to pound. Taking one wobbly step at a time, he continued moving towards the shaman.

"I can save you, Shen. I have an antidote for *gu*," the shaman said.

Shen forced out his reply, his voice came out hoarse, sounding like someone else had said it, "There's no antidote for what you're going to suffer."

"You are dying, Shen. Let me help you."

From the other end of the house, a yell came through an open window. "The food is getting cold. Get to the table, old fool."

Shen looked towards the voice but saw only the shape of the house. Turning his head was enough to make him fall to one knee. His hand landed on something soft. The shaman's book he realized. He used its edge to help push himself upright.

"Shen, I'll save you. Just help me into the house."

Shen took another step towards the moving shape on the ground.

"Out here — help!" Wu cried. His voice was weak, the words too faint to be heard clearly inside the house.

"Stop jabbering and get in here," the wife shouted through the window.

Shen's head spun. He aimed a kick at the shaman and caught the old man in the side. He heard the shaman grunt in pain, but the effort of the kick caused him to swoon. It was no use. He didn't have the strength to finish the old man. He had failed in the first job he'd ever decided on for himself.

What must the Taotai think of me? He kicked again, missing his target, almost falling over.

The wife yelled again, her voice nearer this time. "What's wrong with you, old goat?" There was no reply from the shaman, but Shen heard the man wheezing.

Too weak to get himself over the garden wall, Shen stumbled for the front gate, left open when the women returned home with the shopping.

"You're a dead man," Shen heard Wu say. The shaman's voice was not much more than a whisper. "The poison will kill you, you can be certain of it. There *is no* cure, Shen. No cure, hear me?"

―――◈―――

The toxin coursed through Shen's bloodstream. *Gu*, the shaman called it, wasn't that another name for Jincan? He couldn't be sure. Stumbling along half-blind, his breathing became more labored with each step. His vision worsened, and he strayed off the road, wandering deep into shrubbery by the roadside, eventually dropping to the ground, lying on his front with his head turned to one side. His eyes stayed open, but he hadn't enough control of his muscles to even blink.

The small nick on the edge of his left ear had enabled only the tiniest dose of venom to enter his body. Nevertheless, it was more than a whole day and night before he could move again; first able to control his fingers, and then sometime later, to move his arms and legs. Eventually, he was able to turn his stiff neck.

Shen gradually found the strength to get to his knees. He remembered that Wu was still alive and knew his secret. The shaman might be too weak to do something about it now, but in a few days he wouldn't be. It was more pressing now to get far away as quickly as possible. Shen got to his feet and headed for home, doing his best to remain unobserved, keeping hidden in the bushes that lined the road.

While recuperating, he waited patiently for word from Yan about getting to America. He went to the market daily, listening for any news that could put him in danger. A state funeral was to be held for Governor Cunha. The matter of the governor's death was closed. The rumor mill was seeking out fresher fodder

One morning, the fishmonger called to Shen as he walked past his stall. "I have the best deal for you today. Stop for a look, boss."

Shen paused, listening to more market prattle while examining fresh seafood arrayed on a table. His eyes fell on a red snapper. He imagined enjoying it for lunch, steamed and flavored with sesame oil. "How much for this one?"

The fishmonger put the fish on his weighing scales. "A fine selection, my lord. Fresh and plump. How many in your family?"

"No family, just me," Shen said.

"Then you must be a big eater, master. This one weighs nearly four *jin*. And in this heat, it won't keep for long."

Shen nodded.

"You're a man of exquisite taste, lord. Here's one that I am sure will suit you. And, as one of my first customers today, I will give you an excellent price." The fishmonger picked up a good-sized gray mullet about half the size of the snapper. "Just imagine this beautiful fish on your dinner plate . . . steamed, seasoned with sliced ginger, garlic, shallots," the fishmonger turned away holding the fish and continued to speak, "and a little *Shaoxing* wine." Shen was still considering the purchase when the man turned back to face him and began scaling and gutting the fish. He kept talking. "For you, a special deal, half price." Before he knew it, the fishmonger had the fish wrapped in a piece of cloth. Shen paid the grinning, bowing stall owner. He put the mullet in his basket and then went through the market to purchase the ingredients suggested by the fish merchant.

On his way home, Shen encountered a procession filing out of a church. A line of black-clad foreigners followed a coffin raised on the shoulders of pall-bearers. It was the funeral of Governor Cunha. He stopped to watch the procession pass. Shen recognized some of the somber-faced mourners as foreign dignitaries the Taotai had occasional dealings with.

Shen again remembered Yan's advice about understanding the language of 'Red Hairs', foreign devils. Macau was resident to many mixed-race families that had lived there for generations. Though locally born and able to speak Chinese to varying degrees of proficiency, they were still considered outsiders by the Chinese. Other foreigners, merchants, diplomats, and soldiers jabbered at each other making sounds that to Shen seemed no more intelligible than the bleating of goats. He had accompanied the Taotai to meet with foreigners, always with the aid of an interpreter. At those meetings, Shen stayed in the background watching over his master.

The foreign diplomats were a strange bunch — dressed in black coats and tall top hats, even in the height of summer. Some attempted to speak Chinese, learning greetings and simple phrases, but for the most part, they seemed disappointed, even dismissive that the Taotai didn't speak their language. In truth, the Taotai understood more than he let on.

Though unable to understand any of it, Shen had categorized the sounds and mannerisms associated with people of different lands. Unbeknownst to the Taotai, Shen sometimes after a meeting would mimic the gestures and noises made by the foreigners in front of members of the household staff. His audience would laugh uproariously and beg for more. He spotted the emissary from France walking solemnly in pace with the funeral procession. When the Frenchman spoke to the Taotai, he made *shushing* and *hoo-hoo* noises through pursed lips while shaking his head and jerking his shoulders up and down. Shen couldn't help himself and made a slight head waggle while twitching his eyebrows. Behind the French Emissary came the British Consul. That man hardly moved his mouth or body while he spoke. Behind the stiff Englishman walked a gaggle of Portuguese dignitaries. They also *shushed* and spoke with a roll of their tongues. They were darker skinned and generally smaller in stature, but fatter than Frenchmen or the Englishmen — some of whom really did have red hair. At the end of the line walked several sobbing women. The Taotai never had dealings with foreign women, and so Shen knew little about them. He'd only seen them on the street, his impression was merely that they were generally large and wore frilly dresses that ballooned out around their hips. Both foreign men and women smelled to Shen like rancid butter.

He never imagined he would need to converse with foreigners in their own languages. Now he regretted not taking more of an interest other than for entertainment. He needed someone to teach him, but what language would he need to learn for *Gum Saan*? Was there a common 'Red Hair' language? China had *Guoyu*, the 'national language' that all educated Chinese spoke no matter what part of the Middle Kingdom they came from.

Back home, Shen unwrapped the fish and placed it on his chopping block. He noticed a brownish tip protruding from its mouth and cursed the fishmonger for putting something into the fish to add weight to it. Still, he'd gotten it for half price so he couldn't complain too much. On closer inspection, he saw that a narrow wooden tube had been inserted through the mullet's mouth extending all the way into its empty belly.

He drew the tube out of the mullet's maw and discovered that it held a tightly-rolled note. Shen felt a fool for being so easily duped by the fishmonger. Rather than simply sending him a note, Yan did it in a way to exhibit his control. He would be having a good laugh at Shen's expense. How many more people were in the merchant's employ?

Yan's note provided details of a ship that would depart Xiamen Port for America. The merchant would provide him with a letter which he could exchange for a ticket once he got to the shipping company in Xiamen. Now that his crossing was set, he wondered if he couldn't have made his own arrangements. That Xiamen would be a place where he could board a ship and sail across the ocean came as little surprise, the city which foreigners referred to as 'Amoy', was one of five Chinese treaty ports open for foreign trade after China's humiliating defeat at the hands of Britain.

An American ship, a clipper, would leave for *Gum Saan* in a just over a week. At more than 500 kilometers away, it would take a week to get to Xiamen, giving him little time to prepare for his journey. He would have to leave the following day.

Yan's letter explained that the cost of passage to America had been paid in advance and asked for a refund of 75 American dollars. A sum Yan said could either be paid in cash or advanced and repaid after Shen reached his destination, a deal Yan referred to as a 'credit-ticket.' Shen chose not to be indebted and to repay the sum immediately. That the Taotai had been generous was true, but the amount requested for arranging passage would make an unwelcome dent in his savings.

Shen lifted a wooden box from its hiding place under the floorboards of his room. He pulled off the lid and looked down at the contents: coins, ingots and precious stones separated by compartments. Even after three-centuries of continual occupation by the Portuguese, Macau did not have an official single currency. Instead, a variety of coinage spread through the colony, Shen's money box held respectable amounts of most types: Spanish pieces of eight, silver and gold bars, Chinese coins cast in different metals, and more recently with the British presence in nearby Hong Kong, British currency also circulated. The acceptance of one kind over another depended entirely on mutual consent between buyer and seller.

He picked out a silver coin, an American dollar. Holding it up to the sunlight, he studied it ruefully with the knowledge it would soon be in Yan's possession. On one face, a seated female figure held a flag and a striped shield. The shield had writing across it that Shen couldn't read. He wondered about the significance of thirteen stars that ran across the top half of the coin. The bottom of the coin bore western-style numbers '1841', referring to the year the coin was made, nine years ago, Year of the Ox. The coin's reverse side depicted an eagle with a striped shield over its breast. The raptor clutched three arrows in its talons. Foreign writing ran along the rim of the coin.

Shen picked out more of the American coins, remembering how he'd earned them. It occurred to him that he had more than merely earned his keep in serving his master. Assassin, yes, but he had done many other things for the Taotai as well. Protected him, run the household as a majordomo; even kept the wives and concubines from scratching each other's eyes out. It usually didn't take much, just the threat of hurt was adequate, and if not, then the mere twisting of an earlobe worked wonders. He dropped a coin into the bag as he thought of each of the tiresome women.

Concubines, he shook his head at the thought. *Lìng Zhèng, that deaf old bat, number-one-wife hobbling along on her stinking bound feet, cackling at the others all day long. And the newest concubine, Xuěyīng, silly trouble-maker — bore the Taotai's child, too late for her of course, the child she hoped would secure her place in the household was born a bastard.*

He'd spied, disseminated false information — 'political work', the Taotai called it. More coins slipped through his fingers into the bag. *And all for what?* The Taotai put a price on the governor's head, placed a blockade on Macau. Shen had planned the assassination, even recruited and trained the killers. It resulted in a Portuguese retaliation that destroyed Baishaling Fort. Just imagine, a crumbling nation like Portugal bringing China to its knees. As Yan had correctly said, it left the Pearl River exposed all the way through the heart of Canton. *What a mess!* Macau was not entirely Portuguese yet, but eventually China would have to cede the territory like they did with Hong Kong.

He counted out the last American dollar and sighed, bidding the money farewell as he let the 75th coin fall into the money bag. It responded with a *clink*.

———❦———

Shen held out the bag containing his 75 American silver dollars. A little over 1 *jin,* a sum he could hardly believe he possessed. Yan waved for his bodyguard to receive the payment.

"You look as if you are giving up your ancestor's bones," Yan said with a chuckle. "Be pleased, it is a good thing you are doing — a new life, new opportunities."

Shen's arms felt the loss in weight of over two kilograms in silver coin. "It is such a large amount," he said, watching

Cheng walk out of the room holding the money bag. From the next room, he heard the coins being poured onto a hard surface.

"Not so much if you consider the distance you will have to safely travel, over 20,000 *li*. And, I might add, in luxury. Now, tell me, have you considered how you will carry the rest of your money all the way to America? I suppose you have more, hidden away somewhere."

Shen shook his head. "I have a little saved. No, I had not thought of how to bring it. Maybe just carry a money box."

Yan grinned. He waggled a finger in the air. "I would like to propose an arrangement."

"What do you mean by arrangement?" He regretted voicing the question even as the words left his mouth. He should have flatly refused. With a man like Yan, once a negotiation started, he would continue until it concluded in his favor.

"In America, gold is the most useful kind of money. Do you have gold, silver perhaps?"

"A small amount," Shen said.

"No matter how small, I can take a look at what you have, whether in coins, ingots, jewels even—put a total value on it. Then I could offer you the equivalent sum, all in gold." Shen stayed quiet, not knowing how to respond. Yan went on, "gold pieces can be hammered flat and tied into a belt, kept around your waist at all times. I have done it for others."

The idea made sense to Shen, but he squirmed inwardly at the thought of doing more business with Yan. "I am honored that you would do me such a favor, but . . ."

"Do you think it safe to carry a money box under your arm on such a long journey?"

"I wasn't thinking, 'under my arm', hiding it somewhere, perhaps."

"Even a man as capable as you, couldn't watch over it day and night."

"You would offer an equitable rate of exchange?" Shen said in a tone belying his wariness. He felt like the ground beneath him was starting to give way.

Yan placed a hand over his heart and shook his head sadly, his smile softened a little. "You should not be asking such questions. We are to be business partners. I'll draw up an agreement."

The merchant's response deepened Shen's concern, but he agreed to the deal knowing full well that Yan would get the better of him.

"Good. Now, there is something specific I need you to do for me when you get to America," Yan said. "I am owed money. People have absconded to *Gum Saan,* leaving without honoring their debts to me."

"How does that involve me?"

"Give him the letter," Yan ordered Cheng. The bodyguard had returned and was carrying a document and a small book. He handed the letter to Shen.

"Keep that document safely, you'll need it to exchange for the ticket for your passage to America," Yan said.

Shen nodded and placed the letter into the fold of his tunic. Yan nodded to Cheng, and his bodyguard handed Shen the book.

"That is a copy of the accounts of money owed to me," Yan said. "One of your jobs will be to collect these debts. We can use the money to fund new ventures. You will see that the full amount is substantial, over two thousand dollars."

"What are you owed money for?"

"This and that, credit tickets mostly, but some larger amounts for goods that have not been paid for. That's why I need an honest man like you. You will be entitled to one-tenth of what you collect."

"So, I'm to be your money collector?"

"Nothing wrong with that," Yan said. "Cheng does it for me all the time. He'll explain how it's done if you like." Shen looked at Cheng. The man lowered his chin a fraction; he stood straighter, feet apart, fists clenched loosely at his sides.

"Why not send Cheng?"

"I have considered it, but need him here. You can be sure though, I will send Cheng to go after you if something were to go wrong with our deal."

Shen looked at Cheng. The bodyguard looked back impassively. There would be nothing personal in his going after Shen if he had to, just his master's orders. Cheng was a talented fighter, one that Shen didn't want to face if it could be avoided.

"You have arrived so fortuitously at this time," Yan said.

"And what if the people owing you money will not pay, or cannot?" Shen asked.

"Then you will teach them a lesson, a good one."

"If they continue to resist?"

"You will do what you do best. They must be shown as examples, taught lessons so that others will not take advantage of my generous nature. I'm quite sure you will be quite a success in *Gum Saan*. Foreigners call the town, 'San Francisco.'"

"Sunfrasiko," Shen repeated. "I understand," he said with no intention of following through with Yan's instructions. Once he got far enough away, it wouldn't matter. Shen started for the door.

———— ❦ ————

The blow to Wu's temple would have killed him if properly executed, but in time he recovered from it. Shen's other strike had cracked his collar bone. The pain was unbearable, and it took weeks of self-treatment for it to heal. He was in no condition to do anything about going after Shen, but in any case, so confident was he that Shen would succumb to the poison from the dart, that other than to keep his ears open for a report of Shen's death, he made no further effort to seek revenge.

———✦———

After Shen brought his savings to Yan and an exchange was made for strips of flattened gold, little time remained before his departure. Shen needed to get moving quickly in order to get to Xiamen in time to board the clipper, but a final task remained before bidding a final farewell to Macau: a stop at the *A–Ma* Temple.

There weren't many things that frightened Shen, in truth he could think of just three; the foremost of them being the Taotai's wrath. Though he had personally seen to his old master's death, he believed it possible, likely even, that the Taotai would rebuke him from the spirit world if he were not to behave appropriately. It surprised him that the Taotai hadn't done so already given his bungled dealings with the governor, with Yan and botched attempt to kill the shaman. From time to time he would hear his old master's voice in his head; that was frightening enough, he shuddered at the thought of waking to find the Taotai's ghost appearing at the foot of his bed.

His second fear was of ghosts, not just the Taotai, all ghosts, and malevolent spirits, but as everyone knew they could be warded off by various means: incantations, burnt offerings, and protective measures such as willow branches.

His third fear was of the sea; its vastness. It was a mysterious entity he had little experience of, his knowledge of it limited to the coastal waters surrounding Macau and other Chinese ports he had visited while in the Taotai's service. He feared it less when looking at it with solid ground beneath his feet, but the journey that lay ahead was going to be quite different. The Taotai had mostly traveled by land, but sometimes Shen accompanied him on short boat trips to visit coastal districts. Shen spent most of the time during those trips huddled as near center as he could get on a boat, avoiding having to look at the water, getting up only if ordered to do so by his master.

He had learned to swim in streams and rivers but had never once dared bathe in the ocean. The sea had taken both his parents, so he believed. His memory of it was incomplete. As a child, he'd tried to block pictures of it from his mind. Now, when he did want to remember what happened, he was unable to. How was it that the sea had taken them and spared him? The memories sneaked up on him at times he least expected them to. They caused him to panic; shortness of breath and cold sweat. These were feelings he associated with the whole concept of 'sea.'

Unseen creatures living in its depths could take hold of a man's leg and pull him under, or just as easily swallow him whole or bite him in half. And there were demons and evil spirits concealed in it. What of the *Shui gui*, water ghosts? — Souls of those drowned who try to drag their victims under in order to possess their bodies. Could they be warded off? He had heard stories of sea monsters and demons, as much as he wished to believe them as fantasy, they scared him. Recently he'd heard the tale of a fisherman who, during a typhoon, was grabbed right off his boat by a multi-armed demon. His mangled body was discovered days later washed ashore — the expression on the lifeless face was of a man who had seen a ghost, mouth wide open, eye sockets empty, face white like a dumpling dusted with rice flour, it was said.

The sea, with its shifting colors: blue one day, green the next. On cloudy days it turned silver or gray. At night it was black. How deep was it? The sea gave up its creatures to fishermen's hooks and nets, and it seemed that no matter how bizarre the aquatic denizens were — tentacled, barnacled or spongy — they were usually quite delicious. Was it not rational therefore, to believe that a man would be considered just as tasty to a sea animal?

At the *A–Ma* Temple, Shen prayed to the Taotai's spirit for guidance and to his ancestors for prosperity. He made a donation to the temple and burned offerings to appease any spirits that might wish him harm. Then he asked *Mazu*, Goddess of the Sea for protection and a safe journey.

6

OF THE NUMEROUS BOATS Shen could have chosen to take him to Xiamen, he was drawn to one called *Hai-An*, 'Calm Sea'; a cargo junk that carried no more than 20 people at a time. The captain pointed to two oversized eyes painted on either side of the bow. "To see her way through any weather," he said.

The skipper assured him that it would sail close to shore all the way, adding that nothing could happen to it even if it struck something like an underwater rock or a reef, which only added to his anxiety. The *Hai-An* used a traditional design that ensured a watertight bulkhead. At just 18 meters long, the vessel was nothing like some of the large ocean-going junks that he had heard about. Those behemoths were said to be as long as 50 meters and crewed by 200 men. They operated across long distances carrying over a thousand passengers on board, some sailing as far as the Dutch East Indies. Two years earlier, a junk had managed to sail all the way to Britain. The week-long journey to Xiamen was difficult enough to contemplate; Shen didn't yet dare consider how he might fare on the long ocean-crossing to America. Shen boarded the *Hai-An* carrying his whittled-down fortune concealed in the lining of his belt. Once safely across the gangplank, he admired the lines of colorful flags running from the three masts to posts along the teakwood deck. Given his phobia of the sea, he had little experience of boats. Now he studied the *Hai-An's* rigging and watched the captain and crew readying it for the trip. Hoisting the sails looked simple enough, requiring just one man pulling on a rope to raise each of the sails that unfurled as they went up, the battens running through the sails reminiscent of a bat's ribbed wings. In minutes, the *Hai-An* was on its way. The sails swung to the side to catch the wind.

He studied his fellow passengers, most of them traders accompanying their goods. He had chosen his dress carefully, simple attire of an ordinary working man, not the clothing of one from a wealthy official's household. In a small purse he kept a few coins to cover daily expenses, the bundle slung across his shoulder held a change of clothes and the ledger book containing the names of debtors and the amounts they owed to Yan.

Apart from his collection of weapons, other things in his house had little value; he decided to take the bare minimum, to start afresh in a new land. Of the arms, he kept only the set of deer-horn knives. The rest were wrapped in blankets and then hidden in a pit he dug in the scrub behind his house. The deer horn knives were packed together with a small consignment of Yan's opium, sealed in a wooden crate and secured in the junk's hold. He hadn't decided yet what to do with the small amount of opium that had been pressed together to form a small brick, but agreeing to take it continued the charade of his acquiescence to Yan's plan.

As promised by the captain, they sailed towards Xiamen always within sight of China's coast. Taking a northeasterly course, the junk called in at ports along the way, loading and unloading passengers and merchants with their consignments of trade goods. Depending on what the merchants dealt in, the hold and deck were stacked with everything from urns of liquor and sacks of rice to baskets of live animals and poultry. While in port, the close smell of man and beast was overwhelming. Once under sail however, the odors dissipated, whipped up in gusts and fused with the scent of brine, then the travelers were content to sit on deck amongst crates or beside honking geese. These distractions were helpful to Shen, providing him with a thousand reasons not to look at the undulating vastness that surrounded their little wooden boat.

At Shenquan Harbor, a *jiào*, a palanquin, was hefted aboard the *Hai-An* by four emaciated bearers. The men jostled onto the deck, rotating the *jiào* until they found enough space to set it down. The bearers then stretched a tarpaulin over the *jiào*, tying corners to posts and ropes, protecting the vehicle and its passenger from the sun.

It had been Shen's responsibility to keep the Taotai's *jiào* with its gold-leaf roofing, in pristine condition. The much smaller vehicle that had just been carried aboard was well-made but old and poorly maintained. Cracks ran through its red and black lacquer. Painted lotus flowers on the vehicle's sides, meant to symbolize the four virtues — softness, purity, fragrance and loveliness — peeled away, hanging limp like petals of dying blossoms. Its carrying poles were worn smooth where hands had gripped them thousands of times. The bearers looked like they survived on a diet of no more than opium smoke and black tea; their colorful uniforms were frayed and grimy. Nevertheless, lingering beneath the *Hai-*

An's base odors, the scents the *jiào* brought to the junk were of powdered herbs and incense smoke. Fragrances had been used to infuse its cushions and curtains; little reprieve though from the stink of night soil from fields the vehicle would pass through once back on land.

The chatter was that *jiào's* passenger, a bride-to-be, was the child of a respected merchant, sold off as a third wife for an important landlord. The connubial fate that awaited her at Jinghai was a day's sail away, saving the *jiào's* bearers an arduous trek over hilly terrain and through muddy farmlands where they had the possibility of getting stuck. Shen imagined the bearers knee-deep in muck, setting down the *jiào* in a rice paddy and getting trapped. Then the bride would have to be carried the rest of the way on a bearer's bony back.

To Shen's relief, the sea had been calm for the start of their journey. Even so, the junk tended to roll slightly as it plowed its snub bow through the swells. In the early afternoon, the wind rose, and the *Hai-An's* roll deepened. Shen began to feel seasick. He leaned against a vegetable crate opposite the *jiào* and gazed up, hoping to calm his unsettled stomach by looking towards the pale blue sky. There were few clouds, puffs of white high up. The junk's mast jutted towards them, waving, back and forth. His nausea worsened. He looked down just as the bride lifted up a curtain to peek out.

The girl wore a large 'phoenix crown' headpiece and a shiny red wedding gown trimmed with gold piping. Her powder-white face looked about, as far as the small window allowed — up at the *Hai-An's* rigging, to the crates and cages packed tightly around her vehicle, to shrieking pigs in baskets beside the *jiào*. Finally, her eyes settled on a small crudely painted sign indicating the location of the women's toilet — a concession not afforded to male passengers who had to take their trousers off and hang their buttocks off the side of the junk to relieve themselves.

Shen guessed the bride to be about 14 years old. He observed her sun-browned fingers pinching up the curtain. The sly matchmaker had done well to pass her off as daughter from a wealthy family. *Perhaps in the dim light of a bedchamber, the old groom wouldn't notice he'd bought a farm girl. Maybe the sight and smell of pigs was a comfort to her,* Shen thought, holding back a snigger.

The one time the bride emerged from the *jiào*, drew rapt attention from everyone on deck. It happened several hours after she'd boarded. A merchant sitting near Shen noticed the *jiào's* front curtain being held to one side by its passenger. He immediately elbowed the man next to him, pointing to the movement. The man alerted a couple of others, and soon all eyes were fixed on the girl emerging from the vehicle's cramped compartment. As she exited, the girl carefully maneuvered her large bejeweled headpiece so as not to snag it on the brocade curtain. The effect of the slow, careful emergence looked in imitation of a brightly colored insect's eclosion from its pupal case. The spectators made no secret of their ogling, clearly enjoying the distraction, pointing and commenting on every aspect of her appearance. The child hid her face with a wide sleeve as she tottered towards the toilet, meandering left and right with the junk's rolling motion. Men, women and children stopped whatever they were doing. Shen stayed back and watched as the others got up and closed in behind her like a boat's wake, trailing her all the way to the toilet. The skinny bearers remained, lying asleep over the tops of crates.

The women's toilet was simply a chamber pot concealed behind a blanket with two of its corners tied to a sagging rope. The girl pushed the curtain aside and went behind it. When the human wake stopped on the other side of the screen, men at the back bumped into those in front like an aggregation of flotsam. There were noises behind the curtain, rustling fabric, a *clunk* followed by a tumbling noise as the boat pitched to one side. A man and a woman in front of the curtain put their ears closer to the flimsy barrier. A child lay flat on the deck and tried to lift the bottom of the curtain for a peek. He yelped as his mother bent over and grabbed his ear. The *Hai-An* rolled deeply; the little crowd stumbled a few paces. More sounds came from behind the curtain; a little squeal, grumbling, footsteps, and again rustling fabric.

People moved aside when the bride pulled open the curtain. She emerged flustered, pouting; the hem and one side of her bright red wedding gown darkened by a wet stain. She staggered, taking two short steps to the right and grabbing onto the edge of the blanket. It pulled loose and dropped to the floor. She lost her footing and fell to the floor, dislodging the elaborate headpiece. The spectators laughed. The young bride broke into tears.

Shen had seen enough. Much of his time in service to his master was attending to the collection of the Taotai's women — berating them when needed, but also protecting them. He got to his feet and pushed his way through the crowd. "Stand back. You should be ashamed of yourselves, mocking this child," he said.

"Just a bit of fun," a young man said.

"Well, poke fun at someone else," Shen said helping the girl to her feet. He picked up the headpiece and set it atop her head, at a slight angle.

The crowd parted to allow the bride to make her way back to the privacy of her *jiào*. This time they did not follow but would not be denied the show of her climb back into her vehicle, repeating the slow maneuver involving phoenix crown and curtain. With entertainment over, everyone reluctantly went back to whatever they had been doing.

Shen returned to his spot and crouched with his back against a crate, one hand over his unsettled stomach. He wondered why he'd bothered helping the girl. She was nothing to him. He knew enough about women to guess what would likely come next. He groaned, reminded of the Taotai's women. The *jiào's* front curtain moved slightly. He heard the girl mumble angrily. Inside the *jiào*, she hammered the curtain, its gold 'double happiness' character buckled and shook with the impact of her little fists.

In spite of his nausea and the distasteful thoughts of his former master's wives and concubines, he realized that he actually felt sorry for the girl. *Here it comes,* he thought. The young bride let out a loud wail that once again drew the attention of everyone on deck. She let out all her pent up fear, her anguish, in a penetrating series of howls and breathless sobs that went on until, at last, the *Hai-An* slid into Jinghai Harbor. It docked for only long enough for the skin-and-bone bearers to heft their consignment ashore.

The junk's passengers voiced their relief that once again, they would have enough deck space to sit together and chat.

The *jiào* had reminded him of the world he'd left behind, and he contemplated his new status as a man completely on his own, one who would have to make all decisions for himself. As the junk sailed out of the harbor, Shen pulled Yan's ledger from his bag and flung it into the sea.

Watching the ledger float momentarily before disappearing below the waves, he considered his uncertain future. 'America' in Chinese, *Mei Guo*, meant 'Beautiful Country.' It gave him hope. Everyone had heard stories of being able to pick gold nuggets the size of hens' eggs right off the ground. On the other hand, in one of the Taotai's books he had seen pictures not only of white barbarians but also of wild men; dark-skinned natives who were said to enjoy tearing the flesh and skin off their victims' heads.

On the third day of the voyage, the sea turned emerald green, no longer the color of milky tea as it was near Macau — an effect caused by heavy silt collected by the Pearl River as it cut its way through rich farmland and then dumped into its delta. They had sailed past Hong Kong and were to call at Shenwei, still a day away before reaching Shantou, and then finally Xiamen. A herbalist who introduced himself as Chan had come aboard and sold Shen a cure for his seasickness. The remedy worked well, and he felt well enough to move around.

Shen had thought it best to keep to himself, but the excitement of embarking on his voyage made it impossible not to partake in conversations with his fellow voyagers. In the early afternoon, he saw the herbalist sitting with three other men on deck, chatting in the shade of a sail. The men sat cross-legged in a tight circle. The boat's cat, a scrawny animal with an orange coat, hoping to be stroked, squeezed in between two of them. Shen approached the group and joined their circle. He studied the men surreptitiously, listening and examining each one as they talked. With the herbalist, were three merchants on their way to trade their goods in Xiamen. They knew one another, all having previously taken the same route. Shen told them he was on his way to board the ship that would take him to America, a story they had all heard many times. On Shen's left sat a tall, wiry man with a wispy beard. Like the others, the front of his head was shaved, and a long, plaited queue hung down his back. He introduced himself as a Lin, a liquor merchant. Eager to have his companions sample his wares, Lin brought out a few cups and bottles of rice wine from his stock. They passed the liquor round, sipping and praising Lin on the quality of the drink.

On Shen's right sat Kwok, a portly trader with a large mole on his cheek that sprouted several long hairs which he drew attention to by stroking and tugging on. Kwok boasted of his success in dealing with foreigners. "They think us all stupid, the conceited devils," he said rapping the side of his head with his knuckles.

"*Ayah*, the arrogant, buffaloes," Lin remarked, tipping his head back to drain his cup. The orange cat climbed onto his legs, looked up at him and then settled down. He scratched it behind the ears.

"But brother, the thing is to let them think that," the fat merchant said reaching over Shen to refill Lin's cup. A few drops spilled, the cat dashed nimbly away. Kwok laughed and then filled his own cup.

"What, you mean to let those stinking devils think we're stupid?" Lin swayed while he spoke, face flushed from a combination of drink and sun.

"It's how I get the better of them." Kwok paused for a sip.

Chan the herbalist, a small older man with slope shoulders, pressed for details of the fat merchant's commercial prowess. "Come now, Kwok. Tell us how you do it. Otherwise, we'll think you are just talking to keep the sails full with your breath."

"I act dumb, feign ignorance of the correct value of my goods. I quote them a price which they always reject immediately. Then I tell them I am unfamiliar with the current market price and ask them what they are willing to pay."

"How does that help?" Shen asked.

"It pays to appear weak at first. The pig-headed foreigner invariably says a price that is far too high, which I then try to push even higher. Eventually, I accept, pretending to have suffered a great loss." The fat merchant's belly shook with a hearty laugh, rolling his head back. His satisfied audience laughed along, toasting his cunning with another round.

With several cups of liquor in him, Shen felt emboldened and joined in the chatter. "How do you talk to foreign devils? Do you know their language, Kwok?" The merchants, none of them even half as successful as Yan, were happy to have an opportunity to show off their knowledge to the simple man sitting in their midst.

"The tongue of the Red Hairs? I suppose most of us speak some. We have to," said Lam, a finely dressed tea merchant sitting across from him.

Shen looked around the circle; the men voiced their agreement.

"Is it hard to learn?" Shen asked.

"Not so difficult, that's if you can read and write," Lam replied

"I can do both," Shen said.

"Then, first of all, you'll need the book." Reaching into his embroidered shoulder bag, Lam pulled out a sheaf of papers sewn together with red thread. He flung it across the circle. Shen caught the well-thumbed volume. It was less than 20 pages, several of which were torn or falling out. He read the front: 紅毛通用番話 *hóng máo tōng yòng fān huà*, Literally, 'Red Hair's Commonly used Language.' It gave 1835 as the year of publication, 15 years ago.

"Can you teach me to use it?" Shen said.

"Lam will do anything for money," Kwok joked. "Do you have any to spare, Shen?"

"Yes, he's right. I might, for a fee," Lam replied with a chuckle. "I'd never part with it permanently, but you can read through the book for now," he said magnanimously, grinning from the effects of the liquor. "Keep it safe though, they are not expensive, but hard to come by these days with so many foreigners about."

Shen bowed. "I am indebted to you."

"Used to be just for us traders," Lin the liquor merchant grumbled, "but now the foreigners have servants, and they all want to get their hands them."

"*Eiyaah,* enough of this talk. It's time to drink more, take a few bets and get ready to catch dinner," Lam said.

Shen was anxious to know more about the new language. He thanked Lam again and slipped the book into the pocket of his bag that had formerly held Yan's ledger. The men tossed their drinks down and refilled their cups, chatting and telling stories until the sun was low in the sky.

"Someone said something about dinner. What kind of fish?" Shen asked Kwok, relishing the thought of fresh catch.

"Very big fish, but for tomorrow's dinner. The cook has already prepared something for tonight. You'll have to pay of course. But for now, the captain and crew have started preparations for a little sport to pass the time." He gestured to the junk's high stern.

The junk had slowed. Crewmen were starting to pull the sails down. Shen got to his feet and saw a man ladling something out of a wooden bucket, slopping its contents over the side into the sea. Another of the crew tended a large cauldron on top of a flaming brazier.

"Let's go," the fat merchant said, struggling to his feet and waddling to the stern.

Shen staggered along towards the junk's open aft deck, eager to see what was at hand. He peered into the boiling cauldron. Several globes the size of small cannon balls bobbed up and down. "What are they?"

"Melons," the crewmen said. "Hard, not yet ripe, just the right size.

"For what?

"You'll see," the crewman said with a grin.

The slop being ladled over the side reeked. It was a mixture of fish guts, blood and human urine. 'Drives them mad', Shen was told, but he still had no idea what for.

"Look! Here they come," Lin shouted, pointing at a bloodied patch of water. The other men crowded to the side, jostling for a view. "There's another."

Shen looked over the rail guardedly, curiosity overcoming his fear. He saw a triangular shape cutting through the water towards the junk. There were others, their fins slicing through the surface, circling. *Sharks.* The animals responded each time a ladleful of the vile swill hit the water, turning to it, moving more speedily.

"Get out of the way," shouted the crewman who had been manning the boiling cauldron. The spectators made a gap for him to pass through to the junk's railing. He carried one of the boiled melons gripped in a set of tongs. Another ladleful of fish blood and guts went over.

"Whose turn is it?" asked Kwok.

"This one's mine. Same odds as last time?" said Lam.

"Done."

"Give it here," Lam said. The crewman handed the tongs over, and Lam dropped the melon right into the bloody muck. The globe dipped under the surface for a moment and then bobbed up. One of the sharks went for it, swallowing it whole and whirling away. Seconds later, it thrashed wildly and began to quiver.

"What happened?" Shen asked.

"The thick skin of the melon was cooled a little by sea water, but inside it is boiling hot. The shark that took it is being cooked from within," Kwok explained.

Lam grabbed a long bamboo pole with a sharp hook at the end and leaned over the railing trying to snag the still trembling beast. The gamblers shouted their encouragement. He managed to get the hook into one side of the shark's mouth and dragged it to the boat's side. "Got it. Give me a hand with this," he said, trying to haul the animal up. It was a small shark that he had lifted partly out of the water. The gamblers went to his aid, but the shaking animal was attacked by one shark, and then another and another. They sunk their teeth into it and tore hunks off, flailing their heads from side to side. The merchant still had his hook in it, he wasn't giving up. One of the beasts, quite a lot larger than the others, opened its jaws wide and crunched down across the snagged animal's body, trying to pull away with it. The tea merchant was already hanging over the side struggling with the weight of his prize. Suddenly, Lam was jerked off balance and over the barrier, dropping with the pole headlong into the swirling mass of fins and gnashing teeth.

Shen's instincts took over. Momentarily forgetting his fear of the water, he grabbed the half-full bait bucket and threw it into the sea as far away as he could from the overboard merchant. Its contents splashed out. The sharks that weren't occupied tearing into the half-eaten one went wild. They rushed for the spilled bucket. Shen grabbed another of the poles and hooked it through the merchant's billowing clothes. Others caught on to what he was doing and quickly helped haul the dripping man back aboard.

Lam didn't seem to be hurt. Someone passed him the liquor, and he swigged deeply from the bottle. "You saved my life," he said to Shen.

"Too bad about losing your turn," Kwok goaded.

"To hell with that, it is still my turn to hook one of the beasts." The tea merchant sprung to his feet, ignoring his close brush with death. Acting as if nothing serious had happened, he grabbed the hooked pole. "Quick, give me another melon."

Focus returned to the sport. The junk and the bucket had

drifted closer together, and now the sharks were swimming beside the boat.

"Make way, coming through." Another boiling melon was passed to Lam who dumped it into the sea. It disappeared under water only to resurface and get swallowed by another shark. This time Lam managed to haul it aboard the *Hai-An* with the help of two crewmen. The thrashing animal was put out of its agony by a knife sunk into its head.

Lam gave his turn over to the other merchants. The scene repeated itself with three more sharks killed. Two were attacked by other sharks, but one more quivering shark was lifted aboard the junk. It was enormous, the length of two men and took several men to wrestle it up. The beast whipped from side to side, attacking anything within its reach. One of the crewmen moved in from behind and clubbed the animal's head with an oar. Two others joined him, beating the shark senseless with oars before one of them finished it with a knife to the brain.

Everyone crowded around the dead sharks lying on the deck in a pool of blood. The junk's cook crouched down and began slicing the fins off. While cutting, he described how he would serve the fins in a soup using chicken broth as a base to stew the delicacy with black mushrooms, seasoned with ginger and white pepper. There were seven fins on each shark: the large dorsal fins on their backs, one on each side of the animal, three more along their bodies and finally the lower fins of their tails. The orange cat moved cautiously in, sniffed at the blood on the deck and then went for a small piece of discarded flesh, dashing away with it in its mouth.

By the time the job was over, dusk had settled in. What remained to be done was to skin and soak the fins in preparation for cooking the next day. The finless carcasses were dumped unceremoniously overboard.

Lam moved to Shen's side. "Don't think I am not grateful to you," he said.

"If not me, someone else would have helped."

"Ha! This lot? They would have more likely placed bets on how long I'd last."

"I'm surprised I had the nerve. The sea frightens me."

"Anyone can see that."

"I didn't think I was being so obvious," Shen said.

"You tend to avoid going near the sides of the boat. You look away when someone points to a passing vessel."

"You were in the water, would have died."

"You don't even know me. What am I to you?"

"What I did was preordained. I can't understand why I did it, just that I did," Shen said.

"Well, the important thing is that I am still here. I am in your debt. Earlier, you asked about the tongue of the Red Hairs. Since we still have a few days together before reaching Xiamen, I can try to teach you some. Do you still have the book?"

"Yes, of course." Shen reached into his shoulder bag.

Lam put a hand on Shen's arm. "You misunderstand me, friend. The language book is yours to keep."

The next day, Shen and the tea merchant sat side by side on the deck of the Hai-An. They chose a place as far away from distractions as possible. Though in the limited space available, they pressed into a corner just a few paces from the merchants gambling on deck.

"Let's carry on, shall we?" Lam took the book and covered a page with his hand so his student couldn't see it. "Now, once again, tell me in the Red Hair Language how to ask for the price of something."

"*How muchee cashee?*" Shen said without hesitation.

"Good, good, look again at how it's written. Memorize it, the phrase will be one of the most useful you'll ever learn." Lam pointed to a line on the page. Shen read the Chinese characters '哮抹治加示' and mouthed the sounds, "*haau mut-jih gaa-sih*." The combination of characters bore no relation to asking about a price, or anything to do with money. "This is gibberish," he said with a sigh. Each character held a specific meaning, but when combined they made no sense: 'cough', 'erase', 'govern', 'increase', 'show.'

"It may seem that way, little brother, but you only need to remember the sounds. The Red Hairs will understand what you mean."

"Will I need to remember everything in the book?" Shen asked.

"No, I'll point out the most useful ones. After that, whenever you learn a new word or phrase, write it down the way it sounds to you. Do you see?"

Shen nodded.

"So, let's try it. I will say something, and you write it down in the back of the book."

Shen looked at the back pages. The merchant had written a list of Chinese characters — words and phrases and then another set of characters with their 'red hair' meaning.

"This phrase means 'it is raining.'" Lam pointed to dark clouds on the horizon. "*Haf-got raining com-daan.*"

Shen asked him to repeat it and then wrote characters the way he heard them. He showed them to his tutor: 合威靈 金单. He read the words out loud. "'Hup-gat-wei-ling-gum-daan.' Not bad for a first try." The characters meant: 'join', 'lucky', 'supernatural spirit', 'gold', 'only.'

The tea merchant turned his head to a sharp slapping noise — a gambling tile smacked onto the deck. "Well, since you mention 'gold', I think it's time for me to take some money off the others," he said getting up. "You continue practicing for a while longer. We will talk again tonight when we share a drink with our meal of shark fin soup."

Now that he was learning to speak it, Shen wondered if learning this strange tongue would do any good where he was going. He did not want to tell the merchant and have to explain how he knew, but the words in the book sounded nothing like what he'd heard foreigners speaking. Pondering the situation, it occurred to him that the new language had to be known by both sides in order to work. These Chinese merchants knew how to use it, so did the foreigners they dealt with? Would people in *Gum Saan* realize it too? These unsettling thoughts made him want to stop studying.

He heard the Taotai's voice in his head, *you use any excuse to avoid your studies, have you no shame, idle dog?* They were words he'd heard often as a boy. "Sorry, Master," Shen had said out loud. Face burning in shame, he returned his attention to the book. He did his best to memorize new phrases, silently mouthing them, trying to ignore the noisy gamblers nearby.

Shen smelled the approach of rain, he looked up. The sky had turned overcast, the wind picked up to cause large swells. The herbal cure for his sea-sickness was working, and Shen was reminded to buy more of it for his much longer trip across the Pacific Ocean. The *Hai-An* slammed into a wave with a thud. Shen tried to ignore it, keeping his eyes fixed on the open page of his book. His eyes went over the characters but could take nothing in.

Running his eyes aimlessly over the lessons, an uncomfortable image filled his head. A man's face receding, blurring as it moved away, white hands clawing the space in front of his face. He'd seen this image many times. In his youth, the scene appeared frequently. As he aged, they came less often but still sometimes haunted his dreams. He thought it must be what he remembered of his father's drowning but couldn't be sure. With the scene came sounds of splashing water. He also saw someone diving into the sea: legs scissoring down towards the clawing man. A shoe cast off by the vigorous kicking — was it his mother?

He didn't know how old he was when his parents drowned, but he had been with the Taotai since he was four. Sometimes he remembered being in a small enclosure, an animal pen of sorts. Bamboo stalks bound together with strips of rattan. In the cage were other children, all of about the same size. Was the image a dream or something from his past? Beyond the bamboo stalks holding them in, faces crowded in for a look. He wondered if these were memories or if they were images created by having seen orphaned children for sale at the market.

———✦———

With their baggage and Lam's consignment of tea safely stowed in a dockside warehouse, Shen followed his tutor through Xiamen's streets toward the shipping company where he was to receive his ticket. Even as he walked on solid ground, Shen could still feel the rolling motion of the *Hai-An.*

The seaport city bustled with activity; Xiamen was a town that exuded a sense of affluence. New buildings lined the waterfront. Foreign businessmen, many dressed in dark suits and top hats like the mourners he'd seen in Macau, shouted directions to their Chinese underlings. In turn, the lackeys conveyed commands to gangs of workers. Like an army of ants, the work-gangs scurried in and out of warehouses hefting crates and sacks, either to be loaded onto or carried off boats. Numerous ships were anchored in the harbor, a narrow strait that separated Xiamen from the Chinese mainland. Masts stretched nearly all the way across, their yards furled with canvas.

Lam beamed when he heard the name of the firm holding Shen's ticket, *Qíchāng Yángháng* 旗昌洋行. "Why didn't you say so before?" he said. "It is one of the most important American trading houses in China. In the Red Hairs language, it's called 'Russell and Company.'"

Shen heard the words as *lut-so gaam-pun-yi* and mentally assigned Chinese characters to it: falling whiskers, reduction of stupidity, number two. He shook his head at the ridiculous idea. "So, you have business with them?"

"A little — to them I am but a small tick on a dog's anus," Lam said with a chuckle. "Even so, there is a meal to be had, though not quite as nourishing or fragrant as I would like. But you are in luck, the mǎibàn, comprador, is a relative. Perhaps in time he will smile on me, allow me to climb a bit higher, up onto the dog's back perhaps."

"I am sure you are more than a mere tick to him, brother."

"Still, I will need to earn his trust. Bringing you to him gives me an opportunity to visit him."

"What does the company deal in that it has ships going to America?"

"Mainly opium brought in from India. It exports Chinese goods to Britain and America. Tea, lots of tea, more and cheaper than I could ever supply."

"The tea you brought on the *Hai-An*, is for them?"

"Regretfully, not this time. I'll find another buyer for it."

"Here it is," Lam said, stopping outside a white building. Shen looked up at the four stories, lined all the way across with large windows. On each side of the doorway stood a turbaned guard with their feet slightly apart, their white-gloved hands gripping long wooden poles. The sentries wore waist-length red coats with shiny brass buttons, their trousers were tucked into black boots. A picture of Governor Cunha flashed in his mind.

Lam had gone ahead and up a short flight of stairs that led to the entrance. One of the guards stepped in front of Lam, blocking the way with his pole. The bearded guard said something, and Lam replied. Shen didn't understand a word of what was said, but the Indian lowered his pole to let them pass. "Come on," Lam beckoned.

Shen joined Lam at the door, and they walked through into a cavernous marble-floored foyer. Lam led him towards a desk located at one end of the room. "We're in luck, there's the *mǎibàn*. He serves as a go-between for the Americans and the rest of us Chinese traders, the person everyone needs to go through to do business with the firm. " Lam leaned over and whispered in Shen's ear, "he gets a handsome slice off every trade."

The elderly comprador stopped writing when Shen and Lam arrived. He looked up at the visitors. "What is your business here today?" he said, peering up at them through circular eye-glasses.

"Don't you recognize me, *Mǎibàn*, it's Lam, the tea merchant from Guangdong."

"Ah, so it is. Sorry, Lam, we have filled our quota for the month, you'll have to get here earlier if you want to do business with us." The comprador looked away and resumed his writing.

"Yes, *Mǎibàn*, but this time I'm here to introduce my friend, Shen.

The comprador stopped writing and studied Shen for a moment. "Here to do some business with us, are you? Well, Lam should have told you about the introduction fee I get, has he? There'll be no trading with this great firm unless I say so, understand?"

"Yes, *Măibàn,* but I am here on other business." Shen pulled out the letter Yan had given him and passed it up to the comprador.

The comprador made a show of examining the letter, narrowing his eyes, bringing it close to his face, umming and ahhing before finally putting it on his desk. "Yes, I remember now. I have your ticket here," he said, pulling open a desk drawer. He groped inside it for a moment before pulling out a thick sheet paper about the size of his two open palms. He handed it to Shen.

The paper was covered in foreign writing, some printed and some of it hand-written. Other than a picture of a sailing ship on the upper left-hand corner, Shen couldn't understand any of it. "What does it say?" he asked Lam.

"I have no idea, I can speak a few words, but read . . . Sorry. He looked up at the comprador. "Can you help?"

The old man held his hand out for the ticket. He reached for a magnifying glass on his desk and peered through it. "This is for the *Houqua,* one of our clipper ships, it departs tomorrow."

"What else, *Măibàn?*" Shen asked.

"So, you paid 50 dollars for it, I see."

"Seven . . ." Shen stopped himself in time. He felt the blood drain from his face. He had suspected Yan of over-charging him, but not by such a large amount. He swallowed and managed to nod at the comprador. "Yes, fifty dollars."

"Don't look so distraught. It's expensive, but you won't be disappointed, our ships are the best, the fastest," the comprador said.

Shen cleared his throat. "What else can you tell me?"

"Let's see . . . if you have luggage, to be loaded on board and stored below, it has to be there at the dockside by this afternoon."

"Where should I go?"

"Don't worry," Lam said. "Ask anyone down there where the *Houqua* is, they'll tell you where to go."

"I'll get to it right after I leave here," Shen said. "What else is written on the ticket, *Mǎibàn?*"

"What more do you need to know?" the comprador said testily.

"How long does the voyage take?"

"That's not stated on here," the comprador said, passing the ticket back. "But, you should plan on being at sea somewhere around two months, maybe a little longer, depending on weather and sea conditions. You should be there sometime in October."

Shen slept scarcely a wink that night, his mind repeatedly questioning the wisdom of his decision to flee to America. *What would the Taotai have advised?*

INTERLUDE

1850
THE UNITED STATES OF AMERICA,
WASHINGTON DC

FATIGUE ROLLED OVER TAYLOR LIKE A DENSE FOG. His eyelids drooped, trembling briefly like the flank of a sick foal, then falling closed, a reprieve — stage curtains signaling the end to a tiresome show.

The baying grew more frantic, hounds barking at a higher pitch. A soldier in front turned, yelling above the din, "We have 'em, Colonel." He recognized the man's epaulettes, the broad stripes sewn over the sleeve of his blue uniform. The captain panted, eyes wide with anticipation. "They've reached the river. No place for 'em redskins to run," he said spraying frothy spittle from the corners of his mouth.

The officer turned away and jogged forward. Taylor tried following but was unable to keep up. Looking down over impossibly long legs, he saw his boots stuck deep in muck. He exerted all his strength trying to pull free, but the mud sucked at his feet. "Wait for me," Taylor shouted. His command went unheeded, muted by barking dogs and yells of soldiers rushing past him towards their prey, guns ready, bayonets fixed.

He looked down again at his worn-out legs, both boots mired to the shin in heavy brown sludge.

The captain was suddenly back, facing him now. "Can't wait for you all day to take action. Them red niggers'll escape."

"Where can they go?" Taylor said.

"California, of course," the captain replied.

"There's no need to harm them," Taylor pleaded, mortified by the frailty of his own voice.

The captain responded with a smirk. He drew a pistol from the holster on his belt. The black gun had a barrel that seemed to go on forever. He continued grinning at Taylor while cocking the hammer. The mechanism snapped loudly into place.

"Listen to me," Taylor said. "Why don't you listen?" This wasn't a soldier that Taylor knew. The face seemed familiar, but he couldn't quite place it. Lacking the strength to free his feet, he watched impotently as the captain turned away to join his men, gun held high like a bare flagpole.

Still unable to move, three men in dark dress suits and top hats ran by him. The last one stopped as he came level. "Come on Zachary, you won't get anything done by standing around all day. It *is* a day of celebration, or have you forgotten?" Taylor wasn't able to see the gentleman's face, but he recognized the voice. "Hold on, Clay," he shouted. He watched the tails of Clay's coat flutter out behind him. They looked like hairy bat wings flapping between trees, eventually disappearing behind a copse of birch trees.

The dogs began howling. A mournful bay that signaled proximity to their quarry. Thick woods blocked his view of what lay ahead, but he could well imagine the scene playing out: dogs straining against their leashes snapping at a group of frightened Seminole warriors that had been run ragged from days of pursuit. Cuban dog handlers would be taunting the Indians, laughing; letting their hounds rush in before reining them in at the last instant.

"Don't hurt them. Just round them up like I told you. The bloodhounds have done their job, hold them back." Taylor looked around, nobody was there to hear him. He heard gunfire, *pop, pop.* "Stop!" The firing got louder.

Taylor's eyes opened to see his stockinged feet resting on a dark blue carpet. The shoes he'd kicked off before slumping into his armchair were across the room, one on its side, the other upside down with something whitish stuck to its heel.

There was a rap on the door. He realized the sound was what he thought was gunfire. He cleared his throat. "Enter!"

The door opened half-way, and his daughter stepped through. She stood by the open doorway. "I'm sorry. I didn't mean to wake you. I heard you say something, you were shouting," Mary said.

"Was I? Nothing to be alarmed about, my dear," Taylor said throatily, "a dream. But it seemed so real."

Mary wore a green dress with full sleeves, its high neckline set off with a stiff white collar. She was ready to accompany her father to the next affair. Her hair was done in the style her mother favored, Taylor thought, parted in the center and brushed into puffs over each ear. The perfect Washington hostess.

Mary smiled at her father. "Dreams that seem real," she nodded as she spoke, "I have those too, sometimes."

"And what kind of dreams are those?"

"Of better days, Papa, of the good times that are sure to come."

Taylor rubbed his face with both hands. "It's been a long day, so hot out there on the Mall."

"That's why I came to see if you wanted a drink, something to refresh you before we set off. It's so much more humid here than anywhere else we've lived."

"You've been wonderful, all of you, enduring all those years of living in forts. You're a blessing to me, Mary. Both you and your husband."

Mary blushed. "William's proud to be serving you. Me too."

Mary closed the door behind her and took a couple of steps towards her father. She looked down at him, hands clasped lightly at her waist. "I've had the most exciting life any person could imagine, and now we're here in this great big mansion."

"Yes, we are. And what a place I've led you to. I don't know which are more hostile, Indians or politicians," he said with a laugh. "You were right to stay it today, and it's a very good thing your mother's not here."

"You know what Mama's like, we couldn't drag her to one of those events with a pack of mules."

"That's the truth," Taylor said. The sound of his tired voice reminded him of the dream. "Sometimes I wonder what I'm doing here. What in God's name made me think I could endure politics?"

"You can do anything you set your mind to, Papa, and you're as fine a president as any that served before you."

"An old soldier is what I am."

"I don't suppose there's any chance the old soldier could take a longer rest, is there? You know they're going to pester you all evening . . . about California."

Taylor let out a long sigh. "And to think, before all *this*," he waved a hand, "I'd never voted in my life, never even registered to."

"I worry about you, Papa."

"Oh, don't you fret, I can deal with the likes of Webster . . . and Clay," Taylor said recalling the dark figure in his dream.

"And, Fillmore," Mary added, referring to Taylor's vice-president. She smiled wryly.

"Him too," Taylor grunted. " Yes, it seems Mr. Fillmore has become rather bold of late, outspoken over that slave act. Never thought he'd have the backbone to go against me. But, you know me, 'Old Rough and Ready.' I will be fine, just fine."

"Sure, you will. So how about I bring you a snack and something cold to drink?"

"Now, there's an idea. Something to revive me before having to face those hyenas again."

"I know just the right thing. A bowl of fresh cherries and a tall, cool glass of milk."

"Sounds perfect, my dear."

"I'll get Ben to bring it right up," Mary said, going for the door.

Taylor pushed himself out of the armchair. He peeled off his sweat-dampened coat and tossed it over the back of a chair. He let out a long, weary breath, savoring the couple of hours he still had before more speeches and glad-handing on this Independence Day, the seventy-fourth since the nation's birth.

Still not fully awake, he gazed through a window towards the Mall. Eyes half-focused on the glazing, a ghostlike reflection stared back at him. He allowed his imagination to take hold. The noises of a raging battle floated into his head. The words 'give 'em hell' cut through screams of agony and battlefield din to allow the corners of his mouth to twitch up. Faces twisted in pain, begging for mercy, is how Taylor imagined his enemies. Knowing that he could no longer subdue his enemies is such ways caused the images to fade, and with the receding visions went too his little smile.

Though these days his adversaries were clad in black coats and top hats, Taylor saw them as being just as dangerous, and certainly more treacherous than the uniformed belligerents he faced across battlegrounds. His gray eyebrows pinched together as he clung to a vision of combat mayhem. He fancied blasting those frock-coated politicians with canister shot, shredding them to pieces the way he'd done to Santa Anna's army. Why then, he wondered, did it feel an eternity had passed since that day on the Mexican battlefield when it had only been three years.

It had taken a great deal of persuasion for him to accede to running for office. In moments of honesty, Taylor shamefully admitted to himself that had succumbed to incessant fawning. "What's a sixty-two-year-old soldier going to do now that there are no more wars to fight, General?" he was asked. "You've tamed them all Zachary, the redskins, the Mexicans, what's left? How about running the whole country?"

'Zachary Taylor, 12th President of the United States', had a nice ring to it.

Once described by a fellow officer as looking like an old farmer on his way to market, a political machine took over the moment he agreed to run for president. They dressed him in finery, misquoted his words, exaggerated his deeds and sold him to the populace as the god that would right all wrongs. The ignominy of being drawn into politics through flattery was one of the things that made him dream of annihilating his foes with cannon fire. Now at the helm, he saw his only course to regaining his self-worth was to serve his nation with outstanding leadership.

He tilted his head one way then the other stretching the taut sinews of his neck. He bunched up his shoulders, the effort was rewarded with a satisfying *crack*, relief that felt like the uncoiling of twisted rope. Deep creases in his face, puffy sacs under his eyes revealed all of his now sixty-five years. Taylor had done well to feign an image of robustness through another trying day. Revealing any form of weakness was unthinkable, even more so now that his political rivals were out for blood. He was learning to engage the enemy of this political battlefield in new ways. A broad smile and a firm handshake could be wielded like a concealed weapon, one used to disarm an opponent like a well-timed twirl of a saber.

Taylor's vision cleared and he looked out across Washington's Mall, imagining a tower standing over the open ground where he'd spent much of the day at a fund-raising event. Construction of the obelisk had barely started — all that could be seen at the moment was the tower's base, barely a tenth of its intended height of more than 500 feet.

Ben, the footman, knocked and then entered. The elderly black servant was liveried in a blue coat with brass buttons and white knee breeches. He set a tray with a bowl of cherries and a glass of milk on a table by the window and left the room. Taylor picked up the milk, enjoying the coolness of the glass against his palm. A snack of cherries reminded him of his childhood, growing up on a plantation in Kentucky. *But of course*, he ruminated, *in those days we didn't have the luxury of cooling things with ice.*

Mary's mention of California nagged at him; the matter of whether to allow the territory to enter the union as a free or slave state. With thousands of people flocking there in a rush for gold, the matter had to be urgently resolved. Southerners claimed that slavery was vital to the country's economic survival, the richer, more industrialized north disagreed.

What about the dream? More than just a dream, some of it was a memory; bloodhounds chasing after Indians. A decade earlier, as a military commander, he had imported hounds from Cuba to hunt down fleeing Seminole Indians. It had worked for the recapture of runaway black slaves, why not Indians? But for the most part, it hadn't worked with Indians. It proved to be a flawed strategy in dealing with people who knew their lands intimately; armed groups who would fight back fiercely, killing the pursuing dogs and their handlers. Pro-slavery politicians were now pushing for the enactment of a new fugitive slave law that required officials in all states and territories, including where slavery was prohibited, to actively return escaped slaves to their masters. Life as a soldier was so much simpler — to carry out orders from superiors, but as president, the big decisions were his alone to make. He had long avoided recognizing and dealing with his own attitudes towards slavery, towards Indians too, he realized. Now he had to face them front on.

Taylor picked up a small bunch of cherries and bit one off its stem. Its flesh was firm, tart sweetness filled his mouth. He spat the stone into the bowl and bit into another one. Rolling it in his mouth as he considered his problem. America had slipped well behind countries like Britain and France in abolishing slavery. He was a slave owner too. Slaves still worked right there in the Executive Mansion. Moving closer to the open window, he took a sip from the cool glass. His tongue tingled slightly. He took a sniff over the rim of the glass, wondering if the milk had started to turn. He detected nothing unusual.

From the window, he tried to spot the slave traders' pens in the distance. The founding fathers had declared that America was a nation that believed 'all men are created equal', but more than seventy years on, the country still actively engaged in slavery. The issue had been a thorn in the side of past administrations, but none of Taylor's predecessors had dealt with it adequately, believing, hoping it would just go away over time. Now it had become a matter so contentious, pitting northern abolitionists against southern slave owners, that it threatened to tear the country apart with a civil war. He was a man who didn't take kindly to intimidation, and with threats of southern secession, he was siding with northern abolitionists.

Taylor gulped his cool milk hungrily, downing half of it. He sighed with satisfaction. His tongue tingled again. This time the prickly sensation followed the liquid down his throat.

His stomach gurgled. He placed a hand over it, thinking the combination of milk and cherries might not have been such a good idea. Taylor began to feel an ache in his gut: a dull cramp. He rubbed his belly and took another sip of milk. His stomach rumbled and cramped again, the pain sharpened. Looking at the bowl filled with chewed up stems and cherry pits, Taylor recalled reading somewhere that cherry stones were poisonous. He tipped the glass to his lips, drinking down most of what remained in it and set it down. This time the cramp was painful enough to make him wince and clutch his abdomen with both hands. He sat down heavily in the armchair. Taylor felt dizzy. He was losing control of his bladder but lacked the strength to get up.

He called for Ben who waited on the other side of the door.

The footman entered immediately. On seeing Taylor, Ben's expression shifted from a gentle smile to an open-mouthed grimace. His master slid off his chair and onto the floor. A squeaky breath escaped from Ben's throat. The footman rushed to his master. Kneeling beside him, supporting Taylor's head with one hand. "What's happened, Sir?"

Taylor pointed a finger up at the table. "Cherries."

Ben laid Taylor's head down gently and then went for a pillow to put under it.

Taylor felt another cramp building. Vomit bubbled out of his mouth and nose. Ben pulled out a white handkerchief and wiped the president's lips. Taylor saw the handkerchief and Ben's white gloves stained by something yellowish. He coughed. A fleck of spittle flew into Ben's right eye.

Ben blinked a few times. "Don't you worry none, I'll get help," he said.

Taylor saw that the footman's forehead was creased with worry, there was fear in his eyes. "Go! Call Mary," he said.

"Yes, Sir. Just lie still," Ben said shakily. "I'm going now, Mr. President." He got up and went for the door.

Taylor's body shuddered. He felt incredibly hot. He heard Ben's voice calling out, 'Miss Mary, Miss Mary', and footsteps thumping down the staircase.

The president's physician, Dr. Witherspoon, was called and arrived quickly. He told Mary to make sure her father stayed in bed and was fed only dry toast, and, if he could keep it down, a little chicken soup.

"What's wrong with him?" Mary asked the doctor.

"More than likely it was something he ate. That and the terrible heat, of course." Witherspoon said. "Don't you worry, young lady. Your father has an upset stomach, but he's known for having an iron constitution. He'll be better in a day or two. I'll bleed him and then give him a dose of opium to make sure he gets a good night's rest."

The next day, Taylor was burning up with fever. The doctor tried quinine. It worsened his condition. Taylor slipped in and out of consciousness, babbling deliriously. He could not keep down even plain water, let alone dry toast or soup.

On the morning of the third day, Taylor seemed a little stronger and was able to eat a little bread without throwing it up immediately. Dr. Witherspoon was encouraged. Thinking he had diagnosed the ailment properly and was using the appropriate treatment, he gave Taylor strong doses of Ipecac. Made from dried roots and rhizomes of the Ipecacuanha plant, itself poisonous, the remedy was intended to purge the body of toxins. This it did by inducing vomiting.

By the fourth day, Taylor was barely conscious at all. Those around his bedside, his wife, his children and their spouses, saw the head of their family lying motionless, mumbling weakly. But the images in Taylor's mind were far from the mournful quiet of the dying man's bedroom. His head was filled with the percussion of cannon fire.

For a time, as the withered sexagenarian thought he heard the sound of battle, he was heartened, anticipating a revisit to scenes of a vanquished enemy. But those visions, though horrifying, were naught compared to the images that came now. He saw his beloved nation being torn apart — massive armies shredding each other in a war like no other. Blood in all its hues: crimson and fresh, running and spurting from open wounds; brownish, thick with pus oozing out of severed stumps; black, dry, caked so that the gray and blue uniforms were hardly distinguishable from one another. It was brother against brother, a vision of carnage that was sure to come, something that he was no longer able to prevent.

Those round his deathbed believed the painful groans were corporeal in origin, but what they heard welled up chiefly from another source, the anguish within, the true agony being a realization that it was he that precipitated the inevitability of what was to be.

When he succumbed the following night, July 9th, President Zachary Taylor, the 12th president of the United States had been in office for all of sixteen months.

BOOK TWO

JOURNEY

7

FATHER LEFT ME A BLACK DOG. Other things too: some money, a business and a fine house, but the unwanted part of his legacy, the demonic hound, left an enduring stain. The dog strayed into my father's life when he wasn't much older than I am now. Wandering in as it pleased, we felt its unseen presence by the baleful mood seared into my father's heart.

At my mother's insistence, he attempted to shoo it away. He swore off drink, substituting one form of intoxication for another in the form of religious fanaticism. A devout Presbyterian, whether at home or at work, he recited scriptures at every opportunity in frightening volume and fervor. It got so that people would cross the street when they saw him approaching in order to avoid a lengthy ear-bashing.

Once, in one of his moods, I saw something that simultaneously alarmed and fascinated me. Under furrowed brow, Father's eyes shone as fiercely as if there were candle-flames in his eyeballs. Far beyond my understanding as a child, as an adult I have long since given up trying to make sense of it, explaining it to myself somewhat nonsensically that what I saw was a reflection of his inner torment.

And so for several months, while father spouted *Calvin*, we detected no sign of the dog. Despite the religious discharge, a sense of joy returned to our household. The sun shone more brightly, our dinner-table conversations were filled with mirth. Mrs. Blunt, our housekeeper, planned the most agreeable meals; traditional Scottish fare that delighted us. Conspicuously absent during that time was any sign of the whiskey decanter that had previously held center-stage on our shiny brown table top.

One day, the heavy decanter reappeared. The dog returned. The rooms of our large house darkened. Frosty exchanges replaced conviviality. The most innocent of remarks were met with snapping retorts. My parents hurled angry words like lightning bolts. *Ma* launched Jupiterian javelins, seizing the high ground, demanding that *Da* pledge an oath of sobriety. For his part, with his thunder stolen, *Da* spat invectives back, making up for less potency with augmented frequency. If this was to be a war of the gods, I half-feared that one of them might adopt the role of Saturn and decide to devour their own son. After all, I could not help but feel that it was I, his sole progeny that caused his malaise when he often voiced his disappointment at one thing or another that I'd done wrong. *You lack effort, boy, get that from yer Ma, I s'pose* or *If you spent as much time at schoolwork as playin' th' fool, you just might make something of yerself.*

On occasion, infected by the fury, our faithful Mrs. Blunt tossed a few of her own tempered barbs. During those periods of belligerency, I took refuge in my room shielding my face with one of the many books I had for this purpose until I felt it safe to emerge.

Father made several more attempts to expel the hound but it always returned after short periods. I suspect that sensing it would soon be bad to return, the crafty beast never really left the house at all. Instead, it found a shadowy place to hide until it was once again lured back by the scent of whiskey. With each successive attempt to be rid of it, *Da* seemed more half-hearted. Each time the dog reappeared, it burrowed itself more deeply into the labyrinth of my father's psyche.

In *Da's* later years, the dog took up permanent abode. My mother was resigned to it by then, perhaps in some ways preferring *Da's* drunkenness to his brand of religious fervor that left us exasperated. It is to this day that given half a chance, I would still turn away from any sort of preaching.

My father even gave the hound a name. On occasion, he would speak to it saying things like, "Now, away with ye, *Cù-Sith*, let a man have his dream in peace." As a six-year-old lad, the Gaelic moniker never failed to strike the fear of God in me, conjuring images of an enormous wolf-like creature; the stuff of nightmares.

Soon after Father's death, the beast that had him by the collar for most of his life began to haunt *me*. Immersed in grief, I was at my lowest ebb when the black dog arrived. While my head was bowed, the balls of my palms pressed to my eye sockets to hold back a torrent of hot tears, it nuzzled the crease at the side of my bent knee. When the dog had my attention, it turned its head away. My gaze followed the direction of its muzzle. There, a decanter sitting on a mahogany sideboard promised solace, beckoning me with a wink of its crystalline eye.

The hound appeared nothing like the terrifying beast I'd imagined as a child. It was merely a black dog with a grizzled snout; the kind I'd hesitate to turn out on a chilly night while I sat warmed by the fire, a glass of amber liquid in my hand.

Early on, it didn't bother me much. I accepted its presence as an heirloom like an old rug or a chipped china teapot. As I grew older, however, it rarely left my side and I succumbed to its wicked nimbus with ever-growing self-loathing. The dog would lie at my feet, gazing up with tacit approval while I tipped my head back to glug down the dregs of a bottle.

On a day that was to change my life, I was jarred out of crapulous slumber by repeated jangling. I hid my face under a pillow to escape the clamor only to be haunted by the previous night's excesses in the form of my sour breath.

"Train's leaving in an hour." I forced open my crusty eyelids to see Mrs. Blunt holding a schoolteacher's brass bell in one hand and a cup of strong black tea in the other. Shaking her head censoriously, she said, "Just like your 'da.'" The beverage did little to restore my senses but the mention of my father had the anticipated effect. The old warhorse had witnessed ebriety in our home more often than I am comfortable to admit. I don't recall whether I countered by voicing the words, *I'm nothing like him*, or whether I merely thought them, but her remark jolted me harder than anything else could have.

The thump in my temples told me that Maybury, the man seated next to me on the train probably looked less disheveled than I did. He gave me a lopsided smile, one eye half-closed against a blast of smoke. "How 'bout a snort, Detective Graystone," he said, proffering a pewter flask; other bottles were secreted in the pockets of his brown checked suit. The man had been drinking since the start of our journey. "No sense wasting good tipple. We'll soon be there, I reckon."

Maybury held the uncorked flask to my face. I caught the caramelly scent of whiskey through the reek of coal smoke from the train's smokestack. It took all my willpower to decline the drink, knowing that if I took one sip, I would crave another, and another night would end in oblivion. "Thank you, but no," I said weakly with the sound of Mrs. Blunt's bell pealing in my head. The dog looked up, signifying its disapproval by baring its pink gums, revealing a row of fangs.

The wind snatched away my words but Maybury seemed to understand well enough. He shrugged and then held his head back for a slug. It took restraint not to rip the flask from his hands and pour the drink down my torrid throat, feel the familiar burn in the pit of my stomach. I pushed the craving away, refocusing my attention on the train journey.

I had lost count of the times we'd stopped on the way from New York City, seventeen perhaps. Something in the order of 200 miles of track had passed under us in the past ten hours; a bone-jarring ride made more uncomfortable by the metallic screech of wheels over tracks. Our train car was a rounded boxy thing; as if the upper part of a horse-drawn carriage had been shaved off and set onto a steel frame. With so many mourners trying to get to the capital for President Taylor's funeral, and late as I was to the station, it hadn't been possible to get a place inside one of the cars. Despite the discomfort, I considered myself lucky to have procured a bench seat on the top of a carriage. Travel time by rail was cut by more than half of what it would have been by stagecoach. Unfortunately, my seat was atop the first carriage behind the engine.

Flecks of soot clung to the pink skin of Maybury's bald patch. He dragged the back of a hand across his face, leaving a sooty streak from the bridge of his nose to the stubble under his cheekbone. On both cheeks, reddish spider-veins spread out like a river's alluvial fan. An awning overhead afforded us some protection from the elements, but not from what belched out the locomotive's firebox. He leaned in and put his mouth close to my ear so he wouldn't have to shout, "Tell me about your sleuthing, Graystone. You going to Washington on official business, then?" I couldn't tell whether it was a conspiratorial wink that accompanied his question or if his eye blinked against flying grit.

"No, sir, like most people on this train, my purpose is to attend the funeral."

"Aye . . . aye, but you must admit there's something not quite right about President Taylor's death. Fishy is the word for it." Maybury pinched his nostrils closed and kept it that way for longer than necessary. The veins on his cheeks reddened like bloodworms.

"I agree. The situation raises some questions." I didn't want to reveal much to a stranger on a train, but the circumstances were more than merely 'fishy.' I intended to ferret out the truth. In all honesty, there was an ulterior motive for my coming up with a more plausible explanation for Taylor's death. Succeeding in doing so would put my fledgling 'Graystone Detective Agency' firmly in the national limelight, a triumph that would prove my worthiness and hopefully quell detracting voices; the strongest of which came from within my own head.

The train had last stopped at Laurel Hill. According to my timetable, Washington was the next stop on the line. I looked ahead but was unable to see much through the smoke belching from the engine. A cloud of steam blew into us, enveloping everyone on top of the first two cars with gritty dampness that smelled of grease. Even though Washington's population was only about a tenth of New York's half a million, as we drew nearer, my body tingled with excitement at the idea of visiting our nation's capital.

I pulled out a folded newspaper from my coat pocket to re-read an article on the front page. The diversion didn't last more than a minute before Maybury slurred, "Find anything intrestin' in there?" He gestured at the paper with his flask.

I kept my nose pointed down at the newsprint. "Not really, I've already told you the main points of interest."

"Nothing about them murderin' southerners then, *ey*?" Maybury said, taking another sip. He clearly wasn't going to give up on the conversation.

"There's nothing about a murder, Mr. Maybury," I answered with a smile and went back to reading. Maybury was not alone in thinking Taylor was murdered. Assassination theories abounded; mostly, that Taylor was poisoned by pro-slavery southerners. The newspaper reports made no mention of any poison discovered, though it wasn't clear whether tests had been carried out for that purpose.

"Mighty obliged if you'd read to me, to pass the time . . . somethin' interestin.'" Maybury tapped my newspaper with his flask. The liquid sloshed. A droplet flew out and landed on the back of my hand. Defying the urge to lick away the tawny bead, I turned my hand over and wiped it on my thigh. Boorish and irritating as he was, Maybury meant no harm — after the long day we had spent sitting side by side, humoring this genial drunk for a few more miles was a minor imposition.

"Well, what sort of thing might you be entertained by?"

Maybury scratched the white stubble on his chin, smearing soot into it. "Let'see . . . reckon I've a hankerin' for somethin' *forrin*."

My newspaper flapped against the wind while I unfolded it to search for the heading, 'Foreign News.' All the stories in the section were confined to about half a single column. The accounts were short, not more than a paragraph each. "Here we go, Mr. Maybury." He tilted in to listen. "Three thousand barrels of gunpowder exploded on a boat on Benares River, in East India, resulting in 1000 persons losing their lives."

"Well, fancy that. That would've been a sight . . . all them bodies flyin' through the air, floatin' in the water, crokerdeels tearin' em to shreds," Maybury said.

"You paint a gruesome picture."

"Thank you, sir. The late Mrs. Maybury, God bless her soul, always said I had an eye for the macabre, if you know what I mean . . . ." He took a sip. "Sabotage against the British, you think?"

"Could be . . . doesn't say."

"Hah! Gimme 'nuther un." He elbowed me as if we had just shared a secret and then took a long pull of his flask. I looked away and down at my paper.

"The salary of the French President has been doubled."

"Hmm, that won't sit well with the Frenchies, with the class struggle going on over there."

"No, indeed not. It says here that 150,000 troops have been kept in Paris to prevent outbreaks of violence."

I was about to read out another story when Maybury stopped me, "Well, would ya-look-a-that. . ." He raised his ample posterior from the bench and pointed out towards the passing countryside. In a clearing, about 30 feet from the tracks stood a line of a people watching us pass. "Injuns!" Maybury said. He waved to the other passengers and yelled out the word a couple more times. "Look at 'em redskins," he said waving his arms.

"Well spotted, Mr. Maybury," I called back to him. Springing to my feet for a better look, my first thought at seeing the Indians was that they were not 'red.' Who were these people? I was no expert on the numerous tribes we white men had subdued. My concept of 'tribes' was that they were something akin to what Scots called 'clans.' Then again, America was a vast continent and we had lumped every tribe together under the generic term, 'Indians.' Seen through their eyes, their tribal differences might be as marked as the dissimilarity between Swedes and Spaniards. Tribes were just names to me: Shawnee, Accohannock, Piscataway. I had no clue as to which these people belonged to. They stared at the passing train; their impassive faces looked to have been molded from tanned leather. Colored blankets hung over their shoulders, a few of them covered their heads with the cloths. Their black hair was worn long, loose on some, braided on others. There were women and children in the group of about twenty in all. We turned our heads to watch them as our train drew away. Passengers in the cars behind us reacted much in the same way as we did, pointing and behaving like excited children.

In a few seconds, it was all over. There were smiles all around, slaps on the back as if we'd achieved something worthy. Beginnings of excited chatter quickly gave way to the clamor of the train and everyone settled back to what they had been doing a minute earlier.

Maybury took a self-congratulatory drink. "That was a bit of excitement, weren't it?"

"Indeed, Mr. Maybury. First time for me," I said, slightly out of breath from the thrill.

"Not me, I've seen 'em redskins more times than I care to remember. Shot me a good number of 'em devils too. Good thing those killers have been put in their place. Well, let's get back to it then. What else is in the news?"

"I suppose you've earned it. But just one more, Mr. Maybury, I want to read a bit before we lose the light completely."

"Right, of course, get on with it then . . . ."

I cleared my throat. Having to shout out each story was getting tiresome. "An assault was made upon Queen Victoria in the street by a retired lieutenant who struck her over the head with a small cane, crushing her bonnet, and bruising her forehead slightly. He was arrested."

"That's a good 'un. Crushed her bonnet," Maybury said, forcing the words through a chortle. "Calls for a drink. Sure you won't have one?"

I wasn't sure at all but declined it with a decisive wave. Ignoring the dog's growl, I held the New York Daily Tribune closer to my face to read its small print in the failing light. Taylor's private memorial service had been held. The public funeral procession that everyone was traveling to Washington for was to be held the following day, July 18th.

My reading was interrupted when the engine driver let another blast through the steam trumpet — Washington was up ahead. A short while later, the train slowed, its wheels screeched as it slowed into the station. I refolded the newspaper and stuffed it into my pocket. The train lurched to a stop with a hiss of steam. Maybury had gotten to his feet and would have fallen over had I not grabbed his arm.

We took turns descending a ladder. When all passengers were down, porters climbed up top to retrieve our luggage. Seeing my fellow travelers, I wondered if I looked as tousled as they did. I stamped my feet and shook my coat to dislodge some of the grime that stuck to my clothes. My leather bag had been tied to the top of the carriage with other luggage and had a film of soot on it. I brushed the dirt off the bag with my palm. My Gladstone bag, heavy with reference books, also contained mourning attire. A suit that hadn't been worn since my father's passing a decade ago, and two years before that when it had been my mother's funeral. I headed for the station's washroom to clean up before looking for a place to stay.

Making my way to one of Washington's best-known establishments was nothing short of a foot-race. A good number of my fellow passengers rushed along, bags in tow to the Willard City Hotel, only to find out that no rooms were available at the place that had housed personalities such as Charles Dickens and Mark Twain. The influx of mourners from all over the county made finding accommodation difficult throughout the district. The Willard's management suggested that I try my luck at finding lodgings a little further out, recommending that I venture to nearby Georgetown. I took the advice and walked away from the throng from the train gathered in the courtyard with their piles of luggage.

In Georgetown, I had the good fortune to find lodgings at the Bingham Inn. Located on Bridge Street, the inn had once been a large family home. I was offered the last of their eight guest rooms, all situated above the ground floor public rooms. Mrs. Bingham, the inn's owner, was a small, thin woman who moved with quick, birdlike gestures. Aged about 60, a widow, she peppered me with questions while I filled in the guest register. The way she spoke assured me that she would be a wealth of information about goings on in the federal district.

Though I was relieved to have found somewhere to stay, the Bingham was a place that provided more luxury than I would have customarily permitted myself. Frugality was part of my nature, but in spite of any misgivings, I had to admit that money wasn't really much of a problem. I had inherited the family's printing business which I had helped to run up to the time of my father's death. Our family presses put out a wide range of publications; copies of the better ones often ended up as part of our library at home.

Father's passing allowed me the chance to pursue the dream of a career in law enforcement. Knowing he would have disapproved, I vowed to make a success of it. With the printing company in the care of a capable manager, the business provided a passive income which along with my detective work, allowed me to get by comfortably.

Mrs. Bingham ordered a young woman to show me to my room where I wasted no time preparing for bed. Weary from the long day of travel, I barely noticed my ankles and feet hanging off the end of the bed as I drifted off to sleep.

8

MOST OF THE BINGHAM'S GUESTS left the hotel early to find a good location in the federal district from which to view Taylor's funeral cortege. After breakfast. I opted to stay in my room to reread a newspaper account of Taylor's death.

INTERESTING PARTICULARS
OF THE
LAST ILLNESS AND DEATH
OF

GENERAL ZACHARY TAYLOR

FROM WASHINGTON
Correspondence of the Philadelphia Bulletin
WASHINGTON, Wednesday, July 10.

Mrs. Taylor thrice fainted from excess of apprehension and Colonel Bliss, who had never shed a tear perhaps upon the battle plain, wept like an infant. At 5— two hours previous—the physicians refused to administer any more medicine, considering his case hopeless, and in the hands of God. The Heads of Department, corporate authorities of the city, diplomatic body, and officers of the army and navy paid their respects often during the day, and seemed to entertain lively feelings of solicitude for his safety. Everything that could contribute comfort to the sick, thenceforward, was extended; but the sands of life had run out, and his hours were numbered.

At nine, the vomiting partially ceased, as all pain had ceased about four in the afternoon. But the system had wasted under the shock and gradually sunk beyond recovery. Green matter was thrown from his stomach at intervals until twenty minutes past 10—that particular coloration of bile that best indicates the dissolution of patients thus seized.

I ran a finger down the column, skimming the lengthy article. It listed the people who were at the President's bedside when he died but I didn't see anything that could help me understand Taylor's demise any better.

Gen. Taylor died without a struggle. It was a kind of sinking into eternity without feeling any pain or experiencing its horrors.

When all was over, the chamber was cleared, until the undertakers had concluded their duties. The body was encased in ice and ordered to remain where it was until this morning when it was finally robed for the grave, and laid out in state in the east room. Thus ended the melancholy siege of disease against a strong bulwark of nature.

Died without a struggle? How could the journalist have come to such a conclusion after the suffering President Taylor must have endured over five days?

As a boy, I was drawn to our library and sought out books on warfare, weaponry, and the injuries they caused. That drove me to seek out medical tomes to study about their treatment. As formative and useful as these learnings were to my future career as a detective, nothing prodded me more in that direction than my father's firm's reprints of 'penny bloods' imported from Britain and then recreated for American audiences. Just as it was across the Atlantic, Americans couldn't get their fill of stories of highwaymen and Gothic tales. The more outrageous they were, the better they sold. Immersed in stories of masked brigands, murderers and roués, the medical books provided a complement to my imagination; helping to solve the crimes described in the weekly episodes.

Continuing my research, I pulled out one of the reference books from my bag. Written in 1835, 'Remarks on the Cholera Morbus' described the symptoms and causes of the disease. Not to be confused with the more deadly strain of Asian cholera, 'Cholera Morbus' was a term used to describe a wide range of gastrointestinal disorders such as dysentery or gastroenteritis. It confirmed my earlier hunch that the diagnosis given by Taylor's doctor was far too vague, too convenient to be taken seriously for a calamity such as the one that had befallen our nation's president.

By the time I was ready to leave the inn, the federal district's temperature had risen sharply. The city was packed with mourners, and Mrs. Bingham had mentioned at breakfast while flitting from table to table, that there could be as many as a hundred thousand people out in the streets to pay their respects to the fallen president. She could have well been right, but even with so many people, except for the military drummers leading the funeral procession, the streets were quiet. I pulled the watch from my waistcoat pocket and squinted against a reflection coming off the ivory dial. It had just gone past one in the afternoon. Walking past the back of crowds ten-deep with mourners, I kept pace with the carriage carrying Taylor's coffin.

People stood silently with heads bowed or whispering softly to one another. Occasionally, as the casket passed by a particular section, there would be calls from the crowd hailing their fallen chief or commiserating with the bereaved family. Here and there, hymns would be sung as the coffin passed.

I wanted a closer look at the Taylor family and ran ahead of the cortege before pushing my way into the throng of mourners along one side of Pennsylvania Avenue. Being quite a bit taller than most men in the crowd, I had little trouble seeing over their heads, though top hats and black parasols got in the way of my view somewhat. As the head of the funeral procession neared, I leaned forward for a better look. My clothes hadn't been soiled by soot from the train engine, but I seemed to have put on a bit of flesh on my gangly frame, feeling my trousers pulling taut and jacket stretch across the shoulders as I leaned further over, craning my neck to get a glimpse of the oncoming procession.

Eight white horses drew the hearse, an elaborately decorated carriage topped with a black canopy. Curtains were pulled aside to display the coffin as if it were on a theatrical stage. Behind the wagon, Taylor's horse, 'Old Whitey', followed with an empty saddle on its back; a pair of riding boots reversed in the stirrups. After the hearse came the late president's family: ahead of them, an elderly woman, the widow, head down, shuffling along; Margaret, the 'First Lady.' I had heard that the term was coined by Zachary Taylor when he spoke at a funeral for the wife of a predecessor, Dolley

Madison. Margaret did not live in Washington, preferring to be away from the hectic life of politics. A cynical thought came to me that the widow had ample opportunity to prepare for this moment. She was reported to always dress in dark colors, apparently due to a promise she had made to God; to give up the pleasures of society if her husband returned safely from war. He had returned from many of them, *and now to die like this*. Three of her children had also died, all girls. Two by bilious fever and one of malaria.

A man in his mid-twenties supported Margaret Taylor's arm as they walked. The son, Richard, I presumed — now man of the family with gigantic shoes to fill. Behind them walked another daughter, Ann, the family likeness unmistakable. I put her age at around forty. She walked alongside her husband. Ann's younger sister followed. This one had to be Mary, the one who took care of Taylor in lieu of her mother. Mary's husband walked by her side.

Inspecting each of the family members, I wondered which of them I should try to approach to persuade them that an investigation was needed. One of the daughters, I decided as they passed right in front of me. It was a callous undertaking, but the position provided a rare chance to get their attention. Funeral or not, I had to act quickly.

Pushing aside any inkling of embarrassment, I stood straight and tall as I could. At the top of my voice, I began to sing a Scottish funeral song, *Flowers of the Forest*.

"I've heard them lilting, at our yowe-milking," I began. A few people turned to look at me. I sang louder. "Lasses a-lilting afore the dawn o' day." The woman in front of me burst out into loud sobs.

Mary looked up, turned her head, and stared right at me.

Shamelessly encouraged, I continued, "Noo they are moaning on ilka green loaning, the Floo'ers o' the Forest are a' wede away." Our eyes locked for an instant before she looked away. I continued singing the few lines I still remembered from my school days.

Many people saw me as being rather peculiar looking; tall and rake-thin, with a sharp nose, Adam's apple exaggerated by a long neck. This time, my odd looks, supported by brash behavior, had been an advantage. I wore my red hair unfashionably long, down to my shoulders. I was occasionally ridiculed — to my face as well as behind my back. My ears still rang with childhood taunts of being a 'gilly gaupus.' There had been a time in my youth when I would have resorted to fisticuffs over a slight, but it bothered me less as time drew on. Besides, there was little I could do about it, the die was cast at my birth. I'd wait a day before trying to speak to Mary.

Dignitaries and common citizens followed the grieving family. The newspaper article said Taylor's coffin would lie in state in the East Room of the Executive Mansion where the general public would be allowed in to pay their respects. The body would then be interred in the Public Vault of the Congressional Cemetery. Later, the family would move the body to Kentucky for burial in their private cemetery.

I couldn't see the end of the procession line that stretched down the avenue. With no intention of waiting for the end, I pushed my way out of the crowd to join the funeral march a couple of hundred yards behind the hearse. Walking along, I examined the faces of those lining the roadside. Not sure what to look for, I had to start my investigation somewhere. I wondered whether the saying was true about killers always returning to the scene of the crime. Some mourners wore proper funeral attire; for the women, black or dark gray crepe gowns complete with black bonnets or veils and gloves. The men wore dark suits and top hats. Those without formal funeral wear, dressed as well as they could and added black armbands or pinned strips of black cloth to their clothes.

An hour of marching was enough. I made my way back to the inn. Much research still had to be done. I covered the distance quickly, but the heat took its toll, and I walked the last mile with my jacket off, thrown over a shoulder. I picked up my pace, anxious to return to my room and sit quietly, trying to flesh out a couple of ideas that had come to mind.

9

THE BINGHAM WAS SILENT when I returned, none of the inn's other guests had returned from the funeral. On my way to the stairs, a tinkling of silverware caught my attention. In the public dining room, the young woman who had shown me to my room the previous evening and had served me breakfast was arranging table settings. She wore a starched white apron and had small patches of black cloth pinned to each shoulder of her dress. I waved a greeting to her from the entrance.

"Welcome back. Can I bring you something, sir?" she said in an Irish brogue.

"Thank you. . ." I took my hat off and mopped my brow with a handkerchief, trying to recall her name, "Beth," I said. "Might I have a cold drink?"

"Of course, sir. I'll bring some cold tea to your room. Number three, isn't it?"

Tea wasn't the kind of beverage I craved. I was on the verge of telling her that when once again, Mrs. Blunt's bell rattled in my head. I sensed the movement of something dark in a corner and resisted looking in fear of getting a glimpse of my waiting hound. "It is indeed," I said as cheerily as I could manage and went for the stairs, taking them two at a time.

I had just changed into a fresh, clean shirt when Beth arrived at my door carrying a tray with my drink. She set the tray down and went to a window overlooking the Potomac, opening it to let some air in. A light breeze, warm and humid blew in carrying with it the river's dank smell.

Beth returned to the table and poured a glass for me. The cool liquid caused the glass to frost slightly. "Nice and cold, sir," she said. "Not that tea would be a problem, but you can't be too careful in this heat, with what happened to poor President Taylor," she added, lowering her face to hide her sadness.

"Delicious," I said after a sip, bringing her attention back to me.

"I should hope so, sir. Mrs. Bingham keeps a store of frozen water, keeps filling it to last us through the summer. Prevents our food from goin' off. The same for all the big houses, Executive Mansion included."

The mention of the President's residence grabbed my attention. "Do you know something about the Executive Mansion?"

Beth picked up the empty tray and held it against her chest, arms crossed over it. She bit her lower lip. "Don't know nothin', sir. Just what I hear is all."

"Hear?"

"My sister works there, you see," she said in a voice that revealed a hint of pride.

"She must be very good at what she does to land a job there," I said, sipping tea again.

"Just in the kitchen, though."

"Even so, to work in the service of America's president. That's something to be proud of."

Beth blushed. She looked away with a little smile that exposed her pleasure, a demure look I found quite appealing.

"There's been some talk," I said.

"What talk's that, sir?"

"Well, that President Taylor might have consumed something," I paused, searching for the right word, "tainted perhaps."

Beth's smile gave way to a somber look. "I wouldn't know anything about such talk, sir. Mrs. Bingham doesn't like us talking about such things, especially with guests. Tattletale, she calls it."

"Though it would not surprise me at all if Mrs. Bingham herself were no stranger to idle chatter of all kinds." My comment brought back the smile. "So, what do you think?"

"Wouldn't know, sir. Will that be all?" she said, tone suddenly turning anxious again.

"Being from New York, I'm just curious as to what people here think. For example, whether you or your sister might have any views about it."

Beth held the tray in one hand and passed it behind her back, holding it there with both hands. She wouldn't meet my eyes, looking down at her feet like a child caught in the act of doing something forbidden. Strands of thick brown hair slipped over her freckled brow. "Mrs. Bingham," she said, turning her eyes up at me, "she says to keep ourselves to ourselves. Wouldn't do for Mrs. Bingham to hear I was involved in idle chatter with her guests."

"I shan't tell a soul, and besides, there'll be nothing idle about it," I said. Beth's demeanor softened. I saw an opening to continue. "Surely a lass will have an opinion. There was plenty of talk about it at the funeral today. You wouldn't be the first to speak of it. I was just wondering . . ."

"Some kind of copper aren't you?" she said in the slightly cheeky tone of a girl who knew more than she let on. Her eyes blazed with insolence for just a moment, another guise I took as being quite attractive.

Beth's cheeks flushed. I hadn't realized I had been staring so intently. I felt my own face burn. "Would my being a *copper* make any difference?" I asked quickly in an attempt to redeem myself, already knowing that it wouldn't. I recalled Mrs. Bingham asking what line of work I was in when signing the guest register the previous evening. Beth's reluctance to say anything to 'the law' was a common reaction of the serving classes, even more so with the Irish — arriving in America in droves, taking whatever jobs were on offer, constantly harangued by the authorities.

"Pardon me, I meant to say, policeman. Mrs. Bingham mentioned it when she was assigning us our tables at breakfast is all — told me I was to look after Detective Graystone's table."

"I'm not a *copper* if that's what you're worried about," I spoke gently to indicate no offense was taken. "If there's anything you know, or might have heard about the president's death, I'd be most grateful."

"Can't think of a thing, sir," she said curtly and then turned for the door. "If anything jogs my memory though, I'll be sure to let you know." She exited my room with a swish of her skirts. She'd left the slight aroma of her starched apron. I gazed at the closed door and listened to her receding footsteps.

10

THE WAY BETH CONVEYED HER PARTING WORDS gave me hope that she had something more to say. Two men fishing on the river bank below my window brought to mind Maybury's remark about the circumstances of Taylor's death being 'fishy.' The Potomac was reputed to be rich with a large variety of fish as well as beavers and otters. But wasn't I fishing too? A fisherman with a baitless line cast into a wide, fast-running brown river, and I had not so much as a hint of what I was after. Watching the anglers cast their lines into the river, I whispered the lines of a poem,

> "The springing trout in speckled pride,
> The salmon, monarch of the tide;
> The ruthless pike, intent on war,"

Would the Taylor family want to merely go home and put the loss of their patriarch behind them as yet another death in the family by natural causes? In their position, I surely would not. At least not without first conducting an investigation, even a rudimentary one. But, for them to treat me seriously, I had to go to them with some evidence.

When Beth had come to my room with the drink, she was just making polite conversation with a guest, with the barest mention of Taylor's death. I had grasped that finest of threads and tugged on it. Otherwise, the moment would have been lost. No matter how tenuous a lead it was, I needed to follow it up — the sister she mentioned might also provide some perspective. Experience told me that gut feelings often bore results if acted on quickly. And, that luck, or providence, shouldn't be scoffed at. Time and again I'd found myself in the right place at the right time to hear or see something. Perhaps being directed to Georgetown and finding a room at the Bingham Inn was one of those instances.

My best chance of receiving a mandate from the Taylor family to investigate their patriarch's death was to cast doubt on the cholera morbus assumption. To submit a new theory, and then to convince them that I would be the best man to investigate it. The situation called for more research, more time to think things through. My notebook was filled with hypotheses, random facts, and many unanswered questions.

Along with the rest of the country, I had followed the political strife plaguing Taylor's presidency. Ironically, much of the current difficulties resulted from the successes Taylor achieved before becoming president. As a general, his military prowess in the Indian and Mexican wars had propelled him into politics and set the stage for a presidency that all major parties wanted him as a candidate for. The status of vast new territories acquired as a result of the Mexican-American War had created a political rift between anti-slavery abolitionists and pro-slavery southern states that had lasted years and now reached boiling point. At the heart of it was California. I wondered what would happen with Taylor out of the picture.

Could a war be averted? "No shortage of enemies," I said out loud. Maybe there was a reason for my recollection of the lines from the poem. I considered the words: *pride, monarch, war.*

I pulled a notebook from my bag and began jotting down ideas.

Cause of death: Murder
Method of murder: Poison.
Enemies?
Political rivals: Who would benefit? (would be monarchs),
Southern pro-slavery States. Commercial rivals: Slave
traders/owners (Pride/ arrogance/ intransigence)

Upon Taylor's death, his vice president had assumed the presidency. I wrote the name:

Millard Fillmore

The little I knew of Fillmore was that like Taylor, he was a member of the Whigs. The political party established to oppose Andrew Jackson. Before Taylor, the only other president to die in office was also a Whig, William Henry Harrison, in 1841. Harrison had lasted in office for a little over a month. That time too, it had been diagnosed as the result of natural causes. Pneumonia, I recalled. I wrote: *Whig Party?*

Wars? Indian Wars? Indians? Which tribes? Black Hawks?
Seminole?

It was an unlikely scenario. My mind was drawn back to the sight of the poor wretches I'd seen standing by the train tracks.

Mexican Wars? Might Santa Anna, from exile in Jamaica, be in a position to exert influence?

Would a killer's motive stem from something much simpler? Something personal — the usual things people kill for and get killed over.

Lust/Love?
Money?

The way I liked to think through complex issues was to plant seeds in my mind and then give them time to germinate. Focusing on loose ends only served to tie me into knots of despair. I pushed my notes aside and reached into my bag for a book. At over 700 pages, 'A Treatise on Poisons', discussed the actions of poisons and their detection. It provided an extensive list of individual toxins and how they acted on the human body. There was no possibility of getting access to Taylor's corpse for examination now, but perhaps there were other things to examine for traces of poison, plates or drinking glasses for example, though in all likelihood, after so much time any residue of poison would likely have been washed away.

Detective work required fastidious pursuit of facts and evidence. That, along with analysis, was what solved most crimes. Where others might see those tasks as tedious, I viewed them as a creative process requiring an agile, open mind. I studied the book's table of contents and then tore strips off an old newspaper to use as bookmarks at the beginnings of various chapters of interest: *Of the Evidence of Poisoning; Of the Evidence from Morbid Appearances; With Suspected Articles of Food or Drink, Of the Morbid Appearances of Irritant Poisoning compared with those of Natural Disease.* I also marked several passages that detailed the effects of various poisons.

The sound of guests returning to the inn stirred me from deep concentration; until then, I hadn't noticed that daylight had become almost too low to continue reading. I lit a lamp and changed my clothes in preparation for dinner, wondering whether in a day or two I'd be making my way back to New York with nothing to show for it. What drove me more than merely fear of failure, was the failure of not making a success of a profession I had chosen over the printing business. My father's admonishing voice echoed in my head, telling me I was wasting time, discarding my responsibilities to a business he had built and handed to me on a silver platter.

My ungainly proportions had more than once fooled criminals into thinking I could be easily overpowered. I had proved them wrong many a time, using my height and long reach to significant advantage. My truncheon lay on the writing desk — an implement of my trade that in New York would always hang off my belt. While at the inn, though it could have stayed concealed beneath my jacket, I felt it would be better not to take it into the dining room. I leaned over and pulled up my right trouser leg. No self-respecting Scot would be properly dressed without a *sgian-dubh* strapped to his calf. In my case, the razor-sharp blade wasn't merely ornamental, on several occasions it had been successfully drawn in self-defense against the vermin that populated New York's criminal class. I straightened my brown suit and headed for the door.

Mrs. Bingham greeted me at the dining room entrance. Her silver hair was pulled back into a severe bun, accentuating her sharp cheekbones. The landlady had changed from the black gown she'd worn for the funeral into a simple dark blue dress. She showed her respect for the deceased president by pinning black mourning strips to her shoulders. Epaulettes that denoted her as a part of the army of mourners.

Overhead gas lamps lit the high-ceilinged room. The dining room smelled of roasted meat and tobacco smoke. Most the dozen or so tables were already occupied. The somber mood gripping the nation over the past days seemed to have lifted. With the president laid to rest and a new one sworn in, the dining room assumed an ambiance that approached gaiety.

With Mrs. Bingham leading the way, I nodded greetings to diners as we passed their tables. She showed me to a table farthest from the door, near a large fireplace. A collection of teapots and decorative china plates covered the mantelpiece. A slight smoky smell rose from the cold hearth.

"Look through our bill of fare, Detective," Mrs. Bingham said. "Beth will be here in a moment to take your order. I expect you'd like a cold drink, ale perhaps?"

I forced a polite refusal. "Thank you, Mrs. Bingham. I'll have cold tea, please."

Examining the bill of fare, my eyes were drawn to the price of 49 cents; exorbitant, albeit for three courses. Would it be rude to walk out now? I decided it was, and justified it with the thought that it might be difficult to find a decent meal at a reasonable price anywhere else in the area. I decided on onion soup with crackers, mutton with caper sauce and to end with *blanc mange à la Bingham*. Now it wasn't only my father's reproach I heard — my mother's voice joined in to scolded me for being a wastrel. I hastily put the bill of fare face down and glanced around the busy dining room.

Beth approached the table carrying a small earthenware pitcher. I had expected her to turn away nervously, but her hazel eyes looked directly into mine. Was it a look of defiance? No, more one of determination. The look of a strong-willed girl with something to say.

"Good evening, Detective Graystone," Beth said. "Here's the tea you ordered." She poured a glass for me. "Have you decided what you'd like to eat, sir?" She wrote down my order and then glanced around to ensure her employer wasn't observing. Beth lowered her voice. "I was wondering, sir. . ."

"What were you wondering?" I said teasingly, "Could it have to do with what we were discussing earlier?"

Beth nodded. She turned her head towards Mrs. Bingham, who was busy greeting a couple at the entrance to the dining room. "Can't talk now, sir," she tilted her head slightly in the direction of the door. "It might not be important to you, but there is something I want to tell you about."

"Tomorrow?"

"Sorry, it's my day off, I have a few things to do. The day after?"

"I'd prefer a time sooner. Would it be appropriate to visit your home for a chat later tonight?"

Beth looked uneasy. After the look I'd given her up in my room, I couldn't blame her. "But if you'd rather. . ."

"No, I'm sure that would be fine, I get off here at nine. You could visit at about ten, would that be suitable?"

"Of course. Where do you live?"

Beth turned her head again. Mrs. Bingham had shown the new arrivals to a nearby table. "If you're sure, she said."

"Quite sure."

She shifted so that her back was to Mrs. Bingham and jotted in her order pad. "Thank you, sir," she said, tearing the page off and placing it on my table.

I pocketed the note and watched her walking quickly back towards the kitchen.

———✦———

Mrs. Bingham was more than pleased to learn that I wished to take an evening promenade to explore the city. She led me to the sitting room and showed me a map of Washington and its environs, a patch of land framed within the fork of a Y-shaped waterway; the Potomac being the heavier left branch of the 'Y.' Georgetown, a port settled 40 years before the District of Columbia, sat on the upper left of the map. I committed to memory the easiest route to Beth's house and set off.

A good number of late-evening strollers were still out on Georgetown's gas-lit thoroughfares enjoying the sights. But as soon as I turned off the main road in the direction of Beth's address, I found myself walking down dark streets. In every prosperous city of America, the wealthy needed their help to live reasonably close by but also wanted them out of sight. The serving classes lived in run-down neighborhoods, hidden places that wouldn't offend the aesthetic sensitivities of their wealthy masters.

Except for faint moonlight, my pathway was brightened only by light shining through window panes. Moving further into the poorer part of town, I detected the footsteps of someone tailing me. The clumsy stalker darted into alleyways or ducked into shadows whenever I turned for a look.

Ahead of me, a dark form scuttled quickly behind a building. I touched the handle of the truncheon hanging off my belt, glad to have remembered to bring it. I crossed to the other side of the street and continued past the alley. It was likely that I had been followed right from the time I stepped off the main road onto these dark streets. I was almost certain that at least one other street thug would be waiting up ahead. One or two men behind and one in front. They had the numbers, but their advantage of surprise was gone. Most hooligans relied on being able to scare their prey into submission. Faced with having to fight, they usually fled. Hopefully, this would be the case.

From house numbers, I guessed there would be a few more minutes of walking before I got to Beth's place. Hoping to avoid a fracas right outside her home, I moved to the center of the street, turned around and pulled out my truncheon; twelve inches of ironwood. I slapped the polished, black club into my open palm rhythmically, an invitation for the two thugs following to show themselves. They emerged from their hiding places furtively, one from each side of the street. Even in the darkness, I could see they were young. They approached with a swagger, dressed similarly in ill-fitting suits, stocky and tough-looking but nonetheless just boys, looking enough alike to be twins.

"That's far enough, lads," I said.

"Or what, Stringbean?" the boy on the left said, snickering.

"Or ya might get cut," the other one piped in, " . . . Stringbean."

I didn't mind the childish insult, one I'd heard hundreds of times. I had been at the receiving end of much worse.

One of the twins looked beyond me and the sound of approaching footsteps. I chanced a quick look. Another boy, a dozen running paces away I estimated from his height. "You kids had better clear off while you have the chance. What do you want?"

"We ain't no 'kids.' . . we're protectin' the street," said the one behind me. "You gonna have to pay up, or get hurt."

"I don't want to hurt you lads. I have business with someone just up ahead."

"Hear that?" the left twin said. "He doesn't want to hurt us. Well, here's some business for you." He pulled a knife from his belt. I didn't think I would need mine, my trusty nightstick would be enough.

"That's right. You show 'im how we do things on our street, Mikey," his brother said.

"What do you intend to do with that? Pick your teeth, Mikey?" I said. "Get home to your *ma* and let me get on with my business."

"Looks like Ol' Stringbean ain't getting the message. Let's show 'im what we mean, *ey*, Pat," Mikey said.

I didn't want to seriously hurt these young thugs, but they deserved a thrashing. I heard the one behind running at me. Counting eight steps, I spun, swinging my truncheon in a horizontal arc. It caught the boy on the temple and sent him crashing to the ground. I continued the circle until I faced Mikey again. Seeing how his partner was so easily incapacitated, he came at me cautiously, knife held out.

"It appears you want to join your friend down there," I said.

Mikey looked nervously at the boy lying on the ground moaning and holding his head, and then back at me.

"I'm giving you one more chance to get home to your *ma*," I said. "The two of you. Pick up your friend and go, *now*."

"Why you. . ." Mikey said, moving in quickly with his knife pointed toward me. His face determined, lips squeezed together in an angry line.

"It's like that, is it . . . Tweedledee?"

Mikey slashed with his knife. I stepped back. With my reach extended an extra foot by the truncheon, I could have bludgeoned my opponent in the head. Instead, I decided to go for the arm holding the knife. I whipped the stick onto Mikey's forearm. The knife dropped to the ground. Mikey doubled over holding his arm.

The sole of my boot thumped into Mikey's chest, sending him onto his back. "You two had enough?"

"Balls! You're a dead man," said the other twin, Pat. He moved closer, crouched, and picked up Mikey's knife, not taking his eyes off me for a second. "You all right, Mikey?"

Mikey groaned. The other lad, still on his back moaned in response.

"Seems you want your turn," I said to Pat. "Come on Tweedledum, I'm in a bit of a hurry now."

"Aaargh, ya damn stri. . ." Pat never finished. My fist caught him square in the face while he was running at me. His head snapped back. His feet, still going, slid out in front. The back of his head slammed onto the dirt road.

I picked up the blade. Six inches, blunt and rusty, some kind of kitchen knife with a split wooden handle tied together with twine. I dropped it into my coat pocket intending to throw it into the river at the first opportunity. I walked over to Mikey and squatted over him. "Now, listen to me, boy. My name is Detective Angus Graystone. If I see you lads again, you won't like it. If you see me, run the other way. Do you hear me?"

"Broke my arm, you damned.' . ."

My knee went down onto Mikey's chest, pinning him on the dirt road. I grabbed his injured arm. "Stop whining. It was just a little tap." I squeezed, though not very hard. He yowled. "Did you hear me?" I asked.

Mikey nodded, groaning through clenched teeth.

"Right then. You boys get home now before I get upset," I said. They helped each other up, and the three of them stumbled off into the shadows.

Beth's little two-story house was like every other on the street other than a lit a lantern was placed by the front door. The burning lamp gave off the pungent odor of camphene; a bright burning mixture of alcohol, turpentine, and camphor oil. At 50 cents a gallon, a third the expense of whale oil, it was the cheapest type of lamp fuel. I appreciated the gesture. Whatever the price, lamp oil was a significant expense for poorer households.

My encounter with the young thugs had taken only moments. A glance at my pocket watch told me it was a few minutes after ten when I climbed a couple of creaky wooden steps onto the porch.

Beth opened the door as soon as I knocked. "Detective Graystone," she said, brushing a lock of hair aside. "You found us with little trouble, I hope."

She wore a simple light blue dress with a floral pattern. No longer in the Bingham's uniform, she appeared younger. I had to stop myself from giving her another stare. "Thank you for leaving a lamp burning."

"Least I could do for draggin' you to this part of town." Beth stepped aside for me to enter and then retrieved the lamp and extinguished it. She closed the door and led the way.

"How do you keep safe walking home in the dark?" I asked.

"Most days I try to walk home with my sister. There's a couple of local boys that claim they're watching out for us. Though I wish they wouldn't bother — think they're entitled to more than a simple thanks, if you catch my meaning."

I followed Beth into the sitting room where another young woman was already waiting, seated on a plain wooden chair, mending a dress. "This is my big sister, Jo," Beth said. She turned to Jo, "This is the gentleman I told you about, Detective Graystone."

Jo placing her mending down and rose. She greeted me with a curtsy, one hand slipped into a pocket of her pinafore. Jo was a plumper version of Beth, a freckled brow and scrubbed apple cheeks that reddened slightly at the sight of a strange man in the house. She seemed somewhat breathless.

144

Though I preferred a chair, at Beth's urging, I lowered myself into the place of honor — a lumpy green couch. The truncheon on my belt remained hidden from sight under my coat but rose up awkwardly into my armpit. My knees poked up like a couple of knobby hillocks, causing my trouser legs to rise embarrassingly high. Already the girls were stealing glances at the sight of thin, white hairy calves above my black socks, and to make it worse, the lower part of a knife scabbard.

Beth took a seat next to her sister facing me across a low table. Jo picked up her sewing and went to get tea, leaving Beth to engage me in small talk. I asked her how her family had come to America. For the past five years, mainly due to the potato plague, Irish immigrants had been arriving in the tens of thousands, competing for low-paying jobs in large cities. Her family had settled in America over a decade ago, fortunate to have done so and to have secured decent jobs ahead of the massive influx. Her father had died a few years back, and now they lived in this rented house with their mother. I guessed Beth to be somewhere in her mid-twenties. She wasn't the child I took her for. I encouraged Beth to take her time talking, to feel comfortable speaking to me before I moved the conversation to the reason for my visit.

"What about you? When did your family arrive?" Beth asked.

"I was a wee bairn when we left Scotland for New York, originally from a town known for its stone quarries . . . where the Graystone family gets its name in fact."

"Did you always want to be a detective?" Beth asked.

"Always. Could never get enough of crime stories, much to my father's annoyance. Though ironically, as a printer he was very much the source of it, constantly bringing home copies of books and the weeklies he was involved in producing."

"Ah, the 'bloods'," Beth said.

"Aye, that's them."

"So, what's it like? Policing, I mean. It's dangerous work, isn't it?"

"It can be at times, but my kind of detective work is mostly about accumulating information and interpreting it. A detective can't be too particular about where information comes from. The key lies in its verification, whether it is of any use. Some may think it dreary, but it suits me, in the way my ancestors back in Scotland worked those stones, shaping them to make them useful, chipping away decade after decade, century after century."

"Well, I hope you won't chip away too loudly tonight; mother is asleep upstairs, she works in a bakery, has to be up at four," Beth said.

We looked up when Jo returned with a pot of tea in one hand and three mugs held by their handles in the other. "Don't worry, there's not a chance of waking her," Jo said. "The woman sleeps like a log."

"What's your reason for asking about President Taylor?" Beth said.

"Collecting information, trying to see if there's anything more to his death than just unusual circumstances," I said.

"So, you do think it unusual, Detective Graystone?"

"Most people do, don't they?"

"So it's official business then," Jo added.

My reply was a smile and a slow blink.

"Ooh, very mysterious," Beth said with a sparkle in her eye.

"Don't you go snooping into the detective's private business, Beth," Jo said. "Isn't that right, Detective?" She returned to her seat.

"Hope you don't expect to be served in fine china like at Mrs. Bingham's," Beth said matter-of-factly while she poured steaming tea into our mugs. "You're probably not used to having tea in a house like this is."

These girls weren't putting on airs. What was good enough for them in their own home was good enough for their guests. It pleased me — made for a more honest conversation.

"You might be surprised to know what I'm used to," I said. "Grew up in a house much like this one when we first arrived in America." I spoke the truth but omitted the fact that we owned the property as well as the one next door, and later moved to a much larger home when father's business prospered. We sipped tea in silence. Not an uncomfortable silence, more a quiet family scene of contentment. "What was it you wanted to chat about, Beth?"

"Well, sir, yes, if you remember, I told you my sister works in the kitchen at the Executive Mansion."

"I do remember you saying that."

Beth looked at her sister. "Tell him, Jo. Tell Detective Graystone what happened."

Jo looked down for a moment, then at me. Her words came out tentatively.

"It's what happened that day."

"Which day is that, Jo?" I asked.

"The day President Taylor, well . . . became ill. The holiday."

"July 4th, go on, I'm keen to hear about it," I said.

Beth nodded, encouraging Jo to go on.

"Well, that evening, the things from President Taylor's sitting room were brought down to the kitchen for washing up. That's one of my jobs, you see," her voice held a hint of pride. "We all heard he had taken ill but had no idea of how serious it was at the time."

"Yes, of course," I said.

"There was a little milk left in the glass. I was washing it out and had my fingers in the glass. All of a sudden they began to hurt terribly, felt like they were getting burned by hot coals. I dropped the glass. It shattered into a hundred pieces." Jo began to sob.

"It's all right," Beth said placing an arm over her sister's shoulders. She looked at me and spoke softly. "Jo told me there was all sorts of trouble over that broken glass. But she didn't lose her job, that's what's important." She turned back to Jo. "Show him your hand."

Jo held her left hand out towards me, palm facing down like a monarch expecting a hand to be kissed. The tips of her fingers were darker than the rest of her skin, as if they had been bruised, or scorched by something corrosive.

"Made it hard to do the washing up at first, but they're better now," Jo said. "They don't hurt much anymore, though I wonder if the color will ever go away."

"So, you're saying that there was something in that glass that hurt your fingertips and you think it's related to President Taylor's sickness?" I said.

"I'm not saying anything, sir, just telling what happened."

"Fair enough. I understand. Did you tell anyone else about it?"

Jo shook her head. "No, I was too upset at the time, the housekeeper happened to be there, she shouted at me, and all I could do was to say how sorry I was for breaking the glass. I was so scared of losing my job."

"Not everyone gets to work in the Executive Mansion," Beth said, smiling at Joe, caressing her back.

"I understand. Is there anything else that happened that day that strikes you as . . . unusual?" I asked.

Jo nodded. "Might be nothing. "

"Tell me anyway."

"Well, the footman, Old Ben. The one who was with President Taylor when he got sick. From that day, he had trouble seeing in one eye. It was all runny and yellow, quite disgustin' to see really. Then that eye," Joe gestured to her right eye, "after a couple of days it went blind, completely. Just like that. He wasn't sick or anything, though."

"Did you speak to him about it?"

"I did, sir, when he first started having trouble seeing, he complained about it to everyone. We all thought it was because he was gettin' old. But he said that the President's spittle flew in his eye when he coughed. Am I completely mad in thinking there might be a connection?"

"I don't know if there's a connection. But, no, I don't think you're mad at all."

Jo continued, "At first Old Ben said the President thought it was the cherries he ate, pointed at the empty bowl he brought down. I cleaned the bowl, didn't find anything strange. And then the milk glass. . ."

I stretched out an arm to pick up my mug of tea and took a sip. "Jo, if something in the milk caused President Taylor to get sick, how do you think it could have gotten there?"

"I've been racking my brains about that." Jo paused, she bit her lower lip and fiddled with a loose strand of hair. She continued. "Milk is stored in the cold room, in the cellar, with the ice blocks. Lots of people had milk from the same churn. On that day, Old Ben went down to get it and the storeman would have poured the milk directly from a churn into a jug for the President. That's the normal way we do it. But. . ."

"What happened differently on that occasion?"

"Well, sir, the regular storeman hadn't shown up for work. His helper would have been the one who did it."

"What's odd about that?" I asked.

"Not sure it's odd sir, but since that day we've not seen hide nor hair of either of them, like they've run off or somethin.' It's been awfully inconvenient for us up in the kitchen. A few days ago, someone was sent round to the storeman's house but came back saying it was all locked up and nobody answered the door. People are saying he's run off to California to find gold."

"Won't be the first," Beth said. "All a bunch of fools, if you asked me."

I nodded to Beth and then resumed my questioning of her sister. "What can you tell me about the storeman, or his assistant?"

"Not much at all. But everyone liked the storeman, Mr. Jake. Salt-of-the-earth, he was. Always laughing and joking whenever any of us went down there. Lives alone, not far from here," Jo said.

"I'd like to talk to Mr. Jake, if I can find him."

"I'll tell you how to get to his house." Beth said.

"And Mr. Jake's assistant?"

"Now, he was a strange little fellow. Hadn't been with us long, just a few weeks. An older man, a Chinaman. We called him Bufo. Don't even know if that was his real name. Had one of those strange shaved heads, pigtail and all. Never heard him say a word. Just nodded and smiled while he scurried about. Ask Mr. Jake about him if you see him. He was the one who brought him in. Vouched for him, I heard."

"I will. Is the Taylor family staying at the Executive Mansion now?"

"Goodness, no," Jo said. "Heard that Mrs. Taylor hated it there. They're all staying with his daughter, Miss Mary and her husband, Mr. Bliss."

I recalled that Taylor had appointed William Wallace Smith Bliss as his private secretary, a war hero, said to be highly capable.

There was banging at the front door. "Go see what it is, Beth," Jo said. "Who could it be at this hour?"

Beth excused herself and left the sitting room. We listened to her footsteps as she walked to the front door and opened it. I couldn't hear the conversation clearly, but there were raised voices coming from the front of the house.

"No, you cannot come in," we heard Beth saying. Jo got up and went to see what was going on. I followed.

Beth had the door open halfway, blocking the entrance with her body. Jo moved in behind her. "What is it, Beth?" Jo said peering over Beth's shoulder. "Oh, those good-for-nothings again. Clear off the both of you."

I stepped up behind the girls and looked over their heads. Trying to get into the house, were Pat, face bruised, dried blood under his nose and Mikey standing behind, holding his injured arm. "Did you forget what I told you boys?" I asked. They looked up in shock at me towering over the girls. The twins stepped back and turned to run. Pat tripped on a step and fell with a grunt. Mikey hopped over him. Pat picked himself up and dashed after his brother. The girls opened their door wide and laughed at the sight of the twins hobbling into the night.

I had been enjoying sitting with the Beth and Jo and would have been quite happy to linger a bit longer, in Beth's company in particular but it was getting late. After explaining why Mikey and Pat had run off so suddenly, I thanked the sisters and bid them goodnight.

Remaining for a moment on the dark porch of their home, I collected my thoughts and considered what to do next. From inside the house came muffled giggling followed by a couple of loud gleeful shrieks. I imagined the sisters having the time of their lives, poking fun at the sight of my bare calves. I pushed the uncomfortable image aside by refocusing on my next steps.

My chat with Beth and Jo had taken about an hour. Normally, at this time of night, I wouldn't have entertained the notion of calling at anyone's home unannounced. A visit to the Bliss family would have been out of the question. However, Mr. Jake had been missing for two weeks, and that had to be urgently investigated. Deciding to go there right away, I stepped off the porch and headed towards Jake's place using the directions Beth had given me.

The moon was brighter, higher in the sky, making it easier to navigate the streets and it took only a few minutes to get to Jake's home. The house was dark, curtains pulled shut across all windows facing the street. At this late hour, most working people would be asleep, resting before another long work-day. Respect for propriety was an important element of my professional code of conduct. This situation, however, demanded an immediate response. I would apologize for waking him up if it came to that. The only response to rapping on Jake's front door came in the form of the barks of a neighbor's dog.

From the outside, the house looked very much like the one I'd just come from. Although not having seen much of it apart from the entrance area and a sitting room, I felt I had a reasonable understanding of how the interiors of these houses were laid out. Downstairs: sitting and dining rooms, a small bath and kitchen; two bedrooms upstairs.

At the rear of the house was an unfenced back garden. An outhouse stood at one end of it. Wanting to be sure that Mr. Jake wasn't in there taking a midnight *cac*, I went over and put my fingers through the crescent-shaped hole in the privy door and pulled it open. A squadron of winged inhabitants swarmed out before buzzing back in. No Mr. Jake — I pushed the door shut, allowing the flies to enjoy their malodorous home in peace.

Heading for the back door, weeds in the unkempt garden snagged at my trouser legs. The door lock proved no match for Mikey's rusty knife. A few twists of its point in the door jamb and the door creaked open. I padded into the small kitchen and closed the door. If Mr. Jake were in, he'd get the fright of his life from my being there.

With only a few dozen lawmen in the district, the odds of being undetected were in my favor. Nevertheless, it would be wise not to stay longer than necessary. This situation called for extreme caution. It was one thing for me to lead Beth and Jo into thinking I had official reasons for making inquiries, in truth. However, working on my own with no client, I lacked a proper reason for breaking into someone's home in the dead of night like a common criminal. If caught in New York, I could probably get out of trouble with the support of a well-connected client, but not in Washington.

With a lamp from the kitchen table, I began to explore Mr. Jake's downstairs rooms. Closed up for the past weeks, the air was stale with mildew. Thankfully though, I didn't detect the scent of death, a stench I'd come to know only too well. There were no obvious signs that anything had been disturbed. Mr. Jake kept his home neat, but in contrast to the sitting room in Beth's home — tables covered with frilly placemats and colored cushions — Jake's practical furnishings were arranged at sharp angles around a small fireplace. A single man's abode. Colors were muted in the yellowish lamplight, giving Mr. Jake's residence a drab appearance. I moved through each room, observing. A small larder off the kitchen was stocked with a sack of potatoes, baskets of onions, carrots, some cured meats. Half a bottle of whiskey was pushed back into a corner. From the dust on the bottle, it looked like it hadn't been touched for some time, making it unlikely that Mr. Jake was passed out in some tavern. I moved through the sitting room.

A stack of newspapers lay on the floor by an armchair. The most recent was dated July 3rd — adding to my impression that Mr. Jake's disappearance was unplanned.

A framed picture hung above the sitting room's fireplace. I raised the lantern for a better look. It was an old campaign poster showing a stern-looking Taylor in profile, arms crossed. *Zachary Taylor for President,* it read across the top. Below the image were lines borrowed from Alexander Pope, modified to suit a political purpose: *About party creeds let party zealots fight. He can't be wrong whose life is in the right.* Mr. Jake appeared to be a devotee of President Taylor, not a likely candidate to do harm to his employer.

It was time to check the bedrooms. I called out Mr. Jake's name from the bottom of the staircase. No reply came nor were there any sounds of movement from above. I called again and then started to climb the stairs, slowly. My heart thumped loudly. Each stair creaked slightly under my weight. I pulled out my truncheon. My shadow cast an eerie shape against the wall. At the top of the stairs there were two rooms side by side with their doors closed. I called Mr. Jake's name again; my voice jarred the stillness of the house and put me more on edge.

I cautiously opened the door on the left. The small bedroom had been converted into a study. A writing desk and was set below a window with its curtains pulled shut. The threadbare drapes let some moonlight shine through. The desktop had nothing on it except for Mr. Jake's writing instruments. Against one wall was a bookcase. The walls were bare — nowhere to hide.

One final room in the house needed checking. I moved cautiously to the door of the other bedroom, wincing at the sound of each creaky footstep. Using the end of my truncheon to rap twice on the door, I called out, "Mr. Jake, are you in there?" The cold brass doorknob turned effortlessly. With a gentle push, the door swung ajar, lamplight swept in behind it.

The air was putrid, filled with the kind of odor that comes from sickness: vomit and defecation. My eyes watered. I turned to the open door for a couple of deep breaths before resuming my inspection of the room.

A narrow bed was against the wall facing the door. Contrary to the neatness of other parts of the house, this room was a shambles. The head end of the bed had been pulled away from the wall by about a foot. Surely that would irritate Mr. Jake's sense of order. The bed was unmade, bedclothes hung half off the mattress and lay across the floor. I held the lantern over the bed. The center of the mattress had a dried dark stain that spread out to the circumference of a large melon. The source of the stink. What the dark mess was, I couldn't say, though from its position it appeared to have erupted from the rear end of whoever had lain in the bed, Mr. Jake most likely. The bedclothes were stained too, caked with vile, stinking muck.

At first glance, the contents of a free-standing wardrobe and a chest of drawers appeared intact — clothes neatly hanging or folded. I checked each of the drawers carefully, at the back of one of them, under a pile of clothing lay a small wooden chest. It had some weight to it, and I had to drag it forward before hefting it to the floor.

Once again, Mikey's rusty knife made short work of the lock. The chest held a pile of coins of varied currencies, sizes, and denominations. It looked like several hundred dollars — Jake's retirement money? Surely not his escape fund. I returned the box to its hiding place and closed the drawer.

A suitcase sat on top of the wardrobe. I pulled it down; empty. If Mr. Jake had run off, he'd done it hurriedly and didn't take much with him. It didn't look as if he'd gone to California to try his luck at panning for gold. Why would he go anywhere without taking his savings? The dishevelment of the room, the angle of the bed, suggested he'd been dragged out of it.

Before going back downstairs, I stood by the door and looked at the scene in the room, memorizing it so as to write the details in my notebook later.

Returning to the kitchen, I extinguished the lamp and exited Mr. Jake's house through the back door.

As soon as I got back to my room at the Bingham, I wrote copious notes on what I had observed. Time was of the utmost essence. I had to follow up with Mary Taylor the very next day.

11

MY FEIGNED INTEREST IN THE CAPITAL'S more famous personalities set Mrs. Bingham off on a long-winded explanation of the luminaries and their grand residences. The proprietress not only described the mansions and where they were located but gossiped on the scandalous goings-on of the Washington elite. She gabbed on about a wasp-waisted society matron whose illness resulted from a too-tight corset, and the shenanigans of one Peggy Eaton — the seductress who had brought down the Jackson cabinet two decades earlier — and was still going strong.

No doubt many of the rumors originated from idle chit-chat between Mrs. Bingham's servants and those of other households before being relayed upstairs to her. She was one whose ears sponged up fresh gossip and passed it liberally on to anyone willing to listen, and I felt it important not to let her know what I was up to. I endured it for as long as I could, but soon after surreptitiously getting her to reveal the location of the Bliss residence, I contrived an appointment in order to make an escape and make my way to the home of Mary and her husband, William Bliss.

A mourning wreath swung slightly as the door was opened by an impeccably dressed manservant. Introducing myself as Angus Graystone from New York, coming to pay my respects to Mr. and Mrs. Bliss, I handed the man my card to pass on to his master. The servant, an elderly negro with grizzled hair looked genuinely sorry when he told me in a low voice, hoarse from grief I thought, that his master was out. I was about to ask when I should call again when he deferentially stepped aside to let me in, saying that he would announce my arrival to his mistress. I followed him through a foyer, acutely conscious of each footfall as they echoed off the polished floorboards and through the still mansion. Floral arrangements were heaped against the walls, the scent of fresh and of wilting flowers mingled to produce a heady aroma that bordered on the unpleasant. The servant caught me looking at the flowers as we walked past.

"Just as well you didn't bring no more of them, sir," he said. Leading me into a sitting room, he asked me to wait while he went to fetch Mrs. Bliss. Though my unannounced visit was surely an intrusion into this family's life at a time of bereavement, I convinced myself that it was no time for such thoughts. From what I'd learned in the past day, I was on to something that cried out for tenacious pursuit.

The richly appointed parlor was a far cry from the two sitting rooms I had been in the previous evening. Back in New York, mansions of the wealthy, *nouveau riche* — industrialists and mercantilist — were cluttered with exotic bric-a-brac; talking pieces taken from every corner of a world that the well-heeled inhabitants rarely knew much about. Though the Bliss living room also contained unusual things, the impression it gave was of carefully collected treasures, tastefully displayed within a private living space. Rather than for the benefit of visitors, the artifacts were for the owners' pleasure. Here there were no elephants' feet turned into umbrella stands, taxidermied fowl or curios from the Far East.

William Bliss was reputed to be a gifted linguist, fluent in a dozen languages and well-traveled. Being alone in the parlor allowed me time to peruse the objects. To my untrained eye many looked 'Indian', but Bliss had organized them into sections, each as part of a larger collection but also a collection in their own right. Perhaps this man understood the meaning of 'tribe.' Arranged for display within long cases with glass tops were weapons of various types: arrows of different lengths, their flights and arrowheads all quite different from one another. There were tomahawks and fighting clubs, and in another case were breastplates and different styles of feathered headdress.

I was completely absorbed in examining the articles when startled by a voice, "My husband's." I looked up to see the petite figure of Mary Bliss standing at the doorway. She wore mourning attire; I was pleased to have had the good sense to wear mine too. I stepped away from the display cases.

"Mrs. Bliss, thank you for receiving me at such a sad time. Your father was a great man," I said, bowing my head slightly.

"Thank you, Mr. . ." she glanced at the card in her hand, "Graystone."

"Angus Graystone, of New York City."

"Thank you, Mr. Graystone, for coming all the way to Washington. You seem familiar. Do I know you?" Mary said, tilting her head quizzically.

"I was at the funeral procession yesterday. I sang as you passed."

"That must be it," she said with a flicker of memory lighting her eyes.

"Forgive my manners, Mr. Graystone, please have a seat." Mary directed me to an upholstered chair and sat facing me. "My mother has been quite distraught, as you can imagine. I have been receiving visitors on behalf of our family, so many have called these past two weeks. Thank you for your kindness, but I'm sure you understand, Mr. Graystone, I must. . ."

"Mrs. Bliss, there's a good reason for my being here. Forgive me for being direct."

Mary shifted in her chair. Her back stiffened and she crossed her arms, hands gripping her elbows. "I'd appreciate it if you were," she said.

"The fact is, Madam, I am a private detective."

Mary's eyebrows rose. "Go on, Mr. Graystone." Her mouth puckered.

"I believe there are reasons to question the official reason given for President Taylor's death. If you can spare a few moments, I'd like to explain."

"You show quite a nerve, Mr. Graystone." Mary didn't raise her voice, but it quivered with rage. Her eyes narrowed. The veins at the side of her neck tightened. "Detective . . . ." The way she spat the word out made it sound like a villainous profession. "What kind of man preys on the emotions of a bereaved family?"

"Madam, I can see that my behavior might be perceived as ill-mannered, and if so, please accept my apology. A few minutes is all I ask. If you would just allow me to explain. If you are not convinced, I will leave your home and you will never see me again. You have my word on it."

Mary's features tensed, the muscles at the sides of her jaws bunched and relaxed. I swallowed nervously, feeling my Adam's apple rise and fall like the puck on a carnival's high-striker. Silence smothered the room. In the quiet, I could hear the natural sounds of the house, creaks and clicks of wood expanding in the warm sunshine. The seconds stretched uncomfortably.

Mary drew a deep breath through her nose and exhaled noisily. "I am tempted. . ." she paused and held her head up stiffly, "to have you thrown out," she continued, "but against my better judgment, Mr. Graystone, I will listen to what you have to say."

"Thank you, madam," I said.

"First, tell me something about yourself. Who you are?"

"I got my start in this business of law enforcement as one of New York City's marshals. That was until a short time after they were disbanded five years ago when a *proper* police force was established."

"Your tone suggests it was something not-so-proper."

"Well, yes, I worked with the new force for a while but soon came to see it for what it really was, a farce — a wormholed body fed on by politicians and gangsters."

Mary nodded.

"With little to stop them, the city's numerous hooligans, gangs with names like the 'Bowery Boys' and 'Dead Rabbits', caused havoc and grew stronger by the day. It wasn't long before I decided to go on my own. Fortunately, enough people in New York felt as I did. It allowed me to make a living from detective work."

"What kind of work, exactly?" Mary asked.

"Quite a variety — robbery, extortion, some murders that the police wanted no part of, and missing persons."

While I spoke, Mary listened attentively, asking questions from time to time. Her support for her father as Taylor's acting First Lady meant having to deal frequently with politicians. When I got round to speaking about what I had discovered the previous day, she used her quick, incisive mind to probe deeper into my theories — the burns to Jo's fingers, the footman's blindness, Mr. Jake's disappearance on the very day of Taylor's sickness, Jake's missing assistant. "These things need to be looked into," I said.

"And you've been in Washington for how long?" Mary asked.

"Two days. I arrived by train on the night of July 17th."

"It's quite remarkable that you've gathered so much information so quickly."

"Mrs. Bliss, I would like to offer your family my professional services. It will make things go much quicker, open more doors."

"From what you've told me, I'm sure you would do a fine job, Detective Graystone. My husband and I also feel that inquiries must be made. We are aware of the missing kitchen boy . . . and Mr. Jake's disappearance, of course." Mary looked away for a moment, a sad look on her face. "Actually, Mr. Jake has been found."

"That's good news, Mrs. Bliss, isn't it?"

"Not quite, Mr. Graystone, he was found dead." Mary raised a hand to stop me from speaking and went on. "A few days ago, his drowned body was found washed up on the river bank some miles away. An empty whiskey flask was found in one of his pockets. It is presumed that he missed work on the July 4th holiday because he got drunk the previous evening."

"Fell in the river and drowned," I said.

Mary dipped her chin. "Although Mr. Jake wasn't known for dipsomania. In fact, he rarely took a drink, we're told."

I confirmed Mary's understanding of Jake's drinking habits, telling her about the dusty whiskey bottle I'd seen in Jake's house.

Mary went on. "The kitchen maid's injured hand is something new to us even though it was right under our noses.

And, we had not drawn a connection with Old Ben's blindness. Poor Ben," she said sadly.

Beth's apparent acceptance of my line of reasoning encouraged me. I pushed my agenda hoping to move a step closer to realizing the purpose I'd come to Washington for. "I'm eager to start right away."

"That will not be possible," Mary responded with a bluntness that winded me like a blow to the gut.

"But why?"

"For the very simple and practical reason that we have already engaged the services of another detective agency. A very competent and well-respected one, from Chicago."

"May I ask the name of the agency?"

"Certainly, it's Pinkerton's National Detective Agency. Do you know of it?"

"I do, Mrs. Bliss. Allan Pinkerton and I share some similarities, both having come from Scotland, and we have both served as lawmen, albeit in different cities. But I wonder, does it not disturb you that Mr. Pinkerton failed to uncover some of the information that I have unearthed?"

"It does, Mr. Graystone. However, Mr. Pinkerton has been exploring other avenues, like tracking down the whereabouts of Mr. Jake's Chinese helper."

"Still, I'm certain I could be of service to you. You've seen how quickly I work, Mrs. Bliss."

"Quite impressive, Detective, perhaps if you'd come to us earlier."

"I'm certain I could bring something new to the investigation."

Mary studied me silently for a moment. Her gaze gave nothing away of her thoughts. "There may be a way," she said. "I'll have to discuss it with my husband. I don't want to raise your expectations, but would you come back this evening, at about six?"

Naturally, I agreed and was then shown politely to the door, this time Mary led me past the pungent bouquets.

The next few hours were spent back at the Bingham Inn, finding out as much as I could about William Bliss, studying my notes and doing further research on poisons. The wait was excruciating.

At precisely six o'clock, I knocked on the door of the Bliss mansion. The same servant showed me to the parlor where William and Mary Bliss waited for me. Bliss was about my age. Elegantly dressed in a black suit, he wore a neatly trimmed black chin-strap beard. In addition to his other achievements, Bliss had been a professor of mathematics at West Point. I had to remind myself that this well-turned-out gentleman was a decorated war hero who prior to being his father in law's private secretary had attained the military rank of Lieutenant Colonel.

Bliss came forward and shook my hand firmly. "Mary told me you were inspecting my collection earlier," he said, looking towards the neatly arranged artifacts.

"Extraordinary, sir, though I lack the knowledge to appreciate it fully," I said.

Bliss nodded in resignation though I sensed nothing unkind in the gesture. He invited me to take one of the chairs around a table. Refreshments were brought — a promising sign. With the image of the Indians I'd seen standing by the railroad track seared in my mind, I mentioned the incident to Bliss, asking if he knew who they could have been.

"Hard to say, but from the way you describe them and where they were seen, they could have been members of the Piscataway Tribe, or maybe Doeg." He looked up at the ceiling for a moment, "Could have been Choptank, though. There's no telling without seeing them myself."

"They looked, so . . . forlorn," I said.

"Well, no doubt they were. The tribes I mentioned are mostly peaceful, but anyone whose lands are under threat might take up arms, don't you think? To get what we wanted, to build this great nation, we've had to subdue them." There was no malice in his voice. The words of a soldier explaining the purpose of a mission.

"My wife told me what you've discovered in the brief time since your arrival, we are impressed by the quick progress you've made," Bliss said. "As you also know, we have engaged Mr. Pinkerton to investigate President Taylor's death. We both believe the circumstances require a more detailed look. It's a delicate matter, Mr. Graystone. The country is at the brink of descending into all-out war. It must be avoided at all costs. Any public suggestion of anything other than a natural death would inflame the situation. That is why Mr. Pinkerton is being very careful in the way he is going about his business."

"I understand. I still feel that there are ways I could help, discreetly, of course."

"Mary mentioned to you that Pinkerton has been trying to track down Mr. Jake's assistant, the Chinaman, Bufo. It hasn't been difficult to follow his movements. There aren't many of them in this part of the country. He left Washington sometime on the night of July 4th. An inspection of his quarters turned up nothing useful."

"And, Mr. Jake?" I asked.

The Chinaman may have killed Mr. Jake the previous day, making it look like an accidental drowning, though we have no proof of it. The corpse was in a very nasty state of decomposition, disemboweled, by animals most likely."

"Do you know where the is Chinaman now?

"We've tracked Bufo to New York," Bliss said.

165

"I'm from there. I know every nook and cranny of it. I can find the Chinaman and bring him back." I lifted the teacup to my lips and sipped slowly.

"Too late, Mr. Graystone. Bufo bought a ticket on a steamship, the SS California. The ticket was acquired two months ago, indicating a well-planned escape. The ship left New York Harbor a week ago. He's at sea, on his way to San Francisco. In several months, when and if he arrives in California, he'll melt into a community of thousands of other Chinese already there, a community growing larger with every ship arriving from China. We want you, Mr. Graystone, to go to California, to apprehend him and bring him back here."

I had just taken another sip of tea, and hearing Bliss' request made me cough up some of the liquid I'd just swallowed. I put the cup down with a clumsy clatter and covered my mouth with a napkin, stifling another cough. My eyes watered. My reaction to his suggestion of going after the Chinaman caused Bliss to let out a laugh that sounded like the bark of a small dog.

I eventually managed a response. "What if he jumps ship somewhere along the way?"

"There's always that possibility, even the chance he will board another ship and head back to China, but it's a chance we'll have to take." Bliss sipped from his cup and then went on. "Mr. Pinkerton will carry on with his investigations here, pursuing other avenues. If you agree to go, I will see that you are appointed as a Federal Marshal, giving you all the authority that comes with the job as well as travel money, and marshal's pay of course. You'll be able to appoint your own deputies if it comes to that.

The new president, Mr. Fillmore, will be making changes, selecting his own team. I will not be in a position to make things happen for much longer, I've only been on leave from the army as it is, now it looks as though they want me back as an adjutant general." Bliss paused and looked at his wife who had been listening by his side, they exchanged smiles that to me seemed a little contrived. He cleared his throat, "But while I still can, I will arrange for your appointment via Mr. John Clayton, the Secretary of State, a good friend of our family. That imbecile Filmore will likely replace Mr. Clayton, but he's still in office at the moment. The appointments of marshals usually remain intact for four years. Your principal duty will be to arrest the Chinaman, naturally, but as a marshal you will have other duties to perform as they are called for. As far as I know, there are no other marshal's in California. What do you say, Graystone?"

A hundred thoughts churned in my head at the same time as I tried to make sense of what he was asking of me. I stayed silent, lost in my own confusion.

"Mr. Graystone," Bliss said, calling me back to the present. "I expect you have some questions."

"I know little of California, only what I've read."

"And that would be true of most people outside of the territory," Bliss assured me.

"My understanding is that marshals are appointed because of strong ties to communities they are to serve in?"

"Quite right. But it *is* California we're talking about. A new territory with a new and fast-changing community. Anything else?"

"Would I be able to go about the job in my own way?"

Bliss nodded. "Within the limits of the law, naturally."

"If you are to return to the army, who will I report to," I asked.

"A fair question, Mr. Graystone. Until otherwise informed, you will continue to report to me. There's a need for secrecy and I will ensure our arrangement remains so. Is there anything else?"

Still confounded by the turn of events, I could think of nothing more to say. Bliss took my silence as a sign of assent. "Splendid!" he said, beaming at Mary. She gave her husband a small nod which to me, made it seem that the entire scheme had been her idea. "Bufo has a head start. You'll have to go after him right away. His ship will take several months to arrive in San Francisco. You must find a way to catch up with him, get to him before he disappears completely."

12

MUCH OF THE NIGHT WAS SPENT SITTING AT MY WRITING DESK pondering various ways to get to California and making notes on what I knew about the methods of travel, none of which held much appeal.

The next morning, I returned to the Bliss' home. Though most the flowers had been removed, a faint odor of decay still lingered. I was ushered directly to the library, lined ceiling-to-floor with tomes that I was sure were not merely decorative, a masculine chamber of browns and deep reds that smelled of old leather and beeswax. I wondered if President Taylor had graced this room, perhaps smoked a cigar with a brandy snifter in hand while standing by the now cold fireplace.

William Bliss was waiting with a bespectacled, balding gentleman whom he introduced as Mr. Peters, one of Secretary John Clayton's staff. Bliss sat behind his reading desk and the two of us took chairs opposite him.

"Now, if you will, Mr. Peters," Bliss said, "please officiate over the proceedings that will enable Detective Graystone to carry out his mission."

Peters began by asking questions about my particulars. Head down, he filled the details into the blank spaces of a document with the heading, 'Oath of Office.' He informed me as he wrote that the pledge was little changed since 1769 when first adopted under the auspices of George Washington. When completed, he held it up by its corners, waved the paper gently in front of his face and blew on it to dry the ink. The ink's metallic smell blended in nicely with the other male scents. Peters then placed the oath in front of me. "Peruse the details, Mr. Graystone, if you are in agreement, kindly sign it," he said, pointing a finger at the place for my signature.

I read the document and then replied, "You have written in the details correctly, Mr. Peters." I used Peters' pen to sign the oath.

Peters then reached into his bag and retrieved a bible. Bliss looked on while Peters directed me to place one hand on the leather-bound book and to raise the other while I read the document out loud.

"I Angus Murdoch Graystone, do solemnly swear that I will faithfully execute all lawful precepts directed to the Marshal of the Territory of California under the authority of the United States, and true returns make, and in all things well and truly, and without malice or partiality, perform the duties of the office of United States Marshal of the Territory of California during my continuance in said office, and take only my lawful fees that I take this obligation freely, and faithfully discharge the duties of the office upon which I am about to enter, so help me God."

"Congratulations, Marshal Graystone," Peters said, notarizing the oath with his own signature and dating it. Then he shook my hand firmly and proceeded to pin a marshal's badge to the breast pocket of my coat. I looked down as he secured the silver disk with a five-pointed star at its center.

Peters then provided me with a legal warrant for the apprehension of the fugitive Chinaman, 'known as Bufo.'

"I assure you," Bliss said, "that Mr. Peters and his office will help as much as it is able to in order to facilitate your mission."

"Indeed we will, sir," Peters said.

"How will I recognize the fugitive?" I asked Bliss. "We have arranged for an artist to draw a portrait of the man based on descriptions of those who knew him best. It will be available soon, but you should not wait for it. I will have it forwarded to you."

"Is there anything else, Mr. Peters?" Bliss asked.

"Do you own a firearm?" Peters said to me.

"I have one back in New York, a Baby Dragoon."

"Decent enough weapon for civilians, Marshal. You are now required to carry a firearm at all times, preferably something with real stopping power." Peters went to his bag and took out something bundled in cloth. "Here, take this," he said unraveling the parcel and passing me a holstered handgun.

Even without withdrawing the weapon from its leather case, I recognized it as a Colt Walker. It was a weapon I was familiar with but hesitant to use due to its problematic firing mechanism. The black powder repeating handgun weighed five pounds and had a barrel longer than my truncheon. It fired a .44 caliber lead ball effective to a distance of 100 yards. It indeed had stopping power. I voiced my concern over the weapon's unreliability to Peters. His response wasn't reassuring. Passing me a box of ammunition, he suggested that after loading the gun that I pack lard into the cylinder mouths on top of each bullet to prevent chain fire; sparks from the fired bullet igniting all the other chambers simultaneously.

Bliss reminded me that Bufo had a significant head start and that I had to go after him urgently. I had to wonder whether his sending me to California was a scheme to get me out of the way so that Pinkerton could go about doing whatever it was that they had been instructed to. Nonetheless, I had accepted the mission and needed to leave immediately. As soon as I stepped out of the house, I removed the marshal's badge and put it in my pocket. I was not in the habit of advertising my position as a lawman. Experience told me that unless it was used alongside a threat, it was often more likely to shut people up than get them to speak out. Sticking the holster of the massive handgun into my belt and hiding it best I could under my coat, I headed back to the Bingham to prepare for my return to New York. With the appointment of another detective agency to investigate Taylor's death, things hadn't gone quite as I had wished. In a way, I'd still gotten what I wanted: an official place in the investigation. I consoled myself at being outflanked by Pinkerton with the fact that since things were being done in secret, I wouldn't have been able to publicize my involvement.

When I got back to the Bingham at mid-morning, once again I found Beth preparing the dining room. She had her back to me, arranging a table. I watched her in silence for a moment as she hummed softly, picking silverware off a tray and placing them so that each piece was in alignment. I entered the room and called her name.

"Detective," she said, turning, "You startled me."

"Sorry, Beth. And please, call me Angus."

"I'm not sure I could do that here, sir. You're a guest, and Mrs. Bingham . . . well, you know."

"I suppose I do, but perhaps if we meet again, and if I am not a guest here."

Beth blushed and looked back to the table setting.

A breeze caught a loose wisp of brown hair at the back of her neck that had me staring hungrily at her nape. "Actually, Beth, I'm leaving shortly. I've returned to gather my things and to say goodbye, and to thank you."

172

"No thanks necessary. But don't you have more investigating to do here, or have you concluded your sleuthing so quickly?"

"I'm going to California," I said.

"After our chat the other night, I didn't see you as the type."

"Well, there are all types, and it's not what you think. More detective work. All quite unexpected."

"Well, if you say so. You could do quite a bit of unearthing with a pick and shovel," she said mischievously. "California is a long way. How will you get there?"

"I'm not quite sure, but it has to be fast. The situation is all so new to me, I have to think that through. Perhaps, if you have time to listen, it might help my train of thought."

Beth scanned the room, eyes pausing at tables that still needed attention, and then to a clock on the mantelpiece.

"It would really help if you could spare a little time," I urged.

"Could spare a few minutes, I suppose."

"Course you can, it's quiet now."

She hesitated briefly, biting her lower lip. "Come on, this way." Turning towards the rear of the dining room, Beth led me through a door, then down a corridor and through another door that led out of the building to an attractive back garden that I hadn't been aware of. We sat on a wooden bench in the shade of an enormous oak that hid us from prying eyes.

"Well? Tell me all about it. It's not every day a girl gets to hear about a real live adventure. Can't wait to tell Jo."

Since the discovery of gold in California two years earlier, the way of getting there was an oft-discussed subject that everyone seemed to have some knowledge. Such was the frenzy over newly discovered gold it was impossible not to fantasize at least a little about leaving everything behind and joining the thousands of argonauts heading westwards.

"I suppose you know about the overland route," I said, recalling what I had jotted in my notebook the previous night. Beth nodded vigorously. "Everyone does. It's supposed to be the cheapest way. Is that what you'll do?"

"Thousands of people have chosen to go that way. You're right about it being the least costly, but still, it would be several hundred dollars — and there are other things to think about: a wagon, animals, food for the journey. Then it requires walking or riding two thousand miles across the Great Plains and deserts. The journeys commence from the Mississippi River, that means I would have to get myself *there* first of all, before finding a guide to take me the rest of the way."

"It's a long way just even to the Mississippi."

"A thousand miles. No, I don't think it's the right one for me. With a great deal of good planning as well as luck, the journey could take as little as four to six months, but I've also heard that the trip could take a full year. Choosing that route is far too risky. For reasons I can't go into now, I need to get there quickly. Apart from the time element, one person in ten is said to succumb to disease or fatal accident. I think it's already too late in the year to start on an overland journey, Beth. If I left immediately, winter would set in half-way along, means I would have to spend winter somewhere along the trail."

"There was that incident I read about a couple of years back, said people got trapped in the mountains in winter and ended up having to resort to . . ." Creases formed on Beth's freckled brow.

"Aye, it's a horrifying tale," I said of the tragedy that had befallen the *Donner Party*.

"How about going the long way around?" Beth asked.

I pictured the SS California, well on its way, with Bufo aboard. "Indeed, the Cape Horn Route."

Beth nodded and drew an imaginary 'U' in the air with a finger. "Around the bottom tip of South America," she said. "It is an option, though it means covering a distance of about 14,000 miles, a trip taking several months around Cape Horn and the Strait of Magellan."

"Known for its dangers, so I've heard. Thrilling though," Beth said, eyes animated.

"Other than the dangers of the journey, mind you, I've read that of the 800 or so ships that have departed from eastern American ports last year, most have not returned." Beth nodded, her rapt attention spurred me on. "Ships' crews, even their captains have abandoned their vessels in San Francisco Harbor to join the gold hunters."

"Well, go on then, don't keep a girl on tenterhooks."

"The newspapers report that due to a shortage of vessels, any ship that can sail, whether prepared for the hazards or not, are pressed into service." I shook my head thinking that there would be little chance of catching up with Bufo by following him in the same way he was traveling.

"It all seems far too dangerous to make it worthwhile," Beth said.

"Some dangers are inevitable on such journeys, but you can rest assured I will be on my guard and not take unnecessary risks."

"That's a relief to hear, Detective Graystone."

Pride, or perhaps egotism caused me to reach into my pocket and pull out my shiny new marshal's badge. "It's Federal Marshal Graystone, as of this morning." I handed the badge to her for a look.

Beth's face flushed with pleasure, a look that made my heart skip a beat. "Ooh. Wait until I tell Jo," she said, bringing the badge up to eye level for a closer look before passing it back to me. "So, then, how *will* you get to California?"

"There are two other routes I've heard of. Both involve making the journey first by sea, sailing south on the Atlantic side of the continent to Latin America, then traveling overland and then again by sea on the Pacific side, northwards to California. One of these is referred to as the Nicaraguan Route, the other, the Panama route. I understand that the Panama route is the better established of the two, with regular sailings of postal service steamships on both sides of the continent. It requires sailing first to Panama. From there, another boat ferries travelers upriver. The next stage involves an overland trek through 50 miles of thick jungle to Panama City. From there it is possible to catch a ship bound for San Francisco. The entire trip is supposedly about 5,000 miles.

"Goodness, Marshal Graystone, you seem to have given this a fair bit o' thought," Beth said. By the cheeky look she gave saying my new title, I couldn't be sure If she had meant it in jest. I felt a hot wave roll up from my neck up to my forehead. "That's nearly two thousand miles further than it is between Dublin and New York," she continued in the same playful tone. "That's the one, then. Has to be, if you want to get there, fast, as you say."

I would have relished continuing our intimate chat beneath the shady tree but it was time to go. "Absolutely right. Talking to you has helped me clarify my thoughts. Thank you, Beth. I must go, though I hope we'll meet again, and the next time you'll call me Angus."

"We'll see about that, Marshal Graystone."

On the train on my way back to New York, seated in a carriage this time, energized by the idea of taking the Panama route, I hastily jotted down the approximate time I estimated it would take.

2 weeks to Panama from New York

1 week crossing Panama, approx. 60 miles

2 weeks sailing from Panama to San Francisco

Five weeks, a little over one month, not including the time it might take to find a ship to get me there, but even if it took an extra month, I would still arrive in California before Bufo, I assumed.

13

A THUNDERBOLT HAD ME JUMPING OUT OF MY SOAKED SKIN. It was close enough to taste — metallic, acidic — and to feel its charge in my fillings. Even more horrifying, the light-burst exposed the ocean heaving beneath me. Viscous and black it conjured up the images of my darkest fears — tentacles as thick and long as the ship's mast, curling up, studded with suckers, each ring armed with a beak ready to tear flesh.

A few of us chose to brave the storm up on deck rather than to suffer in the airless hold. Clinging to a pole or rope while being lashed by icy rain was preferable to the below decks. Down there, men groaned with each roll of the ship, clutching their bellies, squirming in pools of vomit. From time to time one would claw his way up through the hatch. The denizens of the stinking hold would manage only a few shaky steps before again spilling their guts and scurrying back down to the stink. Shivering under my raincoat and hat, I hid from the storm as best I could, pressed into a corner.

At dawn, the downpour softened to a drizzle and with a calmer sea, I began to feel safer from the retreating squall.

Then, as if in defiance, the storm released a deep, slow rumble — nature telling me with a belch that it had its fill. Another roar shook me to the core before ebbing away.

Under a burst of light, purple welts lined the sky. Panama seemed to wink at me; a weary gesture from her bruised eyelid that said, "So, now you too."

Hers was a story of turmoil. Thrust off the seabed by its cataclysmic coupling she was smothered in layers of sludge. Driven ever upwards, she eventually broke the surface. With first breaths, she conjoined the landmasses to either side, cleaving the Earth's ocean into two.

Coveted as a prize long before she was named, her slenderness was what made her so alluring. Separating Atlantic and Pacific oceans by a mere fifty miles at her narrowest point she so served as a bond between them. For centuries, conquistadores, mercantilists, and pirates fought to have her. Even my former homeland Scotland had tried its luck at setting up a colony on her Atlantic shore in order to establish an overland trade route. The 17th Century *Darien Scheme* failed miserably after only a few years, resulting in the destruction of the finances of the entire country.

There were several versions as to the origin of the name 'Panama.' A fellow passenger regaled us one evening saying,

Some ascribe it to the fact that a species of tree abounds there. Others say that it is because the first settlers arrived in the month of August when butterflies are plentiful and that the name means 'many butterflies' in native tongue. Perhaps the best-known story is that a fishing village originally bore the name Panamá, named after a nearby beach and that the name meant 'many fish.' Yet still another version says that a Kuna chief gave the land the name 'pannaba', the Kuna word meaning 'very far.'

Whether the name referred to trees, butterflies, a sandy shore or plentiful fish, I had indeed traveled very far, and still had farther to go.

Panama had declared independence from Spain just thirty years earlier and was now part of Colombia. Given the recent interest in California, I wondered what designs America had on her. There was already talk of a railroad straddling her back to link the two great oceans.

And so, *yes, now me too*, I thought in reply to a final burst of light from the receding storm.

Watching from the rail of a boat, that first glimpse of Panama was of ruins. Dawn had broken through low, heavy clouds and a beam of light illuminated crumbling stone buildings on a cliff top. Below the scarred rock-face lay the small port town of Chagres, a row of thatched-roofed wooden shacks sitting at the mouth of the river that gave the settlement its name.

I endured the stink below just long enough to change into dry clothes and grab my things. A hundred and fifty dollars had paid for ocean passage to Panama; a number chalked onto floor planks in one of the holds had served as my berth over which I had laid a bedroll. By the time I went back on deck, many of my fellow travelers were there gawking at the stone walls and at the harbor ahead. Their excitement was palpable — men with the same wide-eyed look of gamblers bent on squandering their last few pennies in a card game or a throw of dice. Some appeared fervent enough to dive into the sea and try to swim ashore in order to beat others to it.

Since leaving New York, I had traversed a mere two thousand miles. After informing the Secretary of State's office of my plans, and even with their involvement, it had taken two weeks to secure a place on a ship headed to Panama. Add to that sixteen days at sea and a whole month, double my original estimate, was squandered. Still, if I moved quickly, I would get to California before the fleeing Chinaman.

Two weeks of waiting in New York had given me time to sort out my affairs: outstanding cases put to bed, and my inheritance, the printing business, left in capable hands. I also used the time to learn as much as possible about the territory I was headed to and to acquire basic necessities for the journey.

Although California had been explored by Europeans since the sixteenth century, so new was the territory as part of America that I hadn't been able to find an up-to-date map of it. The best I could lay my hands on was one created in 1810 titled *Mexico and Adjacent Provinces*. Still, it was the finest amongst those I'd seen carried by my fellow travelers. We sprung from every ilk; only a few were kitted out to look the part of *gold prospector* as we had come to know them from illustrated stories of the west. For the most part, we traveled as we were. It made no difference whether one was a farmer, tradesman or physician, everyone — bar myself — traveled with the singular goal of striking it rich. As before, I saw it as a disadvantage to reveal myself as a marshal. Being the only lawman on board would tear me in all directions and away from my mission. Marshal's badge and weapons hidden away, I fit right in with the motley bunch.

The 241 ft. SS Falcon, a paddle steamship originally designed to carry cargo had been hastily refitted to cater for the sudden deluge of gold-hunting passengers. It still transported freight, but on this trip it also carried 183 passengers; men infected by the gold bug. The vessel was a floating gambling den. Had a piano been set in the large communal space below, the place could have been mistaken for a dingy saloon room. It was a constant battle for me to resist the lure of the whiskey bottle and so far I had prevailed.

Dozens of ships were already at anchor in the wide, natural harbor. As we entered port, passengers scrambled to get their belongings on deck, all wanting to have a head start the moment the boat dropped anchor.

A slight man, balding and sporting a generous gray mustache, stood next to me. Jim Watson had dropped everything, abandoned his old life — and until he struck it rich, so he said, his old wife — in order to make the journey to California. He appeared well-prepared, saying that he tried to learn everything he could before making the trip. The former college professor placed his bags next to mine and we stood leaning with our elbows on the boat's rail. As the sun climbed, its rays drove moisture off rain puddles on the deck planking, stiffening leftover chunks of spew. Feeling the skin searing at the back of my neck, I repositioned my new wide-brimmed hat. Watson lifted the front of his bowler to mop his forehead with a handkerchief.

The gold bug hadn't been the only thing biting. We both scratched at scabs under our sweat-stained clothes. Perspiration dripped off the tip of my nose. I'd spent a good amount of time conversing with Watson during the voyage, eager to learn as much as I could about what lay ahead. He pontificated with the air of one who possessed first-hand experience and not as he was, a first-timer like the rest of us. Nonetheless, I liked the professor and felt that his book-learning might come in handy.

Watson pointed to the cliff top. "Quite a sight, is it not, lad?"

I looked up at the glistening rocks and nodded.

Encouraged, Watson continued, "Fort San Lorenzo. Originally built three centuries ago."

"A formidable position, way up there, though from the state of it, not quite strong enough," I said.

"No, sir. Thing is, when fortifications are erected, they're built to defend against weapons of the day. Not half enough to withstand a barrage from weapons made two centuries later."

I had become accustomed to Watson's style of dangling out bits of tantalizing information and then holding back. I played along. "Barrage, you say?"

"Aye, Graystone," Watson turned to me, "destroyed by weapons in the hands of a man no Spaniard would want to meet on the high seas . . . nor anywhere else for that matter," his voice grew stronger, taking on a slight tremor. "In the year 1671, the Spanish fort was attacked by Henry Morgan."

"The buccaneer?"

"Aye . . . no other, lad. Then he went on to sack Panama City. Morgan, King of Buccaneers, pirate only to his enemies, adversaries of The Crown. San Lorenzo was rebuilt, of course, and then destroyed again by the British Navy. That was a hundred years ago."

Entering the harbor, a collection of ramshackle wooden buildings came into view. They sat on the opposite shore of the river mouth from the cliff face.

"And *that* must be the place we've been hearing about, what they call Yanqui Chagres," I said.

"Imagine," Watson said. "All sprung up in the past year . . . like mushrooms in cow shit."

Drawing closer to shore we were able to read crudely hand-painted signs hanging over the buildings identifying them as a row of hotels, saloons, brothels and gambling halls; all for the purpose of lightening the purses of those headed across the isthmus. By the look of the men aboard the Falcon, it wouldn't be difficult. Afflicted by gold fever, in their minds they had already struck the mother lode.

"You planning on overnighting in that cesspit, Graystone?"

"Not me. I'll try to hire a boat, do a few miles before dark, get up river."

"I agree, no point in staying just to get fleeced with other argonauts," Watson said, laughing at his own joke. "How about we head off together?"

Getting everyone ashore was a chaotic procedure that involved the hiring of rowboats to ferry passenger and baggage to land. Shouting and shoving saw a couple of men in the drink before it was all done. Nearing the landing beach, in their eagerness, some argonauts jumped into knee-deep water and waded the rest of the way.

A market of sorts had been set up. The locals had brought out pots and pans, crude digging tools and anything else they thought they might be able to sell. One man had parrots for sale, another had a couple of monkeys on offer. The little animals were tethered around the neck with twine and clung to him in fear as we rushed ashore. We stopped briefly to buy some fruit for our journey.

Half the men from the Falcon headed in the direction of Yanqui Chagres. The rest of us were mobbed by native boatmen offering to get us to the next stop of our journey, the town of Las Cruces, 45 miles upriver. Watson immediately got into haggling with one of the boatmen, a shirtless, bare-footed man wearing baggy trousers and an old straw hat. I watched my traveling companion negotiate using a combination of basic self-taught Spanish and sign language. It wasn't long before Watson got into an animated shouting match with the boatman.

"What's this about?" I asked.

"Goddam crook," Watson yelled, "wants twenty bucks each. I talked him down from thirty but he won't budge further."

Back in New York, I'd read of colossal prices being charged in California for the most basic items. The price gouging had made its way to Panama. "When we spoke of it on the boat, you said the going rate was a dollar a head."

"I did, aye. But this rascal says a dollar was the old price . . . from a year ago. Twenty is the best I can get from this villain."

The scene around us had thinned, groups of men from our ship followed native guides to their boats. I gestured towards the river mouth; two more ships were waiting to berth. "Doesn't look like there's a shortage of men willing to pay to get to Las Cruces. Let's agree to the price and get moving." Watson concurred but with a look on his face as if he'd just gotten a whiff of something foul. We both took the money from pouches on our belts and handed over the fare. Watson kept up his ranting over the cost with talk about still having to pay to stay at villages as we went.

The river guide introduced himself as Noko and counted the money before stuffing the bills into a pocket of his shapeless pants. He beckoned us to follow him towards his boat a vessel he referred to as a *cayuco*.

Watson scurried beside me, sidestepping puddles in the muddy pathway. "Looks like it's not just Americans going across Panama," he said breathlessly." He gestured with a sideways tip of his head as we passed a couple of men who were conversing in what sounded like Russian.

Noko stopped by the river bank and faced us, showing a half-toothless grin. He pointed to his cayuco. The sight of his boat stopped us dead in our tracks. Two natives waited by a canoe of about twenty feet long and three feet wide.

"Goddam banana boat," Watson remarked, staring at the hollowed-out log.

"Four days in that . . . don't suppose we could get our money back?" I asked without much hope. Looking at the other canoes waiting at the water's edge, Watson shook his head.

Under a loosely woven canopy of palm leaves, two other passengers sat cross-legged in the front end of the cayuco, the baggage between them taking up any space we might have shared under the awning. I hadn't seen these men on the SS Falcon but there were other vessels in port they could have arrived on. A bigger man seated at the front waved his arms angrily. He growled at our guide, "'bout time, let's get going, ya thievin' monkey." He glowered at us as if we had intentionally delayed his departure.

We passed our bags to the native paddlers and climbed gingerly into the dugout canoe, squatting behind the two other passengers. Watson took the rear spot. For what it was, the cayuco was incredibly stable and hardly rocked as we got in. The river guides got into their places at bow and stern. Noko used a pole to push us away from the muddy shore. The other two natives dug their oars into the river, commencing our journey on the Chagres.

14

THE PANAMANIAN JUNGLE was denser than any forest I'd ever known. Foliage prevented us from seeing anything beyond a few feet of the river banks as our cayuco glided over dark water. Vines reached out, twisting and strangling whatever they touched. Trees of different varieties fought for the same space and for any chance to expose themselves to the sun's lifegiving rays. Monkeys crawled along tree branches overhead. Caymans, like beached logs, basked on the river bank. Shrieks pierced the sky; we looked for the source but could never see what made them. Our river guides, amused by the look of our worried faces, imitated the shrill cries and chuckled even harder when the large passenger in front shouted abuse at them.

Watson and I pointed things out to one another: multi-colored parrots, snakes coiled in tree branches, enormous birds soaring high above. There was too much to see and unable to adequately express our feelings of wonder at the extraordinary world we had entered, we settled into silence.

We had taken off our coats and rolled them up to use as padding against the wooden floor of the dugout. I opened my pack to dry out the rain-drenched clothing. While I did so, the passenger sitting in front of me turned for a look at the laid-out contents of my bag. He was a thin ferret-faced creature with a small mustache.

Behind me, Watson noticed the man's stare, "Need something, sir?" he said.

The man nodded. "Salut," he said, grinning at the both of us before facing forward.

Even with the sun beating down mercilessly, our boatmen seemed not to tire from long hours of paddling. They took only brief rests, occasionally heading the cayuco into small clearings on the river bank where we refilled our canteens with river water and ate some of the fruit we had bought.

The two other passengers kept to themselves under the shade of the awning. At one of the stops, Watson sidled close to me and whispered, "Think we have anything to worry about those two?" He angled his head towards the surly pair. In spite of the heat, both men kept their coats on and shirt collars buttoned up as if they had something to hide.

The one who had snarled at our river guide at the start of our journey approached us. He was a bear of a man; not quite as tall as me, but probably half again as heavy. A thick reddish beard covered most of his wide face. He was dressed in an old brown suit and wore a bowler hat. As he neared, he looked me up and down as if he were sizing me up. He stopped a couple of paces away, reached a hand into his coat pocket and pulled out a bottle. "Wet your whistle, mister?" he said, holding out the half-full bottle, its contents brownish, cloudy.

I licked my parched lips. Despite the unappetizing look of the drink, my hand went out towards it. It had gotten halfway to the bottle before I stopped. "No, thank you, sir," I said, changing the motion from a reaching hand to an upwards wave.

"Sure looks like you could use one."

"Water's fine," I replied, taking a sip from my canteen.

Watson stepped over, "Don't mind if I do," he said, reaching for the proffered bottle. He tipped the bottle to his lips, swallowed and then doubled over in a coughing fit. "What is it?" he asked, handing the bottle back to Brown.

"Never you mind what it is, it's what it does that matters. Name's Brown," he said, offering me his hand.

I shook it. "Graystone."

Brown turned in the direction of his traveling companion. "That little fella's Legrand." He pronounced the name *lee-grand*. "Can ya believe it, the name means big guy or somethin', that shrimp. Hey Frenchie, get over here."

Legrand came over, moving quickly. Also dressed in a suit, he had a cravat tied around his neck. Hatless, his face was burned red from the sun. He had a pointy, narrow nose and colorless lips. He took my hand with a firm, rapid shake, "Enchanté."

Legrand took the bottle from Watson and brought it eagerly to his mouth.

"Careful with that, Frenchie," Brown said, snatching the flask from Legrand's lips.

"*Ey, ça* suffit!" Legrand said, flicking drops of whiskey off his sleeve.

Brown laughed and took a swig. "Frenchie likes his drink a bit too much, if ya know what I mean," he said. Legrand shot him an injured look.

The river guides called us back to the canoe. Brown and Legrand moved hastily to take their shaded spots on the boat.

"Strange pair," I whispered to Watson.

"Aye," Watson nodded, adding, "let's keep in mind that talk of robbers we heard aboard the Falcon."

Late in the afternoon, we heard a deep mewing noise. It went on for a time as our cayuco passed a stretch of river the bank. Our guides were again amused by our uneasy response and imitated the cry. Eventually, when they'd had enough fun, Noko looked at Watson and said, "Pantera."

Watson turned to me. "I think that means 'panther'," he said.

I had wanted adventure, but this unhospitable landscape frightened me. Before going ashore at Chagres, I had taken the smaller of my handguns out of my bag, the five-shot Baby Dragoon. Its barrel was pressed uncomfortably but reassuringly against my thigh.

Close to sunset, we pulled onto a small gravel beach where several other cayucas had already stopped. We were disappointed not to continue for a while longer thinking it to be a waste of remaining daylight. The guides urged us to unload our baggage quickly and follow them up a long flight of wooden steps built into a rock face.

Once at the top, we saw a village not far from the cliff edge. Natives went about their business, avoiding our gazes as we passed them on our way to the settlement. The villagers made me again think of the Indians I had seen by the railway track. The word *tribe* drifted into my head, a sorry reminder of my limited understanding of the world. I felt absurd. Other than the made-up designation, *Indian*, there were few reasons for me to compare them, and yet I did. These people had rounder faces than the ones I had seen near Washington. They were shorter. Squat men and women clothed only from the waist down. Strings of colored woven beads crisscrossed their chests. Tattoos covered their torsos and arms. The lower halves of some of their faces were also covered in tattoos from a line extending out from the corners of their mouths and covering their chins. Many of the children were also decorated with inky designs.

"Look at 'em, Frenchie," Brown said, "bunch of goddam monkeys, straight outa th'trees."

Legrand chuckled. "Oui, oui, *monkee*," he said.

The guides led us into a community of wooden huts that were raised on stilts. Dozens of shelters were arranged around a dirt courtyard. Other travelers who were already settled in the spaces under the shacks glanced up at us newcomers. A few nodded greetings or waved wearily. The four of us followed Noko across the courtyard. Passing several more homes, we were shown to a space beneath one of the huts. Hammocks were offered for hire and tired as we were, we didn't have the energy to haggle over the price of two dollars apiece. Likewise, we gladly handed over a dollar each for food. Wooden bowls of boney fish stew were brought to us.

Fires and lamps were lit throughout the village. The reason for the sudden stop to the day's paddling soon became apparent. On my first night on land in the tropics, I wasn't prepared for the speed of transition between day and night. Back in New York, and it was the same during Scotland's summers, when nightfall came it crept in slowly. Sunlight loitered, prolonging the day, clinging to the land by its fingernails until it could no longer resist the pull of night.

Here, when the sun dropped, so did its glow. Once the sun dipped below the horizon, darkness began to envelop everything. Beginning from the jungle that encircled us, blackness rolled in like a slow, cool wave, resisted only by pools of light cast by cooking fires, oil lamps and the odd candle. Lush, dark green foliage transformed into black shadows of reaching, grabbing claws. Above us, the sky was dotted with pinpricks of light that grew in intensity as the world around us grew ever darker.

The two ruffians lay in their hammocks, passing the liquor bottle between them. Before settling down for the night, I placed my marshal's badge in the pocket of my coat. I retrieved my Colt Walker, already loaded and with lard packed over the cylinder mouths. With my money belt secured around my waist and coat pulled over me, I gripped a pistol in each hand. Watson, who also kept his money purse on him, fell asleep within minutes. I lay in the dark for a time, listening to the breathing of my traveling companions, slowing and then turning into snores. Only when I was certain they were fully asleep did I close my eyes.

A shriek jarred me awake; a noise from the jungle that had penetrated my dream now had me staring wide-eyed into blackness. Did I imagine it?

I heard it again. This time it was more like a human cry than the scream of a jungle beast. I lay still, listening. It came again — a woman's scream, and then another. I rolled out of the hammock. The pistols in my hands slammed onto packed earth.

I rose and looked into the dark corner where Brown and Legrand slept. No movement, no sounds other than snoring came from there. I put my boots on and stood.

The screaming started again, high pitched and desperate, and then shouting. Now Watson was awake. I made out his dark silhouette sitting up in the hammock. "What's that bawling?" he said, voice thick with sleep.

Legrand grunted but stayed asleep. "Shaddup," Brown complained.

From the direction of the courtyard, villagers began to run. Some called out warnings as they rushed past our hut.

Brown stumbled out of his hammock. "What the devil?"

I couldn't understand what the natives said, but there was one word they kept repeating. "Hear that? What does that word mean?" I asked Watson.

"I think they're saying, *Cimarrones*. If that's it, we're in big trouble."

I grabbed Watson's arm. "Tell me," I said.

Watson pushed my hand away. "Slaves. Runaways," he said.

"What are you talking about?" Brown said, getting to his feet and coming to us. "There ain't no slaves here, not anymore, far as I know." He went over to Legrand's hammock and gave his friend a kick. "Hey, Frenchie, get up."

"No, not the kind of slaves you're thinking of," Watson said. "Cimarrones are descendants of slaves that escaped from their Spanish masters, centuries ago. I'd heard stories that they were out there but thought it a load of hogwash. Sure, they were freed and pardoned eventually, but there were violent riots. Story is, some of 'em fled into the jungles, formed into robber gangs."

I tried to make sense of what I heard even as the screaming told me the danger was real, and close by.

Watson gripped my arm, "What do you reckon we should do, Graystone? Run and hide until it's all over would be my choice."

Brown and Legrand crowded in to listen for my response.

"Perhaps we could run," an image of my shiny new marshal's badge flew across my mind, "or try to help."

"Hah, help . . . you screwy or something?" Brown said.

"I don't like the idea of taking my chances in the dark in the jungle," I said.

"You could be right about that," Watson said.

As Watson spoke, a man stumbled into our camp and fell dead at our feet. An arrow shaft stuck out of his back. I stooped over him. It was too dark to make out his face, but from a string of beads around his neck, I recognized him as one of the guides from our cayuco. I could still see the image of his laughing face over our fear of jungle noises.

"Without our guides, we'll have little chance of getting to Cruces." Whether I liked it or not, my mind was made up.

"Can't speak for the rest of you, but I going to find out what the trouble is."

"Me and Frenchie's not goin' nowhere," Brown said.

"Suit yourselves," I said, stepping away. Guns in hand, I walked towards where I sensed the danger to be. Women, some dragging their children, and a few white men carrying lanterns and their travel packs ran the other way, brushing past me in the dark.

"Wait for me, Graystone," Watson said, catching up, "figured you'd need some help."

"Ever handled a gun?" I asked, ready to give him one of mine.

"'Course, laddie. What do you think I am?" Watson pulled a pistol out of his pocket and waved it. "This, my boy, is an *1842 Navy*, primed for action, as am I."

It was too dark to see his weapon, but I knew it from its name: a Derringer, a tiny, single-shot pistol that fired a .54 caliber ball. Lethal at close range, but once spent, it was just a five-inch lump of iron and wood.

"Ever shot a man?" I asked. Watson didn't reply. "Put the Derringer away and take this." I handed him my Dragoon, and he stuffed his little weapon back into his pocket.

We hurried in the direction of the screams.

15

DAYBREAK WAS A FEATHERY ORANGE BLUR. In reverse of how quickly it had darkened the previous night, dawn crept in at a snail's pace. Still too dark to see more than shadowy images, we pushed against the surge of bodies fleeing across the dirt courtyard hearing the word *cimarrones* whispered fearfully by terrified villagers as they brushed by. The cries of terror seemed to come from the clearing we crossed when we came from the river.

"You still with me?" I called out, wondering if Watson was still following.

"Right behind you, lad."

Across the square, I retraced the track we had taken when we entered the village, recalling that it would take us past five or six huts before we got to the edge of the settlement. Every home on this side of the community was deserted. In the darkness, I nearly tripped over something lying on the pathway. Watson, following closely, bumped into me when I stopped. I prodded the thing with the tip of my boot; it was soft, heavy.

I sat on my heels and reached out in the dark. My fingertips touched cloth, then buttons, a belt buckle. I caught the coppery scent of blood and the minerally soil it ran into. "A body, dead, I think," I said. Watson scurried off. I cursed him under my breath, regretting letting him have my Dragoon.

I heard him stumbling around in the nearest hut, rummaging about in the abandoned quarters, kicking things over in the dark. I turned to the noise, "Quiet down, Watson," I said just as the burst of a match head erupted. I looked away, a white spot still caught in my vision.

Watson returned with a lit lamp and held it over the body. "What the blazes?" he said.

"You trying to get us killed? Put that lamp out," I said.

"Hold on, Graystone," he elbowed me out of the way. "Let's see what we've got here." Watson lowered the lamp over the body.

The dead man's eyes were open, eyeballs rolled back, I recognized him as one of the travelers who had raised a hand to us in greeting just a few hours before. I pushed Watson's arm holding the lamp toward the body for a closer examination. A deep gash across the corpse's throat exposed white bone. His arms and hands were covered with bloody slashes; the type of wounds received from raising one's arms in defense. The pockets of his trousers had been pulled inside out, hanging out like tongues. Blood still flowed from his fresh wounds, soaking into the bare earth and blackening it in a widening circle.

Watson set the lamp down on the ground and spun away. He stumbled a couple of paces and gagged on the side of the path. "Sorry," he wheezed.

If I had to worry about protecting him in a fight, he would be a great hindrance. "Nobody would blame you for turning back now," I said, resisting the urge to add, 'it might be better.'

Watson sucked in a couple of noisy breaths. "I'm with you, Graystone." In the lamplight, his eyes gleamed with fear but he also showed something more, a look of determination.

"Right, if you're sure. Let's get after the filth that did this."

Watson dragged a sleeve across his mouth. He straightened himself and waved the pistol in the air. "Aye, Graystone, let's deal with the murdering scum."

I cupped a hand over its lamp's chimney and blew out the flame. The sun had risen a mite, but low clouds kept the light dim. We moved ahead slowly, cautiously.

As we came to the last hut, another body lay on the pathway. We stooped over it, eyes trying to adjust to the dark. The man was a native. His lifeless hand gripped a machete. I pried the blade out of the man's hand. A wooden scabbard lay on the ground beside him. I picked it up, sheathed the blade and then put it through my belt.

A bright flash illuminated the scene. Watson had struck another match. "Goddamn. Blow that thing out," I said.

He put out the match but not before I saw that the man had a deep cut in the side of his head. Bare-chested, his shoulder was sliced deeply enough for his arm to be hanging half off.

Watson sucked a breath in sharply. He sensed me glance at him and responded with, "Dinnae worry 'bout me, lad."

"Lower your voice, for God's sake," I said. I was about to tell him to stay back when another yell came from the direction of the river.

"Let's go," Watson said.

As I straightened from my crouch, an arrow whizzed by, missing by inches. "Quick, over here," I said. Watson followed me under the safety of the hut.

I peeped out to see where the arrow came from and made out the silhouette of a man about thirty yards away.

The archer was walking backward, bow lowered with the arrow nocked and ready. Watson leaned forward for a look and I held him back. "What do you see?" he whispered angrily.

We had the advantage of the faint glow of dawn coming from the direction of the cliff. Behind the archer, ten yards nearer the river I saw the source of the yelling. Women were being dragged to the steps at the cliff edge. Cimarrones, descendants of slaves, were capturing their own slaves. Each of them pulled along a woman, screaming and flailing.

"I counted four of them," I said. "Three men, plus the archer acting as a sentry. They've taken captives."

"What do we do?"

"Take care of the sentry first, then the others." I stepped onto the pathway and cocked the hammer of my pistol. The archer heard the distinctive clicks of a gun mechanism. The Colt Walker's weight made for an unwieldy weapon to hold up and aim at eye level. With low visibility and the captives behind the bowman, I couldn't take the risk of letting off several shots and hitting the women by mistake.

I assumed a duelist's stance: right leg forward, left arm bent with a fist balled on my hip. Firing arm held out straight, I raised the Colt to eye level and pointed pistol barrel at the target's chest. With dawn glowing behind him, over the gunsight I clearly saw the shape of the archer, slowly sweeping his weapon left and right, ready to release his arrow at first sight of trouble. I waited for him to point his bow to one side to give me a wider area to target. I was nearly invisible, but not quite enough. Sweeping back again, he stopped, pointing his weapon directly at me.

I heard the twang of the bowstring. Too late I shifted to the side, the arrow tore through my shirt, scoring the left edge of my ribcage and kept going. The strike spun me around, and I hit the ground cursing. I knew that the archer would already be nocking another arrow. This time I didn't bother with attempting a perfect aim. Still down on the ground, I pointed the Colt at the bowman and squeezed the trigger. The gun barrel spat out a yellow tongue of fire, blasting out the .44 caliber ball. The bullet thumped the archer square in the chest, flinging him onto his back.

The three other cimarrones halted, stilled for a moment by the surprise of the blast.

I raised and lowered my arm to check the extent of the injury. My chest hurt like the blazes, but my arm still had a good range of movement.

I rolled over to see that Watson hadn't moved. He had the Dragoon in both hands, raising it to take aim with both thumbs forcing the hammer back. "Don't fire. It's too dangerous with the women back there," I said, also fearing for my own safety.

"What do you suggest then, laddie? Was you who gave me the blasted thing."

The cimarrones exchanged a flurry of angry-sounding words. One of them took hold of the ropes tethering all three native women. He gave a strong yank pulling them towards the river. The women resisted, and we heard the swish of a stick and their shrieks as he whipped them over their heads and shoulders.

The two other men pulled machetes from their scabbards and came towards us. One of them pulled out what could have been a pistol. As they passed the dead archer, they stared down at the corpse, then slowed their pace, approaching with more caution.

Being witness to the butchery they had committed, I had no qualms about killing the marauders. It was two against two, but I'd already decided that Watson would be a hindrance in a fight to the death. "I'll take the fight to them. You stay back," I ordered. "Use the pistol only when you are certain of getting a clear shot."

"Agreed."

It was still too dangerous for me to fire at the cimarrones with the women right behind them. I put the Colt in my belt and pulled out the machete I'd taken off the dead native. I started at them, running and yelling at the top of my lungs. My solitary version of a Highland Charge seemed to work. Still twenty yards from me, one of the cimarrones turned and ran for the river.

The man facing me halted and yelled abuse at his fleeing companion.

I stopped too. Looking back at the ten paces to Watson, I shouted, "Get after him." In the dark, I couldn't read his features, but he jiggled from foot to foot like a marionette; the motion reeked of indecision. I expected him to bolt back the way we came.

I began my run again, adding vigor to my war cry. When I reached my opponent, I brought the machete down hard against his raised weapon. In the dim light, sparks flashed off the clash of our blades. By far the taller man, my longer reach allowed me to crash the machete down repeatedly on my opponent's weapon, driving him backward. This was the man who had drawn the pistol, he had it in his other hand so why hadn't he used it?

The cimarron sprung backward with the agility of a jungle cat, putting two yards between us.

He glanced at my bloody shirt and then looked me in the eye. Now he raised his gun, the expression on his face seemed more of distress than triumph. He held a blunderbuss, a flare-barreled flintlock pistol. The design looked to have been a century old. If still workable, it could inflict tremendous damage at short range, but like the Derringer, it was good for only a single shot. His hand shook while cocking the hammer, but with a blunderbuss, one didn't need great aim. The ball and shot would spread wide enough to kill or maim anything in front or either side of it up to ten paces away. He gestured for me to throw my weapon down. Instead, I transferred the machete to my left hand and pulled out my Colt, showing him the cannon it was in contrast to the antique he held. The cimarron didn't wait to compare sizes.

I heard a click as his finger put pressure on the trigger. I jumped for my life. Dropping to the ground, I heard the hammer on the blunderbuss descended with a rusty creak. Protecting my injured side, I threw myself down onto my right. The pistol slipped from my grip. The blunderbuss exploded in a great puff of gray smoke. Wet pieces stung my face and neck. Pieces of my own flesh and bone, I thought. Strangely, other than in my injured side, I felt no pain.

I looked up through the clearing smoke to see the cimarron had dropped his machete and held his forearm, a look of incredulity on his face. He screamed. The weapon had exploded, blowing off his hand. An inch of bloody stump extended from his wrist.

With the machete still in my hand, there was no need for the Colt, so I left it on the ground. I stood and took three slow steps towards the injured cimarron. He was too shocked to notice my coming at him with my weapon raised. I slashed hard at the side of his neck, driving the blade deep, severing flesh and bone, releasing a torrent of gore that sprayed warmly onto the font of my trouser legs. He fell over, gurgling his last breath.

With another man down, Watson had finally summoned the courage to go after the two remaining raiders. He chased past me, shouting his own version of a war cry. I retrieved the Colt and joined him in the chase.

The attackers had released the women to hasten their own escape and were almost at the cliff edge. Their captives fled in our direction. Sobbing as they reached us, clinging, pleading for help. We pushed away from them. In the loss of those vital seconds, the cimarrones had gotten further away, now only a few paces from the steps leading down to the river.

With Watson running ahead, I cursed at not being able to safely fire my weapon. "Shoot at them," I shouted, casting aside my bloodied machete. I moved to one side, trying to get a better line of sight to the escaping targets and was aware of a group of people coming towards us from the village. The men who had run away had armed themselves and were finally ready to enter the fight.

Watson stopped and cocked his pistol with both hands. He fired at the fugitives. The shot went wide. The raiders scampered onto the stairs and over the cliff edge. I caught up with Watson as we reached the top of the stairway. The cimarrones were already pushing a cayuco into the river. The sun had risen high enough that we could see them jump into the canoe and paddle away. I had little faith in being able to hit them at this distance and at the angle from the cliff top to river. I took aim and fired anyway.

My bullet struck their cayuco, punching a fist-sized hole at the water line.

"Well done, Graystone. They won't get far in that thing," Watson said. He raised the Dragoon and let off a shot in the direction of the escaping men. He seemed more surprised than me when his bullet struck home, hitting one of the cimarrones in the head and sending him over the side.

The men from the village arrived just in time to see Watson's lucky shot. They cheered and urged him to do it again. Watson obliged them. Though the bullet missed by twenty feet, causing a splash in the river where it struck the surface, the villagers cheered heartily.

Seeing that the escaping cayuco had water flooding through the hole, the villagers ran down the steps and took to the river in two of their own boats. The remaining cimarron struggled for the opposite bank, beached the canoe and made a run for it into the jungle. The villagers reached the same spot and followed him into the thicket.

Watson and I walked back to the village passing the dead man with the blown off hand. Watson pointed his finger at my face. "What the devil happened? That looks like blood and meat all over you."

My shirt was covered in flecks of blood, flesh and bone chips. I wiped a hand over my face, smearing the gore from the cimarron's blown hand. The remains of the blunderbuss lay as twisted metal attached to a splintered wooden grip. Exhaustion washed over me. I stared at the cimarron's blackened mangled stump. A pool had spread under the dead man, daylight finally bright enough to reveal its crimson hue.

16

THAT FIRST NIGHT IN PANAMA left six men dead. The fourth raider, hunted down in the jungle, was savagely beaten by his pursuers. Too injured to walk, he was then dragged back to the village and thrown into a cage like a captured beast to await his fate. Execution was a certainty, the decision was merely how it was to be carried out. The term, 'runaway slaves' had me picturing the cimarrones as black Africans. The man in the cage was dark-skinned but not black. He was barefooted and dressed in the same kind of loose shirt and baggy trousers our river guides wore. I recognized some of the traits of our native hosts in him — the result of a couple of centuries of intermarriage with local tribespeople.

Although Panamanian natives had a reputation as peace-loving people, their docile nature had been abused time and again ever since the Isthmus was first discovered in 1501 and later colonized by Spain. They had been known to occasionally rise up against their oppressors. While we gaped at the barely-conscious cimarron through the wooden bars of the pen, Watson told me the story of French pirate, François l'Ollonois. The brigand had a history of inflicting terrible cruelty on the native population. When the pirate's ship ran aground on a shoal, the locals saw their chance for revenge. When l'Ollonois came ashore, the story was that they hacked him to pieces and then put him on a spit to be roasted and eaten.

Brown and Legrand were nowhere to be found. Clothes hung out of our bags, and our personal effects were strewn about our lodgings. Items from both our packs were missing. It didn't take much argument to conclude that our traveling companions were responsible for the thefts. Nothing of vital importance was gone, we both still had our money, but our pocket watches were missing and so was my California map and an excellent compass that I had grown very fond of. Other travelers who had fled from the cimarrones, leaving their packs behind, had also been robbed.

The obvious place for the thieves to try to sell their loot was back at Yanqui Chagres. Everyone else was headed in the opposite direction, unlikely to give chase if it involved back-tracking. If not by the river, the only way out for the robbers was by hiking through the jungle. I estimated that we had traveled about ten miles up-river. It didn't make sense to me, but then the two of them didn't seem to be very bright — carrying heavy packs, they had little chance of making it back alive — a comforting thought.

Back in the village, we were feted as heroes. Watson basked in the praise lavished on him for his bravery, and his expertise with a gun. I was happy to let him take the credit for chasing off the cimarrones. The tribesmen told and retold the story of what they had seen, encouraging him to act out the miraculous shot that dispatched the fleeing raider into the river. I allowed him the use of my Dragoon for his play-acting, after first emptying it of ammunition. That left him shouting, *bang* each time the story was reenacted. It didn't matter, it was always greeted with cheers and had native children running about the village shouting *bang, bang*.

With one of Noko's men dead, it took some persuading for him to agree to leave again. Only when one of the women we had rescued spoke up for us did he consent to take us the rest of the way. Three more days on the Chagres passed with comparative ease. The days went by in much the same way as the first, except now with Brown and Legrand gone, we sat in the cayuco under the thatched awning. We stopped for food and rest each night at small tribal settlements along the river. At the end of each day's journey, we would meet up with many of the same travelers who had arrived on their own canoes. Rhythmic splashes made by the paddles had a hypnotic effect, and I was content to let the jungle slip past us while I relaxed into the journey and allowed my injured side to heal. From the cayucos that had departed the village before us, word had spread of the raid and the part we had played in it. We were warmly welcomed at each place we stopped. Noko warned the people of riverside settlements of the two thieving white men that had fled the night of the attack. So far, Brown and Legrand hadn't been seen, and I was quite sure we'd never see them again.

At last, we reached Cruces. Noko had timed our journey so that we arrived early enough to hire mules for the twenty-mile jungle trip to the Pacific coast. Cruces was a little town much like Yanqui Chagres, full of brothels and saloons hastily erected to cater to argonauts. Again, I resisted the temptation of stopping for a drink and pressed on. We traveled on the *Camino Real*, the ancient 'Gold Road' laid down by the Spanish three centuries earlier. Here too, our reputations had preceded us, and after we bade farewell to Noko and his men, we embarked on the day-long mule-back ride to Panama City.

I discovered that of the many points of congestion along the Panama route, nowhere was more clogged than the harbor at Panama City. Sea transport to San Francisco was in short supply making it necessary for some to wait for weeks, sometimes months before being able to secure passage. The city's dozen or so hotels were constantly full. Local residents took full advantage of the demand for lodgings and rented out rooms in their homes and even spaces on their floors. Travelers who were unable to afford a place to stay camped in a tent city that had grown outside the city walls. On our first night in Panama City, that is what we did.

The next day, we made our way through the crowds towards the Pacific Mail Steamship Company. Men were lined up outside the ticket office. Having made it half-way to California, being stuck here for weeks to await passage could have meant my defeat. When we managed to make our way to the front of the line, the harried clerk told us that we wouldn't be able to leave for another three weeks. Ships sailing the Cape Horn route sometimes called in at Panama for supplies. I asked the clerk if he had news of the SS California and was told it was not expected for at least another month, if it stopped there at all.

We had no option but to give the ticket clerk our names and hand over a deposit for tickets for the next available vessel. Seeing my name in his ledger, the ticket clerk asked, "You wouldn't be United States Marshal Angus Graystone, would you?"

"*Marshal* Graystone, indeed!" Watson chortled.

I reached into my pocket, pulled out my badge and placed on the counter top. "At your service," I said. "Does that make any difference to our chances of earlier travel?"

"It certainly does, Marshal Graystone, but just for you, not your friend," the clerk said, pulling open a desk drawer. He took out an envelope with my name written across the front. "Your ticket," the clerk said handing me the envelope. "You depart three days from now, aboard the SS *Oregon*. There's also this, arrived yesterday." Another envelope contained a drawing. Peters, the man who swore me in as a marshal, had sent me a drawing of the fugitive's face.

After three days camped in Panama's tent city, I said my goodbyes to Watson before boarding the overcrowded paddle steamship headed for California.

BOOK THREE

CALIFORNIA

17

LONG AFTER IT WAS PROVEN FALSE, a popular misconception lingered until the end of the 18th Century that California was an island. Early Spanish explorers were the first to err, influenced perhaps by the writings of Garcí Ordóñez de Montalvo. And who could blame them? Having read a translation of the Castilian author's work, *The Exploits of Esplandián*, I could appreciate how some would wish to hold on to a romantic notion of that mystical place.

> *Know that on the right hand from the Indies exists an island called California very close to a side of the Earthly Paradise; and it was populated by black women, without any man existing there, because they lived in the way of the Amazons. They had beautiful and robust bodies and were brave and very strong. Their island was the strongest of the World, with its cliffs and rocky shores. Their weapons were golden and so were the harnesses of the wild beasts that they were accustomed to taming so that they could be ridden, because there was no other metal in the island than gold.*

Were his writings merely flights-of-fancy?

Premonition was the word that came to mind. Even the Great Seal of California, formally adopted half a year before my adventure began, depicts a goddess said to be the Greek deity, Minerva. To my eyes though, there is little doubt that the seated figure holding a spear was inspired by Calafia, the warrior queen of Montalvo's book. Montalvo was right about California's gold, its cliffs and rocky shores, but his dreamy view of an 'Earthly Paradise' was a distant cry from what I experienced in that autumn of my arrival in 1850.

San Francisco welcomed me with freezing rain. An early-Autumn downpour carried on through to the end of the year and then hardly let up until the following spring. The city's streets flowed slick with mud. A surge of men and their beasts continued to flow in, filling the city to bursting point — and still more people came. According to San Francisco's harbor master, about 70 thousand souls had arrived in just the previous twelve months. Many had traveled in much the same way as I had or by other sea routes; others traversed the continent on wagon trains. But the allure of treasure also drew them from Europe, Asia and from as far away as Australia.

The dismal weather alone was bad enough, but when combined with arduous travel, cramped conditions and exorbitant prices, everyone seemed in a constant state of agitation. Adding fuel to the frenzy were the prospectors that came into town blustering about the abundance of their claims. What they carried in the form of nuggets or dust was spent with abandon in the belief that there was plenty more to be unearthed; for some that was true, for many others though, the single chunk or bag of gold dust would be the last they would ever find.

Overpriced liquor ran freely in the dozens of saloons and gambling halls that had sprung up, reminding me of

Watson's remark about mushrooms growing on shit. I wondered where he was now — in all likelihood still languishing in Panama Harbor's tent city. Fistfights, knife fights and gunfights broke out over the smallest of incidents. To cope with the increasing number of lawbreakers, one of the many ships deserted by gold hunters had been converted into a floating jail. The hundreds of bare masts gave San Francisco Harbor the look of a denuded forest, and with so many abandoned vessels, it took some skill for a captain entering the harbor to pilot his way to a safe mooring.

The argonauts' craving for drink was enormous; the stronger the better. What passed for liquor — no matter the name it was given — was usually some form of rotgut flavored to disguise the poisons in it. I had been dry for most of the journey from New York, but now in San Francisco, with the long wait for the fleeing Chinaman, the weather, the ruckus — I succumbed. And each morning-after, I promised myself 'never again.' It was a sickness, a lust, a variation of the addiction that afflicted gamblers and argonauts. Perhaps in time, my illness would evolve into a full-blown version that encompassed all three vices, and then some. Then at least, I told myself, I could consider myself a success at something.

The hound returned.

It had strayed off somewhere between New York and the jungles of Panama. Its reappearance, a reminder of my frailty, was a cruelty that I had exacted upon myself.

I had been in San Francisco for a little over a month. With each passing day, worry over the task of successfully apprehending Bufo, troubled me more. Though I was sure of having arrived before the fugitive, knowing exactly when he would appear and how to identify him weighed heavily on me. Would my first assignment as a marshal come to naught?

While I leaned back on a rickety chair under a large dripping tent that called itself a saloon, I was aware of the black dog skulking under a nearby table, invisible to the men above him playing faro.

My table, the one closest to the muddy entrance, was a scarred slab of pine nailed to the tops of a couple of crates. Four mismatched chairs were placed around it. It wasn't yet noon, and there was only a handful of us at the Pick and Pan. The proprietor had strewn a layer of straw on the bare earth to prevent customers from slipping and falling down. The straw had become soaked. Strands of chaff, rotten and split gave the place an odor of decay.

The man sitting across the table from me was an old codger with a patch over one eye and a beard like a billy goat. He had his own liquor bottle and was glugging it straight from the neck. I, feigning a higher standard, poured the dark brown liquid into a small chipped glass but knocked it back just as fast. I turned the half-empty bottle to study the name of my swill. The peeling label identified it good-humoredly as Gold Bug Chowder. The 'bug' part of its name I could believe was inspired by its main ingredient. The rest of it tasted like a mixture of turpentine and gunpowder. Almost every shot of it ignited a cough that had me doubling over. Damn gunpowder, I thought.

Saloon keepers gave their specialty drinks names like Forty-Rod, Tarantula Juice or Taos Lightning. There was also one referred to as Coffin Varnish, and for those looking for something even more exotic — one to which my promise of never-again had so far been kept, was the innocent-sounding name, Cactus Wine. The peyote tea that constituted most of it made for an extremely nasty concoction that would cause retching and at the same time induce the drinker to want more.

I pulled a folded piece of paper from my coat pocket and opened it gingerly, attempting to avoid the water droplets leaking through the canvas above. I wasn't possible to shield it completely, a drop or two landed on the drawing, one of them splashed onto the forehead of the moon-faced man who stared back at me from the paper. The portrait showed Bufo to have a flattish, wide nose. I studied what looked to be blemishes on his cheeks. I wondered if I had seen those before, or whether they were newly caused by water splashes. Perhaps it was a scarring, making it easier to identify the man. To my untrained eye, it could have been a drawing of any of the hundreds of Chinese men I had seen since my arrival.

A few days after I landed at San Francisco, a mail ship had brought news that some weeks earlier California had been admitted to the Union as a free state — the entire city had broken into spontaneous celebration. The episode reminded me of Taylor's death and my mission, it steeled my resolve. Now, weeks later, I was a wreck.

As a matter of courtesy, I made my presence as a marshal known to John Geary, the city's first mayor, telling him secretly of my undertaking to apprehend the Chinaman but avoided mentioning the true reason. Geary didn't think much of my chances given the vast number of Chinese who passed through on their way to the gold fields. "A strange bunch," Geary said of them. "Tend to keep to themselves, but good workers, mind you. You'd be better off finding one of them to help you locate the fellow you're after."

Mayor Geary invited me to join a group of local dignitaries to celebrate California's admission. That was the first instance for me to wear my marshal's badge publicly and I concealed it as soon as the ceremony was over. On that occasion, I stood next to the city's first ever elected sheriff, John Coffee Hays, a well-known figure who had made a name for himself as a Texas Ranger and hero of the Mexican-American War. He appeared to be a man more than capable of maintaining law and order without my help — an affable sort who seemed to have been able to read the lay of the land in the short time he had been in the city. "Come for a chitchat anytime, marshal," he'd said and then added, "I've seen you about, Graystone, without the badge, which is your choice of course, but at times that little tin plate could come in mighty handy, 'specially with the foreigners who don't know where the law begins or ends."

Huddled as a group, within the large crowd of spectators were a number of Chinese men. They all had the same shaved foreheads and pigtails hanging down their backs. I had heard the hairstyle referred to as 'the queue order.' Forcefully imposed on all Chinese males, in China it meant submission to Qing rule — non-compliance meant a death sentence; but even here in America, the Chinese still swore fealty to their emperor. Their strange look and the fact that even standing side by side I had difficulty telling them one from another caused me to give serious deliberation to Geary's advice about finding someone in the know to help me.

Of all the drinking holes in town, I had chosen the Pick and Pan because its higher elevation gave me a direct line of sight to the harbor. Without having to rise from my rickety chair, I could see all ships entering the port. Aided by a set of binoculars, I was often able to make out the names of vessels as they meandered between abandoned hulks. Any day now I expected to see the ship I was waiting for. The plan was then to make my way down to the docks and grab Bufo as soon as he set foot on dry land. I refilled my glass and knocked it back. From the corner of my eye, I sensed movement under a table; the approving wag of a dark tail. I turned my shame away from it and for good form brought the binoculars to my eyes to examine an incoming vessel.

My fuzzy vision focused on the incoming ship's name, John Marshall. Directing the binoculars to the shore, I watched an excited mob gather in anticipation of receiving the ship's cargo. American vessels like this one would be stocked to the brim, taking on more freight as they stopped at Valparaiso or other ports along their route. I swept my glasses back to the ship for a better look. On the ship's deck sat six wagons in addition to what looked like two fire engines. It also carried a huge stack of bricks and a pile of lumber. Building supplies were in short supply and anyone getting their hands on these goods was certain to make a tidy profit.

Not the SS *California*. I dropped the binoculars, letting them hang off my neck and consoled myself with another shot.

Sounds of laughter, crashing glass, more cackling, rain plopping onto the tent top, the twang of a banjo. Cold water dripped onto the back of my neck. The smell of mud, vomit, rotgut. My tongue, parched and thick, rasped against the roof of my mouth. I raised my head off my folded arms and forced open one eye. There was a faint glow of sunlight fighting through the gray sky. The low hazy ball of light told me it would be dark in another half hour. I cursed myself for falling asleep.

I reached for the bottle: empty. The shot glass lay tipped over next to it. I shook my head to check if I was in a 'never again' state; it turned out not to be that bad. The saloon had filled up, and the other chairs around my table were occupied. My binoculars were still hanging around my neck by its leather strap. I brought them to my eyes and pointed them towards the harbor to watch a ship coming in. Following its progress, I tried to catch a glimpse of its name as it wove and turned. Eventually, just before it pulled in behind another new arrival, I was able to read the vessel's name, a sleek clipper, the Houqua. Not the one I sought.

I shifted my attention to the ship tied up alongside. The shock of seeing the words SS *California* painted in gold, made me suck in a sharp, loud breath. There was still activity on deck but it was to do with unloading cargo. That meant that most passengers had already gone ashore or were on their way. Still, with binoculars to my eyes, I rose from the chair, knocking it backward and tilting the table with a jolt from my thighs. My table-mates grabbed to steady their drinks and swore at me. After all these months of traveling and waiting, I had missed the arrival of my quarry.

A cacophony of reproaching voices filled my head; clamor punctuated by the clanging of a brass school bell. Bright dots filled my eyes. I took a deep breath, swayed back onto my boot heels and then forward again. I steadied myself with a palm flat on the table. A slow turn to the exit, and then I splashed out into the cold rain to make my way to the docks.

It took ten minutes of hard of stamping and slipping through muddy streets to get to the harbor front. No longer space for a ship to come alongside the dock meant that passengers and cargo had to be brought in on smaller boats. I arrived breathless and soaked but in time to see several boat-loads of Chinese men being ferried ashore. There was no way to tell which boat they had come off. In a panic, I pulled out my portrait of Bufo, looking from face to face frantically trying to find any likeness with the new arrivals. They all bore some similarity to the man in the portrait.

My eyes fell one Chinaman who seemed to resemble the face in the picture more than others. His turn came to go ashore. He had one foot on land to step out of the boat. I rushed forward, leaned over and seized hold of his forearm. The man looked up at me, eyes wide in surprise. I saw a small white blemish near his eye. This surely was my man.

The Chinaman rotated his wrist and forearm and in a split second, pulled free of my grip. I grabbed for him again, but this time it was he who acted first. With a hand clamped firmly around my wrist, he pulled himself up onto the dock. In the same motion, I was pulled forward. Briefly hanging over the edge of the dock, whirling my arms for balance, I plunged headfirst into San Francisco Bay.

Already cold from the rain, the sea's iciness came as a shock. Before dropping into the harbor, I had been barely aware of the noises all around me: the hiss of rain, shouting in different languages, creaking wood, clanking chains. Under the surface, I felt deaf. The water's density blocked out all sound save my burbling cry for help. My open eyes saw only dark gray.

Never a strong swimmer, I clawed water. I breached the surface sputtering and spitting brine, shooting out of the water like a whale I'd seen on the voyage to Panama. Faces stared down at me, fingers pointed. There was considerable laughter at my expense. Treading water, I tried to see where my Chinaman had gone.

Bobbing up, raising my head to look through a gap between spectators' legs, I spied a group of black-clad, pigtailed men trudging away from the chilly shore with their baggage.

A few moments passed before someone snagged my coat with a boat hook and dragged me ashore where I was landed like the day's catch. There I lay in the mud, waterlogged binoculars hanging around my neck, staring up into the darkening sky while Bufo got away.

18

JOHN COFFEE HAYS HAD LOST NO TIME in setting up a comfortable office.

I marveled at the floor to ceiling wood paneling. The sheriff's capacity to secure good quality materials, and find workmen to do his bidding, demonstrated his standing in the burgeoning community.

On the wall to my left, a painting depicted an Indian warrior riding at full gallop alongside a herd of stampeding buffalo. The hunter carried a long lance and was about to thrust it into the flank of the nearest beast. "Comanche," Sheriff Hays said, noting my interest in the scene.

"A fine painting," I said, "but don't Indians hunt with bows and arrows?"

"Mostly so, but Comanches take pride in doing it with a long spear," Hays said, demonstrating his authority on the ways of Comanche Indians. He reputedly had some of them ride with him into battle against other tribes.

Below the painting, a plush claret-colored sofa beckoned, but Hays directed me to a chair opposite his oversized mahogany desk. Perhaps seeing how frail I looked, he feared that once settled into the sofa's red cushions, I wouldn't know when to leave.

Hays stepped to the door and called for his secretary to bring coffee, giving me a chance to look around the room. On the wall opposite the tantalizing sofa was a vast unlit fireplace. Above the mantelpiece hung a great gilt-framed mirror that gave the room a sense of depth and magnified the brightness of a couple of gas lamps. The well-lit room, contrasted sharply with the gray morning, rain-soaked street outside.

The sheriff took his place behind the desk. "Heard you had a little mishap, Marshal."

I gulped sheepishly. "I was in the process of executing my duty at the time. Unfortunately, the man absconded."

"An elusive thing . . . duty, I mean," Hays said, retrieving a smoldering cigar from a little silver plate. He brought it to his lips and drew on it but it had gone out. He put it back down. "Don't you think so?"

"Indeed," I responded not knowing quite what he meant, hoping the comment wasn't a dig at my failure. I let it pass, saved that moment by the arrival of the sheriff's secretary, a thin man in a waistcoat who earlier had shown me in and taken my dripping raincoat. He placed the tray on the sheriff's desk and left the room.

Hays poured steaming coffee for us. His thick black hair was coiffured so that a wave of sorts jutted out from the right side like a cliff's overhang. A mustache and goatee completed the look of a distinguished city official.

Lulled by the sound of coffee being poured, its aroma mixing with the scent of cold cigar ash, I let my mind drift briefly. What Hays referred to as a mishap was an embarrassing affair that I'd not soon forget. No doubt he knew every detail of my unintentional swim. If I'd had my wits about me, I would have gone after Bufo. Recalling that the portrait of Bufo had been destroyed by my soak in the bay, deepened my morosity.

Hays saved me from further self-induced despondency. "Am I correct in assuming that your visit is more than a social call, Marshal Graystone?"

"Quite so, Sheriff."

He gestured to the coffee, and we sipped the strong brew.

"When I last saw Mayor Geary, he advised that it might be prudent to get some help in finding my man, a Chinaman. He goes by the name, Bufo. I believe him to be still somewhere in the city. Could you recommend someone that could point me in the right direction? A person who is familiar with the ways of the Chinese. Yourself perhaps?"

"They're a slippery lot. I got to know Indians better than just about anyone — except for William Bliss perhaps — but Chinese? For that, you'll need one of their own kind." Hays took another sip of coffee. He looked to the ceiling for a moment. "In this case, maybe the help of a China woman."

"There are Chinese women here?"

Hays understood the look of surprise on my face. Chinese women in America were a rarity, more so in the eastern states. The first one to ever set foot in America was believed to have arrived in 1834, a woman by the name of *Afong Moy* who toured the country as a curiosity.

"A few," Hays continued, "flower girls mainly."

"I'm not familiar with the term."

"The name 'flower girl' has a nice ring to it I'll admit, but they are Chinese whores, plain and simple. The way I see it, where there are few flowers, you can bet there'll be plenty of bees going for their nectar." He laughed heartily. I managed to smile, bobbing my head inanely while considering the idea. Getting information from prostitutes wasn't new to me, I had done so on several occasions back in New York with varying results.

Hays continued, "Naturally, these flowers, just buds some of them, no older than twelve or thirteen, have a gardener to look after them. I suggest you speak to the gardener. Here are her name and the place to find her." He jotted in his notebook, tore the page out and passed it to me, hunching over his desk.

I read the name. "Ah Toy?"

"That's the one," Hays said with a smirk on his face.

The name Ah Toy was one I presumed was of a made up character, like so many others that made the rounds in San Francisco; a city that thrived on a scaffold of dreams. Ah Toy's story, one I didn't quite believe, was of a Chinese beauty whose merchant husband had died on the eastward voyage across the Pacific. As the tale went, she had then been taken on as the ship captain's mistress, arriving as a wealthy widow after her exotic charms had seduced the captain into bestowing on her everything he possessed.

"I would wager that a woman like Ah Toy would know something about the man you seek. She's involved with most the goings on with the Chinese here," Hays said.

"I shall go there directly. Should I say you referred me to her?"

"Best not to, Graystone, best not to."

I pulled my still-damp Mackintosh on even though the rain had stopped, no telling when it would start again. The veiled glow in the sky got people out in the streets to do whatever they needed to before the downpour resumed.

34 Waverly Place was several streets inland and uphill from the sheriff's office. I pulled out my pocket watch, newly replaced after the episode in Panama only to register that my

dunk in the harbor had ruined it, but I judged it to be a little before ten in the morning. Taking in the bright red building's three-story façade, I wondered if a woman of Ah Toy's profession would be up yet.

I hadn't any idea of how to approach the subject of a Chinese fugitive with one of their own. Judging by the surprised look on the Chinaman's face when I grabbed his arm, he was unaware that anyone was after him. Maybe he still didn't know. That could easily change after I spoke to Ah Toy. I would have to handle the interview with delicacy. I assumed that in order to ply her trade, she would have to be able to speak some English, but would it be proficient enough to provide the answers I needed? Here, the Chinese that spoke reasonably well acted as translators for those who spoke none at all. Back in New York, they were still a rarity, unusual enough to be seen as curiosities. Since arriving in San Francisco I had observed some of them bargaining animatedly with shopkeepers, making up for their lack of English by communicating their displeasure of high prices being charged with a combination of gestures that involved arms, faces and loud voices.

The windows revealed no signs of life, drapes pulled shut. *Too early*, I told myself. *A drink first.*

Never too early to find a place for a drink in San Francisco, I turned away from the garish façade and began strolling south towards Sacramento Street, looking for the closest saloon. Fifty paces on I pushed my way through a creaky wooden door into a dimly lit tavern.

Other than a sallow-complexioned barkeep, I was alone in a place that smelled of cat piss and spilled beer. My boot soles stuck to the floor with each step, clicking as I pulled them off the planks. "Welcome to the Nugget, what will you have, mister?" The bartender swept a hand across the front of a row of his wares. I scanned the bottles that stood shoulder to shoulder behind him. Tattered labels and mucky-looking liquid filled to different levels gave the bottles a look of soldiers in ragged regalia, minutemen ready for a call to action. Save for one that caught my attention, they were the usual rag-bag that every other sump offered. I pointed to the label I hadn't come across before. "That one, 'Snakebite.'"

"Good choice, just come in a week ago — does the job real quick, like the name says." He gave me a broken-toothed grin and flicked out his tongue in a grotesque parody of a viper. He turned and brought the bottle to the bar. "Leave the bottle?"

It was a third full. What damage could a measly third do? I was tempted, but quickly said, "Just a shot." Behind me there was a low growl; in the reflection of the bottle, I thought I saw something. The bottle's curve lengthened the thing's dark shape as it snuck under a table. I looked away, trying to ignore it. "That place up the street, the red one," I said.

"Chinee whorehouse? What about it, mister?"

"Know when it opens?"

He pulled out his pocket watch and checked the time. "Anytime now, I reckon. It's where I get most my trade from. Men goin' in or comin' out. In an'out." He laughed. "Come here for a stiffener have you?"

The barman sloshed a couple of ounces of brown liquid into a glass, re-corked the bottle and then set it down next to the glass. "Well, go on mister, tell me what you think. First one's free." His grin revealed a row of mossy teeth.

The liquid instantly numbed my tongue. When it hit my throat, I gagged but forced it down with peristaltic determination. My eyeballs rolled back into my skull. It went down hard, like a sharp-clawed animal trying to prevent a fall by raking its's talons against the sides of my gullet. It hit my gut with the kick of a mule. I coughed for a full minute without pause. With each convulsion during that long minute, the remnants of what I had consumed the night before, just a mild fog, seemed to coalesce with the new stuff. The *Snakebite* raised a rallying call to any poisonous brethren still lurking in my body, a battle cry for lingering potency to rise up and attack.

When I had caught my breath enough to stand erect. The barman was staring at me with a knowing a grin on his face.

"Toldya — good hey?"

I nodded. "What's in it?"

"Just what the label says."

I tossed the thought around in my head for a moment, half-believing but not wanting to accept that it could contain snake venom. "How much?"

"Dollar for two."

"A man can buy a whole bottle for a dollar. Besides, you said the first one was free."

"Don't recall sayin' nothing of the sort. What kind of saloon keeper gives free drinks? Dollar for two."

I blinked, confused.

"Want it?"

I fished a dollar out of my pocket and handed it over. The barman poured a brimful. "Better sit yerself down, mister."

There would be no repeat of yesterday's failure, I told myself. "Think I'll stand. Quick one, then I'll be gone." I raised the glass to the tip of my nose, sniffing slowly in an attempt to understand what it was that I had pinched between my thumb and forefinger. Under the pungency of alcohol, it smelt moldy, not unlike the decaying pelt of a small dead rodent. My mind drifted to an image of a decaying rat in the corner of a garden toolshed, the place I'd last smelled such foulness, realizing that here I was about to toss a liquefied rat down my throat.

"Well, go on then," the barman said with a taunt in his voice.

The second shot didn't seem to have as much punch. Perhaps it was that my senses had been dulled by the first, but then a surge came over me like the feeling of deafness and the hunger for air that I sensed underwater in San Francisco Bay. And then, euphoria.

The shelf of lined-up bottles, brothers-in-harm, began to tilt and jiggle, clinking their shoulders together. Bugs, golden ones crawled out of one, their antennae shimmering and waving as they streamed out, inundating the shelf. A hand-sized tarantula burst through a paper label, falling on the golden bugs and devouring them at an alarming rate. Masticating them in its terrible mandibles.

The cork of one of the bottles burst into flames. Bolts of lightning shot upwards, scorching the ceiling. Motionless, I watched in fascination, vaguely aware of the barman facing me. His mouth moved, but I couldn't hear a word, nor was I interested.

A while later, my senses returned.

"Gee mister, you're back. Never seen nothin' like it." He told me I had been standing erect, with eyes wide open, staring straight ahead for about 15 minutes.

Half an hour had passed since I had been in front of Ah Toy's. It was time to head back. Any more time spent in this bar would end in disaster. I staggered out into a light drizzle.

There were hints of life within 34 Waverly Place — drapes pulled open, the glow of a lamp behind the gossamer curtain of a downstairs window. I rapped my knuckles hard on the door. The knocks seemed to reverberate in my head.

Almost immediately I heard locks and chains being released. The door was pulled open a crack. Standing in the dark gap was a tiny person, a child I thought initially, but as the door was pulled the door open a quarter way, I saw it was a woman. The top of her head reached the middle of my chest. She was round-faced with a multitude of skin blemishes around her eyes and temples, her black, glossy hair was pulled back severely into a small bun. She was dressed in a starched white tunic that hung low over baggy black trousers.

"Ah Toy?" I said.

"No Ah Toy, Ah Jun," she replied. Her voice was low and hoarse.

"Ah Jun?"

The woman nodded. "Yu kum pee so?"

"Pee so?"

Ah Jun opened the door halfway. She could have been aged forty or sixty, the unblemished skin of her face was smooth, but the wrinkled, spotted backs of her hands belied someone older. "Look-look Ah Toy, pee so," she said, bringing her hands to the sides of her eyes and crouching forward.

"Ah, you mean peep-show."

"Ayah, wat I say, pee-so, stupit boy. Ah Toy baaf time, look-look see?"

My head reeled, trying to make sense of what the woman meant.

"Madam, I am here to see Miss Ah Toy." Remembering what Sheriff Hays told me, I showed her my marshal's badge. She poked her head forward and squinted at the five-pointed star for a while and then slowly tilted her gaze to my face with a frown. Ah Jun pulled the door open and with a single hooking motion of her scrawny hand, beckoned me to follow. I closed the door behind me and trailed after her bow-legged shuffle into a comfortably-furnished sitting room.

"Wey heeya," she said pointing to a couch.

Ah Jun held her hand out, wiggling her fingers, indicating for me to hand over my raincoat. I pulled it off and passed it to her. She left the room, holding my damp garment up with her hand raised high over her head to prevent it from dragging over the carpeted floor.

Seated comfortably, I studied the room. *Respectable*, I thought. Far more so than some of the establishments of this sort that I'd seen back in New York. A low table in front of me supported an arrangement of bright flowers. By a window facing the main street, a small round table flanked by two chairs sat draped with a frilly tablecloth. The pictures on the walls were exotic, Chinese I thought — vistas of mountains and rivers. A painting on the wall to my right showed a fishing scene and another beside it depicted a horse with its front hooves in the air, long mane flying wildly. The *Snakebite* still coursed through my veins. I wasn't sure if all the things I saw while sitting in that living room were entirely real. In an image of what I took to be Chinese fishing boats, I saw a small boy playing in the water. I heard him laugh, high-pitched and gleeful. There came a splashing sound each time his arm beat the surface. I didn't care whether it was real or not. I felt entirely content and a little disturbed when I heard shuffling noises approach the room.

19

AH JUN RETURNED, her forearm gripped for support by a woman I assumed to be Ah Toy. She took small steps towards me, coming closer I saw that she was much younger than the 'madam' I had imagined. I pushed myself up off the couch. Blood rushed to my head; I wobbled. For a moment, dark spots swam before my eyes.

I studied the approaching pair lit by pale sunlight flowing through the window. The younger woman swayed in a willowy motion, reminding me of heather waving in a gentle breeze. Mesmerized, mouth hanging open, I must have appeared idiotic standing there without uttering a word as they neared to within a few paces.

"No see morning peep-show, why come Ah Toy house?" Her words drifted towards me, shrill, but reaching my ears with an agreeable softness. She tilted her head, eyelids fluttering, ending the question with a winsome smile that reddened my cheeks.

I forced myself to gather my wits, to remember just why I was there. "Miss Ah Toy, it's kind of you to receive me." I hastily tore my hat off, embarrassed that I hadn't done it when I first entered the house. "My name is Angus Graystone."

"Gaystone?"

"Gray, Graystone, like the color, madam, Federal Marshal Graystone." I clumsily fished my badge out of a pocket and held it up.

Ah Toy mouthed my name silently, committing it to memory. "No show law-star in Ah Toy house, Mr. Graystone." She flapped a handkerchief pinched between her fingertips. A fragrant waft caressed my face. "Lawmans scare-way admirer." Ah Toy tilted her head towards the window. There were sounds of the day's first customers arriving, the front door opening and closing. Boots clomped up the stairs.

"Ah Toy haf many, many-mirer," Ah Jun said.

"Right, quite right." I returned the badge to my pocket.

"Why you come?" Ah Toy asked.

"I heard that you know many things, Miss Ah Toy."

"Who say?"

"People say that you know all that is happening in your Chinese community."

"That zageration. Ah Toy know things, not all. What you want?"

"I am looking for a man, a Chinese man. I thought that you might be able to help me find him."

"Many Chinese man in *Gum Saan*. Why Graystone want this one?"

"I am to bring him back to Washington." Ah Toy listened, head tilted. Her fetching pose distracted me from clear thought. "He arrived yesterday . . . on a ship."

"I forget manner. Please sit, Mr. Graystone." Ah Toy gestured to the couch I had just risen from. Ah Jun placed a stool under her mistress's rear as she descended ever so gracefully. I dropped onto the couch like a collapsing scaffold.

Ah Toy said something in Chinese to Ah Jun. The little woman didn't bother disguising her spite, shooting me a look like she'd bitten into a maggot-filled dumpling. She shuffled off, grumbling.

The day brightened. In beams of sunlight coming through the window, I was able to study Ah Toy's features as we faced one another. Me, slouched into cushions; she, perched straight-backed on a stool, resting her petite hands on her lap. Her light green gown flowed loose and long. Embroidered swallows and other small birds, swooped and darted. I saw one of them fly the full length of the gown, from the lacey trim around the neck of Ah Toy's white-porcelain skin, over the slight swell of her breast and continue to the hem above her tiny feet. Another bird flew upwards and I followed its flight up, over her knees and disappear into her high neckline. Over her heart-shaped face, sat an elaborate coiffure, thick glossy hair held in place by a gold hairpin that ended in the shape of a butterfly. It waved its metallic wings.

From the room above, a couple of loud thumps and muffled laughter brought me out of the enchantment. Ah Toy seemed amused by my close scrutiny of her body, smiling, blushing a little. She shifted ever so slightly on the stool. Suddenly aware of my vulgar behavior, I reddened. "I'm sorry, madam. It's just . . .," I said, moving my gaze to her almond-shaped eyes. I was starting to believe the tale of the bewitched sea captain.

"Please, Mr. Graystone, don't shy look Ah Toy. No charge," she said. "But maybe more nice to see peep show . . . next time pay, bath-time peep show." She tittered, modestly covering her mouth with her handkerchief. When her hand returned to her knees, she pinched the gown, fingers bunching up the green silk, raising the hem an inch to reveal her shoes. She glanced down. "You like lotus foot?"

I stared at her shoes. They were impossibly tiny, small enough for both to fit in one of my hands. The shoes were bright red, adorned with floral patterns embroidered in yellow. The tops came a little above her ankles. The lifting of her gown revealed a couple of inches of snowy skin above her shoes. I swallowed noisily.

"Ah Toy, look nice?" she asked.

"You are very beautiful, madam."

At that moment, the older woman, Ah Jun, returned carrying a round lacquered tray with a pot of tea and two little cups. Still grumbling, she set it down noisily on the table between us, giving me a malicious look as she retreated a few steps and observed from a corner of the room.

Ah Toy brought the handkerchief to her cheek and tilted her chin down. "Mr. Graystone too kind." A brief silence, then, "Now, tell me about Chinese man you seeking."

"His name is Bufo. We believe he may have been involved in a crime in Washington."

"He killer?"

"Perhaps. That's what we need to find out."

"No good for all Chinese in *Gum Saan*. Make Chinese get more hard life. How this man look?"

An image of Bufo's portrait appeared in my mind as I tried to recall any distinguishing features. "He has a scar on his cheek. I pointed to a spot near my left eye. If Ah Toy knew who I was speaking of, nothing in her demeanor showed it.

Ah Toy leaned forward to pour; the golden butterfly's wings trembled. The steaming, yellowish liquid gave off a scent of jasmine. Ah Jun spoke quickly, as I received the proffered teacup. "No mind. Ah Jun hate law-mans. Drink tea, Mr. Graystone." The beverage had a floral sweetness to it, subtle but quite distinct. It soothed as it went down.

"You like?" Ah Toy asked.

"Very nice indeed."

She sipped from her own cup, one hand holding the cup by its rim and the other supporting its base. "It call Phoenix Flower Tea. Special from China. Ah Jun bring me. She gone long time, now come back to serve me. Arrive one day-ago." Ah Toy leaned forward to pour again into my little cup.

I looked towards Ah Jun and nodded with a smile. She turned her face away, eyes half closed in disdain. I turned my gaze back to Ah Toy. "She must be quite robust to endure the hardship of a long sea journey and look so well," I said.

Ah Toy raised a hand to cover her mouth and tittered, the mirth adding color to her cheeks. She looked at Ah Jun and said something to her. Ah Jun let out a short burst of laughter, a high-pitched giggle.

"Have I said something amusing?"

"You make mistake. I tell Ah Jun. Ah Jun not *she*, she is *he*," Ah Toy said before laughing again.

Now it was my turn to redden. "So sorry," I said to Ah Jun who snorted out of her nostrils and looked up.

"No worry, Graystone. Simple mistake. You see, Ah Jun what we call yānshù, you say, *yu-nuk*."

"Eunuch?" My open-mouthed mien set off another spell of hilarity.

"He present to me from admirer. Important, rich Chinese-mirer. Say Ah Jun too small, ugly. Voice like cow, not like other yānshù. Is true, but Ah Jun good faithful servant."

Keen as I was to know more about the details surrounding Ah Jun's missing tackle, I raised the matter I came to discuss. "Now, about the man I'm looking for."

"Bufo?"

"Yes. Have you any idea how I might find him?"

"You sure he arrive yesterday?"

"His ship, the California is in port. I saw him, I believe."

Ah Jun went to the window and looked out onto the street, leaning over, palms against the window sill. In front of his face, a circle of moisture formed on the glass.

"Many Chinese know the name, Bufo, but never see. Like ghost. Not usual Chinese name," Ah Toy said. "Name of bad man. Story he do many bad thing. Maybe he in *Gum Saan*, maybe no."

The tea had cleared my head. Finally, someone who recognized the name. More focused, I began to sense the possibility of a pathway opening in the direction of my prey. "How would I go about finding him?"

Ah Jun returned from the window and leaned over to pour more tea for her mistress, as he did, he whispered something into Ah Toy's ear. His mistress responded with a slight nod. Ah Jun didn't bother to pour tea for me, stepping backward he returned to his former post.

"One place in *Gum Saan* all Chinese go. You go there, try see Bufo face," Ah Toy said, filling my teacup.

"Where is that place, Ah Toy? Please tell me."

"I tell, you take care Ah Toy house?"

Perhaps this was a predicament Sheriff Hays had found himself in. "I will do what I can," I replied, safe in the knowledge that soon as I found Bufo, I'd be away on the first available boat.

Ah Toy put her teacup down. Her hands returned to her lap, and she gave me an unwavering stare. Instantly transformed, the demure beauty adopted a bearing of maturity, composed and authoritative. "Chinese Theater. You go tonight. Special opera performance *Palace of Eternal Life*. Many Chinese man go."

"Chinese entertainment, delightful," I said.

"No see opera, you look for Bufo face. Take opera glass," she ordered.

Ah Toy turned and said a few words to her servant. Ah Jun left the room and returned holding my raincoat, signaling an end to the interview.

Ah Toy stayed seated as I rose and thanked her. "Remember promise, Mr. Graystone."

"I understand, Miss Ah Toy," I said.

"Next time Graystone come, pay money. Maybe watch peep show, maybe meet beautiful flower girl. Young fresh flower."

When I took the coat from Ah Jun, he pointed a bony finger in the direction of the entrance. He didn't need to say a word, the scowl clearly exhibited his scorn.

A night at the Chinese Opera. The prospect of catching my man. Things were looking up. I wondered if another dram of Snakebite might not be in order.

—❦—

I decided against another dose of *Snakebite*. Instead, I made a few inquiries about the performance and learned that it was to begin at half-past eight in the evening. I started on my way to the Chinese district some minutes before eight o'clock in order to find the theater and to secure an advantageous position from which to view the audience. Finding the Chinese Theater was easy. I merely followed groups of Chinese as they made their way to number 622 Jackson Street. I joined a line at the door and paid a small fee to enter.

Any expectation of what I would find inside the theater was speciously based on my experience of theatres in New York. Mostly grand, luxurious places with crystal chandeliers hanging from cavernous domed ceilings. What I saw came as a stark reminder that I was too mired in old ideas. To have any chance of finding Bufo, I needed to adopt more flexible thinking, more readily accepting of the new.

The theater was a wooden building that resembled an old barn. It was already full and getting more packed by the minute as Chinese men pushed in behind me. There was a chandelier of sorts. Hanging from the ceiling by a rope was a contraption holding a number of oil lamps. There were lamps hung along the walls and at the sides of a stage that was no more than a dozen feet across. There were no chairs provided. Those nearest the stage were sitting down on bare floorboards. As more people filed in, they pushed forward and sat as close to the stage as they could.

Being a head taller than most in the theater, I looked over a sea of shaved pates and pigtails for a vantage point. It occurred to me that even if I sighted Bufo, getting to him through the thick crowd without him knowing might be impossible. Along the sides of the playhouse, ladders led up to platforms supported on flimsy-looking stilts, providing simple seating in what served as the equivalent of theater boxes. The quandary as to where I should watch from was solved when one of the ushers manning the entrance gripped me by the sleeve and firmly guided me through the crowd to one of the platforms near the front of the theater. He pointed up, indicating that I should watch the performance from above. A Chinaman standing in front of the ladder held his palm out. "Twenysen," he said. He grinned as I paid and then steadied the ladder as I made my way up fifteen or so feet to the stand. It creaked and swayed with my additional weight. There were five Chinese men already up there. They were absorbed in a loud, animated discussion and didn't acknowledge me other than with cursory glances.

I brought the binoculars to my eyes. They had dried out from the soak in the bay, but their lenses were somewhat cloudy. I swept them over the throng. I could tell little difference between the men below, all similarly dressed, most of like stature and with the same queued hairstyle. I studied faces, stopping briefly at each one, looking for a scar, for anything familiar.

After a while of scanning the main floor, I turned my attention to the audience on the other platforms. I sensed the spectators' excitement grow as the time approached the start of the performance. The talking got louder. The audience shouted towards the stage. The din further intensified when music began. A group of six musicians, seated on stools directly in front of the stage, bashed and sawed at instruments unfamiliar to me. There were no curtains, players unceremoniously came through a side door and clambered onto the stage to a renewed uproar. I lowered the binoculars and studied the troupe. The players' faces were heavily painted with long black aching eyebrows and brightly rouged lips. One had a flowing black beard attached to his face by a quite obvious piece of string. Their voluminous gowns were layered and brightly colored; red being the dominant hue, but trimmed with gold, sequined and sparkling in the lamplight. And the headdresses on them, elaborate to the point of disbelief. One, on the head of a man I took to be a warrior of some kind, sported long feathers poking out the top and trailing back several feet. The audience cheered or jeered as different performers took center stage and sang or shouted their lines. As far as I could tell, both male and female parts were played by men. The music was a discordant clash of cymbals and stringed and wind instruments. It was punctuated by clicks and knocking sounds over which the players screeched their lines.

Not understanding anything of the plot nor able to follow it, I was content to continue studying faces in the audience with my binoculars. After some time, my eyes became weary. When I lowered the binoculars, the man beside me gestured, requesting to use them. I passed them to him and he trained them towards the stage. Soon he was pestered by other men on our platform. The binoculars were passed from man to man as I kept looking down and across the sea of faces.

Wanting the binoculars back, I waved to the man who had them, the one furthest from me. He had them to his face, pointed down at the action on the stage which seemed to be some kind of stylized fight scene with two men circling one another and adopting mock-belligerent poses. I finally caught his attention when the man next to him assisted by slapping him on the shoulder. He reluctantly lowered the binoculars and turned his face towards me.

I caught a glimmer of recognition on his face. Not a dozen feet away, was the man I had tried to grab at the harbor.

I rose abruptly. He sprang to his feet, our motion caused the platform to creak and sway perilously. The other men, sensing the danger of an imminent collapse, attempted to pull me back down. I was having none of it. I pushed them away and took two long strides towards my quarry and then threw myself at him in a dive.

I caught him around the waist, and we crashed onto the flimsy boards. The platform rocked and then tilted under our weight. The others on the platform were in a panic, scrambling about inflicting more instability to our podium. Arms locked around my man's waist, I was vaguely aware that a hush had befallen the theater. The orchestra's instruments stopped one by one, the last being a flute's interrupted note.

Our platform began to lean over. I heard the wooden beams holding us up creak and then crack. In a moment, we were falling.

Half a dozen men dropped to the theater floor. My shoulder and the side of my head hit the floorboards with a mind-numbing thud. A shower of planks and broken poles crashed over us.

20

A LENGTHY SCREECH OF STRESSED TIMBERS tore its way into my skull with the delicacy of a dull railroad spike. I steeled myself for the next assault on my sore head, the clang of a brass school bell followed by a tirade delivered in Mrs. Blunt's scathing tone.

What I heard instead of Mrs. Blunt was more creaking. It was accompanied by a slight rolling sensation that was doing my noggin little good, and beneath the thin, musty-smelling blanket I lay on, I heard a gurgle of water. Odors of decaying wood and of the sea's corrosive salt led me to conclude that *California* had been a mere dream. Surely, I was still aboard the *Falcon* en route to Panama. And, somewhere was the faint but unmistakable odor of 'wet dog.' Now came a familiar voice, not Mrs. Blunt's, but another that lacked any sign of good humor. "Wondered if you'd ever come round, Graystone." The voice of one John Coffee Hays.

Confused images of the Chinese theater, of throwing myself headlong at Bufo, came roaring back. My eyes opened to a blurry sight of the sheriff standing over me. I was right about being on a ship, but that was as far as it went towards correctly deciphering my whereabouts.

"Safest place I could think of last night," Hays said.

"Where are you taking me?"

"You're aboard the *Euphemia*, and for the moment you're staying right here."

"The jail boat?"

"The very one."

The sky, colored like dish-water, spilled weak light through the cabin's windowpanes. I was in a barred cell. I sat up, regretting it immediately as a wave of nausea swept over me. A deep breath didn't help. I winced at the sharp pain in my ribs.

"Not under arrest, am I?"

"You ought to be, but no, call it courtesy from one lawman to another." He gave the cell door a shove. It opened all the way. I winced as it clanged against the bars. "Lucky we had the space, Marshal." My title of office was spoken slowly by Hays, one of his eyebrows raised, the other eyelid half-closed. "Other prisoners were moved ashore to the new jail a couple of days ago. You took quite a beating in that theater before my men could restore order and get to you. Had to fire shots in the air to keep 'em back. It was too much of a risk to put you in the new Station House. Reckon the Chinese would've burned it down. Must've been two hundred of them, never seen them so riled up." Hays paused to light a cigar; its burning tip glowed orange and then grayed as he stopped drawing in air. He puffed out a dense cloud that hung for a moment in the cold, still of the cabin. "Usually a pretty quiet bunch, stick to themselves, no fuss."

"Sorry, Sheriff. I was in the process of . . ."

"Yes, I know, executing your duty. You have a novel way of doing it, if I may say so."

"Do you know what happened to my man?" I asked, fingering a great sore lump on the back of my head.

"You mean that one?" Hays angled his head in the direction of the cells alongside mine. In the one adjoining, a figure sat on a blanket in the corner furthest from me. His head bowed, resting on his pulled-in knees. The door of his barred-cell was closed. All the other cells were empty.

"He was out cold too when we got there. You had your arms wrapped tightly around him. Had to pry your fingers loose to get you off. Thought he might be . . ."

"And you thought right, sir. Can't thank you enough. I shall interview him forthwith," I said, rising to my feet. Another wave crashed over me. Down I went.

Through a myriad of scents in the ship's bowels, a single one possessed the strength to lure me to wakefulness. Neither coffee nor salts could have brought me round as quick as the promise of that nectar that is whiskey. Hays had one hand behind my neck propping me up, the other held a glass under my nose. I reached for the cup and hastily tipped it down my throat. A little fireball detonated in my gut. A warm glow came to my cheeks.

"Thanks again, Sheriff." I looked around the cabin for the bottle but didn't see it. "If I might have another of those, I'll be right as rain."

Hays rose and turned towards a window. "If being like rain's what you need, perhaps I ought to put you outside." Sheets of rainwater streamed over the pane. Overhead, the torrent sounded the beat of a thousand tiny hooves dancing on the deck. I held my tongue.

"Maybe it would be safer for you to interview your prisoner from where you're sitting, Graystone. Ought to find out if he is your man in the first place. I'll leave you to it. When you're done, you can keep him locked up here or take him with you. Mind you, if you decide to keep him, here you'll be responsible for his upkeep."

"I understand, Sheriff. Thank you."

"Keys are over there," Hays said gesturing to a desk and chair against the bulkhead. He pulled on his raincoat as he stomped towards the door. Hays placed a hand on the knob and then paused, turning his head to me. "I imagine you'll want to be leaving soon. Not much traffic headed eastward these days, but I'll do my darndest to facilitate your departure." He pushed open the door and stepped out. "You can be sure of that," Hays said, words half obscured by the hissing downpour.

A gust slammed the door shut. Alone in the cabin with the man locked up in the next cell, I gripped the bars and pulled myself up, keeping hold of the cold steel for stability as I studied my prisoner. He raised his head and looked right at me. "Bufo," I said. "I've got you." He rose from a sitting position with the fluidity of a serpent, the blanket falling, pooling around his feet like shed skin. He was of average height for a Chinaman, a head shorter than me. Nothing to fear from this little fellow, I thought. "I say, laddie, Bufo." He took a step closer and now I could make out the scar on his cheek. Seeing that little blemish raised my spirits mightily. Another step and he was inches from the metal rods that separated us.

"Why you tak Shen Xiling?" he said.

"Can't understand a word of that gibberish. Say again."

"Why you tak . . . tak?"

"Tak? Ah, you mean attack, I suppose. Thought that would be obvious to a criminal, but perhaps not where you come from, Bufo."

"No Bufo. Shen."

"Let's not play games now. I know who you are. You fled here from Washington by way of New York aboard the SS

California. I've been after you for months. No point denying who you really are."

"Lo Lew Yok. Shen come China. Shen come Houqua boat. Lo California boat," the Chinaman said, with the effort of those words coughed up like a dislodged fishbone.

I recalled seeing the Houqua through my binoculars the day I went rushing down to the docks and ended up in the bay. The Chinaman's face contorted with frustration, lips pulled wide, brow furrowed. He repeated the thing about coming from China. "Good try, Bufo," I said. "I know who you are, no point in denying it."

In a flash, the Chinaman had taken a step forward, grabbed my wrists, pulled my hands free of the bars and through to his side. Too shocked to react, my face was pulled against the metal. He extended one foot back and with a toe dragged his blanket up. I am not certain how it happened, but in a moment the blanket was wound round the back of my neck, its ends used to secure my arms to the bars.

I was, until anyone came to my rescue, his prisoner. My cheekbones ached from being pulled hard against the bars, arms bound, twisted over each other. Despite the pain, or perhaps because of it, I saw an image of my mother stooping over a dressed chicken; its legs tied together with twine, destined for the oven. What was I destined for?

The Chinaman poked a finger at the center of his nose. "Shen." He reached under his padded jacket and into the front of his shirt. I flinched as he pulled out a sheet of paper and slapped it at my face. Waving the paper in one hand, he repeated his nose pointing and saying, "Shen." He held the paper close to my face so I could read it.

The document was upside down, and it took a moment to decipher what it was. I made it out to be a ticket for ocean passage aboard the Houqua. The passenger's name, written in a fancy hand, was given as Shen Xiling. I supposed that this man, Bufo or not, could have come to have it through theft or trickery. It could have been a forgery.

I saw the best option for getting relief for my sore arms as conceding to the Chinaman's claim. "Alright, I believe you . . . Shen. Yes, Shen, not Bufo." Face jammed against the cell bars, I nodded as best I could. "Shen," I repeated.

"What-you-name?"

"I'm Graystone. Angus Graystone."

"Opun doa Angas Gayston?" Shen asked, stepping back. He stuffed the ticket back into his shirt. "Pomis opun doa?" he said gesturing at the cell gate.

I nodded.

"Pomis, I let go."

"Yes. Promise."

Shen began unraveling the knotted blanket. I slumped to the floorboards, rubbing my painful joints. Shen pointed at his cell door. He spoke in Chinese, but the message was clear. Now free, I weighed my options. It was hard for me to accept that the man that I'd pursued for months over land and sea was not the one I finally had in a locked cell.

He seemed to sense my dilemma.

"Angas Gayston, you pomis," he said.

I got up, again using the bars for support, this time keeping a wary eye on him. I wobbled out of my cell and headed straight for the desk, a scarred old thing with a drawer in the middle and three more down its left side. On its right side was a little cupboard. I pulled open the center drawer. A set of keys jangled forward with the drawer's motion, a black metal ring threaded through the bows of half a dozen keys. I picked up the ring and glanced at Shen who studied my every move.

I laid the keyring on top of the desk. My prisoner began shouting. "You pomis, you pomis." He shook his fist at me.

"Quiet down," I said, holding up a placating palm toward him. My enthusiasm for heading straight for the desk was to search for the whiskey bottle. Unless Hays had it concealed in his coat pocket, which I doubted, the desk was the only place in the cabin I could imagine it being hidden away in.

I leaned over and gripped the knob of the small cupboard. It was locked. From the keyring, I chose the only key small enough to fit the cupboard's keyhole. Unlocked, the little door pulled open with a sharp squeak. There waiting patiently to be freed, a sentinel guarding its dark little cave, was a half-full bottle of 'Forty-Rod.' I picked it up gently and kicked shut the cupboard door. "You are liberated," I said to the bottle.

Shen started yelling at me in Chinese. A pang of guilt struck me. Releasing me in exchange for his freedom, he had been true to his word. With a sigh, I put the bottle on the desk. A low growl comes from behind me. I didn't have to look to know just what I'd see: the black hound with its grizzled snout, baring its teeth at me. The growling got louder, Shen's voice grew more frantic — in Chinese, interspersed with words that I could almost believe were English invectives. I needed to blot out the noise of both complainants. I'd been through enough.

I uncorked the Forty-Rod. The snarling stopped even as Shen's protests grew. Open bottle in my hand, I looked at my prisoner. Memories of the hardships I had borne to capture him came pouring into my head. The trek through Panama's jungle, combat with the *Cimarrones*. I saw Taylor's funeral procession, remembered the faces of William and Mary Bliss, saw an image of my hand on a bible. "Get a grip, Graystone," I said. The growling resumed as soon as I recorked the bottle, intensifying when I put the whiskey on the scarred desk.

Grabbing the jailer's keys, I dragged the desk chair over to Shen's cell and placed it facing the cubicle. The chair's old wooden legs creaked in complaint as I lowered gingerly onto it. Shen watched me make a playful show of inspecting the keys one at a time against the numbers etched beside the cell door's lock. After examining each key and feigning disappointment, I looked up at my prisoner's anguished face, taunting him with a little smirk.

Shen extended his right arm through the bars and said something I couldn't quite catch, but I was ready for him, tipping back just out of reach of his fingers. "Now then, Shen, Bufo, whoever you are, let's have a little talk.

21

SHEN'S FIRST WEEK ABOARD THE HOUQUA had been his worst. Overcome with nausea, he had kept a vomit-pail by the sleeping mat that he was barely strong enough to rise from, occasions necessitated by having to empty the vile contents over the clipper's side. A risky maneuver for anyone, considering the roll of the ship and brisk winds that threatened to cast the bucket's foulness this way and that. In Shen's case, trips to the bulwarks to empty his bucket meant his having to see the churning waters beneath him. After making his way up the ladder, he had to traverse the deck. The pail swung with the ship's movement and with each wary step he took. Underfoot, he felt the clipper's timbers shudder against every wave. Shen gagged at the ocean's distinctive clammy odor intermingled with the smell of pine tar and hemp of the ship's ropes. When he looked away and up, the sight of bloated sails added to his biliousness.

With the passing of each day, Shen became more accustomed to his surroundings. By the third week at sea, more than half-way across the Pacific, he was closer to being his normal self. Urges to retch became less frequent and he was able to resume his practice of the tongue of the 'Red Hairs.' He spent hours repeating the words and phrases written in his book, things he had heard spoken by the crew, mostly orders shouted at him and other passengers. A few passengers that he shared the space of the cargo hold with taught him simple phrases they knew. There were over three dozen Chinese passengers aboard. Shen had transcribed the words, checking them each time he heard them. The issue became whether he had understood the words for what they actually meant. He had written one of the most common phrases he'd heard spoken by the crew as they came below deck to perform their tasks, pushing their way roughly through the passengers: *Mo-wasai-ya-mun-ki*, he wrote in his book. In Chinese characters, they came out as *Grind-say small-ya (element of surprise)-stew-strange*. For the meaning, Shen had taken it to denote 'step aside,' and in that case, it was close enough to the actual meaning of the crewman's words. The barked orders were actually: Move aside ya monkey. And so it went in his study of the language of 'Red Hairs.' He found that if he said the words flatly, without the tonal inflections that differentiated Chinese words and their meanings, he could more or less reproduce them the way had heard them spoken. He had discovered too that often repeating the same word over, prolonging the sound with an *ee* sound at the end sometimes sufficed, and so words like *lookee lookee*, meant to take a look. This suited him well enough as it was the same form of repetition that the Chinese used in their own language to emphasize actions or descriptions.

Many of Shen's compatriots fared no better than he did for those first weeks at sea and several of them were sick right to the end of the journey, hanging their heads over the side of the Houqua, unable to enjoy the sight of dry land, ignoring the excited chatter and view of a harbor cluttered with abandoned ships. The cold rain and fog did little to restrain the excitement of arriving in *Gum Saan*. Poor weather couldn't dampen Shen's enthusiasm at that first glimpse of land, but what did was the memory of Yan's instructions to collect his debts and to begin trading opium.

Was being in America far enough away to ignore Yan altogether? Could Yan's knowledge of the governor's death do him any harm now? He decided it couldn't, he was free, weeks of travel from the likes of Yan and the shaman. He was nobody's man and would do as he saw fit.

His first step on dry land, however, had been an extension of the wretchedness he had endured during the voyage. Upon stepping ashore, the encounter with a tall *white-devil* had been most unexpected. Nothing he couldn't take care of with a simple flick of the wrist and a pull that sent the man into the water, but troubling nonetheless. That episode behind him and quickly forgotten, he settled into a room in a large guest house run by one of his own countrymen. For the first time in weeks, he was able to enjoy a hot meal of familiar food, to sleep uninterrupted by continuous creaking noises, of shaking planks and constant rolling. Life here would not be so bad, he told himself, why there was even an opera house, and a performance of *Palace of Eternal Life* to be held the very next evening.

And that entertainment was ruined by the very man who now sat in front of him. The man who had grabbed him down at the docks was now toying with him with a ring of keys. Why did this man call him Bufo?

The man sitting on the other side of the cell door was a liar. Shen had released him on his word which he had broken immediately. His breath reeked of strong drink. A liar and a drunkard. The way he had made a path straight for the desk in search of the wine like nothing else on earth mattered was proof of that. He wondered how long it would be before he went back to the bottle and forgot all about opening the cell door. Shen had fled one country only to be captured as he set foot in the next. He wondered whether this man was merely a drunken lout or an official. The whiskered man who had brought them here was clearly a man of high office and appeared to own this place. He had the bearing of a leader; he had a badge of office on display, a five-pointed metal star. To get out, he would have to try to reason with this drunkard. It would take every word he'd learned of the Red Hair tongue.

Shen looked up at the ceiling and spoke quietly in Chinese, "Guide me master, Taotai." He looked at the man in front of him and said, "Nice to meet you." He poked his arm through the bars and opened his hand in imitation of the way he had seen the Taotai greet foreigners.

The man leaned back without reciprocating the gesture and started to speak. Shen caught a few words: *Shen, Bufo,* and *little talk.*

22

IT TOOK GREAT EFFORT for our stories to be told and understood by one another. We labored for several hours; admittedly, my knowing naught of the Chinese language meant that the toil was mostly his.

It had started off poorly. Shen shot his hand through the bars, and I pulled away from it, misjudging the gesture of friendship as one of hostility.

Eventually, with a combination of words and gesticulations in a charade-like game, we acted out the histories of our recent pasts. I came to accept that I had mistakenly identified Shen as Bufo, and that I had done so based solely on a blemish on his face, which on the portrait, may have been caused by splashes of water, or whiskey for that matter. By the time I had a grasp of the rudiments of his tale, it was dark. Our shadows cast by the light of an oil lamp on the curved walls of our cabin seemed far too ludicrous for the gravity of our discourse. We waved our arms in a parody of slices of our respective journeys, playing out scenes to one another: his anguish aboard the Houqua, my fight with the *Cimarrones*.

In the end, I performed *there will be no fighting if I let you out,* an act that involved my pretending to be tied by the blanket with my face pressed to the bars of one of the vacant cells. He responded by nodding his head energetically, accompanying it with hearty applause.

His story was that he had merely followed the lure of California gold and claimed to know nothing of Bufo or even of the death of President Taylor. Fearing the effect of showing him my marshal's badge too soon and jeopardizing an open exchange, I revealed my official status to him only when we were far into the conversation. From that point on, his demeanor changed markedly. Officialdom was clearly something that this man respected. Earlier, I had scoffed at the hold the Chinese Emperor had on his subjects so far from their homeland, now it gladdened me that respect for high office meant so much to him. He uttered the name Taotai, several times, each time bowing his head in reverence as he said it. I gathered the name belonged to his former employer, a Chinese official, some kind of district lawman. It stood to reason then, as a marshal, I held a similar status.

Two important things had happened during those hours of the interview. The first is that even though I glanced at the whiskey from time to time, my will-power to resist the drink overcame the ache for it. And, that sometime during our interaction, the black dog had stopped growling. I didn't bother looking for where it might have gone and hoped I would never see the likes of it again.

When I asked Shen to help me find Bufo, he seemed to understand my request but was quite reluctant to become involved, frowning and shaking his head at the idea, saying, "Why Shen help you?"

Eventually, our negotiation came round to talk of payment. I commenced with an offer of forty dollars for two weeks of work, a sum I thought to be generous. Shen immediately refused and countered with seventy-five dollars as his figure, insisting on it, returning to sit in a corner of his cell and covering his head with the blanket until I relented. With terms agreed, we were linked. I had someone who knew the Chinese mind. He had someone who knew the ways of America.

I easily identified the correct key and opened Shen's cell. Recalling how fast he could move, I stepped several paces back. Shen stretched his limbs and stepped slowly out.

Suddenly, he faked a lunge at me, stopping a pace short but not before I had jumped backward in surprise. I lost my footing and tumbled to the ground. Shen stood over me with his hands on his hips, tipping his head back for a good laugh. After what I had put him through, he deserved a laugh at my expense, and I laughed along with him as he held his hand out and pulled me up.

Sheriff Hays wouldn't be happy to hear that I would be staying in San Francisco, but that was the least of my worries. My concern now was how to make sure Shen wouldn't just disappear into the wilderness whenever he liked. I had his promise but no real authority over him. There was something about this man however, that told me the word *promise* meant a great deal more to him than it did to me.

Shen's lips twisted comically in saying the address, "Numba twengty-fi Sakamento."

He reminded me of the seventy-five dollars, all to be paid in American coinage. Making a point of it, and in continuation of our play-acting, he did his best to imitate the image on one of the faces of the coin — stretching his arms out like wings, flapping a few times and then turning his face to one side. "Yes, Shen. I know the ones you mean," I said with a chuckle.

We agreed to meet the next day and that I would pay him before exchanging whatever ideas we had on trying to find Bufo.

"You're free to go, Shen," I said. "Sorry about the misunderstanding." Shen gripped my hand and shook it vigorously.

I watched him go for the cabin door, unsure that I would ever see him again. He stopped briefly to pull his padded jacket over his head and then stepped out into the cold rain.

23

NUMBER TWENTY-FIVE Sacramento Street was a short stroll from my first stop, San Francisco's earliest bank. It had opened in Portsmouth Square the year before, and even with all the gold changing hands, it was still the only bank in town — even though the main prerequisite to opening one was the possession of a large, strong safe.

Most transactions were still being done in hard cash or in gold. Each shopkeeper had secret places for hiding money, under floorboards or stuffed into mattresses. Ships had their own strong boxes, but with many vessels unattended and rotting, ever increasing amounts of cash and gold needed better protection.

The bank's front room seemed more like a saloon. Stools sat along a polished counter that stretched across one end of the room. A couple of roughly-dressed men at the far end were enjoying a morning beverage. They glanced up at me briefly, nodded then went back to their tipple. Behind the counter was a collection of liquor that was far superior to the grog I had become accustomed to: French brandy, real Scotch whiskey, and European liqueurs, some that I recognized from my barroom education in New York. I felt a sudden pang, momentarily forgetting the pressing business I had come for. The *clang* in my head sounded so loud and clear that I turned to look for its source, expecting to see Mrs. Blunt standing in the room wielding her brass school bell while casting a scornful eye at me. "I'm nothing like him," I said.

"Like who?" the barkeep's voice brought me back. He had stopped polishing a glass and looked at me with a bemused look on his face.

"Nothing, just a fleeting thought," I said as I approached him, doing my best to ignore the burning thirst for a tot.

"Won't be the first time in here, a man's thoughts went flyin' off. What can I do for you, sir, keep your gold safe in our vault, or maybe take a little off you in exchange for a nice dram?"

"I'm here to take out a loan," I said.

"Yes, sir, I'll let the boss know. I'm sure Mr. Nagler will be happy to discuss the prospect of a loan. This way," he said, coming out from around the bar, motioning for me to follow him through to a back office.

As banker Nagler's first customer of the day, other than for his fancy liquor, I was greeted heartily with a firm handshake. The barkeep closed the door, and Nagler showed me to a chair in front of his desk. Except for rudimentary office furniture, the banker's room presented the image of a practical man who cared little for creature comforts. I introduced myself, showing my badge, and we exchanged polite conversation for a minute, but when I explained my need, his enthusiasm diminished somewhat. Nevertheless, my marshal's credentials and a letter of introduction penned by William Bliss before my departure from Washington, essentially a guarantee by the government, ensured Nagler's cooperation. He left me for a few minutes while he unlocked a gate and then entered the adjacent room that held his vault.

The memory of Shen's outstretched arms mimicking the regal bird that adorned one side of 'American Eagles', brought a smile to my lips just as Nagler returned cradling a strongbox under one arm. Taking my grin as gleeful anticipation, he said, "Indeed, sir, the very thought of incoming lucre has a similar effect on me."

Nagler thumped the box on the desk and then made a self-important show of fiddling with a bunch of keys that reminded me of my shameful display the previous evening on the jail boat. "All silver dollars, you say?"

"Only those, Mr. Nagler, if you have them, that is."

"Have them?" He cleared his throat and mumbled irritably while pulling open the lid of the strongbox. Nagler returned to his seat and leaned slightly forward. He took on a stern mien, hands jealously gripping the edges of his money box. "You have to understand, Marshal Graystone, that even though California is one of the United States, the coinage you require is in short supply. Are you certain you will not accept other forms of currency that are every bit as acceptable to our merchants?"

"Quite certain — just the eagles, sir."

As Nagler reached into the moneybox, he pushed his eyebrows together in a black 'V.' They looked like shaggy black caterpillars joined at the head but twitching independently. The banker began lifting out a series of cloth bags, naming each one with the air of a man presenting the arrival of notables to a party. With each announcement, his eyebrows grew more animated. "Francs," he said, nodding at me with a smile. "Bonjour mes amis," he greeted cheerily, setting the bag down with a jingle. His voice assumed a higher pitch. "And here come the Pesetas, hola, hola, ha, ha, you lovely ones," he beamed. "Come on now, Guilders. Out you come, Shillings.

And no dilly-dallying ye Doubloons . . . and why not join the fun you laggards?" Nagler peered up at me. "Can't count on those Rupees, you know?" he said with a grin, pulling a bag of Indian coins out. I wondered how often he whiled away the hours, playing this little game with his moneybags.

"American Silver Dollars, sir?" I asked.

"Yes, yes, of course," he said, face darkening as he plucked out another bag, setting it gently on the desk. "Seventy-five, you said?"

"Correct, sir."

Nagler loosened the bag's drawstring and spilled about half of the silver coins out. He began counting, stacking the Eagles, ensuring that they all lay face-up, stopping from time to time to straighten them so that they were perfectly aligned in seven and a half stacks, all the while his eyebrows doing their tricks. With the last coin in place, Nagler made a wheezy doleful sound; his shoulders slumped with the air of a gambler ready to push the remnants of his dwindled stake into one last hand.

I had brought a small sack with me to carry the money in, and when all necessary documents had been signed, I brushed my forearm across the neat stacks of coins sweeping them into the bag. Nagler threw me a scowl that might have been reserved for admonishing a child who had tugged his whiskers.

It was close to noon by the time I arrived at Shen's lodgings with the coins weighing down a pocket of my coat. The three-storied boarding house might have been built in the last year but already paint was flaking off its walls. Like most things in this burgeoning city, it had been erected in haste and more than likely for more than it was worth.

The sun was out, that is to say, I could make out a bright disk trying to burn its way through the flat white sky. The promise of sunshine, however, was enough for residents of the tenement to chance hanging out their washing. I looked up at the building, wondering where in its bowels I would find Shen. Wooden poles with clothes hanging off them stuck out of most the windows, giving the place the look of the frayed sails of a ship that had weathered a storm.

Several Chinese men were out on the street in front of the building squatting over wash tubs, sleeves rolled to their elbows as they scrubbed clothes in water that looked to have been used for well more than one wash. They glanced up at me as I approached the doorstep; their first looks were nonchalant, turning back to their laundering. Then recognition dawned. I was the man who had ruined their night at the opera. They turned their heads to me again, this time the looks were unmistakably hostile. One of them got to his feet and began jabbing his forefinger at me. Others followed his lead and soon they were all shouting, faces twisted in fury.

As the shouts intensified, I considered my options: a dash for the building's entrance in search for Shen or beating a retreat towards Portsmouth Square. The first option disappeared as residents emerged, crowding around the dark entranceway. The mob encircled me, making the remaining option more of a challenge. One of the men threw something black and wet. The garment struck my chest, drawing cheers and jeers. Fists bunched, and the circle tightened. I had the Colt Walker in my belt, but using it would be a last resort. I knew that even showing a gun often led to its unintended use. Even in that moment of imminent danger, my thoughts drifted to the embarrassment of Sheriff Hays suddenly showing up to catch me in yet another debacle.

The mob began to close in. I was trapped like a fry in the center of a black sea anemone. There was commotion from one side of the human ring. An arm poked through between the waists of two men, then another arm, forcing the men apart.

Head and shoulders emerged, and Shen stepped through the gap into the center of the circle. He shoved back his compatriots, widening the ring. The shouts of what I could only guess were curses directed at both of us, grew in vehemence.

Shen stood his ground in front of me. Arms akimbo, he shouted back. He half turned his face to me and said, "Hully, show law-star."

He repeated it more forcefully when I didn't respond. It took a moment for me to recall Ah Toy's admonishment: *No show law-star in Ah Toy house.* I took my badge out. "This, you mean?" I said. He nodded and then acted out how I should show it. Legs apart, holding the badge out at the end of an outstretched arm at face level to my attackers.

As soon as I did, the crowd quietened and stepped back a few paces as if they had been thrust by some invisible force. The shouting ebbed away, first from the men in front, and then through the ones pushed up behind them three or four deep.

Shen spoke to them, shaking his fist. He gestured, pulling a forefinger across his throat, a simple enough sign to understand. He followed with another one that I took to mean hanging by the neck and a few more that I didn't grasp. The crowd dissipated, men went back to their washing and other chores. And although they had ceased shouting at me, their glances continued to divulge the contempt best reserved for those hated but of higher authority.

"Thank you, Shen," I said, pinning the badge to my coat pocket.

"You law-man, you show pa-wa," Shen said, thumping his chest for effect. He lowered his voice, "Got silbadola?" I nodded, patting the heavy bag in my pocket. Shen held a hand out to receive them. "Eat, after eat, talk Bufo." I handed over the sack, and he dropped it into his shoulder bag.

I followed Shen round the back of the building and then down a flooded narrow alleyway. Planks and other debris had been thrown into the mud to provide footing over the muddy ground. I stepped over a rotting dog carcass as I tried to keep up with Shen, moving further away from the city's main thoroughfares. It was evident that the area he was leading me through was inhabited mainly by Chinese. I drew a few curious glances as we went, but nothing that could pass for aggression. We went by open doorways of shops selling food, clothing and several dealing in mining equipment. The pathway was unpaved, slick with mud and with no gutters to carry away rotting refuse. Waste matter cluttered pathways and was pushed into heaps beside entrances, filling the air with a stench. Shen said he wanted to eat, but with the odor of this place turning my stomach, I doubted my ability to.

Shen beckoned me to follow him through a narrow doorway. I crouched under the low door frame into a room with several round tables, each with a few men eating while seated on stools. Thankfully, these men showed no inkling of recognition. Shen exchanged a few words with the proprietor, a short, portly fellow wearing a stained apron who directed us to one of his tables. We took our places between two diners slurping down their meals.

In the center of the table was a large bowl of noodles from which our neighbors were jabbing their chopsticks into and transferring the contents into their own dishes. Beside the large bowl was a platter of fish immersed in a dark liquid, and another of what I later learned were pickled vegetables. The landlord brought us empty bowls and each a set of chopsticks.

Shen wasted no time attacking the food. Filling my bowl before his own. "Eat, eat," he said, waving his chopsticks at me. I had only seen a picture of chopsticks in a book, never witnessed them being used, let alone held a pair. I watched as Shen manipulated the utensils, managing to eat the noodles without dropping a single one. I gave it a try. Each time the slimy strings slipped back into the bowl. The men at the table began to take my failed attempts as entertainment. In a moment, diners at other tables began to watch, soon they appeared to be wagering as to whether my next try would be successful. I finally managed to get a couple of broken strands into my mouth, managing only by using both hands to grip the chopsticks like pincers. I found the taste quite agreeable and was determined to try, if not for a mouthful, then a single noodle. My efforts were being noted and when I succeeded with another slippery strand it was rewarded with a robust round of applause.

I understood there was value in occasionally playing the fool, admittedly I had done so far too often of late, but after the incident at the Chinese boarding house I was content to have laughs and pats on the back continue for a while longer. Eventually, with the food gone, the gaming ceased, and the other diners left the two of us alone.

I brought the conversation round to the subject of finding Bufo. Shen leaned closer to me, using a combination of words, sounds and gestures, he explained what he'd discovered. The name Bufo was familiar to many in the Chinese community, many knew of it, but Shen had not spoken to anyone who had actually met the man. Rumor had it that Bufo was a wealthy landowner in possession of several land claims in the goldfields. He was reputed to be out there, hiring men to work his claims. I ventured that he had no shortage of willing labor. The new State Legislature had levied a monthly licensing fee of $20 to work in the gold fields, a sum few newcomers could afford, particularly after paying the cutthroat prices for equipment.

"How do we find him?" I asked.

Shen took a leaflet out of his tunic and unfolded it. He wiped his sleeve across the greasy tabletop before placing it down. The flyer was printed entirely in Chinese with big, bold letters at the top. Below it was a drawing of a smiling Chinaman holding a sack of gold. Behind him were two other Chinese with long hair queues clearly visible, panning for gold in a stream. Shen pointed at the writing below the picture, translating it, "Get muchee gold, go home richee man." Tapping a finger at a printed seal at the bottom of the page, he added, "This chop, Bufo." On the same line were the characters: 怖栿 bùfo. It was a frightening name, Shen explained, the first character bù, meant 'terror', and the second fo, was a kind of tree from which branches were placed on graves.

Finally, evidence. And so quickly with Shen to thank for it. While I had been sputtering in the harbor, the leaflet had been thrust into Shen's hand moments after he arrived ashore. He had put it away, and until he started asking residents of his boarding-house about Bufo, he hadn't given it a thought.

The leaflet gave the name and address of an agent called *Gold Mountain Fortune Mining Company*, responsible for contracting workers for the Bufo's mining operation. We agreed that the labor broker would be our next stop and that this time it would be prudent for my 'law-star' to go back into hiding.

The broker's tiny office allowed the two of us only a step or two into the doorway. Even so, I had to stand behind Shen and peer over the top of his head at the man sitting behind a little desk. He didn't bother looking up when we entered, focused instead on sheaves of paperwork and whatever he was writing — pen in one hand, the fingers of his other, busily flicking the beads of an abacus. He donned a black skull-cap and a robe buttoned at the neck and stretching over his legs to the ground.

He lifted his face when Shen spoke to him, holding out the pamphlet. The broker didn't respond to Shen. Instead, he looked at me and said, "Chinese only." I feigned an injured look and hastily exited to the muddy alleyway, leaving Shen to get on with it.

A few minutes later, Shen emerged from the ramshackle office signed-up as a laborer for *Gold Mountain Fortune*. He showed me the Chinese documents that included a simple map and directions for how to report to work. Shen explained the terms of his contract: wages, tools and anything else he needed could be obtained at the mine site and then deducted from his monthly wages. The $2.50 a day offered was well below the $4.00 that a white man could get working in San Francisco as a laborer. When I mentioned it to Shen, he mumbled, "Bufo buy many coolie."

For the second time in a day, this time to return the silver Eagles as a deposit in Shen's name, a visit to Nagler had his bushy brows doing gymnastics. Shen surprised both Nagler and me when he started to undo his waistband. He pulled a long flat piece of gold hidden under his belt. The banker weighed Shen's gold and wrote a receipt for it as part of his deposit.

We left the bank intending to secure the provisions and animals needed for our trip into the gold country.

24

SHEN SPRUNG UP like a jack-in-the-box; each bump threw him several inches off the saddle. I wanted to travel faster, but I moved us along at a slow trot to allow Shen to get accustomed to riding on horseback. Afraid that hours of bouncing up and down on a saddle would cause him distress, each time I showed concern, he returned my regard with a grin. I had come to know that Shen could be a bit of a jester when the mood took him, and as he bumped along, he had me in stitches, contorting his eyebrows and screwing up his face in imitation of Nagler. Over the ensuing miles, his happy grin took on the semblance of a grimace. Nevertheless, his feigned mirth was welcome and made our trek eastwards over the rough, wet country more bearable.

The map handed to Shen by the mining agent was a crude one, certainly not a map that would enable safe navigation over nearly a hundred miles of wilderness let alone arrive at the correct destination, except by sheer luck. It revealed few geographical features and those it did were akin to a child's illustrations. Mountains were sawteeth with no indication of height or gradient. Waterways were drawn as wavy lines without a suggestion of actual direction or magnitude. Fortunately, two years into the gold rush it was possible to purchase a map of reasonable accuracy and I spent a few dollars on one. My *Map of the Mining District of California* purportedly showed not only where gold was likely to be found, but also where Indian tribes had their settlements. It could all have been nonsense of course, but I was more inclined to trust my new chart for its geographical accuracy than the sketch Shen was given—clearly a ruse to lure new miners into more debt. Shen told me the price the broker had offered for a rented wagon — I scoffed at the absurdity of an amount that could have purchased a new rig and several pack animals.

My map showed the Sacramento and San Joaquin Rivers running somewhat north-south. From their eastern banks, a series of tributaries fanned out like the tentacles of a sea medusa. These rivers that flowed down from the mountains had the names Stanislaus, Tuolumne, and Merced. It was into that region that we were headed. Just under a hundred miles, I reckoned, and given the terrain, a journey that would take us the best part of a week to get there. I purchased a horse for each of us and a mule to carry our provisions. With no need for tools, compared to real miners, we traveled relatively lightly.

Soon after I had arrived in San Francisco, in the days before falling victim to the demon dog, I had purchased a Sharp's rifle, a carbine well-known for its long-range accuracy. The Sharp's sat in a holster that hung off my saddle bag. I stuffed the two pistols in my belt.

While Shen had been gathered his belongings, I waited in his little room. He packed only a few items of clothing, a small package of something he said was 'medicine', and his phrase book. Then he showed me a pair of vicious-looking knives which he had wrapped in an animal skin. I pressed myself into a corner of his lodging on the second floor of the boarding house while he whirled them in demonstration. Each knife consisted of two overlapping crescent-shaped blades. In his characteristic mimicry, he held them to the sides of his head to explain they were called deer-horn knives.

I tried not to think of the damage they could do. I had convinced myself that my soak in the bay had been an accident. His turning the tables on me in the jail had come as a shock that I'd considered some kind of Chinese trickery. But now, seeing how he twirled the knives gave me a notion of how formidable this jovial little man was.

We hired a barge to ferry us across the bay and then set off on our animals into the California wilderness. There were no settlements marked on the map for the first 50 miles or so, yet signs of human traffic were clear. For many miles out from San Francisco, before argonauts made their separate ways toward their dreams, the ground was rutted by tracks of all kinds. We were rarely alone heading eastwards, often passing more heavily-laden travelers, many of them trudging along the muddy track on foot. We covered close to 20 miles that first day, riding until the sun went down.

Shen had as little experience as I did in setting up camp. The long ride, and his first, had him limping around gathering wood for a cooking fire. We had barely finished eating a hastily cooked meal of beans and dried pork when exhaustion overcame us. In our tent, we pulled blankets over our heads and were asleep in moments.

Over the following days, as we drew ever closer to the goldfields, we came across small mining camps. Those who couldn't wait to get to where richer deposits were said to be, had unloaded their equipment and headed for the barest trickles of running water. A Shakespearian line came to mind, *Though this be madness, yet there is method in't.* We passed enough of these little claims to register that miners focused their efforts on gravel bars that formed on the inside curves of the path of a stream. There, miners would pan behind large rocks or in deeper pools.

One night we shared camp with a man who claimed he'd found *plenty* of gold, panning in isolated places far from the throngs that headed further east. The miner referred to the gold deposits in fast running creeks as *streaks*. Thin streaks of gold, he told us, could be found down the length of a gravel bar where holes tended to be set naturally in line. These were smaller deposits, but enough to make a man rich without having to constantly defend his claim from greedy neighbors. He was continually searching isolated locations off the beaten track.

Shen listened closely and gleaned enough of the miner's explanation to tell me later, "We dig gold, easy rich-man. Find Bufo after." The idea of trying my hand at panning for gold when it seemed to be 'everywhere', had its appeal, but with a good chance of finally catching Bufo, I flatly refused Shen's suggestion. He shook his head and muttered under his breath in Chinese, occasionally looking up at me to call me, "Wood-head," comically tapping his knuckles to his temples.

We heard the river before we saw it. Late on our third day of riding through woodlands, a constant sound not unlike the hiss of rainfall heralded the San Joaquin's proximity. The hiss gave way to a roar as we emerged from the curtain of trees.

Months of rain had swollen the waterway. Shen's frown revealed his dismay at having to cross the roaring surge. We agreed to try to find a place to cross the next day and made camp for the night. I had heard stories of the San Joaquin, its recent history a blight on white settlement of the Americas. In the flickering light of a small campfire, I did my best to relay what I knew of the story to Shen.

Back in the early 1830s, when fur trappers were exploring southwards into the San Joaquin Valley, they were greeted with a horrific sight. An epidemic of smallpox and malaria had swept down the San Joaquin River corridor. Brought to the region unintentionally by Europeans, in a single stroke it was said to have killed up to three-quarters of the entire native population in the valley. The outbreak continued for year after year with until something like 60,000 of the indigenous population lay dead. I had read too that the explorer Kit Carson noted in 1839, that *cholera or some other fearful scourge broke out among them and raged with such fearful fatality that they were unable either to bury or burn their dead, and the air was filled with the stench of their decaying bodies.* That was a decade after he had first encountered natives flourishing in the area. The terrible image of dying natives made for a restless night that was already uncomfortable from the howl of the wind through the trees and the cold and wet.

The next morning, we broke camp and rode a southerly course along the river in the hope of finding a way across, knowing that even once on the far bank we still had a more hard country to traverse. Our pathway to Bufo's land necessitated that we follow the Tuolumne River — a watercourse that flowed down from the peaks of the Sierra Nevada before pouring into the San Joaquin. The Gold Rush had all begun up there, a hundred and fifty miles upriver on the western slopes of the Sierra, at Sutter's Mill.

After a couple of hours, we came upon two figures waiting by a makeshift mooring. As we neared, we saw that the vessel straining against the river's flow at the end of a stout rope was a flat-bottomed barge with low gunwales. I judged it to be about thirty feet long and a dozen wide. I dismounted and led my horse to the ferrymen.

"Your name wouldn't be Charon, would it?" I said, extending a hand towards the man who came forward.

"No, mister, don't know nobody by that name. Name's Jim Doaks," he said, having to raise his voice against the river's roar. He clutched my hand in a calloused paw.

"Pleasure to meet you, Mr. Doaks, I'm Angus Graystone."

Doaks was a wiry fellow, almost as tall as me. Bareheaded, his thick, dark shoulder-length hair flapped in the strong breeze. He had a long weather-creased face and a comfortable smile that put me at ease. He turned to a lad waiting by the water's edge. "That there's my son, Zeke." I nodded at the boy, thin as a rake, in boots that looked three sizes too large. Zeke gave me a bucktoothed grin and nodded back.

"Who's your man?" Doaks said, looking at Shen who was still mounted, the mule tethered behind.

"That's Shen. We're headed up the Tuolumne." Shen nodded to the ferryman.

"Figgered. Soon's I saw that Chinee. They're all headed that way. Some big claims up there. You travelin' light for miners, 'nless you're not."

"We have what we need," I said, tipping my head towards the mule.

"Suit yourself. Getting 'cross'll cost you same whether you got picks and pans or not. Two dollar per animal, three dollar a man." Doaks looked at us and started to count on his fingers. He looked to Zeke. "Much's that, boy?"

"Three animals 'n two men. Twelve even, Pa."

"Twelve even," Doaks repeated. "That's what it'll take to get you cross two-hundred-foot o' ragin' death," he said, holding his palm out, grinning.

I counted out twelve dollars from the purse in my saddlebag and handed it to Doaks who dropped the coins in a pocket of his heavy coat. "Let's getcha cross then," he said.

The animals stamped and whinnied. Panicked by the rocking barge, they pulled back against their reins. Zeke was ready for it and threw blankets over their heads, roping the hoods around the animals' necks so making it easier to coax them aboard. Shen was only slightly less skittish than the animals, crouching and keeping away from the sides of the rocking barge. A long rope had been strung across the entire width of the river and threaded through two stout posts, one at either end of the boat.

Doaks shouted to his son as he was untying the barge from the dock. "Hang on, Zeke, couple more coming."

Zeke looked to where his father was pointing. "It'll save us another crossing if we can get 'em on too. Think we can do it?"

"Oh, she'll make it alright," Doaks said, slapping his hand on a gunwale.

The two men on horseback looked familiar; a big man wrapped in a heavy fur coat and wearing a bowler hat, his smaller companion, just as identifiable. I tensed in recognition of Brown and Legrand, the bear and the ferret, the two that robbed the Panama jungle village the night of the Cimarrones attack.

"Bad men, robbers," I said to Shen.

When they came near, the pair recognized me immediately. "Well, if it ain't the Scotchman," Brown said, snickering, looking at Legrand. "He made it."

"Make good use of my compass to get you here?" I said.

"You're mistaken, mister, don't know anything about your compass," Brown said, hands on the saddle's pommel, leaning forward. "Ain't that right, Frenchie?"

Legrand nodded, smirking, looking more like a rodent than I remembered. His cheeks were chafed red; he licked his dry, flaking lips.

"You robbed us and fled while the rest of us were under attack," I said.

"As you say, we were under attack. We run away from the savages like everyone else, you can't prove nuthin," Brown said.

He was right. I couldn't prove they were the ones that ransacked our bags. It was likely that they had long since sold everything they pilfered that night.

Doaks started counting again, an easier calculation this time since it was a repeat of two horses, a pack mule and two men. "That'll be twelve dollars if you want to get across," he shouted, eyes flicking a glance at Zeke.

"Any objection?" Brown said to me.

Doaks interceded before I could respond, "Nothin' to do with him. It's my ferryboat."

"Well, then it's settled," Brown said. "Pay the boatman, Frenchie."

With Brown and Legrand aboard, as soon as Zeke untied the barge, the pressure of the flow forced our heavily-loaded vessel taut against the creaking rope. Doaks tugged on the line, inching us across the engorged river. He shouted for us to help him pull and we lined up, adding strength and weight to the effort of crossing the San Joaquin. I got behind Doaks, immediately regretting having my back to Brown. Shen was behind me, then Brown, with Legrand at the back. Zeke held the animals still, working to calm them.

"How many times you cross in a day, Ferryman?" Brown shouted.

"Different every day, maybe eight, ten sometimes if we start goin' early," Doaks yelled back.

"Was twelve yesterday, Pa," Zeke said.

"Sounds like you've got yer own floatin' gold mine right here," Brown laughed.

"Work hard for it, mister, it's a darn sight harder 'n pan-nin'," Doaks said, grunting as a wave thudded against the side of the ferry, threatening to tear the line out of his grip. The horses stamped and snorted. Zeke held their reins tightly and made noises to soothe them.

Brown's question about Doaks' earnings raised my hackles. I took one hand off the rope briefly to reassure myself that the pistols were in place. In mid-river it would be foolish for the pair to try anything, but once across, anything could happen with these two.

When we arrived at the far side, we weren't able to do much more than to get the animals onto dry land and sit for a rest on the river bank, but Doaks was keen to push off for the western shore where several men stood waiting by a covered wagon. They started waving their hats.

"Good huntin' gentlemen, maybe see you on your way back," Doaks said, shaking my hand and then turning towards his boat.

"Step back, Ferryman," Brown said. We turned to see Brown lift a double-barreled canoe gun out of his big coat. He leveled it at us. Legrand grabbed Zeke from behind, arm across his chest, a wide blade held close to the lad's throat. Zeke was ashen-faced, ready to drop to his knees.

"Hand over your money, Ferryman, yours too, Scotchman," Brown said.

"Guns too," Legrand said. "Also that nice carbine on your saddle, Scotchman."

"Right," Brown said, "Money, shootin' irons, and whatever the Chinaman's got. No need for dyin' 'nless you make it so."

Doaks took a step towards Brown, face tense with fury. "Let my boy go."

I gripped his sleeve. "Don't," I said.

"That's right Scotchman, you tell him," Brown said.

"Empty your pockets and throw down your weapons or this shotgun will rip your guts apart. Frenchie will give the boy his first shave." Brown pointed to a spot on the ground with the barrels of his weapon.

I took my guns out, slowly, one at a time and threw them to where Brown had indicated.

"Money," Brown said.

Doaks pulled a fistful of coins from one pocket and then from the other. He threw them clattering onto my guns. "Now let the boy go," he said.

"Not so fast. Your turn, Scotchman."

"My money's in the saddlebags. Shen's too," I said, looking at Shen. His fists were clenched at his sides but his face was impassive, calm, eyes on Brown and then shifting to Legrand, measuring.

Brown flicked the barrels of his gun towards the horses. I started to move. "Not you, Scotchman. You stand with the Ferryman. Send your servant."

"Go on, Shen," I said.

Shen went to his horse, opened a saddlebag and, reached in, peering into it.

"Tell the Chinaman to hurry," Brown said. "Go see what he's doin', Frenchie."

Legrand dragged a weak-kneed Zeke towards Shen, stopping a couple of paces away. "Hurry up, Chinaman."

Shen smiled, bobbing his head, hands hidden in the bag, fiddling. "Shen hully-hully." In a blur, he pulled a hand out of the bag and swung it in a shining arc. One of his curved blades planted into the top of Legrand's skull with a *crack*. Legrand's eyes bulged, his mouth fell open. Zeke dropped to the ground. Legrand, standing but starting to drop, reached for the top of his head, unable to raise his arms. Blood ran in rivulets over his ears, down his face.

For a moment, Brown was frozen in place, not believing what he was seeing. "Frenchie?"

I took three long strides and threw myself in a crouch at Brown, shoulder connecting with his side. It felt like I'd struck a tree trunk. My left hand reached for the canoe gun as it went off, firing upwards, splintering a tree branch. Brown went over and I fell onto him, trying to wrestle the gun away. Twice my weight, he stunned me with an elbow to my face and then he was on top of me. He pinned me down with his bulk, pressing the shotgun barrel to my throat. I saw Doaks going for the guns on the ground. Brown saw him too and moved off me raising his weapon, sweeping it, deciding who to target, backing away. He settled on aiming in the direction of Zeke and Shen. He had one round left but the shot would spread over the distance and could kill both of them.

"You fire and you'll be dead a second after, mister," Doaks said. He cocked the hammer of the Colt.

"Well, well, looks like we got ourselves a stand-off," Brown said. "I'm thinkin' I'll take the money and git goin."

"Hell you will," Doaks said. "I'm thinking to blow your ugly face right off.

"Try it boatman and your boy'll be jam."

"Settle down, there's been enough blood spilled," I said.

"Quite right, Scotchman. Like I said, I'll be on my way now, with the money."

Doaks huffed loudly. I held up a placating hand.

Brown kept the shotgun pointed at Zeke and Shen. "Scotchman, you go kick away the other gun on the ground, pick the money up and bring it over. Boatman, you throw down your gun."

I nodded at Doaks and he tossed the weapon to the ground.

I walked to the money, kicked away the Dragoon and crouched to pick up the coins, putting them in my pocket. I faced away from Brown and furtively pulled the knife from my leg scabbard and put it in my pocket with the money. With the last coins scooped in my hands, I walked back towards Brown. "Where do you want them?" I said.

"Put 'em down, right in there," Brown said, pulling out a kerchief and throwing it to the ground between us.

I crouched and spilled the pile of coins onto the cloth. Still squatting, I reached into my pocket. Feeling for the grip of my knife, I pulled it out and sprung towards Brown. I jabbed the blade hard into his thigh. The sharp steel went in a full six inches before stopping at its bolster.

Brown growled in pain.

Shen took his chance, grabbing Zeke he pulled him away behind some trees.

Brown held the shotgun in one hand and reached for his leg in the other.

Doaks went for the Colt. "Step aside, Graystone," he shouted.

I rolled away.

Doaks shot at Brown from a crouching position. The bullet entered through the bottom of Brown's jaw, smashed upwards and took off the dome of his head. Brown flew backward and crashed to the ground.

I walked over to Brown's lifeless body. The lower part his face was gone leaving a gaping bloody hole of splintered teeth.

"Zeke?" I asked, looking towards the boy. Shen had him safe, seated on the ground. Shen crouched by his side with a hand on the boy's shoulder.

Legrand was on his back where he had fallen, the curved blade jutting out the top of his head like some kind of ornamental headdress.

Doaks went to his son and embraced him tightly. "Thank you," he said to Shen.

Shen grinned and nodded. He went to Legrand, planted a foot onto his face and yanked the weapon out of his skull.

In a moment, Zeke was well enough to stand. He walked over, looked down at Legrand and swung an oversized boot, connecting with the dead man's side. The boy stumbled backward from the effort, almost falling over. Then he lurched forward, hands across his belly. Doubled over, Zeke made a gurgling sound and then released a stream of spew onto the dead Frenchman.

"Right. Let's get rid of this trash in the river," Doaks said.

"Want to check their pockets first?" I asked.

"Don't really want nothin' from these shits."

Zeke went to his father and pinched his sleeve. "I guess we oughta look, Pa."

I went through Brown's pockets and found my compass. Legrand had nothing of value on him. Their saddlebags yielded some money and an assortment of goods, likely stolen. Seeing the valuables, Doaks changed his tune and was happy to accept the loot. I kept the shotgun and ammunition for it.

"The likes of these snakes don't deserve a prayer, I reckon," Doaks said, looking at me.

"I'm with you on that," I said, bending over to grab one of Brown's legs. Shen got the other limb and helped me drag Brown to the river and tip him into the swiftly moving water. We lost sight of his corpse after a few seconds. Doaks and Zeke, each holding a leg, dragged Legrand to the river and rolled him in.

"Better'n they deserve," Doaks said. "What about their animals?"

"They're yours," I said. "Me and Shen have what we need." I looked at Shen who nodded his agreement.

"Then here's your money back," Doaks handed me twelve dollars. "I owe you more than money, Graystone, and I'm a man who repays his debts."

"I may call on you to do so, Mr. Doaks."

Doaks walked over to Shen and shook his hand. "Thank you again, Chinaman."

"See you, Doak," Shen said. Zeke went to Shen and surprised him with a hug. Shen broke out into laughter and slapped the boy on the back.

A shot rang out from the other bank. The men waiting with the wagon were waving again, impatient to cross.

"Think they saw what happened?" Zeke asked his father.

"Won't matter a fart, boy. The fever's got 'em."

The boatmen started their crossing and we watched the barge for a few minutes making its way back across the river.

I flattened the map out on the ground and pointed out our position to Shen, tracing the distance we still had to travel. The Tuolumne River lay a dozen miles south of us. We were nearing Bufo's land, but our success of finding him and then apprehending him depended on a great deal of luck.

25

TEN MILLION YEARS AGO, a massive block of the earth's crust ripped through the surface as it tilted to the west. Rivers cut deep ravines on both sides of the new mountain range. Lava boiled up and then flowed down into canyons which over millennia, eroded to leave high plains along the ancient river channels.

Still, the gods were not done sculpting. Glaciers carved out crescent-shaped gorges throughout the range. Working hand in hand, river and glacier exposed the uppermost portions of the plutons forming Sierra Crest. Long before Garcí Ordóñez de Montalvo dreamed of gilded Amazons, or the Franciscan missionary and chronicler Pedro Font, named the serrated peaks 'Sierra Nevada', the mountains were home to America's native peoples.

It was many years later that I heard the story of the birth of the peaks explained in Yokut lore:

> There was once a time in the world when nothing existed but water. At the place where Lake Tulare is now, a pole

stood far out of the water. This pole provided a perch for Hawk and Crow.

First, Hawk would rest on the pole for a while, then Crow would knock him off and sit on it. Thus, they took turns sitting on the pole above the water for a very long time. At last, they created the birds which prey on fish; Kingfisher, Eagle, Pelican, and others. They also created Duck. Duck was very small, but she dived to the bottom of the water, filled her beak with mud, and then died when trying to return from the depths. Duck floated on the water, lying dead. Then Hawk and Crow took the mud from Duck's beak and began making the mountains.

They began at the place now known as Ta-hi-cha-pa Pass, with Hawk building the eastern range and Crow forming the west one. They tamped the mud down hard into the water and piled it high, working toward the north. Finally, Hawk and Crow met at the place we call Mount Shasta. Their work was done, but when they looked at their mountains, Crow's range was by far larger than Hawk's.

Hawk said to Crow, "How did this happen, you rascal? You have been stealing earth from my bill. That is why your mountains are the biggest."

Crow laughed at Hawk.

Then Hawk chewed some Indian tobacco and it made him wise. At once, he took hold of the mountains and turned them around almost in a circle, putting his smaller range where Crow's had been. And that is why the Sierra Nevada Range is larger than the Coastal Range.

Our trek towards Bufo's camp proceeded with renewed vigor. The Tuolumne, largest of the waterways draining the southern Sierra, flooded a wide expanse along its banks, forcing us to ride some distance from it as we traced its flow off the peaks.

My map indicated Indian settlements lying along our route though we encountered none. Once friendly to outsiders, as the trickle of white men into their tribal lands turned into a flood, they responded to the usurping of their lands with belligerence, ambushing travelers and raiding mining camps. I was only partly mollified by their absence. My curiosity for this country's indigenous people, kindled by the incident by the train tracks on the way to Washington several months earlier, remained unsated.

Two centuries earlier, a chronicler on Francis Drake's circumnavigation of the globe described Indians as *people of a tractable, free and loving nature, without guile or treachery.* White settlements had turned a peace-loving society into 'savages.' I was certain that before long, the Indians of this part of the country would meet the same fate as the tribes of the eastern states where the Indian Removal Act had been in place for two decades — a policy that Zachary Taylor played a significant role in enforcing.

The temperature dropped precipitously as we climbed towards the upper reaches of the Tuolumne. Snow, merely a dusting on the trail when we started our climb grew heavier, slowing our ascent.

The sky was pierced by a high-pitched wail. We turned our heads in unison, looking up and behind us and then to each other.

"That was from far away," I said, wanting to believe it.

"What animal?" Shen said.

"Wolf . . . big wild dog," I explained.

"Wolf," Shen repeated. He nodded. "Same China, but I no see, Guangdong no wolf. We go faster," Shen said, kicking his mount.

An hour went by with only the sounds of snow-muffled hoof beats. Feeling we had outrun the danger, we relaxed our pace. The whitish light was fading, and I told Shen we would soon have to stop for the night.

Shen looked back again. "They follow?"

"I don't think so, but it's possible," I said, though from what I'd read of wolves, the tenacious creatures weren't likely to give up on a meal, particularly since there was little meat in these wintry elevations. I hadn't seen so much as a hare since we started our climb. The prize of a couple of men and their horses was well worth a long chase.

After another half -hour of riding we stopped to set up camp against a cliff face, below a rocky overhang. We settled down for a sorry meal of biscuits and salted pork in front of a brushwood fire.

Shen pulled a blanket over his head and moved closer to the heat. His shadow cast a wavering pyramid on the cliff wall. Firelight flickered over his face; the shifting shadows distorted his true features. For a moment, my thoughts drifted to an image of the Indians I'd seen so many months ago.

A bursting twig brought me back. I watched Shen poking the fire with a stick. "I never asked why you came to America, just assumed you wanted your fortune in gold. But, you don't seem so interested in it. Why did you come, Shen?"

Shen's head dipped. He dropped the stick and picked up a little stone and threw it in the fire.

"Well, it's your business. You needn't tell me," I said.

He flung another pebble at the flames, harder this time. It sent up a crackling shower of sparks.

"Shen run-way."

"Ran away from China?"

Shen grunted.

"From what?"

"My master, Li Taotai, fore he die, he order me kill-man. When I go, man ready-die . . . from sick. So, I no-bey Taotai order. Some man say I kill. So I run-way."

From his display of martial skills, it shouldn't have surprised me that Shen had killed in his past. He saw my wide-eyed reaction. "You no kill many-man, Graystone?" he said.

"Not many, a few. Shot them in the line of duty, as a lawman. One with a knife."

"Law-man kill, no-problem," Shen flapped a hand and tossed his head back. "Now, Taotai come visit Shen. Every-night he come. He all skin-bone. Ugly. Point finger. Say 'why Shen no-potec-Taotai.' Why Shen no-bey order.' Sometime daytime he come. I scare." He scattered a handful of stones into the campfire and pulled the blanket tighter round himself. "Graystone scare what?"

"Me?" I looked around, searching the perimeter of the fire's glow. "I'm scared of a dog. A black one. It comes to me mostly in the day, not in my dreams. It's when I want a drink. Like at this very moment. Something to ward off the chill. My father gave it to me. It's my burden now."

"I help kill, but . . ." Shen looked about. "I no see black dog."

"And I don't see your Taotai."

Shen's smile was interrupted by a shrill note. It was long and mournful and raised the hackles on my neck. Shen sprang to his feet. The horses snorted and stomped, pulling against their restraints.

The cry was answered by another one that seemed much closer and then another and another joined the chorus. I stood up and looked into the blackness. The howls reverberated across the peaks from every direction.

"Wolf hungry, eat Graystone," Shen said.

"You, my friend, will be the first course."

"We get-ready. You know-how fight wolf?"

"No, you?" I said.

Shen shook his head and took the fighting blades out of his saddlebag. I readied my guns and then gathered more wood for the fire.

The cries went on for a while longer and then fell silent. The quiet was a new worry, at least with the howling we had some sense of their distance if not their location.

"Wolf come now?" Shen said.

"I think so."

"How long-time?"

I didn't have an answer and worked at preparing my Sharp's rifle. It might not be much use at close range but I loaded it and placed it at my feet. The two handguns were ready too. "Can you use a gun?" I asked Shen, holding the Dragoon out to him. "This is good for five shots."

"I no shoot before. Waste bullet," he shook his head.

"Use the canoe gun then," I said pointing to Brown's shotgun.

He shook his head. "I make, how say . . .?" He gestured as if holding a long stick and jabbing with it.

"You mean a pike."

"Pike," he repeated. "Make pike, we pike to wolf."

Shen made a good point about wasting bullets. I had plenty of ammunition but only eleven bullets loaded in the two weapons and one round in the long gun. In a fight, there wouldn't be time to reload once the chambers were empty. "I agree, maybe they'll run off without too much of a fight. We'll use pikes first," I said.

"In China, we put splosion on spear. Poke enemy, enemy have splosion. Maybe we use shotgun bullet?"

"It's worth a try, Shen. Show me how."

Risking a run to trees beyond the glow of our fire, Shen came back with two fairly straight branches, each about six feet long. He used the edge of one of his knives to carve out a hollow with a sharp point at the bottom of it. I handed him a shotgun shell and he lodged it firmly into the gap.

"Poke strong to wolf –body. Make splosion," he said demonstrating the weapon with a firm jab at the air.

"I understand. Let's try it."

We decided not to use the other stick for an exploding spearhead, instead sharpened it and then hardened the pointed tip in the glowing charcoal of our fire.

Our horses warned us of the approaching pack, they snorted with their ears flicking back and forth. The animals stamped and curled their upper lips, sniffing the air.

For a while, we saw nothing. Then, squinting into the dark trees, the first we saw of them was a set of eyes reflecting the yellow of our campfire. She grabbed the loaded spear. We stood side by side with the cliff face to our backs and the campfire in front, between us and the line of glowing eyes.

More sets of glowing dots appeared beyond the firelight. The wolves growled and came closer but stopped beyond the ring of light. As our eyes adjusted, we spotted their dark shapes moving amongst the trees. I picked up a burning stick and flung it hard at a cluster of gleaming dots. The stick spun, whooshing, leaving a trail of sparks. It struck a tree and a cascade of embers rained down, scattering the wolves. They yelped and retreated into the woods.

"Wolf scare," Shen said, nodding but not altering his defensive stance.

The branch burned for a moment where it fell in the snow. As soon as it went out, the wolves were back. This time they came closer. A large gray one wandered to within twenty feet of the fire. When I bent to pick up another burning stick, it snarled, bared its fangs and then retreated.

We had a stack of firewood but it wouldn't last long if we kept throwing branches. Even so, we each threw a couple more flaming sticks at the beasts. The pack scattered only to return when the branches burned out. Each time they dared to come closer than before. There were several hours more of darkness; our firewood would be gone well before dawn.

"Graystone shoot, kill-wolf," Shen said. "Maybe runway."

"I agree. Even if I miss, the noise might do some good."

We counted six wolves in all. The one that showed itself first was the largest, standing at close to three feet at the shoulder. It had a torn left ear and was always the one that ventured in closest. Our fire dimmed and the gray led the pack in an ever-tightening semi-circle. It stood a dozen feet away, baring its teeth and growling. I lowered my spear and then leveled the Dragoon's sight at the wolf's large head and cocked the hammer.

As I began to squeeze the trigger, a wolf slammed into my side, knocking me over. My gun went off, missing my target by a mile. In the moment of my tumbling to the ground, I understood the ruse. The one with a mangled ear was a decoy, drawing our attention while the pack planned its attack. I crashed into the ground with the wolf on top of me. The pistol flew from my grip.

The wolf sunk its teeth in the padded front of my coat, but I still felt the points of its fangs tearing into my flesh. Shen came to my rescue, driving his loaded pike into the back of the wolf. The animal yelped from the strike to its spine, but the shell didn't detonate. The wolf kept trying to rip into me. Shen jabbed the pike into it again. This time there was a loud, smoky blast that stopped it for good.

The explosion drove the other wolves back.

"You hurt?" Shen said.

I felt under my clothes. The bite to my chest left deep scores, bloody and painful, but no serious damage. I nodded and picked up the Dragoon. We readied for the next attack.

"Wolf clever," Shen said.

"Yes, we were tricked. I'm going to shoot the next one I see."

The wolf with the mangled ear came out again, same as before, taunting from a safe distance. Shen looked to the sides, ready for another attack. Fearing I would lose my chance, I fired without taking careful aim. The Dragoon's 31 caliber ball dropped the animal, tearing a hole into its skull. The other four animals scattered but the killing two of their members drove them into a frenzy; snarling and gnashing, pacing in front of us, measuring. Without more wood, the campfire was reduced to a pulsating orange glow. Flames no longer a danger to them, the wolves spread out, two in front and one on each side of us. I could only see dark shapes moving from side to side that didn't allow aim at a stationary target. I wasted a bullet firing the Dragoon at a shadow. The blast drove them off, if only for only a moment.

"You ready, Shen?"

Shen nodded. He had a blade in each hand and stood in a low stance, his legs wide. I had a loaded pistol in each hand ready to club or shoot.

Four wolves charged at once, dark shapes hurtling in from different directions. I fired at the first animal coming straight at me. The wolf sprung into the air, its ribcage exposed, front limbs outstretched. The tongue of fire that spat from the Colt's barrel singed the shaggy torso as it crashed into me. It knocked me onto my back. Blood gushed from the hole punched into its chest, staining the front of my coat. I pushed the dead wolf off me just as another sank its fangs into my leg. I pressed the Dragoon in my left hand against its body and fired. Even with a bullet in it, its jaws stayed clamped to my leg. I fired again, killing it and emptying the revolver's cylinder. I pulled free of the dead wolf's jaws and got up with a searing pain in my leg.

The swirl of Shen's knives kept the two wolves from rushing him. I limped closer, trying to get a shot at the animals. One of them turned towards me. I raised my Colt at the dark shape and cocked the hammer. At the sound of the loud click, the wolf turned away and bounded for the trees.

The remaining wolf turned its head, giving Shen an opening. It yelped as one of Shen's blades sliced into it, catching it on the shoulder. It shambled backward. Shen ran at it, slashing and catching the wolf in the neck. He hacked the other knife into its skull; the force slammed the animal to the ground.

Five members of the wolf pack lay dead, their blood pooled beneath them in dark circles where it melted the snow. The wolf that ran from the fight watched us from the edge of the trees, snarling, showing us sharp white fangs. I picked up the Sharp's and tried to take aim at the dark silhouette. The wolf backed into the trees and disappeared.

"Run-way wolf, black. Same black-dog, no?"

I lowered the rifle. "Yes, Shen. Same."

We rebuilt the campfire and then moved the stiffening carcasses away from our campsite. My injured leg had stopped bleeding but throbbed with pain as we dragged each wolf some distance away.

Seated side by side, warming ourselves, Shen asked to see my wounds. The scratches on my chest were covered in dried blood. We rekindled the fire and melted snow into a cooking pot, using warm water to clean the gashes. The bite to my left leg was more serious. Shen cleaned the wound and then took a wad of brown gummy substance out of his bag.

In the bit of water remaining in the pot, he began to mash the stuff.

"What's that," I asked.

"Dàyān, pow-ful China medicine. Help pain."

He smeared the warm paste over the bite marks and then told me to drink the mouthful of dark liquid remaining in the pot. I gulped the bitter liquid down, and it wasn't long before the pain in my leg was forgotten. I pulled a blanket over me, and caressed by the warmth of the fire began to doze. Shen again pulled a blanket over his head and sat with his legs crossed and the deer-horn knives ready in front of him.

I woke shortly before dawn. Shen was asleep, sitting with the blanket over him, chin slumped onto his chest. The fire had burned down to embers. My sense of hearing seemed oddly acute. It was as if I could hear the actual glow of the fire, orangey-red streaks pulsing through bits of ash. Above me, the inky sky was studded with bright yellow dots. From where we had piled the wolf carcasses came noises of ripping and crunching. Alarming noises that would have normally had me rushing to investigate, but in my peaceful state, I cared not at all. I lay still watching the sky brightening as Shen began to stir. First, eyelids twitching and then one eye opening at a time. At full daylight, we revived the fire. Shen cleaned and reapplied the tincture to my leg wound.

We saddled our horses and started on another day of riding upwards. Passing the dead wolf carcasses, we saw that the remains had been torn into and partly eaten.

26

GOLD MOUNTAIN MINING'S CAMP was situated on a tributary identified on the map as *North Fork*, a place that corresponded to a mark on Shen's map as the uppermost tine of a sideways trident.

At higher elevations, the number of mining camps increased. At some places, men were packed closely together working claims that were not more than ten feet square, some even smaller. Bundled in layers of clothing, they squatted by the cold river or operated their equipment, barely looking away from their work as we passed them. Some sizeable camps had been established — villages of canvas and wood — where there was endless talk of rich strikes. Merchants had set up crude stores that sold everything from mining implements and clothes to the most highly sought-after items: booze and tobacco. Larger camps took on the feel of rowdy towns that reminded me of Yanqui Chagres, the wild frontier town in Panama.

We stopped for food at a settlement called Sonorian Camp. Leaving our animals at the stables, we made for a building that touted itself as the Empire Hotel. As we walked towards it, a Chinese man trotted up to Shen. They spoke for a moment, Shen clearly enjoying the opportunity to speak in his own tongue.

"Chinese no-go hotel. Chinese have Chinese place," Shen said when they had finished their conversation. We were aware that Chinese miners never worked alongside white prospectors, though we did pass groups of Chinese working their claims in their own all-Chinese camps. We agreed to part ways and to meet again after filling our bellies. Shen followed his compatriot to another part of Sonorian Camp while I continued to the Empire Hotel.

The guesthouse was a one-story building with a dirt floor. A few planks served as walls, but the sides of the place were mainly constructed of canvas laid over saplings. Had it not been for the cold wind whistling through the place, its rank odor might have prevented my entry. The one room served as kitchen, dining hall, saloon and bedroom. Tables and benches, already crowded with miners, were placed in the center. The room's edges were lined with five-decker bunk beds built from posts and crosspieces tied with rawhide, each layer of bunk bed allowed just enough space for a miner to crawl in and lie down.

The proprietor identified himself as Dooley and then gave me the choice of paying for a meal with a pinch of gold dust or with coins. Handing over coins, Dooley passed me a tin plate, a knife and fork and directed me to squeeze onto a bench between two miners. In the center of the table sat a platter of roasted meat and potatoes. When the man on my right left his place, it was immediately filled by another ravenous miner. Diners were eating as fast as they could, so they could get back to working their claims. As one of my neighbors was finishing his meal, I asked him whether he knew anything of the *Gold Mountain Fortune Mining Company*.

"Going up to watch? Which side you bettin' on?" he asked, picking his teeth with the tip of his knife.

"Betting on what?" I said while munching a piece of gristly meat. The hotel owner said it was roast beef, but I hadn't seen any cattle up in these mountains, the chewy stuff was more than likely roast mule. Through gaps in the wall nearest the kitchen area, I caught a glimpse of the carcass of a large animal roasting on a spit.

"You must be the only one who don't know about the Chinese War. Whole bunch of us heading up to watch," he said. "Blacksmith's been making all sorts of weapons for them. We get so little amusement up here it'll be worth giving up a few pinches of dust and a day of wading in the freezing river. Chinese killing each other will be something to remember."

The man responded briefly to a few more questions before rushing back to his place by the river. The news stunned me. Here, up in California's mountains, two rival gangs of Chinese were going to wage battle, one of them being Bufo's company. I gobbled down a few more chunks of meat and went looking for Shen.

My dining companion hadn't been jesting about the blacksmith. I joined a small crowd, peering through his open door, observing him at work. Inside the workshop, several crates were filled with spear points; others held blades that could be fitted to the ends of poles.

Looking for Shen brought me past a carpenter forming wooden shields. Outside his shop was a wagon stacked with shafts of different lengths. I guessed they would be put to use as pikes and spears.

Shen found me listening to a man taking bets, giving odds for the *Gold Mountains* over the *Cantons*. He gripped my

293

sleeve and pulled me towards the stables. "We go-now, Bufo fight, maybe run-way."

We wasted no time retrieving our animals, leaving the pack mule and taking only whatever we could onto our horses. While we rode, Shen told me he had found out that the *Gold Mountains* had used explosives upriver, diverting water from a rival Chinese camp, the *Cantons*. Back in San Francisco, I had heard that miners were using gunpowder to blast the bedrock of riverbeds. It was experimental and highly dangerous work, but the Chinese were said to be the best at it, having mastered the use of explosives centuries before Europeans ever came to know of it. In damming up the river, Bufo had stopped the *Cantons*' mining operation, channeling the flow into what Shen referred to as a 'water cannon.' The conflict had escalated into war.

The *Cantons* were larger in number, about 400, Shen said, but *Gold Mountain*, with half the number of men, possessed explosives and some Cantons were believed to have defected to the enemy side. I had witnessed the blacksmith forging spear points and blades, Shen had seen his compatriots making clay pots. He used a combination of words, noises and gestures to explain that the pots were to be filled with gunpowder and rocks and then lobbed at the enemy as grenades.

We pushed on with the hope of arriving before the confusion of battle would make it impossible for us to find Bufo. The weapons we saw at Sonorian Camp were ready for imminent delivery. The miner I sat next to at the hotel said he and his friends would be going up to watch in two days' time.

———

Silhouetted against the flat gray sky, a dark figure surveyed our ride towards North Fork. For some miles we had caught glimpses of sentinels perched on higher ground, watching as we rode by. The watchers didn't bother concealing themselves or try to prevent our progress; rather, they often stood or leaned forward for a closer look. When Shen shouted out in Chinese, the only responses to his greetings were his own words echoing off cliff faces.

We saw that the pathway ahead led between two rocky escarpments, high and steep they reminded me of the narrow paths designed to herd cattle toward their slaughter in the *shambles*, the open-air slaughterhouses of English and Irish towns. I tried to push the image of bloody carcasses from my mind as we neared the pass.

There was no sign of sentries, but wary of a trap, we slowed our horses to a walk and then paused once we arrived at the mouth of the rift, fearing that once boxed in there was the chance of an ambush. The horses snorted out steamy clouds, the snowy ground muffled the sound of their nervous stamping.

Animal tracks and furrows made by cartwheels indicated there had been substantial movement through this gap. We looked up again for signs of the watchers but saw nothing. Trying to find another way through would take time we didn't have.

"What do you think, Shen?"

Shen looked up from the cart ruts and frowned, "You give silbadola, Shen get Bufo."

Without another word, he leaned forward and kicked his mount into a full gallop. I was taken aback by Shen's recklessness and for a moment just sat there, mouth agape, watching the Chinaman's hair queue flailing out behind him. In the few days since the start of our undertaking, Shen had become quite the horseman.

I went after him at speed. I had the larger and faster of the horses and soon caught up, galloping through the unknown pass just as recklessly as Shen. It posed risks, but I respected Shen's determination and followed less than a length behind, peppered by sand and ice kicked up by his horse.

Being so close behind, I had no time to react when Shen suddenly slowed. He leaned back, tugging hard on his reins. His horse slid on the slick ground, turning to one side. Unable to avoid a collision, my horse slammed into his, throwing him to the ground. I was already off balance when at the next moment, my legs were grabbed, and I was hauled off the saddle onto the snowy pathway. My injured leg slowed me from getting to my feet. I reached for my pistols but was pinned down; one man held me on each side and another pulled my guns from my belt. Hard blows rained onto my head. I felt a hand grabbing for the knife strapped across my leg. Dazed and unable to see clearly, I struck out, connecting, fighting my way to my feet before taking a hit to the back of my skull that made me see stars and then drop to my knees. Another blow to the same spot put me face down, out very cold into the snow.

My eyes opened to the sight of a spear point aimed at my throat. I was seated, propped against the bottom of the cliff face. Shen sat beside me; our arms were roped behind our backs. Five Chinese held us at spear point, one had my pistols in his belt. I recognized the spear points as the same kind the blacksmith had been making back at the mining camp.

The men guarding us panted nervously. They licked their lips and shifted back and forth rearranging their grips on the spear shafts. Any of them might just thrust their spear into us out of fear. These were miners; men who might have been more accustomed to rakes than pikes, and before becoming miners they were likely merchants or farmers, men who had never wielded weapons, let alone know how to use them properly.

The leader, a stout fellow with a round, flat face, shouted a question at Shen. The man was wrapped in animal hides that looked poorly cured, the skins of different kinds of animals of varying sizes, roughly sewn together. The coat was secured around his middle with a length of twine. Shen responded in a calm voice. He had gone down hard off his horse and had a bloodied cheek. He had a look I had seen after the river crossing, assessing our captors. One of the men went to check Shen's saddlebag.

"Who are they?" I asked.

"Canton. Bufo enemy." Shen looked at my leg. The ripped trouser leg glistened with fresh blood.

"I'll be alright," I said.

Commotion flared up when Shen's fighting blades were discovered. The man who found them brandished the weapons in outstretched arms, waving them about comically, making high pitched noises. His unskilled movements brought the hooked blades dangerously close to his face. Shen shouted for him to stop but the man, intent on playing the fool, continued the dangerous folly. A moment later, we noticed blood dripping down one cheek. The man waving the blades didn't notice and had to be told.

He dropped the knives and touched his ear and then looked at his bloody hand. He had inadvertently sliced off a piece of his own ear. The shocked look on his face caused the others to laugh uproariously. The leader scolded their foolishness and ordered the deer-horn knives to be returned to the bag. The man with the bloodied ear could hardly bear to touch the knives. Another guard was given the task of resuming the search of Shen's bags. From the saddle bag, he pulled out the pack containing Shen's papers and brought it to his chief. The leader gripped his spear under an arm and began to read the mining contract. He made a show of studying it, holding it this way and that, eventually giving up and asking for another guard to read it to him. The reader held it close to his face and stuttered out one word at a time.

The discovery that Shen was contracted to the enemy camp raised tensions markedly. Our weapons had been taken away but now we were more thoroughly searched. They found my marshal's badge, deep in one of my pockets. I bawled insults, hoping that the 'law star' would mean something. Unlike the effect the official standing had in San Francisco, my credentials were of little consequence out here. The men yelled back at me, neither of us understanding the words of the other.

Shen's contract had been a way of getting into the Gold Mountain Camp, now it had become an obstruction. It was clear that we had to get away from the Cantons, to continue our mission. When I said as much to Shen, he replied, "See Canton Camp."

I hadn't a better plan and so nodded in reply.

Two sentries marched us at spear point for about half a mile to the Canton's mining camp; another led our horses along behind us causing me to wonder if these men could ride. Our arrival at the camp added frenzy to the camp that was already abuzz with preparations for war. The Canton miners crowded in for a look at us.

With mining operations at a standstill, the Cantons were being drilled as soldiers. Straw dummies had been set up and lines of men armed with pikes, spears and swords took turns attacking them, yelling as they struck. Even with my limited knowledge of military affairs, these ragtag troops looked as if to be play-acting at being soldiers, laughing and joking as they wielded their weapons.

The mining process at Canton Camp was as sophisticated as any I had observed since the start of our journey, their modern equipment had been set up on an expanse of ground beside a tributary, but the damaging effect of the blockage upriver was clearly evident. The Cantons' process depended on an array of sluice boxes that washed rock and gravel taken from the river bed. Though the river bed was exposed with only a trickle of water still running over it and making it easier to reach the gravel, there was insufficient water to wash through the grit. Machines sat idle beside mounds of snow-covered dry dirt. Stamps, machines that pounded gravel into fine particles for washing went unmanned. The vitality of four hundred miners had been diverted towards a fight for the camp's very survival.

We were led to the tent of the camp's commander, a man of about fifty years. A roughly beaten conical helmet sat on a side table. The commander wore a protective jerkin of thick animal hide. He looked up at us from his seat behind a table; two deputies were beside him studying a hand-drawn map on which round wooden pieces, each the size of a thick coin was placed.

The headman listened to the explanation of why we had been brought to him. Shen's contract and my marshal's badge were placed on the table. The commander addressed me directly in English. "Is it true you that you are a law officer?"

"It is, sir. Marshal Angus Graystone. I am on a mission to capture a suspected murderer. We want no part of your fight, just to pass through."

"Your injury," the commander said, "did my troops do that?"

"No, sir. We had an encounter with a wolf pack."

"Yes, they are around but rarely bother us here with so many men around. Occasionally an animal is taken in the night," he said. "Have you any military experience?"

"I am afraid not."

"A pity, you might have been of some use to us. I am Yangwa. You see me in this," Yangwa waved his hands over the front of his chest, "this costume, dressed for war." Yangwa's shaky voice revealed his fatigue. "Before coming to America, I was a school teacher. Now I am charged with trying to teach men how to kill. Something I have little experience in."

"Can the conflict not be resolved in another way?"

"We have tried, there is no choice. Insults were made and now honor demands it. The men demand it. I am held in high regard because I am a scholar, chosen to lead an army only because I am an adept player of *Xiangqi*. Do you know it?"

"I do not, sir."

"*Xiangqi* is a game played on a board, something like your game of chess, a war game with pieces representing soldiers, cannon and the like. The object is to capture the opposing general." Yangwa picked up one of the wooden disks. "Like this," he said. "This little piece of wood represents their general. If only it were so easy. Most of the men here cannot read or write, let alone play a board game that requires an understanding of strategy. Now I have to treat a real battle as I would a chess game. What do you think of that?"

"Rather a risk, I would say."

"Risky indeed," Yangwa replied. His voice softened, "Quite a pity that you are unable to offer us assistance. Still, I suppose, we have the advantage of more men than the other side."

He ordered my hands to be untied. My badge was returned but not my pistols or knife. I pointed to Shen, "What about my friend? It was never his attention to work for Gold Mountain, the contract was a way for us to enter the camp to get to our man."

"Your friend has fighting skills. The weapons we found can only be used by one who has certain talents. If we release him, can you guarantee that he will not fight against us, that you will both stay out of our way? It is a matter of principle that we conclude this battle."

"You have my word."

Yangwa considered my response for a moment and then ordered Shen's release.

"Tell me the murderer's name, Marshal Graystone."

"Suspected murderer," I corrected. "His name is Bufo."

Yangwa raised an eyebrow. "Bufo, are you certain?"

"I have been trailing him for several months since leaving New York."

"I know the name Bufo, Marshal Graystone, but I very much doubt you will find him at the Gold Mountain Mining Company."

"If not there, where can we find him?"

"Bufo is a name used as a convenience, to recruit Chinese miners. I question whether you will have any success asking for him there. And if he is there, he will certainly be protected. I suspect that Bufo exists but in name, a mere cipher to conceal the identity of someone else. Discovering who that person is must be your true mission," Yangwa said, picking up another disk.

"Perhaps the man I want is their general. If it is your intention to capture Gold Mountain's general, then we share the same mission."

Yangwa shook his head. "No, their leader is Li Guang, a man I am familiar with, chosen by his men to lead them in the battle against us. I will capture or kill him. He will try to do the same to me. Either way, you and your companion will not be allowed to interfere. As a precaution, you will stay here as our guests. You will be free to leave on the day of our battle."

"And if we do not wish to accept your hospitality?"

"Then your treatment will not be as guests but as prisoners. And that, Marshal Graystone, will not be as pleasant."

They herded us into a storage shed crammed with mining equipment. The door was locked from the outside and we were kept in the shed for the next two days, though fairly well looked after. Yangwa sent a man to take my clothes. They were returned the next day, washed and repaired. We tried to understand what Yangwa meant about Bufo, but had no plan other than to proceed to the mining claim as soon as we could. The conundrum, discovering the identity of whoever was behind the name Bufo, was a name concealed in a Chinese box with layer upon layer of intrigue.

27

MORNING OF THE BATTLE, we were woken by the sound of a key turning in the lock of the storage shed's door. During our incarceration, a constant din of maneuvers had filled the camp. It had erupted into a crescendo the previous day when the Cantons began its move towards the battleground. Our door opened to a largely deserted camp. True to his word, Yangwa had our weapons and property returned to us. We were eager to get to the battle and set off immediately on horseback, following the tracks left by the hundreds of soldiers that had left the day before.

Two thousand miners had arrived from neighboring camps to witness the battle. The spectators watched from a hillside that sloped down onto the battlefield. They braved the cold while seated on blankets, bundled in thick clothing, eating and drinking, awaiting the grand entertainment that was about to unfold. Some of those who had arrived on wagons chose to remain in their carts and watch from elevated positions. We found a place at the edge of the crowd overlooking Gold Mountain, where several Chinese miners from other camps had come to watch.

The combatants faced each other across a plain covered in a layer of fresh snow that had fallen the night before. The armies appeared to be in no hurry to do battle. From what I understood from the conversation with Yangwa, and then hours of talking to Shen in our cell, this was as much about honor and showmanship as real fighting, and a great deal of posturing was required.

In no hurry to rush towards their deaths, the armies took turns trudging through the snowy field for a couple of hours, hurling insults and threats back and forth accompanied by much gong-banging and trumpet-blaring. The scene brought back stark images of what I had seen that night in the Chinese opera house in San Francisco. I had to wonder whether all this posturing, the braggadocio, was borrowed from the opera. Or was it Chinese opera imitating what happened on real Chinese battlefields? As shameful as it was for me to think of the night at the opera house, I was nagged by a thought, an unanswered question — was my finding Shen up on the platform truly a coincidence? Perchance, but it seemed unlikely. I ruminated over the possibility while we laid a couple of thick blankets over the snow. Shen had his eyes fixed on the action on the battlefield and ignored my first attempt at getting his attention. I tapped him on the shoulder. "Shen, remember the night I grabbed you in San Francisco?"

He launched into an angry rant, all in Chinese, but the meaning was clear as he gesticulated wildly, moving to a parody of our crash to the floor below and then ended it in a boisterous laugh that had us both in stitches.

"Yes, I'm sorry, Shen. The thing is," I said, breathlessly, "I wonder how we both happened to be up on the same platform. Have you ever wondered?"

He blinked a few times, tilted his head in thought. "Opra-man say good-lookee-see up, I pay fi-sen," he said holding his hand up to show 'five.'

I'd paid twenty cents, but that hardly mattered now. "And before that, did someone ask you to go to the show?"

"I get goo-luck welcome ticket from Sakamento-house-owna. Say welcome-to-America."

"The house owner, what's his name?"

"No he-name. Owner boss-lady. All Chinese know."

I heard Ah Toy's words clearly in my head, *You go tonight. Special opera performance Palace of Eternal Life. All Chinese man go . . . you look for Bufo face. Take opera glass.* "This boss-lady, was it Ah Toy?"

Shen shot me a cheeky grin, "You know, Ah Toy. Graystone like Ah Toy, maybe?"

A heated argument broke out a dozen yards downhill drawing our attention away from the idea of Ah Toy somehow being involved in our chance meeting. Spectators had grown weary of the display on the battlefield and had begun to yell for the fighting to start. One of the miners got to his feet. Swaying from the effects of a liquor bottle still in his hand, he pulled out a pistol and fired several shots into the air, shouting for the armies to begin the fight. Yells from nearby miners telling him to put the gun away were met with swearing and gun waving.

"This could get ugly," I said to Shen. "Drink and guns are a bad mix."

"Show law-star," Shen replied.

"That's likely to get us both killed," I said leaning back on my elbows intending to make a smaller profile against stray bullets. Shen did the same.

When the man next to the gun-wielding miner rose to his feet and tried to get the drunk to sit down, his effort was met with a poke to the chest with a gun barrel. Unable to placate him, he pulled out his own weapon. The drunken miner, unsteady and half blind from rotgut, gripped his weapon in both hands. While he tried to cock his pistol with his thumbs, the second miner shot him in the chest. At point-blank range, the blast knocked him several feet, landing on his back in the snow.

Rather than spur the armies on, the gunshots had the opposite effect, both armies immediately went quiet and all eyes looked to the direction of the shooting. The gunfire provided a brief interlude to the main event, there was shouting amongst the white miners and threats were hurled about with men getting to their feet and waving their fists at one another.

On the battlefield, both commanders yelled orders to their men. Gongs started up again, this time with renewed vigor. Eager to watch the show, the argument on the hillside soon dissipated and the spectators went back to their places, quickly agreeing that the dead man got what he deserved for unsportsmanlike behavior.

Finally, the two armies began to draw closer together. The white miners cheered, some threw their hats in the air. Money changed hands.

If the Chinese had guns, none were evident. Yangwa leading the Cantons, walked out before his men. His soldiers in the front rows were armed with pikes and spears. Behind them marched swordsmen.

The Gold Mountains had half the number of troops. Their general led, taking strong, confident strides across the white field. With no official uniforms on either side, the Gold Mountains identified themselves with strips of red cloth tied around their arms. Their ranks were arranged in a similar way to Yangwa's men, but at the back of the 200-strong army, stood a machine on a wheeled platform. The stand supported a tall, stout frame that narrowed at the top. Shen explained its purpose by placing the tips of his fingers under his forearm as a fulcrum, then indicating a throwing motion. The Gold Mountains had brought a catapult.

The Gold Mountains made the first move, rushing their opponents and striking at the enemy line of wooden shields. The spectators roared. As quickly as they had advanced, the Gold Mountains stepped back. Still, neither side had an appetite for killing; it still appeared to be play-fighting. From the back of the Gold Mountain army, the catapult flung its first projectile. A clay pot made a whirring sound as it was lobbed in a smoky arc over the heads of the front lines. It exploded somewhere in the center of the Canton ranks, sending out splinters of rock and flaming oil in every direction. About six men went down, creating a small gap around a dark circle. The bomb attack started the battle in earnest.

The front lines of both sides began to use their weapons, jabbing between shields with pikes and spears. More men went down. Another bomb was released. The white miners hooted and whistled, watching the projectile's arc, cheering wildly when it landed, exploding with the same effect as the one before. The swordsmen rushed into the fray. And so went the battle for another hour. Injured soldiers who were able to move on their own rushed away from the fighting. Even a minor scratch was enough for some of the men to flee, leaving fewer and fewer men on the battlefield. The Cantons attempted to hack their way through the Gold Mountain ranks to get at the catapult but were repeatedly forced back.

The battle ended after three hours with the Cantons routed and their leader, Yangwa, captured. A total of about thirty men, either killed or wounded had to be carried off the battleground — a number that certainly would have been much higher had both sides been intent on really killing, or if guns had been used.

It was still early afternoon. The spectators would still have time to get to their camps before nightfall. They got stiffly to their feet; some of them had to be roused from drunken slumber, pulled up and helped back to their wagons or onto horseback.

"Shen, you still have your contract, don't you?" I asked. Shen opened his bag and pulled it out to show me.

"Good. Let's go try to speak to the commander of the Gold Mountains." We rolled up our blankets and led the horses down the snowy hill towards the battlefield where the victors were celebrating.

A line of Canton miners had formed in front of a table that had been set up at the edge of the battlefield. They had shed their weapons and stood in line waiting to put their name to new contracts for their new employer Gold Mountain, effectively the new owner of the Canton Mine as part of their spoils.

A few men began to chant the name of their commander, Li Guang, the man who led them in victory. More men joined, pumping their arms in the air. The chanting grew in volume and vigor, bolstered gradually as the hundreds of men who were no longer the enemy joined. Li Guang was at one side of the battlefield, overseeing the care of injured soldiers. He raised his arms in acknowledgment and strode towards the center of the chanting troops. They moved aside, creating a clear pathway for him. Li Guang called for quiet then and began addressing his men.

"Tell me what he's saying," I told Shen.

Shen held my arm to quiet me while he listened. "He say, Gold Mountain soldier fight good. All miner get special pay."

"Go on, what else?"

"He send rider to Sunfrasiko. Tell good news to mine owner. Tell owner come see new Canton mine."

"Does he say the name, Bufo?"

"Wait, quiet," Shen said. "Now he say Bufo name."

"We have to get Bufo before he arrives. Once he gets here, he'll have 600 men backing him up."

"How we catch Bufo? What track he take?"

"There's one place everyone uses."

Shen thought for a moment then broke into a grin. "Cross river," he said. "Doak place."

"We'll prevent Bufo from coming to this side of the San Joaquin River."

"Go-fast. Chinese rider no-stop. Change new horse, new rider every-day."

"A relay team of riders could get to San Francisco in a few days, but they still have to come back. We have time on our side," I said.

"Go now, Graystone."

We led our horses to the edge of the battlefield and then began retracing our ride off the high peaks along the path of the Tuolumne. I was well aware, as surely Shen was, that only a few days remained of the two weeks he'd promised in exchange for seventy-five dollars.

We passed a train of drunken miners, snoozing in wagons or slumped over their horses and mules.

The chase across California, bad weather, rough terrain, jailed by the Cantons and then a wolf attack, drove us into an unexpected bond. Shen, a man from a world so different from mine had proved a trustworthy companion.

He still asked me to repeat or explain things, but these occurrences lessened as I learned to better communicate with him using gesticulations as part of my vocabulary. Shen's talent for face contortions enabled an impressive range of expression, whereas I, rarely one for exuberant display, struggled to 'talk' to him as best I could. My exaggerated gestures often likened to a game of charades. The effort honed our senses of perception for one another's thoughts. Approaching Sonorian Camp at dusk, Shen's queue whipped round when he turned to face me.

"What is it now?" I said.

His eyebrows converged and his lips pushed into a pout. "We-eat, we-go. No-stop."

"There's ample time, Shen. It will be a few days for the rider to get to San Francisco and a few more to get back. We'll be right on time. No need to charge off so quickly. We should have a short rest."

"You see dog?" Shen said.

"No, why? You're seeing your Taotai, perhaps?"

Shen snorted at me. The truth was, he knew I wanted a drink. He may have suspected my desperation in having one. And not just one; to down a string of good-sized slugs of something that would bring tears to my eyes and cause me to break into a sweat. I had been dry since the night of the Chinese opera, but now whether it was the promise of success or fear of impending failure, abstinence burned a hole in me.

"Some hot food, good sleep and a hot bath, doesn't that sound fine?" I licked my lips.

Shen's glower didn't let up. I continued, "Have our clothes washed, you might enjoy some . . ."

Shen stopped me with a hand held up. "I-gree."

"Good, settled then. We could both use a little rest."

"But no *chi-nanigan*." Shen fired an angry look of at my laugh. "What? I say-funny?"

"I'm sorry, just surprised. I'm not sure what you mean."

"Stop one day. No-trick, drunk-whiskey-fall-down." He held up a finger. "One day. You-gree?"

"Don't worry, Shen. There's time," I said as we stopped in front of the stables.

I ignored Shen's snuffle. In my mind, I was already inside the Empire Hotel.

We had out-paced most of the returning miners, but as one of the few places to get food and a bed, at sundown the

Empire was bustling. I gave Dooley a few coins for a meal and a bed and then sat at one of the tables. The meal was little changed from the one I'd had before, and I filled my belly with chunks of whatever the meat was.

Dooley had his shirtsleeves rolled up to the elbows, hairy forearms in a tubful of suds containing dinner plates and utensils. He raised his head as I approached the bar. Behind him, bottles of liquor were displayed along a slightly lopsided plank.

"Take your pick, mister, they all do the job," Dooley said watching me peruse his wares.

I studied each bottle, the same stuff I'd guzzled in San Francisco but with different labels made to appeal to argonauts. I chose one called 'Sluice Juice.'

Dooley dried his hands on a stained apron and reached back for it. I declined his offer of a glass and handed over what amounted to thrice what I had expected to pay. I held it in the crook of my arm and eased into the assigned bunk. I sat up in the sagging bed and uncorked the bottle. I chuckled at Shen's way of picking up new words. I respected his stalwart sense of duty and trusted him with my life. I hoped he considered me a friend, as I did him. He missed his master; perhaps the mere memory served as an invitation to his Taotai for nightly visitations. I knew what summoned my demon; bequeathed as it was, nothing could be done about it.

I tilted my head back and took a big swallow. Through the bubble that floated through the amber liquid, I spied a black shape, more wolf than dog. I'd conjured up *Cù-Sith*, the demon hound of my nightmares. I lowered the bottle for a better look. My scuffed black boots stood up like two great ears at the ends of my outstretched legs.

28

SHEN'S CHINESE FRIENDS' panning brought in paltry amounts of gold and so they augmented their income by taking in washing. Building materials in short supply, the three men that shared a little claim, lived in a shanty built of odd-sized planks and scraps of brushwood.

As the first Chinese to arrive with news of the 'war,' they gave Shen a warm welcome, peppering him with questions about the battle. Wet sheets hung over stretched ropes served as a backdrop for the snowy battleground, a pair of trousers suspended on a hook was the catapult. Shen regaled his hosts by employing his considerable talents at mimicry to deliver a detailed if somewhat embellished account of the battle and ultimate routing of the Cantons. For his effort, they rewarded him with a hot meal. The four men sat cross-legged in a circle around a pot of steaming noodles.

"That tall devil you travel with, is he your master?" asked Kwan, the man who first approached him outside the Empire Hotel.

"He is a high ranking official with the government," Shen said.

"Like one of our mandarins?"

"Just so, sent on a mission from the nation's highest officials. He hides his badge of office, a five-pointed silver star," Shen lowered his voice, "It is hidden because of the secret nature of our work."

Shen's audience looked wide-eyed at each other and bobbed their heads. "Who would have thought that one of us would reach such heights?" said one of the others.

"He paid me to help him, but he isn't my master," said Shen, "we are more like partners. My master, another high official, died back home in China."

"You sound like you miss it back there, brother. Not me. There was nothing but a bitter life with nothing to show for," said Kwan.

"And, this is better?" Shen said, pointing at wooden tubs filled with wet clothes and ropes draped with sodden sheets.

"I tell you, there's only one thing I miss about China," Kwan said.

One of the other men slapped Kwan on the shoulder. "Don't keep going on about that stuff. We're better off without it. We were all skin and bone with nothing to live on, spending everything we had for a few pipes every night."

"So, how did you pay to get here?" Shen said.

"We borrowed money for credit tickets, all three of us, from a man called Yan."

Shen stiffened at hearing the merchant name.

"So, it seems you know the money lender," Kwan said.

Shen nodded as he recalled seeing the ledger floating on the crest of a little wave after he had tossed into the sea. The names of these men would have been in it. "I've heard the name, Yan. Best stay hidden up here where you can't be found."

"We intend to, even if we get rich we are never going back," Kwan said. "But what I wouldn't give for a good pipe or two."

Shen rose and retrieved something from his bag. "Well, my brothers, that is something I can help you with."

Like the ledger, the opium belonged to Yan. Allowing Yan's debtors have some of his opium would be a fine way of snubbing the merchant, Shen thought.

An old bamboo pipe that Kwan had kept was passed around as the men helped one another partake. Shen's hosts eventually succumbed to the drug by falling into a deep sleep. Half awake, Shen listened to the howling wind and creak of the building. A single window allowed soft snow-reflected moonlight into the shack. He could hear the tapping of individual snowflakes as they struck the windowpane. Through the gloom, Shen's eyes fixed on a dark shape hovering a few inches off the floor. Each of the Taotai's visits were preceded by different forms; sometimes a gust of wind or a wisp of smoke, once he rose from the reek of a chamber pot — this time Shen saw a tall thin shadow.

Shen knew of men in his former profession who were haunted by the ghosts of people they killed. Thankfully that didn't happen to him, but seeing the Taotai was frightening enough. He knew that trying to run was futile. The Taotai's nimble spirit wouldn't allow such foolishness. And why should he be so insolent as to run from his master?

As a sign of respect, Shen tried to rise to a *kowtow* position, kneeling and prostrating by touching his head to the ground just as he had done on his master's previous visits. Unable to move at all, he watched while lying on his side while the Taotai's form materialized from opaque shadow to more or less solid form. The Taotai was dressed in the gown he'd been buried in; shiny blue silk edged in brocade and embroidered with designs of clouds. Below it, his skeletal feet floated a few inches above the ground. His hands were clasped, bony fingers entwined. Smooth white skin pulled tightly over his cheekbones, eye sockets and mouth were no more than black holes. A dark line circled his neck where the sash had been tightened to strangle him.

Shen heard the Taotai's words not through sound but as ideas floating into his head. *You are nothing on your own. Without a master, you are as fickle as a cobweb caught in a breeze.*

BOOK FOUR

DEMONS

29

COMMOTION OUTSIDE THE HOTEL woke me. I knew enough not to move my head too quickly on a morning after a night on the bottle.

The tables and benches of the Empire were empty. A boy half-heartedly pushed a broom over stained floorboards. I shifted my weight to investigate an uncomfortable lump under my back and discovered that I shared the bed with two empty bottles. One of them I didn't recall buying. I squinted at the torn label, 'Blast Hole' it read.

The disturbance outside grew louder with a lot of shouting; one of the voices was unmistakably Shen's. I had slept fully clothed with my boots still on. I swung my legs out of bed and stood up very slowly.

"Well if it ain't Rip Van Winky," Dooley said.

"What's all the noise?"

"Some Chinaman wants to come in," he said with a shrug. "Got my boys to throw him out. Said he wanted gray stone. Figure that . . . everyone else is after gold and the dumb chinee wants gray stones. Told him I didn't care what kinda stones he wanted, he ain't welcome in my hotel. My boys're taking care of it."

"Graystone, that's me," I said, staggering to the doorway. I held a hand level with my brow to diminish the brightness and peered out.

Three men surrounded Shen, another one lay unconscious on the ground with blood dripping from his nose.

"What's going on here?" I said.

One of the men around Shen looked up and said, "Gonna teach the Chinee some manners."

"He's with me," I said, "leave him alone, I'm Federal Marshal Angus Graystone." I held it up my badge.

"There's no law 'round here but our own law. Put the tin star away or you'll be getting a lesson too."

"We go, Graystone. No time fight."

"I'm not ready to go, Shen. We have plenty of time. It'll take days for a rider to get to San Francisco and back again."

"Only place you're going Chinaman, is to the floor. The man who spoke swung a fist at Shen. Shen easily ducked under it, infuriating his attacker. "Let's get 'im boys," he yelled. They went for Shen all at once. But as if it were some game, Shen turned, ducked and somehow evaded all the blows and grabs. It took a few confusing moments with the men looking about to finally see him standing a few feet away.

"What I say? No *chi-nanigan*. We get horse, go."

"Told you, I'm not ready to go. I'm the one who makes the decisions. Go enjoy your friends for a day or two. We'll go when I'm ready." I stepped onto the street and immediately fell face-down into the snow. Shen helped me up.

"What about him?" one of the men pointed to the man with the bloody nose.

"Get him up, I'll buy him a drink," I said. "I'll buy all of you drinks."

One of the men looked past me and spoke to Dooley who was standing at the Empire's doorway. "That alright with you, boss?"

"Fine with me if he's paying," Dooley said. Two of Dooley's men picked their bloodied friend and carried him into the hotel.

"Get yourselves a drink," I called after them. "I'll join you in a moment."

Shen yelled at me in rapid Chinese, shaking his finger. "Calm down, Shen. Just a day or so, then we'll be off again. There's hard country out there . . . wolves even," I said.

Shen turned and walked off still muttering something under his breath, his head hung low. "A day, two at most," I called after him as he turned a corner towards the Chinese quarter.

Four days after we rode into the Sonorian Camp, we were still there. I can't be sure whether Shen returned the next day but I guess that he did and was turned away. In fact, I remember almost nothing of that day and very little of the next two. Now, the hound, more wolf-like than before, was my constant companion. I had become a fixture at the Empire and enjoyed convivial relationships with Dooley and many of the characters that frequented the place.

I guzzled away the feelings of guilt that surfaced, telling myself that we still had *days to get there.*

30

GRAYSTONE'S SNUB HIT SHEN HARD, but the man's facility for mirth along with the newfound camaraderie he enjoyed with his compatriots soon soothed any feelings of bitterness. He adapted to the rhythm of camp life, accepting that it might be the beginning of a new life that was meant to be. He did his best to push away thoughts of Graystone and Bufo. Hadn't he had wanted to be as far away as he could from Macau from the accusation of murder? Well, this was it — what was it to him if Graystone failed in his mission?

He more than earned his keep by pitching in at the laundry while his pals tried their luck panning for gold on the freezing riverbank. Carrying buckets up from the river, he filled large wooden casks with heated water and spent hours churning filthy clothes and sheets with an oar-like implement, stirring and scrubbing until his hands were rubbed raw.

Shen also tried his hand at searching for gold: shoveling river gravel into buckets, pouring it into a sluice and then sifting the rock and gravel through layers of mesh in search for the tiniest specks of glitter. Though the back-breaking work yielded little, his companions were never deterred, always hopeful that at any moment their dreams would be fulfilled.

Each night as fatigue forced his eyelids to sag, unsettling feelings nagged at him, insinuating that important work was left undone. These thoughts often preceded the Taotai's visitations. As usual, Li Taotai 's wasted figure emerged from the most unsavory places such as the stink of a shoe or a pile of reeking, stained sheets. Though Shen recognized them for what they were, they always frightened him. The Taotai's messages floated into Shen's head — sometimes as whole sentences but often just single words: *duty; honor; trust; mission*. Shen understood these concepts well — ideas drummed into his head and for which the Taotai in life, constantly berated him for not succeeding in.

It was after the visit by his deceased master some hours before dawn of the fifth day at Sonorian Camp that Shen crept into the Empire Hotel. He lit a lamp, turned the flame down low and pushed open the front door. Even with a kerchief tied across his face, the stink of the hotel sickened him; scores of unwashed, snoring bodies confined in the closeness of a single room that served as dormitory, kitchen and saloon.

Clad entirely in black as he was on the night he hid in the folds of a Banyan tree, his mission this night was not to take a life, but to save one — to get Graystone out of the place.

He slunk from bed to bed, holding the lamp above each man, examining their faces until he found Graystone. The marshal lay face up, open-mouthed with his long hair over his face. The crook Graystone's arm cradled an empty bottle.

Shen had a long coil of rope with him and now he tied it round one of Graystone's legs. This was an inelegant solution designed for the task of extracting Graystone from the hotel. The plan called for force and speed rather than finesse. He retraced his steps to the hotel's doorway, uncoiling the rope as he went, exiting the Empire and this time leaving the door wide open. The other end of the rope was tied to the saddle on his waiting horse. Shen had considered the possibility that Graystone could be injured in such a plan but felt the risk well worth the result, which if successful might even appease the Taotai's restless spirit. Once Graystone was jerked out of his bunk, there was a direct pathway from Graystone's bed to the doorway, over the porch and then a few bumps down the stairway onto the snowy ground. From there, he would drag Graystone over the snow all the way to the laundry.

The open door allowed frigid night air to blow into the Empire and Shen began to hear some murmurings inside. The miners were in deep drunken sleep but before long, one of them would rise and shut the door.

Shen got onto the horse and kicked it into action cantering straight ahead in a line from the doorway. He felt the tension change in the rope as Graystone was jolted out of bed and thumped onto the floorboards. He went straight on, turning around to see Graystone slide over the porch and then fly over the steps. He hit the snowy ground with a thud. Shen kept going making a wide turn, dragging Graystone away from the hotel and round a corner towards the Chinese sector.

31

A PUNGENT FOG ENGULFED ME. Conifers towered overhead, their branches weighed down with clusters of pine cones that added woodiness to the green odor. But there was more to the smell — something medicinal, complex and rich that left a bitter taste at the back of my throat. Close by and quite distinct was a burbling sound. I turned to look for its source expecting to see a mineral spring bubbling through thick mud, but all around me were the great pines, their scaly trunks like oversized fence posts encircling me. Giant roots forced upwards through the earth released yet another smell into the mix, this one of minerals and damp. The roots extended towards me and tangled around my legs, tightening they pulled me off my feet. I fell face down onto the crumbling earth.

I heard the bubbling sound again and forced opened my eyes. My chin was turned over my right shoulder and now I saw blurrily where the sound came from. A pot boiled above a cooking fire, near to it, a dark figure used a long pole to stir the contents of a steaming container. I gasped as my mind raced to an illustration in a picture book. In the picture, a black man stirred a steaming cauldron in preparation for cooking his next meal, a trussed-up missionary. Closer to me on the floor sat plates of what appeared to be bundles of dried grasses and sticks along with a stone mortar and pestle — seasonings for a meal for which I was to be the main course. The black figure heard my gasp; he looked up and then came towards me.

I tried to move away but my muscles betrayed me. The figure squatted down and did something to my back. I realized then that I was completely naked. A sucking noise came from my back. I felt my skin being pulled up and then heard a slight *pop*, like the sound of a cork being pulled from a bottle. Normally, just the sound of a cork would send me looking for a bottle. Oddly, this time I felt no desire for a drink. Three more times I felt the pulling sensation on the skin on my back and heard the sucking and popping sounds, and then the figure spoke to me.

"So, you wake-up, Graystone. How head?"

My response came out as a sentence made up of a gagging noise followed by a cough and a stream of mucus from my nose.

"Ah, you-beta," Shen said. "Gé good-for drunk-man. See? I make special tea to take-care." He picked up one of the pungent dishes and brought it close to my face. It looked like a plateful of wood chips. "This one *gé*, make blood clean," he said. He showed me a dish of dried yellow blossoms, "This one *quan ye lian qiao*, make Graystone no-like drink whiskey." He placed a dish of dried mushrooms under my nose. "This one, *lingzhi*." I gagged at the intense woody smell. "No worry. Womit-good for drunk-man."

I was beginning to regain some movement and mumbled something about my back. Shen showed me a glass jar. "Suck-out bad blood. Graystone feel-beta soon," he said.

"Where the devil . . .?" My question came out as a hoarse whisper.

"China wash-shop," Shen said with pride in his voice.

I managed to push myself up on my elbows and saw hanging sheets and dripping clothes. I immediately regretted the effort and collapsed, my face once again pressed to the floorboards.

"How long here?" I said

"You sleep two-day." Shen made a 'V' with the fingers of his right hand.

"Bufo?"

Shen shook his head. "Bufo maybe leave Sunfrasiko. Maybe we miss-a-ready. Why you no-listen I say no *chi-nani-gan?* Black dog bite-you-ass, maybe?"

It hurt my chest to laugh, but I did anyway. "Yes, and a few other places, too. But thank you for getting me out of the Empire. We have to go after Bufo right away."

"Tomorrow," Shen said. He pointed to a pile in the corner. "I get Graystone bag from hotel. We back Sunfrasiko you give Shen more silbadola. You-gree?"

"I agree, Shen. Another fifty dollars," I said.

Shen contorted his eyebrows in imitation of Nagler forcing me to hold my breath to suppress the painful laughter.

"You drink more special-tea. Sleep. Tomorrow find Bufo."

As ingenious as Shen's plan was, and though grateful for the rescue, the wear and tear from being dragged over hard-packed snow at speed had left me battered. We rode out of the camp shortly after daybreak and proceeded slowly down the mountain.

Retracing the path, we rode on the ascent. In the late afternoon, we passed the place we had camped the night of the wolf attack. It didn't take much discussion for us to agree not to stop there again and we rode on for another hour before stopping for the night. We neither heard nor saw wolves but decided to take turns as sentry while the other slept. Just before dawn on my watch, I heard a distant sound. It was faint, but clearly not the shriek of the wind. The cry of a single wolf came and went and though I decided not to disturb Shen, the animal's wail woke him and he sat up wrapped in blankets and looked around.

"Wolf look for family. But far-way," Shen said.

Hearing the howl unnerved us to the point that we decided to break camp and get off the mountain as soon as we could.

32

WE MADE UP FOR THE DEAFENING ROAR of the San Joaquin River by signaling to the ferry by waving and jumping to catch Doaks' attention. Shen leaped onto a boulder and waved his arms at the ferry that was a third of the way across, coming in our direction. Doaks and Zeke freed their hands from their ropes just long enough to return our greetings.

The ferry carried a couple of horses rigged to a *prairie schooner*, the kind of covered wagon that carried settlers and gold-hunters westwards. We saw two passengers, one seated under the front bow of the wagon, the other stood in front and between two horses, steadying the animals. Still more than two hundred feet away, I couldn't see the men clearly, but by the look of their loose-fitting dark clothing, they appeared to be Chinese.

"Could that be Bufo?" I asked Shen.

"Maybe Bufo. We wait, maybe catch," Shen said, grinning as he skipped off the rock.

The man seated on the wagon had seen Doaks waving to us. He turned towards the interior of the wagon as if speaking to someone inside. Even at this distance, I could see the change in his patient demeanor to what seemed like agitation. He jumped off his seat and moved quickly to the man holding the horses, talking, pointing at us. Then he hurried to Doaks. A moment later, Doaks and Zeke shifted positions and began pulling the ropes in the opposite direction. The ferry began pulling away from us, reversing its way to the other bank.

As soon as the ferry docked on the western shore, the wagon backed onto dry land and drove away at a rapid pace.

Doaks would have normally waited for another load of passengers to bring across, but now he wasted no time setting off again in our direction. Even with no load to haul across, it still took another half-hour for the ferry to get to the eastern bank. We boarded and greeted each other with handshakes and slaps on the back.

"I guess seein' you so soon means you've made your fortune already," Doaks said.

"We've been on quite a different mission, but what happened to your passengers back there?" I asked.

"Wanted me to turn back."

"Didn't give no reason, did he Pa?" Zeke piped in.

"No siree, but payin' double's reason 'nough," Doaks said, jingling the coins in his pocket.

"Were they Chinese?"

"They was, far as I could tell. Looked like all the rest. Like Shen here," Doaks said. "Why are you so interested?"

"We were hoping to intercept a fugitive, Mr. Doaks," I said, showing my marshal's badge.

Zeke stepped in for a closer look at my credentials. "That a real marshal's badge?"

"It certainly is, Zeke, Marshal Angus Graystone at your service. Now, back to those Chinese passengers — did they say where they were going?"

"No, but 'bout a week ago, I brought one of them across t'other way. Was in a real hurry too. Took off like his ass were afire. Now he brung these two others back with him."

"I saw only two men," I said.

"There was three," Zeke said. "One of 'em never got out the wagon. Never got a good look at him."

"One of them must have been Bufo," I said to Shen. "What did the one driving look like?"

"Big fella, not tall as me, but wide shouldered, never smiled or said nothin' — not the one that come through before, that were the one with the horses. But what's all this about?"

"I've been tracking a man for months, since leaving Washington. One of those might have been him. He's wanted in connection to a murder, perhaps more than one," I said, recalling the death of Jake the storeman. "We must get after them. They already have a lead of an hour, it'll be more like two by the time we get across and on our way."

"We go," Shen said.

"Be nightfall by the time you get movin', sure you want to ride after 'em in the dark?" Doaks said.

"We have no choice. Let's get across, Mr. Doaks. Same price as before?"

Doaks held his palm up to stop me trying to pay him. "Keep your money. I am in your debt, Marshal Graystone, yours too, Shen. I'll help you go after 'em Chinee too, if you want."

"No thank you, Mr. Doaks, just getting us across will be help enough," I said.

We put our backs into pulling our way back across the San Joaquin.

It wasn't yet fully dark when we got across the river and, we set off immediately in pursuit of the wagon. The fresh wagon tracks were easily seen as we rode after it. As darkness descended we could only guess at the direction they took, getting off our horses and feeling the ground for tracks. I recalled our route toward the river, but there were any number of ways to get to and from San Francisco if, in fact, that was where they were headed. It made the most sense — a place Bufo could to go back into hiding.

Riding on horseback was a great deal faster than a wagon, but in the dark we had to ride cautiously, even more so when the trail headed into the thick woodland. We kept moving, trusting that we would eventually find Bufo somewhere ahead of us, perhaps camped for the night.

An hour later we saw a pinprick of light, the glow of a campfire. We dismounted and led our horses off the trail. Shen took out his set of knives from the saddlebag. I checked my handguns and drew the Sharp's carbine from its saddle scabbard.

We pushed through the undergrowth towards the campfire, stopping thirty paces away to peer through the scrub at the campsite. A blanketed figure with his back to us sat motionless before the fire. There was no doubt that this was the same wagon we had seen on Doak's ferry, distinctive with its dun-colored top. The very notion of being so close to Bufo got my heart thumping.

"Graystone stay, no-talk, I look-see," Shen said.

I nodded, and he used his knives to part the bushes, approaching the sentry from the rear. I brought the carbine to my shoulder and trained the sight at the slumped figure.

Shen stooped over and hooked a corner of the blanket with the tip of one of his blades. He pulled it up slowly. As he began to lift the blanket away, I tightened my finger on the trigger. The blanket slid to the ground over the figure's back, revealing it as a skeleton of branches and twigs.

Shen turned to his head to a sound coming from the wagon's dark interior. A sonorous *twang*, a sound we both knew as the release of an arrow.

Shen raised his knives as the shaft hissed its way towards him, slashing, catching and ducking away at the same time. One of his blades caught the arrow's fletching, diverting it from its true path, but not enough so. The arrow's tip ripped through the cloth above his shoulder. He looked at the wound and staggered slightly but didn't wait for a second arrow to be loosed. He stumbled for cover towards trees at the edge of the clearing.

I fired my carbine through the cover of the wagon, not knowing what I was shooting at, hoping to give Shen a moment to escape. I lay the single-shot rifle down and drew my Colt. I got up and pushed my way closer to the campsite. As I cleared the bushes, I caught movement from my right side; I turned just as something smashed into my face. The force knocked me over, slamming the back of my head to the ground. I dropped my gun. At the moment before complete blackness overcame me, I imagined being back at Ah Toy's bordello. Ah Jun's grinning pock-marked face grinned down at me.

My eyes opened to a lamp swinging overhead. I was in the wagon, bumping along at a brisk pace. A face blocked out the light as it peered down. The same pitted face, this time it certainly was no dream. I recognized Ah Jun's gleeful expression as one of triumph.

"Ah Jun?" I said.

"That the name you know me by, lawman."

I attempted to sit up. My arms and legs were tied, and I was able to raise my head only a few inches off the floor before falling back. Ah Jun giggled, coquettishly placing a hand over his mouth.

"What other names are you know by, Bufo perhaps," I said.

"Bufo?" Ah Jun looked amused, tipping his face quizzically to the side. "Sometime I Bufo, sometime Bufo other person." Ah Jun turned his head to face the rear of the wagon. Another man sat watching us; the one who was driving before, a bow lay across his thighs.

"Where are you taking me?" I said.

"No matter. You die soon, Graystone. We find good place where nobody find you. Lawman disappear, not murder. Cut to small piece. Maybe wolf eat. You like wolf, Graystone?"

"Shen will come for me."

"Shen Xiling? No, Shen no come. He dead. Or soon die. Maybe animal eat body. Nobody find. Nobody care dead Chinese." Ah Jun giggled again looking at the bowman.

"I don't believe you. Shen will come after you," I said.

"Arrow cut Shen," Ah Jun said, patting his scrawny left shoulder. Very bad poison Shen know before — Jincan. I get good pay from Jincan-man to kill Shen." Ah Jun, turned again and gestured towards the other man. "He Cheng, come allway from China. He job kill Shen, so I say, you can do. He master Yan say Shen steal money. I already get money from Wu. So many want kill Shen. Shen good for kill-business, no?" Ah Jun laughed again.

I had no idea about 'Wu', but Shen had told me about Yan. So, now Yan had sent an assassin to settle debts.

"Why did you kill President Taylor — it was you, was it not?"

"Just job," Ah Jun said.

"For who?"

"For my master, of course. I only do job for master."

"Your master, you mean . . ."

"So difficult understand, Marshal Graystone?" That grotesque giggle again.

"You mean, Ah Toy?"

Ah Jun's expression hardened. "She say, you do — so I do. She have many-mirer. One-mirer pay good money, say kill Taylor before Taylor change many-thing."

My head reeled with what I'd just heard. I wondered if I'd live long enough to discover the name of Ah Toy's customer who'd paid for the assassination of the President of the United States. The key to the puzzle was Ah Toy, and both Ah Jun and Ah Toy would have to face justice. Ah Jun seemed to sense my thoughts. "Soon you die, Graystone. Lawman job stop now. We cut to small piece, you never see ancestor," he said.

33

SHEN HADN'T FORGOTTEN what it felt like to be poisoned by the shaman. A loud noise, like the rushing wind, filled his head as he made for the trees — just shapes, too far away to reach, he thought. He was vaguely aware of still holding his deer horn knives and tried to grip the handles more firmly. His only chance of survival now was to run. Wu's voice echoed in his head. *You're a dead man. The poison will kill you, you can be certain of it. There is no cure.*

He kept moving, stumbling to the trees and through them. In total darkness now, well-beyond the glow of the campfire. Snow began falling, a light dusting reaching the forest floor between the pines. *Keep moving,* he told himself. Eventually, not able to take another step, he dropped face down.

He awoke to bright moonlight. The space around him illuminated by light reflected off a layer of fresh snow. Again, as it was when the shaman's dart nicked his ear, Shen was unable to move. His shoulder ached mightily. He could see clearly in the direction of where his face was turned to, and his hearing was acute, but no movement at all. *Is this what it has come to? A frozen death in Gum Saan.*

Shen heard snarling: a slow, deep growl. It came from behind his head. He could feel the grips of the knives, useless now in his paralyzed hands. The growling came nearer, and he imagined the approaching wolf, teeth bared, just as he'd seen the night he and Graystone had fought them off. *Graystone*, he thought for just a second before the snarling got his full attention. *Help me, Taotai.*

He felt the animal's hot breath, its snout sniffing his neck. Attracted by the dried blood on his shoulder, it sniffed the wound a couple of times. Then as if struck hard, it whimpered in fear and shied away. The venom had saved him from the wolf, he wondered if it would kill him now. *Help me, Taotai.*

Shen became aware of a stench emanating from his mouth. *Surely this is the end. The poison has entered deep into my bowels.* Then, from wisps of his cloudy breath, the gaunt figure of Li Taotai began to slowly materialize. First, the bony feet, the white skin covering scrawny calves, knees, thighs, until a whole body was formed from clouds of his stinking breath. The Taotai's body hovered horizontally a few inches off the ground, facing him.

"*So you will just lie there and die, Shen Xiling?*" he heard the Taotai say. "*What of your new master — Have you no honor?*"

"But . . ."

"*All you've ever been is 'buts', you disgusting piece of frog spawn. But, but,*" he heard. "*You can still redeem yourself. The lawman is alive, not for long though. That venom will not kill you. The first dose still courses through your blood. It hardened you to its effects. Now, get up, you dung heap.*"

The Taotai's body grew fainter and fainter until it was gone. Whether a vision or not, it had stirred Shen into action — shamed him. He put every ounce of strength into trying to move his hands, then his feet. In a while, he was standing. He walked on wobbly legs in the direction he thought he had come from and was soon seeing broken twigs where he had crashed through while escaping. In a few moments, he was at the clearing where the wagon had stopped. No sign of it nor of Graystone. Wagon tracks in the snow revealed the direction it had taken.

"Shen, that you?" a voice called out from the edge of the clearing. He turned to see Doaks approaching on horseback. He had their two horses in tow, still saddled. "Found your horses back there, reins tangled in the brush."

"Doak. Why-you come?" Shen said.

"Figured by the way you took off after 'em other Chinee, maybe you'd need some help. We don't get much business after dark, left Zeke to manage the ferry and started after you. Where'd the marshal go, and what happened? Looks like blood on your shoulder."

"Bad-man take Graystone," Shen said, wasting no time stowing his blades in the saddle bag.

"What, which bad man?"

"No time talk. We-go," Shen said through gritted teeth, pulling himself slowly into the saddle. "We follow track." Shen pointed at the wagon tracks in the snow.

"I'm with you," Doaks said. "Me 'n Zeke owe it to you both."

"Thank you, Doak, we-go." Shen kicked his horse and winced at the pain in his shoulder as the mare jumped ahead.

34

WEIRD GIGGLING AH JUN inspected me as if I was a trapped animal. When he prodded me in the chest with a finger, I growled and jerked against my restraints like an angry beast. This set off an intense round of high-pitched titters.

I sensed we were moving deeper into the woods as the wagon slowed and bumped, and took big turns. I wondered why they didn't just kill me first and then dispose of the body in a secret place, but I didn't give voice to the query in case they liked the idea.

Just after sunrise, the wagon lurched to a stop. Ah Jun crawled to the front and looked out and exchanged a few words with the driver.

Ah Jun sniggered, then turned to me saying, "This good place, time-come for you-die, lawman."

Cheng untied the rope around my legs but left my hands stayed tightly bound. Then Cheng stooped over and with one hand clenched to the front of my coat he hauled me to my feet as if I weighed no more than a child. He pushed me towards the front and then off the wagon.

Ah Jun said a few words in Chinese to the driver, the miner from *Gold Mountain Fortune* that had been sent to fetch Bufo. The man nodded, dragged me to a small pine tree and tied me to it, standing upright with hands behind my back and another rope tight across my chest to hold me up. Ah Jun looked on while Cheng came to me and tested the ropes. The broad-shouldered Chinaman had the typical Qing hairstyle with a long, plaited queue hanging down his back. He wore a padded gown of dark blue, its shape not unlike a priest's cassock; across his waist, off a heavy leather belt, hung a knife in an ornate scabbard.

It was Ah Jun's turn to approach me. While the small eunuch stood before me, inspecting me, poking and pinching my arms, chest and legs with his fingertips, the wagon driver took care of the horses and Cheng started a campfire.

"We feast tonight, Graystone. But not you. You, not guest, you food," Ah Jun said.

My legs turned to jelly, and I sagged with my entire weight supported by the ropes. Ah Jun covered his mouth and let out a high-pitched cackle that lasted for a full minute.

I had spent so many years spurning prayer, but in seeing the maniacal Chinaman squealing in delight over my fate, it just seemed natural to turn my eyes up to the overcast sky and pray in silent fervor. I begged for deliverance, promising the Almighty that I would live a life of sobriety and good deeds if only . . . .

"I say wolf eat Graystone. Maybe, maybe, first, you be breakfast, then lunch and dinner. We cut you small piece, cook, eat, cut again." The giggling started again, this time causing tears to run down the pockmarked face. "You know *lingchi*? No? I tell you."

Ah Jun took great delight in explaining the details of *lingchi*: the ancient form of Chinese torture intended to prolong a victim's life and agony by slicing small pieces of flesh off. The torture could last for days, Ah Jun expounded with glee in his voice. I had read an account of such torment being used in China to punish missionaries but had never heard it in connection to cannibalism.

"We start leg part," the eunuch said indicating the top of his thigh. "After, we see." He gave my chest a squeeze. "Maybe here good," Ah Jun said as if considering a choice piece of meat at a butcher shop. He turned and shouted a question to the wagon driver who was stooped over a steaming cooking pot. The man nodded back.

"Graystone big man, we lucky, can cook two-way. One-way *geng*, make soup, we put together noodle, very-licious. Nother-way we do *fu*. How to say . . . ah! Slice, dry. We got good fire, no?"

Indeed, there was a good fire going and a nice pile of firewood stacked and ready for what that my captors expected to last all day, perhaps longer.

"Please, Ah Jun, kill me first, then cut me," I said.

"Cannot-do, Graystone. Must keep meat fresh. Also, punish lawman. Graystone give many sore-head," Ah Jun said rapping his knuckles lightly on his temple. "Me sore-head, Ah Toy sore-head. Now, too much talk. We start breakfast." Cheng came to me and used his knife to cut off my coat and then sliced open my left trouser leg from cuff to hip. The wolf bite had left a white, jagged scar on my shin.

"Wait, Ah Jun," I said. I had to do something, anything to stop this. "What about Jake, the storeman, did you kill him too?"

"Ah, poor Mr. Jake. Yes, I kill Jake. I try Jincan for Jake. Jincan work-good, next day I use kill President Taylor."

"Jincan? What's that," I said.

"*Eh*? What Jincan? Jincan magic poison. Poison all-way from China. But enough talk. We-hungry."

Ah Jun urged Cheng towards me. Cheng didn't like being ordered about by the eunuch and let him know with a scowl and a couple words spat out with bile. I wondered if there could be the slightest chance that somehow, I could work the hostility between them to my advantage.

The eunuch's voice softened, he smiled and batted his short eyelashes at Cheng. He pointed to the top of my thigh, tilting his head to one side quizzically. Cheng huffed and then nodded and approached me with his knife drawn. With his other hand, he pinched up my flesh between his fingertips and then looked up to Ah Jun for approval. The eunuch nodded enthusiastically, looking at my thigh and then up at my face with a wicked grin. I looked up at the clouds wondering if they were dense enough to thwart my pleas for escape.

I turned away, not bearing to look as Cheng put the tip of his blade to my thigh. I'd been on the receiving end of myriad weapons: bludgeoned, shot and stabbed, but none of those experiences prepared me for the agony that accompanied that first cut. The incision itself was done cleanly, and with Cheng's sharp blade, I felt not much more discomfort than the press of cold steel. No, it was the anguish of it being the first of many, and that each one would be regarded as a *fillet* to satisfy the cravings of these twisted heathens. I screamed at the top of my lungs.

My ankles were tied to the tree, but that still left a little room for my knees to bend. And bend I did. My banshee scream was accompanied by wild gyrations of whatever parts of my body I could move even an inch to prevent Cheng from completing his task.

Cheng's scowl didn't stop my struggling. He pulled his blade away from the thin piece of flesh hanging loosely off my thigh and rose. Blood ran down my knee and as I went on flailing, flecks of blood flew onto Cheng's robe.

Ah Jun said something to Cheng that seemed to anger him and then held his hand out as if to take the knife. Cheng responded by flinging back his own invective, one that angered the eunuch who glowered and muttered under his breath, hand still held out to take over the *lingchi*.

Cheng held the knife out holding it by the blade, and as Ah Jun was about to take it, Cheng let it drop to the ground, a satisfied grin on his face.

Ah Jun stooped over to pick up the knife, cackling in his bizarre way. He came to me, still hooting and snorting, staring up at my face from just a few inches away. I made use of the slack the ropes allowed me for movement of my upper body and neck. I thrust my head and shoulders forward, slapping my forehead into the bridge of the eunuch's nose.

Blood spurted from Ah Jun's face as he reeled backward and dropped into the snow. He was still conscious, moaning and lolling his head from side-to-side. The knife had been flung out of his hand.

Chen bellowed out a laugh, continuing as he walked to the eunuch and bent over him for a good look at the bloodied nose. Ah Jun pushed himself up onto his elbows and shook his head. He spotted the knife, crawled over to it and picked it up. Still on all fours, he stared at me, looking like a beast that had spotted its prey. He got to his feet and stumbled over, knife held out. Chen followed him close behind.

There was a deafening blast followed by a crash above our heads at the top of the tree. Clumps of snow and branches rained down. Cheng moved back a step and looked up. Ah Jun scuttled to one side, brushing himself off.

Beyond the campfire, Doaks stood with his feet apart, cradling Brown's double-barreled canoe gun. A plume of bluish smoke curled up from the barrel. "Now, you just stop whatever you're doin' to the marshal and step away," he said.

Cheng and Ah Jun took a couple of steps back. Doaks drew a pistol and motioned for them to get further away. "Drop the knife," Doaks said. Ah Jun tossed the weapon down.

The man minding the cooking pot began to rise off his haunches. "You stay right there," Doaks said, pointing his weapon at him. When the man didn't heed the warning and took a step closer, Doaks extended his arm and shot him in the head. The man was knocked backward onto the campfire.

I felt the ropes being cut away from my hands. The cord around my chest was sliced through from behind the tree. Still jelly-legged, I slid to the ground. Shen stepped from around the pine tree. Ah Jun's mouth dropped open in shock. Cheng pointed at Shen and shook his head in disbelief.

"Doaks, Shen, how," I spluttered.

"Tell you later, Marshal. First, let's take care of these criminals." Doaks walked forward with his gun ready. The dead man in the campfire was aflame, his flesh already starting to blacken, giving off a rancid, sulfurous odor. Doaks kicked the cooking pot over and doused most of the fire. He walked over to me and passed me the canoe gun. I leveled it at Ah Jun and Cheng.

"Nasty cut, Marshal," Doaks said staring at my bloody leg.

"I need the little one alive," I said.

"Cheng, I kill," Shen said. "I no-kill, he never stop try kill-me."

Doaks grabbed Ah Jun by the scruff of the neck and with the pistol jammed against his ribs, marched him to the wagon and roped him to one of the wheels. For good measure, the ferryman slammed his fist into Ah Jun's cheek, knocking him out. Coming back past the fire, he pulled out a branch, its tip still glowing orange and then came to me.

"This'll hurt more 'n a porkeypine up yer ass," Doaks said looking at my leg.

I nodded. "Do it."

Doaks pressed the smoldering stick onto the cut on my thigh to cauterize the wound. I stifled a scream as best I could as smoke curled off my seared flesh. It was over quickly and Doaks helped me to my feet and gave me the extra pistol he carried in his belt.

Shen called Cheng over to him and the two assassins spoke face-to-face for a time. The tone was calm, but as I watched them, their bearing revealed that something very grave was about to take place.

"These men were going to eat me," I said to Doaks.

He shook his head slowly. "It'll make a gruesome tale for the young'uns, I reckon. Can't wait to tell Zeke."

"How did you find me?" I asked.

"We were headed in the right direction anyway, but that scream of yours told us how close we were."

"What now, Shen?" I asked when they had completed their parley.

"I fight Cheng. This no you-problem, Graystone. Cheng kill-me, he do job for Yan, he go-free.

"We can't let him go," I said.

"Chinese honor. You pomis, Graystone. Doak, pomis?"

Shen looked at us with such conviction that we both nodded our assent. Secretly, I decided promise or not, to blow Cheng's head off with the canoe gun if he came anywhere close to defeating Shen.

Cheng had arrived in America ready for war. With Doaks watching him at the back of the wagon, he unloaded an assortment of Chinese weapons: a kind of halberd that combined a spear and a long-bladed ax, two different kinds of swords, a heavy battle-ax and a spiked mace. Shen added his deer horn knives to the fearsome collection. The combatants eyed the armory without touching any of the weapons and then moved away to prepare.

I pulled a blanket over my shoulders and we sat side by side at the front of the wagon, the best seats in the house for a fight to the death. I saw that Shen's left shoulder was injured; the cloth over it, torn and crusty with dried blood. He swung his arm in a circle in one direction and then the other to ease the stiffness.

It started much in the same way as the opera and the 'war' had, with much posturing. Both men went through a series of exercises staying on their respective sides, bending, stretching, whirling and leaping. They boxed the air, shrieked and hissed as they went through their paces. Cheng had the advantage of weight and height, but I had seen Shen in action and held on to the belief that he would get the better of his opponent. They had stripped off their winter outer-clothing and wore only thin, loose shirts and baggy trousers.

The combatants stopped their exercises at the same time as if a gong had sounded calling them into action. They went to the weapons laid out on the ground. Cheng chose first; he selected a sword with a wide blade and long handle that could be gripped with both hands. Shen glanced at the sword and picked up the halberd, testing it for weight and balance. The men went back to the open area near the smoldering corpse and faced one another. They exchanged a few words and bowed to one another.

Cheng lunged forward with his broadsword, extending his arm to its full length. Shen turned sideways as the blade passed his chest. Shen used the halberd's pole to strike upwards at Cheng's outstretched arm, catching his elbow and knocking the sword arm upwards and then stepping back a pace. Cheng changed the sword to his other hand and struck again, this time in a continual series of slashes. Shen countered with the long weapon, rotating it and using the back of the ax-blade to hook Cheng's sword. It caught, and Shen began to tug at the sword but Cheng pulled his weapon free before Shen could complete the move. Shen spun his body in a full circle with the halberd's blade rotating at waist level, Cheng ducked under it, escaping by an inch of being sliced. He rose quickly and swung the sword in a diagonal arc. Shen caught the blade with the halberd's axe again. The weapons were locked, the fighters closed in a contest of strength, their faces only inches apart.

In anguish, I grabbed Doaks' shoulder and placed my other hand on the canoe gun.

"Go on, Shen," Doaks shouted.

Cheng raised the locked weapons, forced a slight turn and then slammed his elbow into Shen's injured shoulder. Shen grunted and pulled back. But with weapons still locked, he pulled away hard and swung his leg into Cheng's ribs. There was a crack from Cheng's side like the snapping of a branch. Both men disengaged and staggered backward. Both were injured now.

Doaks and I were at the edge of our seats, leaning forward. "You've got him now," Doaks whispered. I eased my grip on the shotgun.

Cheng began breathing heavily, his body slightly bent to favor his injured side, the same side where Shen had struck his elbow with the pole. Shen spoke to him. He yelled something in response and then flailed with the sword, clearly wincing in pain as he did. The strike had no power in it.

Shen swung the halberd down hard. It caught the sword just above the weapon's hilt. The force ripped the broadsword out of Cheng's hand and Yan's man was left standing empty-handed with a spear point at his throat.

"Give no quarter, Shen," Doaks said in a hoarse whisper, raising a clenched fist.

"He will not," I responded. On one of the cold nights along our journey from San Francisco, Shen told me of his three mottos, one of which was to show no mercy. He pressed the spear point closer but held it for a moment, allowing Cheng to fully realize his predicament.

Cheng gave an almost imperceptible nod, a bow of acceptance and respect. Then Shen calmly took a pace forward and skewered his opponent through the gullet. The point exited the back of Cheng's neck. He pulled the spiked point out and then lowered it and thrust it into Cheng's heart.

Blood poured out of Cheng's mouth, throat and chest. He dropped to his knees and then fell forward onto the sparkling white snow.

35

TIME HAD COME FOR REFLECTION as to just how much of my mission I'd succeeded in. As we took turns at driving the wagon, I had hours to deliberate on my course of action, and of course, to hear Shen's thoughts on them.

In capturing Ah Jun, Bufo — or at least *the Bufo* that had killed Taylor — I had only partially succeeded in carrying out my duty. The fact remained that Bufo was not a single assassin but a cabal of murderers that shared the name, with possibly Ah Toy as its mastermind. There were still too many unknowns to declare success. For one thing, I still had to deliver Ah Jun back to Washington. Ah Toy, also had to be apprehended for ordering her eunuch to commit murder, and I had to find out the name of Ah Toy's patron that paid for the murder.

"What we do, Graystone?" Shen asked after I laid out the facts.

"As soon as we get back to San Francisco, I'll put Ah Jun in a cell on the jail boat. Then we'll arrest Ah Toy."

"How you-rest Ah Toy? She portent-lady in Sunfrasiko. Have many-friend. Same China. Have money, have power, law no-can-touch."

There was truth in Shen's words. It wasn't just China, it applied the world over. Sheriff John Coffee Hays would probably have something to say about my trying to take Ah Toy away. I'd have to speak to him first and get his support. "You may be right about that, Shen," I said, "but I have to try. I'll have to bring them both back to Washington."

Ah Jun sat bound and gagged behind us with wet cloth stuffed into his ears so that we could converse freely without being overheard. So far, he had been relatively docile, but when we were about a day out of San Francisco, Ah Jun started to wail like a banshee. The gag stuffed into his mouth was there mainly to suppress the giggling and the eunuch's incessant bawling was loud and quite unbearable. Shen spoke to him in Chinese and then released the gag for a moment.

"What's the matter?" I asked.

"He say stomach-pain," Shen said, stuffing the rag back into Ah Jun's mouth.

"Nothing much we can do about that," I said.

"Say he want," Shen acted out a man squatting on his haunches to take a shit.

"Well, if it'll shut him up, I suppose we could stop for a minute," I said.

Letting him do his business meant untying his wrists and ankles, something we'd done several times along the way. Given the eunuch's diminutive size, he didn't pose much of a physical threat to us. I stopped the wagon and Shen pulled Ah Jun to his feet. I noticed that the man's left shoe had been kicked off. I was quite willing to let him walk shoeless on the cold ground and ignored his fuss, shouting through his gag and pointing to his bare foot.

Shen kept his wrists bound but untied his ankles and led him towards the curtain closing off the back of the wagon. Cheng's cache of weapons lay there in a pile covered with a blanket. We thought nothing of it as Ah Jun, tied up, would be incapable of wielding any of them with any adeptness. Ah Jun gazed at the mound of arms as he went by. The only weapon in view was a single arrow. I hadn't noticed it before as it lay pressed up against the wagon's sideboard, presumably where Cheng had dropped it after I fired my carbine blindly into the wagon's cover.

Shen pulled the curtain aside and Ah Jun shifted to the left, making like he was preparing to jump off the wagon. He swung his leg, kicking his bare foot into the arrowhead. The arrow tip tore into the sole of his foot.

Shen jerked Ah Jun back and flung him to the ground. He grabbed the arrow's shaft and jerked the point out.

"Poison," Shen said.

"Can we stop it?" I asked, shouting above Ah Jun's cackling.

Shen shook his head. "Too late.

The Jincan had entered the eunuch's blood. Ah Jun's eyes rolled back. He shuddered violently, kicking and frothing at the mouth. Shen stepped away. In less than a minute, my prisoner, the murderer of President Zachary Taylor, was dead.

36

JINCAN HAD TAKEN ANOTHER LIFE, this victim literally getting a taste of his own medicine — for us, a rather incommodious affair, to say the least.

We rolled Ah Jun's corpse into a blanket and loaded it onto the wagon intending to show the remains to sheriff Hays in explanation of our petition for his support in the arrest of Ah Toy. With no proof that Ah Toy was in any way connected to Bufo other than being Ah Jun's mistress, the arrest warrant for Bufo was useless. However, after just a few hours, not even cold air could prevent the body's deterioration. The putrid odor in the confines of the wagon was too much to bear. When we uncovered the body for inspection, we found a gaping hole where the stomach should have been. The Jincan appeared to have liquefied Ah Jun's internal organs and begun to eat its way through the gut, caving it in. I recalled Bliss' description of Jake's remains about the body appearing as if disemboweled by animals. We had no choice but to toss the carcass, blanket and all into the bush where it would continue to decompose and disappear altogether.

Shen was silent for a long while after this occurred. When I queried him about it, he told me that he had once tried to use Jincan to murder a high official, and now, happy he hadn't succeeded despite the Taotai's displeasure at his failure. I sensed a change in him, defiance. His mood lifted after this and he took over the reins and with a new liveliness, reverting to his old comical ways, even so far as imitating the giggle of the dead eunuch.

There had been no sign of the black dog and I hoped it would stay that way, wondering as we lumbered along whether my oath to the Almighty was a binding one since it was interrupted before I could utter it fully.

We arrived in San Francisco after dark. Nevertheless, when we drove past the sheriff's office, I was encouraged by a light coming from his office window. Shen waited while I went up to speak to Hays.

On our way back to San Francisco, I was fortunate to have been able to purchase an old suit of clothes from a miner. Ill-fitting as it was, the black suit at least made me somewhat presentable though more in the guise of an undertaker than a marshal of the United States of America. Hays' secretary looked me up and down and asked me to wait while he entered the sheriff's office, giving me one more look as he closed the door to Hays' inner sanctum. I heard a mumbled conversation through the door and then a moment later, the secretary opened the door.

"Marshal, the sheriff is just about to leave for home. Would you be kind enough to return tomorrow?" the secretary said.

"I'm afraid it's a matter of some urgency, sir. Kindly relay that to the sheriff. It really cannot wait."

"Well, sir, if you insist, but it has been a rather long day," he said, opening the office door for me to enter. "Marshal Graystone to see you, Sheriff."

Hays got to his feet and shook my hand. He stepped to the window overlooking the street and looked down. "That your rig, Graystone? Seems like one I've seen before."

"Borrowed," I said.

He looked at my strange attire and waved me to a chair in front of his desk then went to his own seat. "So, what is it that can't wait until tomorrow?"

"This may take a while to explain, Sheriff, and it's best that I start from the beginning," I said.

"Just a moment," Hays said. He called out to his secretary and told him he could leave for the night, saying that he would lock the place up. Then he asked me to proceed.

Over the best part of the next hour, I told Hays the entire story beginning with my visit to William and Mary Bliss in Washington and ending with the disposal of Ah Jun's body. Hays asked a few insightful questions as I spoke, but mostly just listened.

"That's quite a tale, Graystone," he said at the end.

"And every scrap of it, the truth. I know how well-liked Ah Toy is, so I would genuinely like to have your agreement before I formally arrest her."

"You'll need a new warrant. The one you have is for the apprehension of someone called Bufo," Hays said.

"Correct sir, but I believe it is Ah Toy's alias. But I'll gladly obtain a new warrant if that's what it'll take for your agreement.

"There are some things that are hard to believe, Ah Toy being the head of a criminal gang, for example, but I'm inclined at least to give you my support for obtaining a warrant for her arrest. That'll take some time though, probably a day or so, Chief Justice Hastings is a busy man. The rest will be up to you."

"Thank you, Sheriff," I said, starting to get up.

"A word of advice, Graystone, go there in the morning before the place opens for business. Her customers are likely to start a riot if they see you trying to take her away."

Shen had gone back to his old place in the Chinese quarter. I had found lodgings at the Niantic Hotel, a grounded ship turned boarding-house. The next morning, I went to the courthouse situated on the corner of Kearny Street and Pacific Avenue.

I submitted my application to a clerk who repeated Hays' line about how busy Hastings was. My pleas for exigency went unheeded. Each time I pressed, the law clerk told me to 'come back later.'

The long wait gave me time to write a full report to William Bliss. I ended by informing him that Ah Toy would be arrested the following morning, after which I would make arrangements to return to Washington with her as my prisoner.

It was late afternoon when the warrant for Ah Toy's arrest was issued. Recalling Hays' caution about correct timing, I went to find Shen to plan our early-morning raid.

EPILOGUE

SHEN'S FOOTSTEPS THUMPED up the creaky stairs of the Niantic. It both amused and irritated me that one so capable of stealth could demonstrate his displeasure in such a boorish way when it suited him. At any moment, he would be at the door. This time he'd be unable to barge in as I'd taken the precaution of locking the door so I could finish the letter I'd been writing to Bliss. The area around my feet was littered with scrunched up paper balls of earlier unsuccessful attempts. Finally, I was having better luck and needed privacy, *keep it simple*, I'd told myself.

Shen turned the doorknob and then jiggled it. When the door didn't budge, he began knocking.

"Graystone, you come-fast," he said through the stout barrier. "We miss-boat."

"Give me a few minutes, Shen. I have to make sure this gets on the mail boat before we go."

"You say same las-time. You-pomis we go. All bag on ship, soon ship-go. Come now."

"One minute, Shen," I said.

I read through what I'd written one more time.

November 18th, 1850
San Francisco, California

Adjutant-*General William Wallace Smith Bliss*
United States Army, Western Division

Dear General,

Though only a day has passed since my previous correspondence, there has been a sudden and quite tragic turn of events. I am afraid, therefore, that this letter carries dreadful news. By the time you receive this communication, I shall no longer be in San Francisco, and Sir, no longer even in the United States.

The aforementioned news is that when we went to detain the woman known as Ah Toy, one I suspect to be the diabolical mastermind behind the death of your father-in-law, our beloved President Taylor, we found her premises locked and empty.

The culprit is now on the run. Apparently, warned of her impending arrest, she and members of her household staff boarded a China-bound clipper the previous day while I awaited the issuance of the warrant for her arrest.

Somehow, word of my impending action reached her ears and I see her escape as a further suggestion of guilt. To investigate the source of betrayal, the leaked information regarding her arrest, though necessary, would take time that I do not possess.

I am certain you will agree, General Bliss, that my duty and the only course of action is to follow her to the

Celestial Empire, and once there to take steps towards bringing her to justice. I have therefore secured passage on a China-bound vessel departing San Francisco on today's afternoon tide.

Traveling with me as deputy, guide and interpreter will be Mr. Shen Xiling, whom I wrote about previously. Naturally, you will receive further correspondence regarding my whereabouts, and of my progress in due course.

"Alright, Shen, stop banging, I'm coming now. Just have to sign this thing and get it into an envelope." I picked up the pen again and wrote:

Until then, I remain, your faithful servant,
U. S. Marshal Angus Murdoch Graystone

AUTHOR'S NOTES

Having conjured the characters in this book to life, to me, they are like old friends. Shen, though based on a real-life assassin involved in the death of Macau's 74ᵗʰ governor, João Maria Ferreira do Amaral, other than in name, was entirely made up. In my previous book, *Mesquita's Reflections*, Shen played the part of the manservant to a Chinese official. I felt there had to be more to his story and so cast him as one of the main characters in *Jincan*, and set him off on a journey across the Pacific on a collision course with Angus Graystone and the America of 1850, where the tumult of the gold country served as an intriguing backdrop.

The cause of Zachary Taylor's sudden death has long been the subject of speculation. Due to the vitriolic politics of the day, it has often been suggested that Taylor was assassinated. One idea behind that thought is that he threatened to block the expansion of slavery into western territories. Readers might recall that in 1991, Taylor's remains were exhumed to test for traces of poison. None was found.

I have tried to be as faithful as possible to the events surrounding Taylor's death such as his medical care and funeral. The newspaper account which Graystone reads in the Bingham Hotel was in fact taken from the Philadelphia Bulletin of July 10ᵗʰ, 1850.

Angus Graystone came to life as a character completely opposite to Shen as I could make him. Arguably the leader of the duo due to the financial arrangement they arrived at, he is also the bumbling one (in this story) who needs rescuing from time to time. Think Cervantes' Sancho Panza, the sidekick that often provided the words of wisdom to stem Graystone's impulsiveness. Creating Graystone's character satisfied my hankering for a reconnection to my family's Scottish ancestry, just as Shen's did in connecting me to familial links to Macau.

While researching San Francisco's history and the Chinese diaspora, I came across the intriguing story of Ah Toy. From there I had fun recreating the madam into a diabolical femme fatale, and little Ah Jun into an assassin.

I took some liberties with the timings and locations of certain events for the sake of story-telling, one example being my description of the war between the Chinese miners. Such an event did take place, but it happened at a place called Weaverville in 1854 — somewhat further north from where I describe it, and a few years later.

And finally, the poison, Jincan — its creation by the shaman provided me with hours of enjoyable research which eventually provided a solution to my poison problem; one that could do its job and disguise the outcome as caused by a natural ailment.

I look forward to bringing you further adventures of Graystone and Shen. If you have questions or comments on this book or anything else, I would be very happy to hear from you via email at marco@lobomarco.com or through my website https://lobomarco.com.

CPSIA information can be obtained
at www.ICGtesting.com
Printed in the USA
BVHW041207021219
565396BV00014B/166/P